2.14 Miles
of
Interstate 91

Here's to you Pat.
any kid of Norrine's
is okay in my book.
She's one classy lady!

Bob Keifel

2.14 Miles
of
Interstate 91

A Novel by R. D. Veitch

Writers Advantage
New York Lincoln Shanghai

2.14 Miles of Interstate 91

Writers Advantage
an imprint of iUniverse, Inc.

For information address:
iUniverse
2021 Pine Lake Road, Suite 100
Lincoln, NE 68512
www.iuniverse.com

This is a work of fiction.
Any resemblance to real persons living or dead is purely coincidental.

Author's Contact Information
E-mail: rdveitch@mninter.net

ISBN: 0-595-25653-8 (Pbk)
ISBN: 0-595-65236-0 (Cloth)

Printed in the United States of America

"We come along and drill a million holes in this rock. We fill'm full of dynamite. Blow the rock into little bitty pieces. Then we take the rock and glue it back together with concrete and tar. We call that progress."

Côte

To Tom, Lisa, and Rob

Anything is possible.

And

To Mary Jane, *who made this possible.*

With special thanks to Bill

for the push that got it started.

Contents

Chapter 1 Entrance Ramp, Interstate 91 North 1

Chapter 2 Côte 13

Chapter 3 Charlie 20

Chapter 4 John Cashman 26

Chapter 5 The Duke 30

Chapter 6 Church 34

Chapter 7 Lightnin' 41

Chapter 8 Chip 49

Chapter 9 Edgar 55

Chapter 10 Kelly 61

Chapter 11 Tommy Mac 72

Chapter 12 Judge Rubenstein 79

Chapter 13 Barrel-ass 83

Chapter 14 Big Jim 94

Chapter 15 Sneakers 108

Chapter16 Crackers 118

Chapter 17 Dad 130

Chapter 18 Ellen 143

Chapter 19 Rest Area 151

Chapter 20 Whitey 154

Chapter 21 Henry 168

Chapter 22 The Tycoon 181

Chapter 23 D-d-donnie 192

Chapter 24 Strong 205

Chapter 25 Mora 216

Chapter 26 Mom 226

Chapter 27 Jack 244

Chapter 28 BVD 261

Chapter 29 Santee 289

Chapter 30 Magus 313

Chapter 30 PH 340

Chapter 31 Teach 355

Chapter 32 I-91 South, Exit 40—Bradley Field 362

Chapter 1

Entrance Ramp, Interstate 91 North

June 2002

The highway shot north like an arrow. Rick could see the map in his mind, the road ricocheting off Mt. Tom, burying itself into the Green Mountains, and the heart of his past. He stared at the road over Ben's shoulder as the plane banked for its final approach to Bradley Field. Ben, not yet six, was in awe of everything, but the highway held all of Rick's attention. Interstate 91—he'd helped build it, and it was part of him. It was the place he started, and the surest path back to where he was from.

This was a special trip: just Rick and his grandson, Ben. Tim, Rick's oldest, and Ben's dad, was enjoying a four-day second honeymoon in Hawaii with his wife, Laura. Rick's wife, Mary Jo, was doing a two-week Spanish immersion in San Antonio. Business was slow in Rick's consulting practice, and he jumped at the opportunity to take Ben on this four-day adventure. Rick had family in Vermont who had never met Ben, which was a great excuse for the trip. But it wasn't just about meeting family. It was a trip back in time; a chance to dig for roots, and to give Ben some idea of the place his grandfather had come from. It was a trip to the "old country," American style.

The trip wasn't just for Ben. Rick had a need to go back. There was some unfinished business, or some uncompleted thoughts that would wake him sometimes at 2:00 in the morning and persist until he gave up on sleep and went downstairs to read. He didn't know exactly what it was or why it bothered him. He only knew it had to do with that final summer on Interstate 91, and his mind worried it subconsciously like his tongue might probe the broken enamel of a chipped tooth.

Of course he had been back to Vermont many times over the past 38 years. But those trips were different. They were filled with family events like weddings and funerals. And Mom and her second husband, George, Rick's stepfather, dominated. The two participated in nothing, wallowing in self-pity in their cluttered apartment, but every trip back focused on their needs. She even dominated the last trip for her funeral and burial, which, as she had instructed, was next to her mother in the old St. Charles Cemetery, rather than next to her husband, who had died just a few months earlier. Rick looked forward to a trip that didn't center on "Mom," and then felt a twinge of guilt for the sense of freedom it gave him.

Ben and Rick flew from Minneapolis into Hartford, Connecticut's Bradley Field. Bradley Field was handy for the drive to Vermont. Just hop on Interstate 91, the gateway to Vermont.

They would stay with Rick's sister, Willa, and her husband, TK. Willa was more than happy to have them, and Rick always felt comfortable in Willa's lovely little house overlooking the Connecticut River. Of all of his siblings, he was closest to Willa. Her husband, TK, was more like a brother than a brother-in-law. TK and Willa had been together since early high school.

The landing was smooth. Everything they had was in their carry-on duffel bag and backpacks, so they made their way quickly to the exit, and waited for the rental car bus. Rick had rented a small Mercedes convertible—a two-seater. He wanted the whole trip to be fun for Ben, and he couldn't see the fun in sitting alone in the back seat. The Mercedes had a switch that turned off the airbag if you had a child in the passenger seat.

"Wow, Grampa, is that our car?"

"You bet, Ben. Like it?"

"Wow, it's like a racing car. We can go really fast."

"And really get a ticket?"

"Oh yeah. Well, can we go *kinda* fast?"

"Sure. The speed limit on the Interstate is 65 miles-per-hour. That's faster than a mile a minute. It will feel real fast in this little car."

They got the paper work done quickly, and in moments they were on the road, top down, singing and laughing.

"You know what, Grampa?"

"No what Ben?"

"I think you need a car like this at home."

"Great idea, Ben. Do you think you can convince Grandma Mojo to let me get one?"

"Wouldn't she like it?"

"Nope. She'd think it was too chilly, and too impractical."

"Yeah, well it's fun!"

They joked and kidded as the little car whisked them through the traffic around Springfield, Massachusetts. Gradually, the traffic thinned as they headed north through Holyoke, Deerfield, and Greenfield. As the terrain became more mountainous, Rick felt a sense of coming home.

Ben asked, "Who am I going to meet in Vermont, Grampa?"

"Well we're staying with Aunt Willa and Uncle TK. And when we have the family reunion, you'll meet Uncle Charlie and Aunt Brigitte, Uncle Larry and Aunt Helen, Uncle Moe, he's the guy who created all the monsters for the Creatures of the Swamp game, and his wife Celeste, and Uncle Steve and his wife Dotty. You'll probably meet a whole bunch of their kids and grandkids. I don't know who will make it."

"Are they, you know, going to hug and kiss me and stuff?"

"Well my family aren't much into hugging and kissing. But you know if you say some of those smart things you say, people can hardly help themselves. They just want to give you a squeeze."

"Yeah, I know. I mean, when Grandma Ellen lost her keys and found them, she said, 'They're always in the last place you look.' So I said, 'Grandma. That's 'cause you stop looking when you find them.' And she started hugging me and saying 'Oh you're so smart.' But Grampa, it was just logical."

"Yeah I know. But sometimes people don't expect kids to be logical."

Ben was quiet for a moment, then he said, "You know what it is, Grampa?"

"No what, Ben?"

"It's 'cause we're short. If people look down on you they don't think you know anything and then they're surprised when you do."

"I think you're right Ben. But that idea is just the kind of thing that will get people hugging you if you say it."

"But they just pop into my head. How do I stop?"

"How about I give you a *nougy* if I hear you say something like that. Then maybe when you get an idea, you'll think of the *nougy* and decide whether or not you want to say it."

"What's a *nougy*?"

Rick reached over and ran his knuckles lightly over the top of Ben's head. "That's a *nougy*. We used to call it the *barber's itch*."

"I'll give you a *nougy* Grampa."

"Not in the car Ben. Or we'll end up in the ditch."

There were few cars on the road as they crossed the state line into Vermont. Tired from the excitement, Ben dozed.

Interstate 91 carved out a new plateau into the side the foothills tracking the Connecticut River, which separated Vermont from New Hampshire. In the Midwest, people thought of Vermont and New Hampshire as pretty much the same, but Rick knew differently. They might as well be on different planets. Vermont was one of the last havens for grass roots liberals, shocking the nation with its "domestic partners" law. New Hampshire was second only to Montana as a fortress for radical conservatives, proudly displaying the motto on their license plates "Live free or die."

Rick thought about the road. It had changed Vermont. When he was a child, the major route in and out of Vermont was U.S. Highway 5, a tortuously winding, narrow road where a single farmer pulling a manure spreader could bring interstate commerce to a halt. He remembered the interminable trips with his father to visit his grandparents on Long Island. How marvelous it had seemed to finally reach the Merritt Parkway with two lanes each way.

Interstate 91 had ended Vermont's innocence. Before the road, Vermont had been a long way from anywhere. Tourists came, but they stayed for a week or perhaps the whole summer. The towns were small— some hardly more than an extended family. The larger towns had two or three thousand people. Vermont had only two cities: Rutland in the heart of marble country, and Burlington in the Northwest corner on the shores of Lake Champlain. It had a handful of large towns like Brattleboro, and Bennington, and dozens of smaller towns, large enough to have their own high school, but little else. These middle-sized towns: Bellows Falls, Springfield, Barry, Montpelier, Windsor, White River Junction, St. Johnsbury, Newport, and others, were centers of commerce for the myriad of little villages and hamlets that sprinkled the rocky hills. The villages often had little more than a gas station, general store, and a church with perhaps a half-dozen clustered houses before giving way to the farms and sugarbush that had once been the mainstay of the state economy.

Cut off as they were from mainstream America, these small towns had a simplicity that Rick doubted could be found today anywhere in America. It wasn't that people were especially good and kind or that kids didn't get into trouble. People ranged from near saints to the mean-spirited and narrow-minded. Kids raised hell then, as they do now. But the nature of the crimes was different. Back then; the prejudices were among the Irish, Poles, and Italians, or perhaps between Catholics and Protestants. There were no racial minorities in Vermont; the last of the Abnaki, Vermont's dominant Native American tribe, vanished or were assimilated in the early 20th Century. Kids' crimes were pranks, not vandalism. Sometimes the results were just as devastating, like when the school board president's son and two other Boy Scouts burned Mount Kilburn, but they lacked a malicious motivation.

Interstate 91 changed all that. It opened a vein that increased the outflow of smart kids fleeing the state for the big city, and it also let in elements that had always found Vermont too remote to bother with. Bikers had always come to Pearly Bell's hill-climb in Grafton. Interstate 91 brought the Hell's Angels. Before the Interstate, high school kids drank beer, raced their cars, and killed themselves in fiery car crashes. After the Interstate, they did drugs, killed each other in alleys, and committed crimes to feed their habits. Once cheerleaders with bouncy tits and loose sweaters had rewarded local football heroes by going all the way in the back seat of Dad's car. After the Interstate, hollow-eyed waifs had bored sex in alleys for the price of their next fix.

Interstate 91 changed Vermont from a distant place to a suburb of New York City. Tourism became not just the biggest industry; it became the only industry. "Flatlanders," as locals call them, moved north and bought up old farmsteads and opened bed & breakfasts. The big chains came and destroyed the small town merchants. Vermont became a theme park, a parody of itself.

Rick chuckled at his silent rant. He had left while the change was in process. He had enjoyed the last taste of innocence, but had it been all that innocent? He had been part of Interstate 91, working summers while he was in college, helping to build the road that changed Vermont. Wasn't he to blame for the changes? What right did he have to bitch?

He knew he was being unreasonable. The Interstate brought good as well as evil. Its real crime was that it brought change, inevitable change, and in his heart he wanted home to be like it had been when he was a child. Or did he? He laughed out loud.

They cruised through the rolling hills. It was June and already it was brown in Minnesota. But here, in the cool wooded hills, the world was green and Rick soaked it in. The highway turned away from the river and cut behind Bellows Falls, climbing gently.

"It's a flatlander's road," Rick thought. "Real Vermont roads go with the land. They're like Route 5, up and down, winding around the rocks too big to push aside. They follow nature. Flatlander roads cut their own path, adding curves and hills more to break up the monotony, than to respond to the land. Interstate 91 pretends to be a Vermont road, and the views sometimes fool you into thinking it is. But you could plunk this road surface down in Nebraska, and it would fit right in."

Their exit was north of town, dumping them off in Rockingham, on Route 103, a quarter mile from where 103 and old Route 5 split. They were still a half-mile short of the 2.14- mile section where Rick had spent his last construction summer doing grunt work for B. V. DeBoni & Sons.

"Wake up guy!" he said giving Ben a little tap on the shoulder.

"Ohhh. Are we there yet?"

"You bet. Just around the corner. Wait till you see Aunt Willa's horse."

"Aunt Willa has a horse?"

"Yep. And Uncle TK has a tractor. What do you think about that?"

As they turned into the farmyard, it erupted in dog barks, chickens scurrying, and TK and Willa shouting hellos. After the mandatory hugs and tour of the little Mercedes sports car, Willa took Ben in tow to introduce him to her horse, Barb. TK and Rick sat on the edge of the porch step, looking out over the Connecticut.

"Whatcha got planned," TK asked.

"Mmm. Show Ben Ellen's farm, some stuff like that. Who's hosting the gathering of the clan?"

"We'll have everybody here who's still speaking to everybody. Never know how many that will be."

"They never change, do they?" Rick laughed. "I've been thinking about Interstate 91."

"The sewer that poisoned Vermont?"

"The very one. Something's been bothering me about the year I worked the ledge up there. Can't put my finger on it, but it chafes."

"You worked for DeBoni didn't you? Wasn't that the year of the big union brouhaha?"

"Yeah, and all those deaths. A lot of people died that year.

"Police solved all those didn't they?"

"They think they did, but I don't know. Maybe Ben and I will hike out onto the ledge. Isn't that little quarry supposed to have some fossils?"

"Supposed to. Don't remember hearing that anyone found any lately. But people don't go in there any more. Too hard to get to."

"Used to be a good path in from Ellen's place. Part of the old Boston Post Road, I think. It was pretty grown over, but passable. Heck, I drove my motor scooter over it 35 years ago."

"Rick, it was closer to 40 years ago, and trees do a lot of growing in 40 years."

"Hey, Uncle TK. Will you show me your tractor?" Ben had raced ahead of Willa.

"You bet, Ben. Come on. I've got to move some manure over to the big pile. You can ride along."

"Oh boy," Rick joked to Willa. "Nothing like moving a little honey with the tractor to make a kid's day."

"Why don't you go in and get cleaned up and I'll take your little car for a spin," Willa said, her hand out.

Rick laughed and tossed her the keys.

TK hadn't asked the obvious question. Why did he care about those deaths? Rick thought about it that night, as he lay in bed staring at the stars through the skylight. And if he cared, why hadn't he looked for the answers before? He wondered if he hadn't asked the questions because he had been afraid of the answers.

Rick and Ben were off early the next morning. Willa packed them a lunch, a thermos of coffee, and a couple of cans of pop. She packed it in a daypack with the admonishment, "You do the carrying Rick. This is too heavy for Ben."

"I can do it Grampa!" Ben chimed.

Rick held a finger to his lips and winked. "Of course, Willa."

Rick drove back along Route 103, and turned off on Williams River Road. He showed Ben where his grandmother Ellen, Rick's first wife, had grown up. Some of the farm buildings were still there. The little hired hand's house had been expanded. Others had been replaced with modern summer homes. New homes had sprouted in the fields on both sides of the road. The narrow country road still alternated patches of decaying tar with sections of hard-packed gravel. "See where all those houses are, Ben?" Rick pointed to a half-dozen multi-story homes, each perched on an acre or so, hanging on the hillside, with big picture windows overlooking the Williams River Valley. "Your great-grandfather used to have about 150 cows right where those houses are."

"Where did they all go?"

"They were all sold when he died. That was a long time ago. Your dad was only about your age then."

The little house where Ellen had lived was now just a small fraction of a sprawling country manor that filled the space between hill and brook. Just beyond where the barnyard had been, there was a grassy turn-off that led to an old farm lane. Seeing no sign that it was in use, Rick pulled in and parked, leaving enough room for a tractor or pickup to pass if some-one had a mind to get into the lower field. He locked up out of habit, and he and Ben set off, Ben carrying the pack, which Rick had lightened by plucking out the heavy steel thermos.

The lane was so overshadowed by towering maples that brush and shrubs had little chance to grow. The path was slightly overgrown but still easily passable. The lane curved downhill, towards the river. It crossed a small brook and then turned into a simple logging road. There were remnants of ancient stonewalls here and there, with no sign that the intervening spaces had ever been cultivated. But Rick knew that two hundred years ago, the whole state had been under plow or put to sheep pasture.

They made their way down the steep hill, recrossed the small brook, and finally intersected an ancient roadbed, perched on the north bank of the Williams River. Here, the towering maples gave way to red and white pines, and the roadbed was a mat of rotting pine needles. The acidic soil kept the trail clear of brush.

"This is the Boston Post Road," Rick said. "It used to go all the way to Boston. They'd carry the mail between Vermont and Boston on this road. Ethan Allen, and the Green Mountain Boys used it."

"Are they a rock band?"

"No, they fought in the Revolutionary War. This was probably an Indian trail before they made it into a road."

"Will we see any Indians?"

"Not too likely in Vermont. This area used to belong to the Abnaki but I don't think there are any members of that tribe left."

Ben picked up a bent stick. "If we see'm, I'll shoot'm. Blowey! Pow!"

"Careful who you're shooting there, big guy. We're supposed to be part Abnaki."

"Really? We're Indians?"

"Well just a little bit. Want me to carry that pack?"

"No I can. Is it far?"

"Not too far. Been a long time but I think it's just over that rise."

Memory shortens distance, and it wasn't over that rise, or the next three. They trudged along the old road, enjoying the quiet of the deep woods. Ben looked dwarfed by the adult-sized daypack, but he hiked along briskly, and Rick was glad that he had maintained a strict regimen of morning walks. It wouldn't do to have *Grampa* call for the first rest because *he* really needed it. They walked for another 15 minutes, starting up a long hill. In the distance, they could hear tires singing as southbound trucks barreled off the mountain, and down to the Williams River Valley on I 91. Northbound trucks changed gears as they lost momentum near the top, climbing out of the valley.

Ahead, they could see a break in the hill, and the Post Road petered out and disappeared where the margins of the Interstate right-of-way had been graded and planted.

"This is the quarry, Ben. I'm tired. You want to rest?"

"You rest, Grampa. I'm hunting for fossils. I bet I'll find Tyrannosaurus Rex."

They stood and surveyed the quarry. The floor was level and about half an acre across. The walls were terraced with sheer rock faces five or six-feet high, and then a narrow ledge, and another face. The rock was greywacke, a kind of slate-like rock that was layered in chunks, eighteen inches to two-feet thick. Here and there, patches of marble and white quartz interlaced the rock. The rock faces turned this way and that, as quarrymen had sought out the best flat surfaces. Mostly the rock had been used for stoops and foundations. Small trees and bushes grew from the niches and on the ledges. A path followed the old access road, curving around the north side of the quarry, and climbing up the hump that overlooked Interstate 91.

"Well maybe not Tyrannosaurus Rex. But maybe you'll find a trilobite or a starfish. I'm going to climb up the hill where I can see Interstate 91. When you get tired, come on up and we'll have lunch up there."

Rick looked down on Ben as he climbed. Ben was well taught by his mother, a naturalist for the State of Minnesota, and was already busy examining the ledge for likely spots, tapping it with the rock hammer TK had lent him. Rick patted his pocket and felt the small lump. Ben would find a fossil one way or another. Rick observed the traces of the old access road where it had come off the Interstate right-of-way, and curved around to the quarry. They had driven down this road to park their cars in the quarry, safe from the dust and debris of the job. It was steeper than he remembered, and he was puffing as he emerged on top of the hill. Looking southwest, down the valley, Interstate 91 dropped off the ledge and swept down across a mile-long bridge over the Williams River, and then climbed again into ledges on the other side.

He didn't have a real plan of attack. He thought he would treat this problem as he treated his clients' business issues. He would lay out the facts in his mind like the pieces of a mosaic, and then tell the story they revealed. Consultants, like archeologists, have to be good storytellers.

Rick found a tree where he could sit and gaze down the valley. He opened the thermos and poured himself a cup of steaming black coffee. The smell of coffee on the morning air enhanced his memory. So many other mornings he had sipped hot coffee from a thermos and looked down off this ledge.

He let his mind wander back, and, as always, when he thought back about those times, he thought of people, not events. The first person that always came to mind was Côte.

Chapter 2

Côte

June 1964

They sat like feral goats astride the rock hummock, leaning into the hill, heads down, plumes of rock dust streaming into the air. Air tracks. Rock drills, tethered by thick air pipes to Conestoga-sized compressors, thundering in early morning sun on a day that promised to be hot and humid.

Côte stood just upwind from the topmost drill. A fireplug of a man, he was square in every dimension. A silver hard hat, styled like a World War I home guard helmet, was cocked rakishly on his head. He stood quietly, reaching over from time-to-time, to nudge the drill control levers with his grade-stake, and then settled back, leaning on the stake, and surveyed the raw gash that sliced through woods: up and down steep hills, muddying clear mountain streams, 2.14 miles of Interstate 91, being carved from the Vermont hillside. Not virgin. No, Vermont had been raped and healed before. But the new road violated once again the green canopy of century-old maples and firs that had all but obliterated the signs of past violations.

Côte smiled a wide, gap-toothed smile. "You know," he said. "We come along and drill a million holes in this rock. We fill'm full of dynamite. Blow the rock into little bitty pieces. Then we take the rock and glue it back together with concrete and tar. We call that progress."

He reached over and tapped the controls again.

"Maybe progress for us. Not much progress for the rock."

He smiled again. "Hear that?"

He laughed. "You don't hear nothin' do ya? All you hear is *whack, whack, whack*. The drill hammering on the rock. It all sounds the same. But you stand here long enough, and you can tell the difference between *whack* and *whock*. See, it's slowing just a little bit. I think we hit some marble. You'll see the dust change color pretty soon. Lot of marble in these hills. Marble and granite. Hard rocks."

As he talked, the plume of rock dust changed from dark gray to almost white.

"Life don't make no sense," he laughed again. "Man works all his life. Works hard. Makes a million dollars!" Côte wiggled his square butt in a parody of a dance. "Takes his million dollars and lives it up. Quits working. Eats. Drinks. Has some fun with the ladies. He thinks he's got it made."

The drill sound changed and Côte leaned over and tapped the controls to stop the drill. He reversed the drill, unscrewing the hammer from the coupling, and ran it up to the top of the boom. Rick leaned another steel drill rod into place, turning its threaded end into the coupling. Côte brought the drill head down and let it screw itself into the coupling topping the new steel. He gradually increased air pressure until the drill was hammering away again, and the plume of white rock dust billowed back into the sky.

"He gets fat." Côte continued the story as if it had not been interrupted. "He has a heart attack. Goes to the doctor. Doctor tells him, 'You're too fat! Get some exercise or you are going to die.' So the man hires some guy. Pays him good money to make him work harder than he worked before so he can lose weight. Now does that make sense?"

The sun was hotter now. Below the hummock, Old Clyde's big Northwest power shovel worked the remains of the last shot, dumping big scoops of gray rock into a giant pale green Euclid dump truck. Further down, great yellow Caterpillar-built "pans" scooped dirt through the open maw in their bellies, pushed by a monstrous D-9 Caterpillar bulldozer. Then, fully loaded with fresh dirt, they roared off the hill and snaked their way across the newly formed plain, spewing their belly-loads and adding a layer to the fill that would bridge the valley.

Rick stood by Côte, listening to him talk. Côte never called him by his name. He was *"College"* or *"hey, you"* to Côte and Henry. But Côte talked to him like he was a human being. Henry just grunted at him, pointed at what needed to be done, and then did it himself if Rick was too slow or too unsure of himself to do the job quickly. Nothing made Rick feel more worthless than having Henry push him aside, and take over the job.

Rick was actually Henry Baldridge's "chucktender," a minimum-wage grunt whose sole purpose was to grease up the couplings on the 12-foot steel shafts, sharpen bits, and put on and take off the steel pipes that drove the drill bit 50 to 60 feet through the solid Vermont ledge. Today he was serving both Henry and Côte, because Côte's chucktender, Dale Rudge, an older guy who was known as *"NN"* for *Numb Nuts*, had called in sick. Rick figured Dale was either nursing a Monday-morning hangover, or looking for other work, most likely the former. Rick didn't mind the extra work. Here, where the rock was hard, there would be nothing to do for half-an-hour or more, as the drill hammered its way through twelve feet of ledge. Then he'd add a steel and wait another half-hour. It was tedious, and he broke the tedium with cigarette after cigarette, sometimes smoking three packs in the ten-hour workday.

"Damn!" Henry's voice cut through the incessant pounding. Then Henry's drill stopped.

"Hey you. You seen *PH* around here?" Henry growled at him, a stub of a cigar working in his jaw. Henry ate five cigars a day. Oh, he lit them from time to time, but mostly he chewed them down, biting off and spitting little pieces of tobacco wrapper as he wore down the chewing end.

PH was Patrick Harris, the assistant "super" responsible for the rock cut. To the crew, *PH* stood for *Pecker Head*. They didn't like or trust Harris.

"I saw his truck heading for the yard, five minutes ago," Rick answered.

"Damn sonofabitch ain't never around when you need him." Henry snorted. "You got that little scooter thing up here?" he asked referring to Rick's Vespa motor scooter.

"Yep."

"Well get on the little scooter and pedal your ass down to the shop, and have them send back Calvin, with his torch. We ain't gonna drill no rock with the base plate cracked like that."

Rick looked down at the point where the boom set firmly on the ledge. Sure enough, he could see a hairline crack in the plate. He shook his head, marveling at how Henry could have known that the base plate was cracked when the drill was hammering away and dust was flying everywhere. He wanted to ask Henry how he knew, but Henry wasn't Côte. He had no patience with *dumb college fucks*.

"Are you gonna lay your hands on it and cure it? Or are you gonna get your ass on the scooter and get somebody who can fix it?"

"I'm going, I'm going." Rick hiked down the rock ledge and the dirt track to where they parked their cars. He kick-started the Vespa, and putted off down through the job-site, keeping a wary eye out for monster trucks, bulldozers, belly pans, and the like, that would flatten him out, and never even notice.

As he rode down through the right-of-way he thought about just how insignificant he was.

Construction jobs have a pecking order. Actually, they have two pecking orders. There's the boss pecking order that runs from the owner at the top, down through super and assistant supers, to grade-foreman at the low end. Then there's the labor pecking order. Top is the big shovel operator, old Clyde Renslaw, a veteran of some thirty years or more. He was the highest paid hourly man on the job at $22.45 an hour, a damn fine wage in 1964, and nearly nine times what they were paying Rick, the Federal job minimum of $2.56. Below Clyde were the backhoe operators and dozer drivers. Maybe Côte and Henry fit in there, or maybe down a notch with the Euclid drivers and the cowboys who jockeyed the big belly scrappers across the fill. Truck drivers came next. They were a transient lot, some of them even owning their own rigs.

Next, were the full-time laborers. This included the oilers who kept the shovels greased and clean. They were mostly the kids of other top-end workers: apprentices learning the trade by taking care of the equipment. There were also some regular old-timers, with no particular skills, who were kept on more out of habit than need. Everett was one of those. He was about sixty, and too frail for heavy work. He ferried stuff around in the old pickup or took a stint at flagman from time to time. The time-keeper, Tim McDermott was forever after old Everett to cash his checks. "What's the matter, you going out of business?" Everett would ask.

"Please, Everett. I can't close the books until those checks clear the bank. Please cash them."

"I don't need the money right now. I'll need it in January maybe."

Tim would try to explain about putting the money in the bank, but it was clear that Everett didn't understand or like the idea of banks. The conversation would be repeated about once a week. Once Rick asked Tim how many checks Everett had outstanding.

Tim had laughed, " Fourteen at last count. About $3,000. Fuck, you could buy a damn nice car for $3,000."

Next down the pecking order were the day laborers, drunks, and dropouts. Guys like Numb Nuts, who spent a few days or weeks on the job and then disappeared after payday. Sometimes they would show up again two or three weeks later. Most often, they wouldn't be seen again.

But low men on the totem pole were the college kids. *Dumb college fucks* they were referred to, partly out of envy, and partly out of accurate observation. Without exception, Rick and the half-dozen or so college students and one teacher on summer vacation, lacked that uncanny sense of what needed to be done and how to do it, that even the dumbest, most worthless drunken day laborer seemed to have. Job smarts, like street smarts, could only be learned on the job through painful trial and error. Over the course of a summer, each *dumb college fuck* would learn some, or quit, or get injured. Those who learned might retain a little bit the next year if they came back. This was Rick's third year, and he knew he wasn't quite as dumb as he had been the year before, but to him it was still an alien world, with every event a strange adventure.

Rick knew that the envy was real, too. The regulars knew that this was just a summer lark for him, not a lifetime commitment, and they resented him and envied him for that.

Over lunch the other day, Côte had talked about his own kid, Pierre. "He just found what his pecker is good for this year. Now he has a job and a little money and he bought a car. He cruises in the car and picks up girls and practices with his little pecker. He spends all his money on beer and gas. No way he's gonna be able to pay for school. Pretty soon he'll knock up some girl and they'll get a shack, they'll have eleven kids and he'll be here all his life. The boy just don't have no sense, *College.* You can't tell'm nothing. He's just as thick-headed as me when I was his age."

An air horn blasted Rick out of his reverie and he lost control of the scooter, running it in and laying it down on the soft sand at the edge of hard-pack road. Crackers, the most notorious of the belly pan cowboys, laughed and waved as he roared by. He had swung well out of the normal track to give Rick a scare. Last year Rick would have been completely pissed off. But now he just sighed and flipped Crackers the bird. The scooter was still running, so he flicked it out of gear as he picked it up. He remounted, popped it in gear, gave it some gas, and turned down the access road off the right-of-way, and headed for the yard.

He thought about the mechanics. He hadn't included them in his pecking order review. They were like doctors. Outside of the normal order of things, with their own internal pecking order, but with universal respect and not a little fear from everyone else on the job. Any one of the shop crew could pass judgment on a piece of equipment and take it out of service. If the equipment didn't work, neither did the man, and if you didn't work, you didn't get paid.

Swinging into the yard, he parked the scooter behind the maintenance shed. He looked at his watch. Ten o'clock. Sandwich break. He lifted his lunch-bucket off the back rack and sauntered into the shed. He thought to himself, "Hey, a year ago I wouldn't have remembered to bring my lunch-bucket."

Chapter 3

Charlie

As Rick walked into the maintenance shed, the mechanics were pulling out their lunch-buckets and pouring coffee from their thermoses. There was a collective groan of envy as Whitey, DeBoni's only black employee, and maybe the best diesel mechanic in New England, swung his 12-pack sized lunch-bucket up onto the tread of the partially disassembled D-9 that was today's major project. Whitey's wife was the cook at the Village Inn, and Whitey's lunch-bucket usually was stuffed with gourmet delights. Today it was simply southern fried chicken. Everyone's eyes followed Whitey's hand as he pulled a leg from the bucket and sank his teeth into the crispy meat. His eye's rolled back. The juices ran down his chin. He brought his other hand up with a napkin and dabbed at the drool. "Man, that woman can cook," he sighed.

Around him the crew looked at their paste-board sandwiches, mostly purchased at the little lunch counter called Mama D's, next door to the Evergreen Motel where they bunked. "You are one rotten bastard, Whitey, torturing your friends like this," Calvin, the torch man, whined.

"Did I tell you guys I was down to D-d-d-donnie's Cadillac showroom this weekend?" Whitey ignored their complaints.

"You get a raise Whitey? Buying yourself a brand new Cadillac?" Arnie Amesworth, the hydraulics man, already half-believed that Whitey was getting a raise and he was getting screwed.

"No, no. Are you shitting me? Out of DeBoni? Give me a break. I was getting a part. My neighbor has a '56 limo he bought from Shaughnessy. I do a little work on it from time-to-time. He swears he's gonna cut it down and turn it into a pickup. But listen to this. This really big black dude came sauntering in. I mean big! I thought maybe one of them professional basketball players or something." Whitey took another bite of chicken.

"There is this really gorgeous, brand-new Eldorado sitting there on the showroom floor. Baby blue, top down, tan leather upholstery. Sweet. This dude saunters over, opens the door, and plops down behind the wheel. One of D-d-donnie's little shit-ass nephews comes running over. Says to the black guy, 'What can I do for you?'"

"Black guy looks at him. He's almost eye-to-eye and the black guy is sitting down. He says, 'Son, what do I look like to you?'"

"Well the kid may not be too smart, but he's got balls. He says, 'Well, to tell you the truth, you look like a nigger sitting in a Cadillac.'"

"I about bust out laughing. I step back in the shadow where nobody'll see me unless I smile." Whitey flashed his perfect white teeth.

"Black guy is not fazed at all. He stretches out, puts his right arm up along the seat back. Rests his left elbow on the door, one finger touching the steering wheel. He smiles this great big smile and he's got a gold tooth right in front with a diamond in it, I swear to God. 'Now what do I look like, boy?'"

"Still a nigger in a Cadillac, to me sir," says the twerp.

"Black dude grunts. He reaches into his breast pocket and pulls out the biggest damn *ceegar* I ever did see."

"Big as yours, Whitey?" Calvin asked.

"Ain't nothing that big, boy. But it was big for a ceegar. Anyway the black dude jams the big ceegar in his teeth, turns, and smiles at the boy and says, 'How about now?'"

"Look like a big nigger, with a big ceegar, in a big Cadillac, sir. Much as I want to sell you this car, it don't make much difference. You still look like a nigger in a Cadillac."

"The black dude says, "How much, boy?""

Well I though the little shit would swaller his tongue. "It be $7,500 for the car, sir."

The dude flips out his roll, and man, it's bigger than my fist. He whomps off C- notes till he gets to 75, then takes one more and stuffs it in the kid's shirt pocket.

"Wha…what? The kid is stammering worse than D-d-donnie. I-I-I…"

"Big dude grinned and said, 'I just had to be sure I didn't look like no *Eye-talian* Contractor.'"

The mechanics whooped, falling off their perches, and holding their sides.

Just then, Charlie DeBoni walked into the shed.

The mechanics whooped it up again, laughing until tears rolled down their cheeks. Charlie was their very own *Eye-talian* Contractor.

"What's so goddamn funny?" He stood with his hands on his hips, up on his toes, trying to add an inch to his five-foot-five frame. "Whadda you guys doing sittin' around? I need that damn D-9 out on the fill. I gotta get the new one out here and up to Granby by Friday."

"Hey Charlie," Whitey chuckled. "Give us a break. It's our sandwich break. You don't want to go pissin' off these guys with the union sniffing around."

"Union! I'll give you sonsofbitches union!" Charlie turned beet red. "I swear I'll shut the whole fuckin' thing down if I hear union. Goddamn it! You think the union's gonna give you a job Whitey? Get me that dozer quick."

He turned and stormed out of the building.

"Don't think that man likes the union, much," Calvin said in a stage whisper.

B.V. DeBoni was a non-union shop. In fact, it was the only non-union contractor on the entire Interstate 91 project. Behind them, Paligrinni, one of the top ten contractors in the country, was pure union. Ahead of them, Hanes, a regional powerhouse, was pure union. DeBoni was the non-union sausage in a pure union sandwich. And if Charlie DeBoni had anything to say about it, it would stay that way.

The company's full name was B. V. DeBoni & Sons, and Charlie, at 42, was the only "son" left in the business. He ran the show. Once in a great while, old BVD himself would show up at a job site, but mostly the old man stayed down in Massachusetts and worked the politics. Charlie ran the jobs.

His two brothers, Antonio and Mario, both had a taste of the business and decided it looked too much like real work. Antonio, the older brother, was a numbers guy and still did the books for DeBoni. But his main interest was, what he called, "the short-term loan business."

Mario had just turned 30. He was Momma's pretty baby and he just played around, spending the old man's money. He had a reputation as the *Eye-talian Stallion* among what passed for a jet set down on Cape Cod.

Charlie had an Italian's true love for contracting. Charlie, like his father, loved to build. Benito came to the United States after Mussolini came to power, and bought his first cement mixer the next year. *Old BVD,* as the crews immediately christened him, started as a sidewalk contractor, and built the business slowly, moving up to small road projects. It was Charlie who got DeBoni in the Interstate business, going head-to-head against some of the biggest contractors in the country. He won his first Interstate job on I 89 up near Montpelier, largely because no one else knew where it was. The Montpelier job was all hard rock drilling, and B.V. DeBoni made a lot of money. This job was different. Only a third of the 2.14-mile segment was rock cut. The rest was fill, and a bridge—a mile long bridge, that spanned a 120-foot deep ravine over the Williams River. B.V. DeBoni had never built a bridge before.

Charlie had just two passions—or maybe obsessions would be a better word—and the shop crew had just been treated to both of them. He hated to pay the township taxes on his equipment, and did everything in his power to avoid the annual property tax levy of 1 percent of the depreciated value of production equipment. He always tried to move his best gear out of town before the annual assessment, scheduled for June 15th each year. The beat up old D-9 they were rebuilding was to replace a nearly new machine, out on the fill for at least a couple weeks while the town tax assessors, called *listers*, in the local parlance, did their thing. He'd bring the good dozer back later in the summer after the tax bill was set. Everybody on the job from Super, John Cashman, down to the lowest truck driver hated Charlie's obsession, because for two to three weeks, they'd have to get the job done with pure junk. The mechanics hated it worst of all, because they had to make the junk work. Cashman tried to show Charlie that moving this equipment around was actually costing him money, but Charlie couldn't be reasoned with when it came to paying taxes.

He also hated unions. He swore he would shut down the company before he would let B.V. DeBoni & Sons be unionized. Most everybody who worked for him believed it.

The mechanics began repacking their lunch-pails. Whitey tossed a chicken leg to Calvin who munched down on it and sighed, "Goddamn Whitey, if I was married to your woman I'd weigh 1000 pounds."

"Like hell you would, Calvin. That woman likes her lovin', and she done make you work for every bite. With your little thing she'd wear you right out. Why I bet she'd wear you down to where you'd have to wear suspenders 'cause you couldn't find a belt small enough to keep your pants up."

Rick was chuckling as he walked over to Calvin.

"What'cha laughing at College?" Calvin tried to give him a mean look, and then burst out laughing. "That damn Whitey's a piece of work, ain't he?"

"He sure is. Say, Calvin, old Henry sent me to get you and your torch up on the rock."

"What, he want me to cut him a new asshole?"

"Don't know if you've got enough acetylene for that. He's pretty hard. But he's got a crack on his faceplate. Says he can't drill till you fix it up."

"Yeah, yeah. Tell him I'll be along shortly." Calvin began packing up his gear.

C h a p t e r 4

John Cashman

Rick walked out of the maintenance building, blinking in the bright June sun. About ten yards ahead of him, halfway between the maintenance shed and the office trailer, Charlie and John Cashman, the job Super, were arguing. Charlie's arms were waving, his voice a near scream. John stood quietly, arms folded, his voice a low rumble. At six-foot-one, Cashman towered over the diminutive Charlie DeBoni.

Rick couldn't hear everything being said, but it sounded like John was trying to tell Charlie that if he moved equipment out, they were going to fall behind and maybe even have to pay a penalty. Charlie clearly wasn't buying it.

"Don't give me any grief, John. We're sending that stuff to Granby on Friday. You'll just have to make do." Charlie stomped off, jumped in his baby blue Cadillac, and roared out of the yard churning up a rooster tail of dust.

Rick rolled his scooter out from behind the maintenance shed, and was fastening his lunch-bucket when he heard John Cashman call him.

"Wallace come here a second."

Rick rocked the scooter back on its stand and trotted over to where Cashman stood. Cashman's weathered face and white-blond hair made him seem ageless, but Rick guessed he was in his mid forties. He stood, arms folded, just as he had when he talked to Charlie. He wore a plaid short-sleeved shirt, with an open collar, and the mandatory pocket protector stuffed with pens that all the "bosses" wore. He wore chino pants so low on his hips the crotch was just above his knees, and the cuffs folded over his work-boots. Rick liked and respected Cashman. He always treated Rick like he was an intelligent human being, and that was a rare experience on this job.

"You're working up with Côte and Baldridge aren't you? You doing Rudge's job as well today?"

Rick nodded.

"Well I just hired two guys who claim to be experienced chucktenders. They're looking to learn the rock drilling trade. I'm sending them up to work with Côte and Baldridge. I'm going to send you down to work with Duke on the fill."

Rick's heart sank. Shit. He liked working with the drillers. It was dirty, but it was one of the better "grunt" jobs. "You're the boss," he said without enthusiasm.

"Before you head down there I need you to run into town for me. Duke ain't happy with the nozzle on one of the fire hoses he's using to soak down the fill. Fire department said they'd lend us one. You mind picking it up? You can zip over there on that scooter of yours and we'll give you a tank of gas."

"Sure thing."

"If you get back here by lunch-time, I'll run you down to the fill."

Rick kick-started the scooter and zipped out of the yard. As he cruised along the highway, he thought about Charlie and his ploy to move the gear before the local listers put it on the tax role. One of the listers was Rick's girlfriend, Ellen's father. Edgar McCormick was the guy who would be assessing Charlie's equipment to determine how much tax Charlie would pay this year. Rick wondered if he should say anything to Edgar. It was a bit confusing to him where his loyalties should lie. In fact, just about everybody but Charlie would be happy if the listers caught Charlie and prevented him from shipping out the heavy equipment. No question that Charlie would blow sky high, though. "If I rat on him and he finds out, I'm toast." Rick thought.

Mike Hennessy, another college kid, was already working the fill with Duke. Rick had talked to him a bit. He said the work wasn't hard; just running the hose over the fill as the pans dumped fresh dirt. All you could do was try and keep the dust down. But it was pretty tedious. The thought struck Rick that he might be able to give Crackers a soaking when he was dumping his load. That made him smile. The crazy sonofabitch would probably jump off the pan and beat the shit out of him, but it would be worth it.

It was only a ten-minute ride into town. The firemen at the Bellows Falls Volunteer Fire Department were friendly, and happy to tell him all the details about the top-notch nozzle they were letting DeBoni borrow. They were also anxious to talk about the new chief. Old Jim Murphy who had been chief for twenty years was dying of stomach cancer up in the Rockingham Hospital. Elmer Blodget was the temporary chief, and from what Rick gathered, the fireman didn't think Elmer's Marine drill sergeant tactics were going to be much help putting out fires. Rick could have easily spent half a day jawing with them, but his sense of duty forced him to cut it short and head back to the job.

As he cruised along the Connecticut River, rounded the corner by the *setback*, and climbed the hill past the Jehovah's Witness "Kingdom Hall," he thought that there were worse things in life than being paid $2.56 per hour to drive your motor scooter around and get a free tank of gas to boot. He was more than a little sorry when he came to the turn where Route 103, and Route 5 split. He followed Route 5 across the Williams River and turned into the dirt track that led to the job.

He parked the scooter in the shade of the office trailer, and poked his head in the door. "I got the nozzle Mr. Cashman," he said.

John Cashman got up from his desk and grabbed his white hardhat. He pointed to the dark red pickup with DeBoni & Sons on the door and said, "Hop in."

As they drove out on to the right-of-way and turned down towards the fill, Cashman asked, "You like that drilling work?"

"It was okay," Rick answered. "I like Côte and Henry. Côte at least isn't afraid to try and teach a college kid something."

"He's a piece of work," Cashman mumbled. "Both them guys get the job done. Any talk of union up there?"

"Oh there's talk about it," Rick answered. "Côte and Henry don't have much use for the union. But they talk about it. Some of the other guys don't seem so sure it ain't a good idea. Best I can tell it's just talk, though. I think they talk it up when PH is around to get his goat. He gets pretty hot under the collar when he hears union talk."

"Yeah, they're all a bunch of jokers," Cashman pulled off the main roadbed. "I'm sure most of them know they'd never get a job in a union shop. I've run some union jobs and it's okay. They have a lot of extra rules about who can do what, and how hard they have to work, but generally the union guys know their stuff better than the guys we hire. And that counts for a lot. Fewer mistakes. You can get the work done on time."

As they sat in the truck, a tall, lean man, with unruly hair sticking out sideways from his baseball cap, sauntered towards them. It was Bob Duke, Assistant Super in charge of the fill and the bridge footings.

John got out of the truck and met Duke over by the edge of the bank. Rick stood holding the new nozzle and watched as the two talked in low tones. They came back to the truck and John got a roll of blueprints out from behind the seat. He stretched them out on the hood, and he and Duke talked some more, pointing here and there on the blueprint. Rick had no idea what they were talking about, but it seemed to lead to agreement between the two.

Duke hollered, "You, *College*. Follow me and bring that nozzle."

Chapter 5

The Duke

Rick hurried to catch up to the lanky "Super" as he strode across the freshly compacted fill. It was midday, and the temperature on the fill was easily 100°. Bob Duke, known to just about everybody as *The Duke*, had a reputation as a hard, but fair man. While the crew disliked and distrusted PH, they trusted Duke. He made no effort to be liked, and that was okay. One of things the crew distrusted about PH was that sometimes he tried to be one of the boys. But of course he couldn't be. He was management. They were labor. Duke understood that and respected the line.

Duke also had a legendary temper. He'd chewed just about everybody's ass at one time or another. When he did, you knew you deserved it. He didn't bother with praise. It was your job to do it right.

Rick could see Mike Hennessy spraying water out across the fill, hanging onto the business end of a fire hose. He worked the water from one edge of the fill to the other and then back again.

"Need more water," Duke said. "Ain't enough to just keep down the dust. We need water to compact this fill. Got to meet certain compaction tests."

Beyond Hennessy, Rick could see one of the grade foremen holding a second hose with a feeble spray.

"You're going to run that second hose," Duke said. "Soon as we change the nozzle. You just go over the same ground the other *College* is wetting down. You think you can handle that?"

"Sure."

They passed Hennessy and came up on Dana Andrews, the grade-foreman who was running the second hose. "I brought you a *College*. You can get back to pounding stakes. Now let's change that nozzle."

Duke pointed to the bank. "At the bottom of that bank is a pump. It's an old fart, and it's hard to start. I don't want to shut it off. I want you to run down the bank and turn off the valve to this hose. When you do, the pump is going to labor some, and try and stall. If it stalls, it will take forever to get it started again. So you are going to turn the water right back on. I'll change the nozzle between the time you shut off the valve and turn it back on. You got that, College?"

"Yep. Off, then right back on. Don't let it stall."

"Listen again. Off, then right back on. Do not let the pump stall."

"I got it."

"Then what are you waiting for? Get down there. When I yell, you turn off the water and then turn it back on."

"Yes sir," Rick said, and headed over the edge of the fill. It was about thirty feet down the bank to the edge of water. The old pump sat on two wheels with its tow-bar propped up on cement blocks. An intake hose ran from the pump out into the little backwater. Another hose ran up the bank.

Rick positioned himself at the valve. He heard Duke yell, "Shut it off!" He spun the valve closed and immediately the pump began to labor and cough. He waited a second or two, and then turned the valve back on. He heard some commotion up topside, but didn't think much about it as he climbed the steep bank.

As he cleared the edge, he found himself face-to-face with Duke—a wet, steaming mad Duke.

"By the holy o, rip-roaring, jumping Jesus Christ! You are the dumbest college fuck we have ever had on this job. Get your ass off my fill, and now!"

"Wha…wha." Rick stammered. "But, but I just—"

"Get the fuck off my fill!"

Rick turned and began the long trudge back to the yard. He was stunned. His summer job was gone. He'd just been fired.

A pickup pulled up along side of him.

"Hop in, College." It was Everett, the old codger who did odd jobs here and there. He was cackling with glee.

Rick climbed in.

"You should' a seen it." Everett cackled. "Old Duke, he just about got the nozzle to the hose when the water hit. Hee hee."

"I don't get it. I just did what he told me. I thought he knew how long it would take to change it."

"Ain't your fault, College. He had Andrews holding the nozzle while he unscrewed the old one. Andrews dropped it when he went to hand it to him. Old Duke, he ain't gonna screw on no nozzle with sand in the threads. So he hurried up and wiped it clean. Course, that took some time. Hee hee. He was one mad puppy. The water was turning to steam he was so fucking hot."

"Yeah, funny," Rick moaned. "But there goes my job."

"No way, College. I'll talk to John. He won't fire you over this. Like I said, it ain't your fault. But God, Boy, you are gonna be a livin' legend."

"You'd do that for me, Everett? Thanks. I really owe you."

"Worth it Boy. Funniest damn thing I ever seen on a job and I been working these jobs for forty-five years. Hee hee!"

Rick sat on the ground next to his motor scooter while Everett went into the office and told the story to John Cashman.

Cashman came out and motioned for Rick. Rick got up and walked slowly over. He could see that Cashman was making an effort not to smile.

"Wallace, I don't think you're going to work out down on the fill. Take the rest of the day off. Tomorrow report to the dynamite crew. Oh, and Wallace, be a little more careful will you. Mistake like that on the dynamite crew might be fatal."

Chapter 6

Church

The dynamite crew met in the main yard every morning and rode out to the shot in DeBoni's dynamite wagon, a converted World War II combat ambulance. The ambulance was painted DeBoni red. The insides were lined with plywood, presumably to prevent a metal-on-metal spark from setting off the dynamite. It was one of the few concessions made to treat dynamite as if it were dangerous.

The dynamite crew consisted of Wilber *Church* Halbert, the *blaster* grade-foreman, and Billy *Barrel-ass* Brennan, his assistant, plus assorted laborers. Mike *Teach* Merryweather, an art teacher from a local high school who worked summers on construction for "drinking money," was pretty much a regular on the crew, as was Danny Dombroski, another *College* from Westminster West, a near-by hamlet. Rick and Danny had gone to high school together, but weren't really friends. Rick was a *townie*, Danny was a *woodchuck*, and their social circles didn't cross much.

"You working with us today, *Squirt?*" Barrel-ass's voice thundered across the yard.

Rick had a nickname. Not exactly the kind of nickname he had hoped for, but at least for the moment he had been lifted up from the faceless masses of *dumb college fucks* and was recognized as a person.

"I hear they're going to award you the *golden nozzle,*" Teach chuckled.

"Wow, I hear the Duke was plenty pissed off," Danny said.

"He'd have been hot under the collar if Squirt here, hadn't cooled him off," Teach put his arm around Rick's shoulder. "Wonder if you would do the same for our friend PH? What was it the Duke said?"

"He said, 'By the holy o, rip roaring jumpin Je—'"

"That's enough of that," Church said. "No reason to be taking the Lord's name. Get in the truck everybody, we got to blow some rock today."

Profanity and cursing are part of the natural language of construction. Take away the word "fuck" and its many variations, and most guys on the job would lose half their vocabulary. Some might not be able to communicate at all. Church was a rare bird. He never cursed or used profanity.

"Strongest thing I ever heard him say," Côte had confided one day over lunch, was 'dang!' Heard him say that over in Springfield the day he had that shot go *bang* instead of *whomp*. Rocks flying everywhere. One skipped under the shovel and hit old Clyde right in the gut. Took him to the hospital. He was okay. Good thing 'cause you can't hardly find a good man on the shovel like Clyde. Rocks coming down like rain. There was a greenhouse over about a half-mile away, broke every window. There is still a big dent in Hannibal's Euclid. Go look some time. Right in the right door. Old Church, he said, 'Dang!' "

Rick remembered. That was last year, and he had been on the crew that reglazed the greenhouse. He had learned how to putty a window—about 100 of them to be exact.

Rick swallowed the rest of the Duke's curse. He respected Church. Church was a Jehovah's Witness, but he never handed out literature or tried to convert anybody. He just didn't "talk the talk" everyone else on the job talked.

Church reminded Rick of Walter Mitty, from the Thurber story, or maybe more like Wally Cox playing Walter Mitty in the movie. He was slight, had a narrow face, and a sharp, pointed chin. He wore wire-rimmed glasses, and looked like he should be afraid of his own shadow. But Rick had never seen Church back down from a confrontation. He stood his ground, told people what he thought, and never showed any fear or anger. He always had a little smile on his face like someone was whispering a secret in his ear, or telling him a little joke.

Church climbed into his own pickup and hollered over to Barrel-ass. "Take'm up to the magazine and pick up 25 Hi Pro, 10 Special Gel, 10 Toval, and 30 bags of fertilizer. Grab some caps—a box of each. I'll be up checking with PH to see when he wants to shoot."

Barrel-ass appropriated the driver's seat in the dynamite wagon, the only actual seat. The rest of the crew piled into the back, and they roared out of the yard and headed up on the fill.

The magazine was a small cement block shack, built into the side of the hill. It was situated midway between the two interstate lanes, such as they were, at that stage of construction. The lanes would be about a quarter-mile apart here, with a knob of a hill in between. Rick thought it would be picturesque when it was done.

You'd have missed the turnoff to the magazine if you didn't know where it was. DeBoni didn't advertise its location. It wasn't all that unusual to have somebody steal a few cases of dynamite from a construction job. Farmers always needed to blow a stump or something, and dynamite was expensive. But it wasn't exactly a secret. The magazine had a big padlock on the door but that wouldn't have stopped anyone who really wanted to steal some dynamite.

Barrel-ass parked the truck with the back door facing the magazine. He lumbered out of the truck, and unlocked the big Master Lock padlock. He swung open the thick plank door and reached in and grabbed four boxes of caps, each color coded for the electrical delay. Then he went over and sat down in the shade.

"You heard the man, boys," he hollered. "Twenty-five cases of Hi Pro, 10 Special Gel, 10 cases of Toval, and thirty bags of fertilizer."

Barrel-ass was not exactly a boss, and should have been working with them. The crew didn't hesitate to give him a load of grief over what a fat, lazy, good-for-nothing slob he was. But the truth was, that there was barely room for three to work, and the work wasn't hard. All three preferred to be working rather than sitting, so they formed a line. Rick grabbed the cases from the magazine and handed them to Danny. He handed them to Teach, who stacked them in the truck.

There were four major kinds of dynamite being used, all made by Dupont. Hi Pro was the workhorse. Packed fifty sticks to a case, each stick was an inch-and-a-half in diameter, made of hard, waxed cardboard, and contained a pound of packed yellow powder. Special Gel was similar, but if you broke a stick, the inside was a yellowish crumbly clay-like material.

Toval sticks were about the same size, but more pliable. It felt more like modeling clay that had been worked. Fertilizer was ammonium nitrate—literally a fertilizer. People found out how explosive it could be when a shipload exploded and leveled Brownsville, Texas. Now they used it as filler. It was much cheaper than dynamite, and every bit as effective. Fully loaded, the old ambulance carried about 4,000 lbs. of explosive.

By 8:30, they had loaded the truck. Barrel-ass, who had finished off his first lunch-sized snack of the day, climbed in and started the engine. With no room inside, the crew clung onto the sides, standing on the running boards and the back bumper. The overloaded truck lurched its way back onto the right-of-way, and began the long climb up, where Rick had been working with the drillers just the day before.

They parked near the compressors, leaving room for the air tracks to maneuver when it came time to move them. Both Church's and PH's pickups were pulled up off the side of the right-of-way. Rick could see the two of them standing on the forward edge of the ledge, talking.

Côte and Henry were working well back from the edge now. They were drilling near the top, and by looking at the neat rows of plastic bags, stuffed in the holes to prevent dirt and debris from being kicked in, there seemed to be a perfect square, 40 feet on a side, holes about 24 inches apart. It looked as if there were only a half-dozen or so more holes required to complete the grid. The two new drill tenders were standing up behind Côte and Henry, talking together. They looked to be in their early twenties, lean, and narrow-faced. Rick thought they looked like brothers, or at least cousins.

"Let's start haulin', boys," Barrel-ass boomed.

The procedure was simple. Haul boxes up the hill, and distribute them around the holes. The aim was just to get the dynamite up on the hill. Later, they'd sort out how many sticks per hole, and what kind.

"PH wants to shoot at noon," Church said as he came down to the truck. "Guess he doesn't want to lose any time. We won't make that though. Probably be two, two-thirty. Just too many holes to fill. Haul them boxes, boys. Let him see we're working."

They hauled boxes until their ten o'clock sandwich break. Rick carried his thermos over to where Côte and Henry were sitting on a log in the shade, off the edge of the drill grid. The two new chuck tenders were perched on a rock behind them.

"Hello there Squirt," Côte smiled. "Still talking to us lesser educated folks?"

"Hey, come on Côte. I just do what I'm told. Cashman says go down on the fill, I go down on the fill."

"Do what you're told a little too precisely, is what I hear," Henry laughed. "Think you can come up with something to drown PH?" He took a bite from the end of his cigar, rolled it on his tongue and spit it out. "Maybe blow him up? That would be okay too."

"These here boys are the Marstons. Dig and Dab, or Dob and Dump, or something like that. They're from over Haverill way." Côte waved his hand back at the two lean-faced men sitting on the rock.

"Dodd," said the taller of the two.

"Ding," said his brother.

"Rick," said Rick. He poured coffee into his thermos top and lit a cigarette. "Cashman said you guys are looking to be drillers?"

"Gonna take our jobs, Henry." Côte laughed.

"Okay by me," said Henry. "I'm ready to retire right now. I've had enough of this shit. You, Ding, or Dang, or whatever. Go run the drill. I'm takin' a nap."

"Hey, we're just learning a trade. Gonna be some good jobs on that cut when Paligrinni starts it. They say they're gonna run 24 hours a day. Big bucks. Union job."

Rick knew he was referring to the other side of the ravine, where the other end of DeBoni's bridge would be anchored. It was a solid granite ledge about a half-mile thick, and a good 90 feet above grade. "You guys union?" he asked.

"I got a card," Dodd said. "Ding ain't yet. But it's the coming thing. Everything's gonna be union pretty quick. Good deal, too. Pays better than this chicken-shit outfit."

"Another 50 cents an hour." Henry spat. "Shit, they take that back in dues. Seems like just one more bunch of guys trying to tell ya what to do. You like it so much, how come you ain't working one of them union jobs?"

"Aw it ain't like that. They only take back thirty cents, and it goes for pension and insurance and stuff. It's a good deal. Soon as Ding gets his card, we'll probably hook up with a union outfit. Of course, this outfit may go union first. I hear there's a meeting on Thursday night."

"Yeah I heard that too." Barrel-ass chimed in his two cents. "Gonna be down on the boat landing. Beer and barbequed chicken. I can go for some of that."

"They know the way to your heart, Barrel-ass." Côte laughed. "Feed him and he's yours."

"Any you guys show up at the meeting, don't bother coming to work on Friday."

They all looked up. PH was standing there glaring at them, hands in his pockets, jingling his change.

"Well shit, on that note, I'll be there too." Henry laughed. "Anything PH is against, can't be all bad."

"Watch your mouth Henry, or somebody'll shut it for you."

It got deadly silent.

Henry stood up. He stretched himself to his full 5-foot-eight. He held his grade-stake like a baseball bat. "You think you're that somebody, Pecker Head?"

PH just spun on his heel and strode away.

Côte broke the silence. " I don't think he wants to pitch to you Henry."

Everyone laughed except Henry. "Cocksucker," he said. "Come on Dang, let's drill some rock."

Chapter 7

Lightnin'

By eleven they had all the dynamite up on the hill. Church had distributed a cap to each hole, figuring out how he wanted the delays to work. A good explosion is a carefully planned event, with different holes fired microseconds after other holes in a planned sequence that first cracks the rock, and then pulverizes it with lines of pressure crashing into each other, the full force of the explosion being absorbed into the stone. A good shot goes *whump*, and the whole chunk of mountain lifts a foot or two into the air and settles back down, broken into millions of pieces. Each cap is color coded to indicate its delay; that is how long after the electricity hits the circuit, that the cap fires. Get it wrong, and the shot might go *bang* and send rocks flying every which way like the shot in Springfield. It was an art, but a learnable one. Church had gone to school at Dupont for three weeks, learning the ins-and-outs of dynamiting.

Even when you got it right, it could go wrong. The exploding dynamite creates pressure, and pressure follows the line of least resistance. They figured at Springfield that there had been an undetected crevasse that ran through the rock. All the energy of the explosion escaped through that fault blowing the top off, rather than being absorbed into the ledge. It not only sent rocks flying for a half-mile or more, but it didn't succeed in busting up the ledge. It left giant boulders that had to be individually drilled and shot. It was the kind of mistake that cost the company money, and made the blaster the butt of industry jokes. Some guys would have quit and moved to Alaska after that kind of fiasco. Not Church. He said, "Dang!" smiled, and went on to the next job.

Church told them how many Hi Pros, Special Gels, and Tovals per hole. Basically, his strategy was to run half-a-dozen Hi Pros, and one or two Special Gels down the hole, and then a Toval, with the cap in it, was carefully lowered down. Two or three more Tovals, another half-dozen Hi Pros, and a couple or three Special Gels followed. The hole was then filled with fertilizer up to within two feet of the surface. Dirt and stones were tamped in to seal the hole flush with the surface, with just the cap wires sticking out.

When they took their lunch break at noon, Church estimated that the shot would go at 2:30. He looked down the valley towards Bellows Falls, where thunderheads were building. "Hope that storm holds off till then," he said.

"Why?" Danny asked. "Thunderstorms make a difference to dynamite?"

"See them caps," Church said. "They're electrical. You get electricity in the air and they can go off. That's why they have those signs that tell you to turn off your two-way radio in a blasting zone."

"Really? You could set'm off with a radio?"

"You bet, College. That's the way they do it some places. Have radio caps instead of electrical caps. But you can't do that for a shot like this where you need to set off the caps at different times. That's why we use wire and a battery."

"Battery? What battery?"

"That's what's in the little black box, boy. Just a battery like a car battery. When I push down the plungers, it sends a current through the wires and sets off the caps."

Rick was surprised that Danny knew so little about how dynamiting worked. But then that's what it meant to be a *dumb college fuck.*

"Hey Teach," he yelled, holding up one of the safety flyers from inside the dynamite boxes. "I've been checking *The Do's and Don'ts of Dynamite,* here, and best I can tell, we have a perfect score. We have done every one of the *don'ts,* and we have *don'ted* every one of the *do's.*"

"Well Squirt, that's the secret of success in this business. What do a bunch of jerks at Dupont know about real life? They just print that thing to keep their lawyers happy."

"People who make mistakes with dynamite probably don't get to sue," Côte said.

"Sure, they get the pieces together and file a class-action suit," Teach responded.

Everyone looked at him a bit strangely.

"You see...ah, never mind. Bad joke."

"Let's go people. Lunch is over and we need to hustle to beat that storm." Church was up and agitated. He grabbed Barrel-ass, and the two strode out onto the shot and began loading holes.

The drillers had finished their work on this shot. They began maneuvering the air tracks down the hill to where the compressors stood. They would drag the compressors a half-mile or so up the right-of-way, and park them until after the shot.

Teach and Rick filled and tamped holes after Barrel-ass and Church loaded them with dynamite. Danny began hauling boxes and stuff off the shot area.

As soon as the last hole was loaded, Church began wiring up the shot. He worked quickly, stripping wires and twisting them together to connect every hole with the main wire that would run to the battery box.

The sky darkened and the wind picked up.

"Better get off the shot till this blows over, boys." Church said. He waved to them and led them off the shot. Just as they got to the bottom, the first lightning flashed and thunder roared.

Danny yelled, "My lunch-bucket!"

Rick looked over his shoulder as he hustled toward a pile of stumps, and could see Danny's lunch-pail sitting up on the knob.

Danny ran back up the hill. He grabbed his bucket, turned, and began running back down towards where the rest of the crew had already huddled behind the stumps and brush.

Suddenly the whole air went blue, and thunder crashed, immediately followed by a monstrous explosion.

"Ooooh, shit." Teach moaned.

Dirt and debris rained down on Rick and the others. He heard a crash nearby as something smashed into the brush heap.

Rick lay very still, his arms over his head. It was quiet. Rain pelted down for a minute. Then hail. Then nothing.

"Danny?" he said.

He heard a moan.

Rick got to his feet. Teach, Barrel-ass, and Church were standing up. He heard the moan again. "Danny?"

He crawled his way over downed branches and boulders to the brush heap. It was a tangle of raspberry bushes and cut branches, heaped up, ready to be burned. Danny was lying in the middle of the heap. He held up one hand with the handle of his lunch-bucket clutched tightly in his fist.

"Danny!" He yelled. "Hey guys, over here! He's alive. Sonofabitch. He's alive!"

Danny sat up. He looked a little bewildered. Then he grinned. "I think I got blowed up," he said. "Shit. How am I alive?"

"Thank the Lord," Church murmured.

"Well come on, *Lightnin'*, " Barrel-ass bellowed. "Don't lie there. There's work to be done."

"Another *dumb college fuck* retired, and another nickname born," Rick thought, shaking his head over the miracle. It must have been Danny he heard crashing into the brush. He must have flown through the air and crashed down into the raspberries and puckerbrush. It was a genuine miracle.

The drillers had walked back from where they parked the air tracks and compressors. Henry looked at the shot and asked, "Whole thing blow? Or just part?"

Church looked at the mound. "Just part, I'm afraid. I didn't get it all wired."

"Shit," Henry said. "Better get Chip up here to clean it off."

Church nodded, and walked off to his pickup.

"What's the big deal?" Rick asked.

"The big deal is unexploded dynamite," Henry said. "The big fucking deal is that somebody, probably me, is going to have to drill out those live holes.

"Are you an angel?" Lightnin' asked. "You don't look like an angel. You look like Henry. And Henry looks like—"

Henry spat a wad of cigar tobacco on the ground and walked away.

"Danny, are you alright?" Rick asked. Danny looked right past him. Rick could see that Danny was shaking.

"Teach, I think he's in shock. We should get him to a hospital."

"You're right. Let's take the ambulance. Hey Barrel-ass, we're running Danny into the hospital in the ambulance," he hollered. Barrel-ass gave a little wave of permission and turned back to his lunch.

Together, Rick and Teach lead Danny over to the ancient truck. Rick opened the back and helped Danny up on the floor, and climbed in beside him. Teach jumped into the driver's seat and fired up the engine.

"Go slow, Teach. It's rough back here."

"You bet, boy." Teach eased the old truck onto the northbound right–of–way. The road back to the yard was blocked with debris so he headed in the other direction. "We can get off on the old Alden Hill Road," he hollered over the growling roar of the engine.

In the back, Rick put his arm around Danny, braced his feet across the Truck bed, and held on tight. Danny was humming to himself. Rick noticed a little trickle of blood coming out of Danny's ear. Danny turned and looked Rick right in the eye and said, "Take care of Kelly, Rick."

"Kelly? Who's Kelly?" Rick asked. But Danny didn't answer. He just closed his eyes and hummed to himself. Rick could feel Danny's body trembling uncontrollably.

Teach worked the truck down a steep pitch onto the graded town road.

"Better go faster now, Teach," Rick said. "I think he's in trouble."

Teach gunned the engine and the truck lurched up the hill. "We'll catch South Street and come into the hospital the back way," Teach said. "This is my country. I live just up here a half-mile or so."

South Street was blacktopped, but not much smoother than Alden Hill Road. Teach put the pedal to the metal, and the truck gained momentum, topping out at about 35 miles-per-hour. "It don't go too fuckin' fast," Teach said in his best construction voice. "But it's probably fast as you'd want to go in this thang."

Rick said nothing. He just held Danny. He wondered if they would become friends here on the job, when they had never been friends back in high school. Then he wondered if Danny would be back on the job soon, or ever.

Teach brought the old ambulance complaining and groaning down the hill, and into the emergency port of Springfield Hospital. He leaped out, came around and opened the back doors. Together, he and Rick eased Danny out of the truck. Danny's eyes were glazed. He had trouble walking.

A nurse came out and brought a wheelchair. They sat Danny down and the nurse wheeled him into the emergency room "You boys go tell the desk what this is about."

"There was an explosion," Rick said to the nurse. "He was on the shot and lightning hit. He flew twenty feet into some bushes."

The nurse just waved at him and hustled Danny through the door into the examination room.

Teach was already over at the desk, leaning on it and smiling down at a pretty young girl. "It was a dynamite accident, Miss. The young man was on the rocks. The dynamite was all in place and lightning set if off early. He got blown about twenty or thirty feet, did a full flip, and landed in some bushes and brush. We thought he was okay at first. But then he didn't seem quite right so we rushed him to your tender care."

"Name?" the young woman said.

"Whose? Mine or his" Teach asked.

"The patient's name, please," the young woman said in a firm tone.

"Mmmm, Danny, something Polish. Rick, what was Lightning's name?"

"Dombroski," Rick said. "Daniel Lewis Dombroski. He's 20 years old. He lives in Westminster West, out off old Route 7. His father is Peter Dombroski. He's a farmer."

"Telephone number?"

"No idea," Rick said. "You'll have to look it up."

"Insurance number?"

"How would we know that?" Rick stared out the window. "We hardly knew him at all. You probably should check his wallet or something."

The girl at the desk was ignoring them as she typed up a form.

"Miss," Rick asked. "Can we find out if he's going to be alright?"

"The waiting room is down the hall," she said not looking up. "They usually only tell things to the family. But you can wait if you want."

"Well, will the doctor want to ask us anything about the accident?"

"What could you tell him?"

Rick and Teach looked at each other and shrugged. "Nothing I guess. Well, you should write down that it happened on the DeBoni job on Interstate 91. Maybe the cops or somebody will want to know."

They went back out and climbed into the ambulance. Teach got in the driver's seat and Rick sat on the floor on the passenger's side. Teach started it up. "Let's stop at my place on the way back," he said. "Maybe have a cold beer."

"Okay," Rick answered. He looked up through the filthy windshield. The world looked yellow and grimy. It matched how he felt.

Chapter 8

Chip

A dynamite misfire is a dangerous thing. The rock is cracked but not broken. Plenty of dynamite is still in the ground, unexploded with live caps. It all has to be removed before the shot can be redone.

The first step is to bulldoze the top of the ledge clean. For that you need a big bulldozer. Not because the job requires power, but because if a hole should blow, the operator has a better chance of surviving if he has a big bulldozer under him, rather than one of the little *Cats*. Rick and the dynamite crew stood around smoking and sipping coffee as they waited in the early morning haze for Chip to bring up the D-9, and clear the ledge. Then they would begin the tricky job of removing dynamite from the holes.

Steve "Chip" Johnson operated the biggest bulldozer DeBoni had, a Caterpillar D-9. Chip was down the hill on the north side of the road, on Ed McCormick's land, where the big belly scraper pans picked up dirt to dump on the fill. A pan would roar into the gravel pit and over the edge, dropping the jaws of its belly scoop. As the pan filled, it would lose momentum and eventually stop. Then Chip would run up behind the pan with his D-9, and give it a goose, tracks churning as he pushed the pan through the gravel pit. The pan would close its maw, and with a final shove, be off down the hill to dump its load on the fill. Every pan load was money in Ed McCormick's pocket, with DeBoni paying him a few cents a yard for suitable fill.

Chip was glad for a break in the routine. Donny, the other dozer operator, would try to keep the pans moving with the D-8, but the pans would probably have to run three-quarters full until Chip returned. He turned the big cat uphill, and crawled his way up to the misfired shot.

There was little doubt how Chip got his nickname. He was a short, muscular little man, with big round cheeks, which he kept stuffed with *Day's Work* chewing tobacco. He had big beaver teeth in the front, a little pug nose, and tiny eyes. He looked like a chipmunk stocking up for winter.

"Hey you fuckin' chipmunk. Get up here and clean this ledge." Henry waved his grade-stake and hollered with mock belligerence.

Chip pulled the D-9 up short and leaped down. He ran at Henry and bumped his belly up against him. "Who you callin' a chipmunk you sorry-assed dust-eater. I resemble that remark!"

The two laughed and pushed each other. "See this chipmunk, Squirt?" Henry chortled. "This little sonofabitch is the best goddamn bulldozer jockey in the state. I'd love him even if he weren't my son-in-law."

"Aw Dad, gosh." Chip crossed his legs and curtsied like a bashful little girl.

"Hope his daughter is better lookin' than Henry," Church said, and gave his little smile.

Everyone was dumbfounded. It was the first time they had ever heard Church make a joke.

"Let's get this show on the road," PH was standing down by the bulldozer, hands on hips. "Johnson, push the rock right up on top of the last shot. Clean off this road first, though. You guys hang tight until he cleans some space. Then start looking for those holes. This is going to put us behind."

It took Chip less than an hour to scrape the ledge clear of debris. Once Church waved him to stop, and hiked over and pulled a stick of dynamite out from under the blade, still trailing the wires from the blasting cap. That made everyone pause for a minute. But there was nothing to do, but to do it, so Chip put the dozer back in gear and kept scraping.

When he finished, he jumped down and walked over to Henry and Côte. "There's the hard part. Now you guys do the easy part." He gave Henry a playful punch. "Take care, Dad. Don't make my wife an orphan."

Henry grinned and spat out a piece of tobacco.

Church directed Barrel-ass, Rick, and Teach to fan out and look for the telltale wires that showed an unfired hole. Some were easy to find. Others they had to scrape around for. Henry and Côte had laid out a neat grid so that once they found one or two; the locations of the rest were easy to figure out. As they found a hole, they pushed in a grade-stake, and went on to look for the next.

Church showed them the next step. One hole at a time, they scratched down, getting the dirt and debris clear. Then they took a long wooden rod with a metal spike in the end, and went fishing down the hole trying to spear and lift up the dynamite sticks. Finally, when they had all they could reach, they used the wires to wiggle the stick with the blasting cap back up the hole with any of the sticks that remained on top. When it worked, it worked slick. Sometimes the ledge had shifted in the hole and you couldn't get anything out. Sometimes they got part of it out, and the wires pulled loose. By noon, they had all they could get.

"Your turn," Church said to Henry.

"What's next?" Dodd Marston asked.

"Henry here drills out each hole." Côte smiled.

"Ain't that dangerous?" Ding was wide-eyed.

"Well a little bit. See, concussion is what makes dynamite blow. So that drill thumping on it just might be enough to set it off. You try to be gentle, but..." Côte shrugged.

The group was sitting in a small grove of trees near the top of the ledge. Behind them, to the northwest, was seemingly endless forest. Rick thought about Ellen McCormick. This land went right up to her doorstep about a mile-and-a-half away. Her old man owned it all. They had walked down this way more than once, looking for a good place to neck. There was an old quarry just over the hill that had some fossils in it. They were using it for a parking lot now. It was far enough away from the ledge so that it was pretty safe from any debris. But it was close enough so you didn't have to walk a mile from where you parked. He thought maybe he could run his scooter up the old logging road after work, show up on Ellen's doorstep, and maybe cage some supper.

He heard Ding ask, "How come Henry? Why not you, Côte, or both you guys?"

"No sense risking both," Henry said.

"Henry's top dog," Côte said. "I'd be happy to do it, but he won't let me."

"Which of you guys is going to help?" Henry asked.

"No fucking way," Dodd hollered. "Ain't my job to get blowed up."

"Not me," Ding chimed in. "I'd quit first."

"Brave ain't they," Henry laughed.

"I'll do it, Henry." Rick spoke up and wondered why he had.

Henry looked at him. "All right Squirt, let's move the rig up here."

Rick followed Henry over to the compressor. They fired it up and waited for the air pressure to build. Rick kept the air-hoses from fouling while Henry ran the drill back up on the ledge. There were ten loaded or partially loaded holes. Henry set up on the hole nearest the outside edge. "If it blows, it might vent out that way," Henry pointed with his grade-stake. "Course you never really know."

Rick lined up four extra pieces of steel, greasing each coupling and threaded end.

Henry took one of the long wooden rods they had used to spear dynamite. He used that like a grade-stake to tap the controls while he and Rick stood off the edge of the shot.

There was almost no resistance. The drill ran down twelve feet in a couple of seconds. Henry tapped the controls off. They slipped the coupling bracket around the coupling and ran the drill head back up the boom. They added a second steel, then a third, fourth, and a fifth.

"Like drilling through butter," Henry said. "But this butter can go boom. Don't forget it."

They moved to the next hole, and it went the same. So did the third, and the fourth. The fifth hole had some ledge in it, and had to be drilled a bit. They had the same problem with the sixth, and the eighth holes. The others were quickly drilled clean.

"That's it," Henry said. He walked off the ledge and got a drink of water. Rick could see from the stains on the back of his shirt he had been sweating profusely, something Henry just didn't do. Rick figured that this was a lot more dangerous than it looked.

Côte moved the other air track up, and Rick went back to the dynamite crew. Church had laid out a half-dozen new holes that needed to be drilled. He pointed to Barrel-ass, "Go get about twenty Hi Pro and Special Gel, ten Toval, and 25 fertilizer. Bring a box each of the caps."

The crew headed back to the magazine and loaded the truck. By the time they got back to the shot, Henry and Côte were finishing up. Without a word, they hauled dynamite up on the hill and distributed it to each of the holes.

Church wired the shot quickly. He had Rick hold the end of the heavy yellow wire, and Church himself took the spool and walked a hundred and fifty yards up the hill, and behind a small rock outcropping.

When he got back to the shot, he looked up at the clear blue sky and nodded. Then he took off his hard hat and waved it downhill. PH was standing by Clyde's shovel, looking up his way, took his hat, and waved back. Clyde shut off his shovel and it was like a signal. One-by-one the Euclids shut down, their air horns blaring. It was quiet.

Noise is like profanity on a construction site. It's most noticeable when it's not there. The quiet was so solid you could almost feel it.

Together the crew walked with Church to where he had set the detonator. He opened the terminals and screwed a wire down on each. He crouched before the box, a little smile playing on his face. He pressed the circuit tester. It flashed green.

Church stuck his thumbs up, and then turned them over and ground them into the two "Fire" buttons.

There was a *whump*, and a little dust cloud rose over the shot.

"That's it?" Rick asked.

"That's it." Church said. "Good ones aren't exciting. We don't need exciting."

The crew was all smiles as they walked back to survey the shot. They could see Tim, the timekeeper's pickup speeding up the hill toward them. "Wonder what that's about," Teach muttered.

McDermott halted his pickup at the edge of the shot. "Any stuff that's Dombroski's up here?" he hollered.

"Dombroski? Oh, the college kid. No, I don't think so?" Church looked around at the crew. Everyone shrugged.

"They just called from the hospital. He died," Tim said. "Wallace can you stop down at the office?"

They stood and watched Tim get back in his pickup, back it around, and head out.

Without a word they headed back to their machines.

Chapter 9

Edgar

The day dragged to a close. The drillers positioned their rigs on the ledge to begin drilling for the next shot. The dynamite crew picked up boxes, trash, wire, and other debris, tossing the combustible stuff on the brush pile for a scheduled burn later in the week. Barrel-ass wrapped all of the wire up into a large ball.

"Good copper in this shit," he said to no one in particular. "Burn off the insulation and turn it in. Probably enough to buy a six-pack right here."

No one paid any attention to him.

Finally the air horns from the Euclids signaled shutdown for the day.

Rick tied his lunch-bucket on the back of his scooter and putted off over the hill and down through the construction-site. Some of the drivers walking to their cars yelled insults at him and he waved the finger at them in an automatic gesture. He pulled into the yard and shut of the scooter. He could see Cashman was busy giving instructions to the Duke, so he sidled over to the maintenance shed to watch the mechanics pick up.

"Hey Whitey," he hollered. "You guys going to have the D-9 out on the fill by Friday?"

"Yeah, boy." Whitey was carefully cleaning the grease from his hands with a strong-smelling degreasing agent. "We'll have the fucker out there. I doubt that it will be able to push a wet fart from a whore's asshole. But it will be out there. Man wants it out there. It'll be out there."

"How come no guts?" Rick asked.

"No guts because this old piece of shit has about a bazillion hours on it. The pistons are rattling in the cylinders. You got more compression when you jack off than this thing can work up in a whole day. It needs a new engine."

"Yeah," Arnie, the hydraulics man chimed in, "once you put a new engine in it you'll find it ain't got enough hydraulic pressure to lift its blade. So you gotta add a whole new hydraulic system."

"Course," Calvin chimed in, "the metal so damn tired you can about break pieces off with your hand. Old Charlie bought himself a beaut here. Hope he didn't pay more than scrap for it."

"Chip ain't going to be too happy driving that," Rick laughed.

"Chip goes with the new D-9 up to Granby. I don't know who they got driving this pig. Shit, they may let you drive it Squirt."

The mechanics all laughed at Whitey's suggestion that DeBoni would let a *dumb college fuck* drive any bulldozer, even this piece of crap.

Rick looked over his shoulder and saw that Cashman had finished with the Duke. He waved at the mechanics, "Maybe I can get the Duke to put in a word for me."

"He's got a word for you all right." Whitey laughed. "But I don't think you want to hear that word. It might make you blush."

Rick left them discussing among themselves the particular epithet that the Duke would use as he kicked Rick's ass over the bank, and walked slowly across the yard toward John Cashman.

"You wanted to see me, Mr. Cashman?"

"Oh, Wallace. Mmm, yeah. Do you know Dombroski's family? I've got to go down to Shaughnessy's and talk to the family. Charlie wants me to give them a little something."

"I know them a bit. You know we're not close friends or anything. But I know who they are."

"Would you meet me there at seven-thirty tonight? Introduce me to the family? I would appreciate it. This isn't fun but it's easier if somebody introduces you."

Rick said he would, flattered that Cashman would ask. As he walked backed to his scooter he thought, "Oh shit. Ellen is back from Boston tonight. I'm supposed to see her."

As he kick-started the scooter he had an idea. "Maybe I'll just mosey over the hill and see her right now. I'll tell her what's up and how I got to go to the union meeting tomorrow night and set something up for Friday night."

He rode back up on the job and made his way up the hill. As he passed the turn-off to the dynamite magazine, he saw PH's pickup on the access road. He wondered vaguely what PH was up to. "Probably doing a count," he thought.

He pulled off the job into the old quarry where they parked, and then picked up the ancient roadbed that followed the Williams River. The little Vespa wasn't the best off-road vehicle, but it putted its way over rocks and through the scrub brush that grew back in the ancient roadway. It was light enough so that he could lift it over a small tree that had fallen across the road. After a few minutes, he turned up the hill on a newer logging road. Ten minutes later, he emerged on the edge of one of the McCormick fields. He found the tractor path and followed it, letting himself out of the gate and taking great care to reset the gate latch; a piece of baling twine looped over a post.

As he drove into the yard he could see Ellen's father, Edgar, sitting on the back stoop smoking a cigarette. Rick liked Edgar. He had a lean, hard, weather-beaten look of a man who spent his life outdoors in all kinds of weather. He worked hard, milking about 120 Herefords and raising some chickens. He had inherited the farm from his wife Mora's father. He had added to it, buying derelict farmsteads that abutted his place. He owned well over a thousand acres now, and farmed a little less than half. The rest was in sugarbush and pine. Edgar treated Rick like a human being, and that raised him high in Rick's book. Ellen's mother, Mora, was pretty sure that Rick was subhuman and certainly not worthy of her daughter's attention.

"Hey Ed," Rick hollered as he shut off the scooter and set it back on its stand. "You cutting hay already?"

"First cutting's raked and ready to bale. You coming up Saturday and helping us haul it in?"

"Sure, Ed. You need me, I'll be here." Haying was not Rick's favorite chore, but some things you just had to do to keep your love life less complicated.

"You're the head lister, aren't you, Ed?" Rick asked.

"For whatever that's worth."

"You have to assess all Charlie DeBoni's equipment?"

"You bet…every last pump and shovel." Ed grinned. "Old Charlie doesn't like me much."

"Well I don't understand something. Old Charlie is planning on moving half of his equipment to Granby for a couple of weeks. He seems to think that if he does that, it won't be taxed. Is that right?"

Edgar whooped. "That stupid Dago. I've told him a hundred times that it doesn't make any difference. Shit, I walk down to his job every weekend to check how much of my fill they've used, and I take a count of the equipment. I know more about his equipment than he does. He'll get charged for each piece that was on the job for more than sixty days, and he hasn't moved anything new on the job since May."

"Well it sure does upset Cashman and the operators to have their stuff moved. And the mechanics are about ready to revolt trying to patch up old crappy stuff to substitute for the new equipment."

"I don't know how Charlie got it into his head that he only got taxed for what was on the job as of June 15. It ain't never been that way. It ain't never going to be that way. Maybe other towns do it different, I don't know. But we have always taxed on a months-in-use basis. Course it ain't like it's going to put him out of business. One percent of the depreciated value per year. If it's been there six months, it's half a percent. I'm thinking $15-$20,000 for everything he owns. But he should have included that cost in his bid."

"Well don't go saying I said anything, Ed. He'll fire my ass so quick I won't know what hit me."

"I won't even let on I know you. I certainly won't tell him you're dating my daughter. Where is that girl? Ellen, get down here. Your beau has come sparkin'."

"Hi Rick. I saw you drive up. You haven't been home to change yet?" Ellen was smiling at him from the doorway, short, blond, and sexy in her tight plaid shorts and halter. Rick felt his knees go wobbly. He felt himself blush. Damn, nothing was so uncomfortable as talking to your girl when her dad was sitting right there.

Edgar jumped up as if he could read Rick's mind. "Got to check on that splay-toed heifer down at the other place. See you on Saturday, bright and early, Rick."

Ellen came out on the lawn and stood close to Rick. At 5-feet-four, she came up to his nose. He resisted the urge to bury his dust-covered nose in her hair, as they watched Edgar climb into his jeep and roar off down the hill.

"Uh, have a good time in Boston?" Rick thought about how to break the news to Ellen, and then figured he might as well come out with it. "Uh...I got to go to Shaughnessy's tonight. Danny Dombroski died. Mr. Cashman wants me to introduce him to the family.

"Danny died? Oh how horrible." Tears flooded her eyes. "What happened?"

Rick realized Ellen had been away. It was only a couple of days, but it seemed like a year. He told her about the accidental detonation, and Danny getting caught in it. He told her how he and Teach had taken Danny to the Springfield hospital. "Danny only said one thing to me, he said. "Take care of Kelly."

"That's so sad," she sobbed. " Poor Kelly."

"Who is Kelly? Do I know her?"

"Kelly Dalton." Ellen sniffed and wiped her eyes with the back of her hand. "Danny and she were engaged. I think maybe she's pregnant."

Suddenly the tragedy seemed even bigger. Rick didn't know what to say. He mumbled, "I have to go to a union meeting tomorrow night. Maybe we can do something on Friday night."

"Oh, I'll be at the union meeting. Dad's running the chicken barbecue, and Lorie and I have to help."

"Wow. Be careful. Some of those guys are rough."

"Oh don't worry. Dad keeps us behind the grills, boxing up the lunches. Besides, you'll be there."

"Yeah. Well, bring earplugs. The language can get pretty raw."

Ellen laughed. "You better get home and get clean. You can't go to a funeral home looking like you just came out of a coal mine." She gave him a quick kiss, getting a little smudge of rock dust on her nose.

She waved from behind the screen door as he putted out of the yard and down the hill.

Chapter 10

Kelly

It was nearly seven by the time Rick got home. His mother and father were sitting in the living room watching television. Dirty dishes on the table indicated that supper had come and gone. Rick wasn't sorry. His mother was a terrible cook. He grabbed a beer from the refrigerator they called the "green monster," and poked around looking for something that didn't have mold on it. He settled for a chunk of cheese, and a couple of slices of bread.

"You're late." His mother said.

"Stopped off to see Ellen. Gotta go to Danny Dombroski's wake tonight."

"You friends with those Pollacks?"

"Not close. Mr. Cashman wants me to introduce him to the family. He's going to give'm a check or something from Charlie."

"Humph. Buy them off, you mean. That Charlie DeBoni's afraid the Dombroskis will sue him for everything he's got."

"Maybe. If so, he sure doesn't understand how people like that think. It would never enter their minds to sue him."

"Why you brown-nosing Cashman? This job doesn't mean anything. This is just summer work. You don't need to put yourself out for these people. It isn't like they are paying you anything."

"Yeah, well I know. But I like Mr. Cashman. He's okay. He asked me to help, and I said I would."

His mother got up and went back into the kitchen to refresh her drink. "You find something to eat?"

"Yup."

"You want to eat with us, you have to get home on time. I'm not setting up meals on your schedule."

"I know Mom. It's okay." He looked over at his father. His father's eyes never left the TV. He alternated between sips of scotch, and drags on his cigarette. "'Lo Dad."

"Hi Rick." His father never looked up from the TV.

"Well, guess I'll wash up."

No one said anything. He clumped up the stairs in his work boots, and went into his room. He shrugged off his clothes, tossing them in the laundry basket in the hall. Naked, he wandered down the hall to the bathroom.

He wished they had a shower as he ran the water for the tub. But once he'd settled into the bath, and sat back sipping his beer, he thought a bath was pretty good too. "Danny must have died last night," he thought. "Otherwise they wouldn't have him at Shaughnessy's so quickly." He wondered if Danny really did see angels.

He looked down at the tub as the water ran out. A huge black ring showed the level where the water had been. He grabbed a washcloth and gave the ring a half-hearted rub, getting off some of the greasy residue. Then he dried himself, wrapped the towel around his waist, and headed back to his room.

He found a short-sleeved shirt in his closet, and a clean pair of chinos. His mother couldn't cook worth a shit, but she did do laundry. That wasn't all bad, he mused as he dressed. He checked his watch: 7:25. Better hurry.

He bounded down the stairs, gave his parents a wave, and bolted out the door. He thought for a second about walking, but kick-started the scooter and putted down the driveway.

It took less than two minutes to get to Shaughnessy's. He parked the scooter, and sauntered up the walk to big veranda that looked out over the river. He stopped outside, and gazed across the river at Mt. Kilburn, or *Fall Mountain,* as the locals called it. It was recovering pretty well from the fire three years ago.

"Hello Rick. Are you here for the Dombroski viewing?"

He looked around. Michael Shaughnessy, the town mortician, was smiling at him. Shaughnessy was tall and thin. His skin was pale, with eyes sunken well back in his head. He looked to Rick like what Count Dracula might look like; his unctuous smile perhaps hiding pointed teeth, and some sinister motive. But in fact, Michael Shaughnessy was the kindest of men, and truly carried the sorrow of loss for the bereaved families. And, if in his sincerity he became very wealthy, there was no harm in that.

Michael was the third Shaughnessy to provide funeral services for the town and its surrounding villages. His nearest competitor was more than twenty miles away. His grandfather had added the funeral parlor as an adjunct to his furniture business. It was the normal thing. People who ran furniture stores sold coffins. It took little imagination to add the other trappings. Michael's father was the first Shaughnessy who was also a licensed embalmer. Michael had followed in his father's footsteps. Rick always wondered whether Peter Shaughnessy would follow the same course. Peter had been in his class in high school. Peter always said he wanted nothing to do with the business. But people changed.

"Hi Mr. Shaughnessy. I'm meeting Mr. Cashman from DeBoni's. He wants me to introduce him to the family. Is the family all here?"

"Yes they're having a private viewing and service right now. We'll open to the public in five or ten minutes. Do you think many of Danny's friends will come?"

"I don't know, Mr. Shaughnessy. I just heard today that he had died. I don't know if people know yet."

"Yes. It is a bit of a rush. But his father doesn't like embalming, so we have to get him buried quickly. We have some ice under the casket, just like in the old days. But the weather is hot." He shrugged.

"There's Mr. Cashman. Hey, Mr. Cashman. This is Mr. Shaughnessy, the funeral director. They haven't opened the room yet. The family is having a private service."

"How do, Mr. Shaughnessy." Cashman extended his hand. "You look a bit cleaner than when I saw you last, Wallace." Cashman laughed.

"I'll go in and open up. You folks can come in a minute or so."

"Say, Mr. Cashman. Uh…uh, my girlfriend's father is Ed McCormick, the town lister." He stopped. Then he blurted out what Edgar had told him. "Ed says it doesn't matter if Charlie moves that equipment. He'll charge him for the time on the job anyway. His property runs right up to the edge of the right-of-way. I think you are even buying some fill from him. He says he knows that equipment better than Charlie, and Charlie will get a bill that counts every piece that has been on the job more than 60 days, whether it's there or not on the 15th."

Cashman was staring at the mountain as if Rick had said nothing. He sighed. "Wallace, it don't matter. Charlie's going to do what Charlie's going to do. He owns the company. It's his right, I guess."

"You folks can come in now." Mr. Shaughnessy was holding the door open.

As they walked in, Rick was conscious that the smell of flowers was a lot less than usual. Most of the other times he'd been to Shaughnessy's, it was for a great-aunt, or an old uncle, and the place was crammed with floral arrangements from top-to-bottom. In the viewing room there were only two bouquets, set tastefully on either side of the plain wood casket.

He and Cashman walked up to the bier first, to look at Danny's corpse. That was the custom. Rick knelt on the kneeler and thought through a prayer. Cashman stood, his hands crossed in front of him. He was holding an envelope. Danny looked like a wax statue. "Maybe they didn't embalm him, but they sure did use the cosmetics," Rick thought.

After what seemed like an acceptable amount of time, Rick got up, and Cashman followed him over to where the family was standing. Danny's father had his hands in his pockets. He looked uncomfortable and glum. Danny's mother was crying. His sister and brother stood there as if they didn't know what to do.

"Mr. Dombroski. This is Mr. Cashman from DeBoni's. Mr. Cashman, this is Mr. Dombroski."

"John," Mr. Cashman held out his hand and smiled.

"Peter," Dombroski said, shaking his hand slowly. "That boy of mine, he didn't do no damage did he?"

"No. No. Mr. Dombroski…Peter, Mr. DeBoni sends his personal regrets and sympathy. These accidents happen. God knows why."

"Well I was hoping Danny didn't do nothing wrong. He was a good kid, but you know kids."

"Peter, Mr. DeBoni wants you have this. It doesn't make up for a lost son. But it's something."

Mr. Dombroski took the envelope and opened his. His eyes went wide. "A…a thousand dollars. He give me a thousand dollars for my boy?"

"I know it isn't…"

"Tell Mr. DeBoni I thank him. He don't have to give me no money. He paid my boy good to work there. I can't take this. Danny didn't earn this."

Cashman put his arm around Dombroski's shoulder. "Take it. Charlie wants you to have it. Peter, your son was a good man. It's the least we can do."

Rick turned away, embarrassed to watch Dombroski's gratitude. He looked around the room. More people had wandered in. Some were Danny's friends and relatives. He saw a young girl standing at the end of the coffin, weeping. Suddenly he recognized her. "Kelly," he said softly to himself.

She was a couple of years younger than he was, and had been in Ellen's class in high school. Her sister, Mimi, had been in his class. They were part of that strange group in Westminster West, neither *woodchucks*, nor *townies*. Sort of rural intellectuals, he guessed. He remembered that the two girls lived with their mother, and that she taught at Putney School, a private school with a reputation for being a little nutty and artsy.

He and Ellen had even double dated once with his friend Dieter and Kelly. She had been lean, with an almost boyish figure then. Rick could see she had filled out nicely in the three years since.

"Ricky, my boy." A voice from the shadows interrupted his thoughts.

"Gramps. Hi Gramps. You working tonight?" Rick peered into the shadows to see his grandfather, Tommy McGuire, standing quietly against the wall.

"I am, boy. Will you stay and help an old man put away, and walk me home?"

"Sure, Gramps. I will."

"Good, boy. Now go comfort that young thing by the coffin. I think she's got more sorrow than she can carry."

Rick's mind groped for the right thing to say as he walked slowly over to Kelly Dalton. He put a hand on her elbow and said, "Kelly, I'm so sorry."

"Rick," she wailed, and threw herself on him, burying her face in his chest. He found his arms wrapping around her and holding her close, with his body rocking gently as if calming a baby. He was conscious of her breasts pressed against him, and felt guilty that he felt himself reacting sexually.

"Oh Rick. What will I do? Oh God."

Rick could think of nothing he could say that would make it better, so he just held her tight. Then he remembered Danny's request.

"Uh…Danny…uh…Danny asked me to help you if I could. Is there anything you need?"

"Need," she wailed. "Rick, I'm pregnant. We were going to be married this weekend…secretly. We had our blood tests and marriage license and everything. Now how will I manage? My mom doesn't know. The Dombroski's don't know. Everyone will just think I'm a whore."

"Maybe you could be married last weekend." Rick didn't know where the idea came from. "Maybe…uh…maybe I know somebody. Thad Booth's stepfather. He's a judge, and a justice of the peace. And he's a pretty good guy. Maybe we can get him to, you know, just date the certificate last week. Then I think you'd at least get some help from Social Security, and maybe your folks and the Dombroskis would be able to help too."

"Oh Rick. Do you think so? Do you think he would do it? Can you ask for me?"

"Sure Kelly. I'll ask him tonight. He just lives down the street from my grandfather, and I've got to walk Gramps home. I'll stop in. When did you get your blood tests?"

"Two weeks ago. We went as soon as I knew I was pregnant. We got the results a week ago last Friday in the mail, and got the license the same night. We were just looking around for where the best place to get married would be."

Rick stood with his arm around Kelly. She leaned against him, tears still flowing, but the convulsive sobbing was now under control. "Thanks Rick," she smiled, maybe for the first time since she heard about Danny's accident. "Call me when you know. Do you have Mom's number?"

Rick shook his head, no.

"It's hard to forget. It's like a cheer." Kelly whispered in his ear, "463-2468." She made a sound that was half sob, and half giggle. " I think I can talk to some of Danny's friends now." She squeezed his hand. A group of girls were standing in front of the coffin looking down on Danny. Kelly walked slowly over to them, dabbing her eyes with a sodden handkerchief.

Rick felt himself blush. He looked around to see who else had come, that might be looking at him. He was surprised that several people from the DeBoni crew were there. Teach and his wife, June, were talking with the Dombroski's. Whitey and the Duke were talking quietly together near the doorway. Côte and Henry were in line, shuffling their way toward the casket, both looking a little uncomfortable. Côte had cleaned up, and changed to a sports shirt and dress trousers. Henry, who never seemed to get dirty, wore the same green work shirt and work pants he wore every day on the job.

As he looked around the room, he saw Church come through the door. Church's head was down, and he walked slowly, like a man in a trance. He queued up to view the body. His eyes were closed and his lips moving as if he were mumbling a prayer. Rick wasn't sure, but he thought he could see tears on his cheeks. But maybe it was just sweat. It was warm in the room. He thought about Shaughnessy telling them that Danny hadn't been embalmed. He thought he could smell the body starting to rot, but maybe it was his imagination.

John Cashman motioned to him as he shook hands with the Dombroskis and headed for the door. Rick obligingly made his way through the room and out into the hallway. Cashman headed for the front door and motioned again for him to follow.

It felt good to be out in the air, even if it was a sultry June evening. Cashman put a hand on Rick's shoulder. "Thanks Wallace."

"I was surprised to see Duke and some of the other guys from DeBoni here."

"Why? They're all real people, Wallace. They may talk rough sometimes, but you know they are just people. And seeing a kid killed gets to people."

"Yeah, I guess. Church sure looks upset."

"Mmm. I hope he isn't taking this personally. Church is a pretty serious guy. Say, Wallace are you going to that union meeting tomorrow night?"

"Yes sir. I thought I might look in and see what it was all about. Besides, as Barrel-ass says, it's free food and free beer."

"Do me a favor and just keep your eyes open, will you. Something is cooking, and I don't know what. I don't want problems with the union. They can put us right out of business if we piss them off. Law says we have to let them talk to the men, and the men have a right to vote. I aim to go by the law, no matter what Charlie says. I don't think these guys will vote union."

"Not unless something really pisses them off," Rick said. "I could see some of the guys voting union just to take a whack at PH."

"Nah. They're smarter than that. They'll give Harris a hard time, but these guys want to keep their jobs. This is the best pay most of them have ever had in their lives. Anyway, keep your eyes open, and tell me if you see anyone who looks like he's set on making trouble."

"Will do, Mr. Cashman."

"Oh, and Wallace. Thanks for the information about the tax assessment. I don't know if I can do anything with it, but thanks for passing it on."

Rick watched Cashman stride down the walk. He wanted to leave too, but he'd promised his grandfather that he would stay and help clean up.

"Getting pretty cozy with the big boss, Squirt?"

Rick wheeled around. The Duke was standing behind him. "H-hello Mr. Duke," Rick stammered. "I didn't know that you knew Danny."

"I didn't. Just heard it was a college kid, and thought it might be you. No such luck though."

Rick was stunned, his jaw dropped.

Duke laughed. "Just kidding, Squirt. Dombroski worked down on the fill for a bit. Sad to see a promising young kid get killed. I lost my son pretty nearly the same way."

"Ohh…I didn't…I'm sorry…" Rick stammered.

"No reason for you to know. It happened in Maine, two years ago. I thought I would tell you that I'm sorry I hollered at you. Wasn't your fault. It was my own damn fault."

"Th-that's okay. I sure didn't mean…"

"Made you a bit of a celebrity, didn't it?" Duke laughed again. "Well it's good for the men to have something to chuckle about, 'specially after an accident like what killed Dombroski. So, no hard feelings, okay?" Duke stuck out his hand.

Rick shook the Duke's hand.

"But keep the hell off my fill," Duke growled.

Rick stood and watched the Duke saunter out to his pickup truck. He was totally dumbfounded. "The Duke apologized. Who would ever believe?"

Other people started filing out. Rick nodded to them, and said a word or two to Whitey, Teach, Côte, and Henry. Church walked out, head down, looking neither right nor left.

"Wallace?"

Rick turned. Peter Dombroski was standing there, hat in hand. "Thanks for taking Danny to the hospital."

"I just wish we had got him there sooner."

"Wouldn't have made no difference. Doc says everything was broken up inside. Amazing that he walked around as long as he did. He never did quite come back right in the head. Kept saying he saw angels, and that you were one of the angels."

"It was…it was…" words failed Rick.

"Thanks for bringing Mr. Cashman. I can't believe that Mr. DeBoni would give us that much money. Pretty unusual for an *Eye-talian* to do anything good for a *Pollack*."

"Yeah, well, Charlie's a pretty good guy, I think. A little strange and excitable, but underneath a good guy. And I guess he can afford it."

"Just the same. Thanks."

Gradually, the people left. Rick went back inside. Mr. Shaughnessy was closing the casket. His grandfather was folding up chairs, and stacking them on a cart.

"Here, Gramps, let me help."

"'Bout time, Boy. Thought you had skinned off home."

"No chance, Gramps. I got some stuff I need to ask you. I'm not letting you get away."

He began folding and stacking chairs, and in no time they had cleared the room.

"Are you done, Tommy?"

"We're done, Michael. With the help of a strong lad, it was no job at all."

"Should I be giving him your pay, then?"

"You should not. He has more money than brains now. Besides, he was working for me, not you. I'll decide what pay he should get."

"All right then, here's your wage." Shaughnessy handed over a crisp five-dollar bill.

" I thank you sir. We'll be on our way."

Chapter 11

Tommy Mac

"Darn! I've got my motor scooter," Rick said, as he and his grandfather walked down the stairs to the parking lot. "I don't suppose I can talk you into hopping on the back, Gramps?"

"Not on your life, boy, or my life either, for that matter. Can't you push the thing? It's not very big."

"Yeah, I guess so. It's a pain, though."

"We all have our little crosses, boy—"

"Some bigger than others, I know," Rick finished his sentence.

"And how's my little Maureen?"

"Mom's okay, Gramps. Same as ever."

"And does she ever talk about her father?"

"Yeah, like you have been dead for 45 years."

"Ahhh. Such a shame. She's not a forgiving woman."

"You got that right."

"Don't you be bad-mouthing your mother, boy."

They walked in silence for a while. Rick thought about the weird estrangement between his mother and his grandfather. All his life, his mother had treated his grandfather as if he'd been dead for years. She talked of him only as a girlhood memory. She said nothing about him in his later life. He might not have even known he had a grandfather if his Aunt Elizabeth hadn't invited Gramps up when Rick was staying there with his cousins. Rick had been six at the time.

When Rick told his mother about seeing Gramps, she treated him as if he'd had a vision from the dead. She simply wouldn't acknowledge that her father was still alive. It left Rick very confused.

Finally, his aunt had taken him aside and told him the story.

His grandfather and grandmother lived in a little house near the church. His grandfather worked as a machinist at the big paper company, rebuilding the big presses. Life had been very good. They had one daughter, Elizabeth, and then his grandmother got pregnant with Rick's mother. It had been a hard pregnancy. The baby was born, and as was all too common in those days, his grandmother had hemorrhaged, and died. His grandfather was crushed. He'd taken to drink. His sister, Rick's mother's Aunt Rebecca, herself a widow, moved in with her brother, and took care of the children.

About that time, the unions were making a rumpus in town. Rick's grandfather somehow got caught up in the union mess. He was fired. Not just fired, he was blackballed. No other paper company would give him a job. Eventually, the union won, but the paper company just shut its doors. All the workers lost their jobs.

Rick's grandfather left the girls with his sister, and traveled New England looking for work. He'd find a bit here and there, and send money home. His sister, whose husband had been killed in a railroad accident, had a small pension. She was able to make do, and raise the girls.

His aunt said that when her father would come home from time-to-time, Maureen would have nothing to do with him. Somehow, the little Maureen had decided this man had nothing to do with her. Instead, as she grew up, she invented a fanciful mother and father, who had been tragically killed. To this day, she kept up that myth, even though she knew full-well her father was living with his brother's widow, just a few blocks from where Rick lived.

Grampa McGuire moved in with his brother Charlie's wife, right after Charlie died. Charlie had been gassed in the First World War, and had been sickly ever since. Nonetheless, he had lived until his mid-sixties. Tommy Mac was just a year younger. When Charlie died, Tom said to his widow, "Martha I need a place to live."

Martha had said, "Move in then, but you'll be giving me your Social Security check." And that's how it worked. Gramps and Aunt Martha almost never talked. He lived in the front bedroom, and spent his days on the front porch, much as his brother, Charlie had done. Martha went about her business. Gramps liked his *Jameson's* every day, but Martha wouldn't give him back a nickel for booze— "the Devil's own medicine," she called it. Gramps did little jobs here and there, like stacking the chairs for Shaughnessy, to earn enough to buy a half-pint per day. Each morning he would rise, take a cup of coffee, and read his paper. Then, at 10 o'clock, he would walk downtown to the State Liquor Store, and buy his half-pint. They always kept a regular supply for him. He would walk home, make himself a sandwich, and sit on the front porch if the weather permitted. He'd sip his whiskey, making it last most of the afternoon. He'd take a small nap, and then go find an odd job to earn tomorrow's whiskey.

Once his grandfather moved in with Aunt Martha, Rick had made a point of stopping in a couple of times a week to talk with him. His grandfather appreciated the company, and they had become good friends.

"You said you wanted to talk to me about something, boy." His grandfather's voice cut through his revelry.

"Unions."

"Unions? What are you doing messing with unions, boy?"

"Well I'm not, exactly. The union is trying to get DeBoni's crew to vote it in. They're having a rally tomorrow night. I thought I would go and see what's up. Besides, my girlfriend is working the barbecue. I kind of need to be there."

"Well, I can see that. But unions, you've got to be careful with unions."

They didn't say anything more until they reached Aunt Martha's house. Rick parked the scooter and they climbed up on the porch and sat quietly as the early June light faded, and the first stars appeared.

"Now I don't know all there is to know about unions," Rick's grandfather spoke quietly. "But I know my own story. So why don't I just tell you that, and let you make up your own mind."

"Okay."

"You know I was always a mechanic. Learned it at my da's knee, I did. He was a big strong man, a blacksmith who didn't care for horses. So he took to making parts for machines. And his timing was pretty good, too. The age of horses was coming to an end, and the age of machines was going strong."

"But he liked a drop now and then, and sometimes more than a drop. When I was just twelve, he came out of Murphy's Tavern, stumbled into the street, and didn't one of those horseless carriages run him over. First man ever killed by an automobile in this town. Old man Shaughnessy, the first Shaughnessy, did him up nice. There was a big wake and funeral. Then we wee ones were on our own. My mum had died many years before. There were no other neighbors or relatives to take us in."

"We had this house. Charlie, me, and Rebecca. Thirteen, twelve, and ten. Just babies. Charlie was hauling wood and doing okay. Rebecca had a bit of a job cleaning some people's houses. I went down to the paper mill and walked into the shop. I said, 'My name's Tom and I'm a mechanic.' Well didn't the boys have a hoot."

"Old man Reilly says, 'They're making them mechanics kinda small these days, ain't they.' Gerry Adams says, 'We works on gears bigger'n you.' But Alphy Langdon, bless his soul, he pipes up, 'Give the kid a chance, Reilly. Somebody small could be useful getting inside some of those rollers.'"

"To make a story short, they hired me. They worked me hard. There wasn't a dirty job in the place I didn't get first crack at. But I loved it. I loved them big presses with their giant rollers and cutters. Some of them machines were already fifty, sixty years old. We rebuilt'm from top-to-bot-tom. Most of them didn't have a single piece left that had come from the manufacturer."

"This was a busy town in them days. We lived together, me, Rebecca, and Charlie, for about ten years. Then the War came, and Charlie was off to be gassed in some ditch in France. Could have been worse, I guess. But he was never the same after. Never had the energy to do anything. Just sat and rocked."

"A busy town. Must have been four hundred worked at the paper mill. Two shifts. Got paid one dollar and fifty cents a day. Railroad was boom-ing. Town was growing. Built the high school then."

"Wasn't no unions in this town, then. There were unions popping up across the country and there was trouble everywhere. Wilson sicced the army on'm. Killings. You've never seen the like. The bosses would hire gangs of thugs with clubs to beat the union people."

"There wasn't all that much support here for the union, though. People had work, and they were pretty happy with that. They didn't expect much more. 'Course, it was far from perfect. Bosses didn't give a damn about workers. Guys with green eyeshades were making all the decisions. It always seemed cheaper to them to let some poor schmuck get killed or maimed, than to spend a nickel making the job safer."

"That's how I got involved with the union. Safety." Rick's grandfather held up his left hand, the last two fingers had been sliced off—the ring fin-ger at the first knuckle, and the little finger right at the base.

"There was a cutter we were having problems with. They wanted me to replace a loose feeder bracket. I wanted to shut down the machine, but the bosses said, 'No.' They told me a real mechanic could fix it on the fly, and they couldn't afford to have it down. So, fool that I was, fool that all young men are, I set about fixing it. Wouldn't you know I slipped, and my ring finger went under the knife. Sliced it off as neat as you please."

"I let out a holler. Foreman comes down and said, "What'd you do, Tommy?"

"I said, 'Cut off my finger, goddamn.'"

"He said, 'How'd you do that?'"

"I said, 'Just like this.' And I stuck my pinky under the knife and cut that off too. I was a hotheaded kid in those days, and none too smart."

"Well, they staunched up the wound. Cauterized it with a hot iron, and sent me home with no pay for that day. That pissed me off some. I was back the next day working, but from then on, I was not one to side with the bosses. There were a couple more big safety problems, and I spoke up. Most of the time it was a simple matter of putting in a guardrail or some such. Stuff we could do in a couple hours. But no, the bosses wouldn't hear of it."

"Then the unions came to town. They held some meetings, and one of things they talked about was simple job safety. That struck a chord with me. I signed up, and pretty soon you could say I was a union agitator. Well, that did it for the bosses. They fired my ass. Not only that, they spread the word. There wasn't a paper company or machine shop in the country that would give me a job, and me a damn good mechanic too."

"By then I was married, had a little girl, and your mother on the way. I was desperate for some income. I tried hiring out under different names, but a man with two fingers trimmed like this is pretty hard to hide."

"I ran booze across the border. That was prohibition days. And wouldn't you know, I got caught. I was in Windsor, doing a year and a day, when your mother was born, and my sweet *Magee* died. My sister Rebecca's husband was killed in a rail yard accident. He worked for the Burlington & Boston, and it was union. They saw she got a bit of a pension. She moved in when I went to the slammer, and helped Magee until she died. Then she took care of the girls, God bless her. When I got out, we talked, and figured it would be better if I moved away for a bit, and the little ones didn't have to face their jailbird da every day."

The story gave Rick a different look at his mother, and her strange rejection of Gramps. He thought about it, and then shrugged. "Still too long to carry such a grudge," he thought.

"Gramps. How about the union? Good? Bad?"

"Well, after a bit, the paper company workers voted for the union. Like I said, mostly it was about job safety. They were losing one or two a year into one machine or another. Three days later, the paper company locked its doors. Just shut down, and moved its operation to Canada. Four hundred jobs disappeared. Four hundred families went hungry because there weren't any other jobs to be had. You might say that this town started its Great Depression a little early because of the union."

"Good or bad?"

"Ahh, I don't know Rick. I've thought about it all my life. The union was right. It was reasonable. But it lost people jobs, and that didn't help them. The union organizers were good men. They believed in what they were doing. They kept saying that 'you have to look at the long run, not just today.' But me, I say 'In the long run we're all dead. Without jobs, that happens quicker.'"

"Maybe you're saying a person has to look out for himself and his family first," Rick said.

"Maybe I am. I guess it's for you to figure out. Now, I got to go to my bed, boy. Thanks for the help, the walk home, and the company."

"'Night Gramps."

"'Night Ricky. Say a hello to your mother for me. Tell her I'm sorry."

Chapter 12

Judge Rubenstein

Rick didn't bother starting his scooter. He just walked it down the sidewalk another four houses. The lights were on. He knocked.

A plump woman with a pretty face answered the door. She was in a short nightgown, but seemed to think nothing of it. It was Thad Booth's mother, Bonnie.

"Why, Rick. Thad's not here. He's off chasing fish, and poking around the rocks in Woods Hole."

"I know, Mrs. Rubenstein. I came to see the Judge. Is he here?"

"Well yes, he's in the living room studying something or other. I never know what he's reading. You're not in trouble are you?"

"Not me, Mrs. Rubenstein. But I do need the Judge's help. Do you think I can talk to him?"

"Well, come in. Let's ask."

"Oh, Aaron. Rick Wallace is here. Can you see him?" Mrs. Rubenstein sang out in her natural soprano."

"Come in, Rick. Come in." The diminutive man, with an eagle's beak nose, and small reading glasses poised at the tip, turned from his desk, smiling.

"Hi Judge. Hope I'm not disturbing anything."

"No, no. Just reading some Shakespeare. It will be there tomorrow…and tomorrow, and tomorrow…"

Rick laughed. "Well if you'll listen to a tale told by this idiot, I'd appreciate it."

"Tell me."

Rick poured out the story of Kelly Dalton, and Danny Dombroski, and his idea that the Judge could sign a marriage certificate that said they had been married a few days earlier.

"Hmm. Basically you are asking me, a judge, sworn to uphold the law, to commit a crime. Do I have that right?"

"Uhh…uhh." Rick had never considered that this was a crime.

"Did you know that by just asking, you committed a very serious crime? Suborning a judge? Probably would get you three years in jail, perhaps with two suspended."

"Oh, no. I didn't…"

"Just so that you understand that this isn't a trivial thing. So why should I do it?"

"Well, well what I was thinking, I mean, maybe I'm wrong and everything, but it seemed to me that if they had already gotten their blood tests and their marriage license, they had really committed themselves to being married. And what with the kid coming and everything, well, that probably God would see them as married."

"And maybe God would, and does." Judge Rubenstein smiled. "But marriage, Rick, is a civil contract. Whatever the religious beliefs or ceremonies, the state accepts marriage as a legal contract. The state is not empowered to determine what God thinks."

"Oh. I guess because most people do it in the church, I always thought the religious thing came first."

"Not at all. The minister or priest is authorized as an officer of the state, to execute this contract."

"Oh. Well the state will see Kelly as just another unmarried mother. Her kid will be a bastard. I guess I should tell her to get an abortion or something."

"Not so fast. As you so astutely argued, they have demonstrated intent. The state recognizes intent as being as valid as a signed contract. The pregnancy might be written off as just hormones out-of-control, but taking the blood test, and getting the license, are clear signs of intent."

Judge Rubenstein reached up on a shelf and took down a volume of Vermont statutes. He flicked through some pages. Then, his finger pressed against an entry, and he said, "The law suggests that a valid marriage exists in a number of different instances that clearly show intent. For example, living together for seven years constitutes a valid marriage. There are other examples. None precisely dealing with this case, but the intent of the legislature is clear. They wish to promote valid marriage. Therefore, they accept a valid demonstration of intent to marry as constituting a valid marriage."

"You mean you could just rule that they are married?"

"Precisely. However, like most things in the law, it is not that simple. There would have to be a hearing, witnesses called. The state would have to have the opportunity to object, as accepting the marriage would clearly obligate the state and the federal government to support this unborn child."

"Oh." Rick's heart sunk yet again. "That sounds like it would take a long time."

"Precisely. Probably two to three years."

"Wow. I don't know if Kelly could stand that."

"But of course, now that we know what the law says, we are obligated to seek justice as well, provided that it can be had within the law. There is no justice in dragging this on for years, the outcome assured, but the process exacting its pound of flesh. So the simple answer is to do exactly as you requested. We will execute a marriage certificate dated to an acceptable date prior to death. The pregnancy is proof enough that the marriage was consummated."

"You'll do it? But I thought…"

"Not another word. But secrecy is important, and to assure secrecy I intend to make you complicit to the crime. I name you best man. Have the girl here tomorrow night, along with another witness, and we will catch up on this past-due paper work."

"Wow. Thanks Judge. This is super. You're the greatest."

"No, just a talkative old man who enjoys a little run around the legal pole from time-to-time. You know that in this family, we have utmost sympathy for people who get the proper order of marriage and children, confused. Now, I need to get back to my reading. I'll see you tomorrow night, at 7:30 sharp."

"Yes sir!"

Rick walked out to his scooter, and punched the sky. "Damn. That was great." He kick-started the little bike, and putted down the street. Realizing he had better call Kelly, he headed for Sam's Twist Cone to use Sam's pay phone, and to stock up on some burgers and fries. Suddenly, he was famished.

Chapter 13

Barrel-ass

Rick got home at about 11:30. Both of his parents had passed-out watching TV, cigarettes smoldering in their respective ashtrays.

He clicked off the TV, ground out their cigarette butts, shuddered, and headed upstairs, leaving them asleep in their respective chairs. Morning would come early.

Rick awoke at 5:00 A.M. As long as he could remember he had risen early, no matter how late he'd gone to bed the night before. He dressed quickly in the dark, and tiptoed downstairs, shoes in hand. Sometime in the night, his parents must have come to and wandered off to bed.

He put the coffee on, and made up his lunch of ham and cheese sandwiches, tossing in a small pie for desert. He lit his first cigarette, and smoked it with his first cup of coffee. He had no appetite for breakfast. Nicotine and caffeine would suffice. He poured the remaining coffee into his quart thermos and slipped out the door. Thermos and lunch-bucket fit into the carrier nicely. He patted down his pockets. "Shit. Got to get cigarettes."

He rolled the scooter out of the driveway and jump-started it on the hill. Turning out on the Atkinson Street—really Vermont Route 5—he gave the scooter some throttle, and putted off in the dank chill air. It was just 6:00 A.M. He had plenty of time.

He stopped for cigarettes at the Motor Mart, a little gas station that had added a few grocery items. Rick thought it was a pretty good idea. The station was open long hours, and got a lot of business from people who were up early, or didn't get home until late. Plus, they could charge outrageous prices because there was no competition. He picked up a devil's food cake to eat on his sandwich break. "Shit, two packs of cigarettes and a *Devil Dog*, and most of a dollar gone."

It was light, but a heavy morning fog reduced visibility to about ten feet. The drive to the job was slow. Rick had his headlight on. He found that even in good weather, drivers didn't see the little scooter. In fog like this he might as well have been invisible. He wasn't sorry to pull off the highway and into the yard. He was early, but not the first to arrive. Cashman was in hot discussion with Charlie DeBoni. Whitey and the other mechanics were laying out their tools.

Rick hauled his lunch-bucket and thermos over to the dynamite wagon. He poured himself a cup of coffee, and sat on the bumper, watching the yard wake up.

Church drove into the yard, parked his truck, and walked over to Cashman and Charlie. He stood patiently and waited for them to finish. Charlie threw up his arms, and stalked over to the maintenance shed, obviously bent on giving the mechanics a piece of his mind.

Rick watched Church and Cashman. The discussion was quiet. Cashman was obviously not pleased, but finally, he nodded. Church turned and walked back towards his pickup. Rick heard Cashman holler, "You better teach him good!"

By now the rest of the crew had arrived. Church waved Barrel-ass over to his pickup. He hollered over to Rick and Teach, "Take the wagon to magazine. We have a truckload of dynamite coming in. Empty out what we got, count it, then load in the new stuff in back and stack the old stuff up front so we can get at it."

"I'll get this started," Teach said. "You go get the magazine key."

By the time Rick got back, Teach had the old ambulance running. Rick jumped up on the running board and hollered, "Let'r rip!"

"Damn, Teach," Rick hollered as the little ambulance lurched over ruts and holes, making its way off the main right-of-way and up the narrow trail to the magazine, "you drive this fucker like it was a tank."

"Tanks for the memories," Teach crooned. He cackled with glee.

"You know, for a teacher you ain't very respectable," Rick shouted.

"Fuck respect! Who cares if the little shits respect you as long as you scare them shitless!" Teach pulled the wagon off the track, leaving space for the dynamite truck to back in.

"What puts you in such a crazy mood," Rick asked.

"Big union meeting tonight! Gonna join the Wobblies. Become a card-carrying communist."

"I thought teachers already had a union."

"Hell, that ain't a union. That's just a glorified chapter of the PTA." Teach spit. "We're talking Jimmy Hoffa's boys here. Or maybe the AFL-CIO, or the United Construction Workers of America. We're talking power! We'll be marching with picket signs."

"Let PH or Charlie see you with a picket sign and he'll shove it up your ass."

"P. H., *patooo*!" Teach spit again. "That weasel. He don't scare me." Teach was hamming it up, strutting around. "I'm writing a musical."

"What? What'n hell are you talking about?" Rick was nonplussed by the sudden change in direction.

"Not a musical. An operetta."

"An operetta. Like the Pirates of Pensantz?"

"More like the HMS Pinafore. But you have the idea."

"An operetta? About what?"

"This. About this." Teach made a sweeping gesture with his hand.

"The job? An operetta about the construction job?"

"In fact, I call it B.V. DeBoni-fore."

"Go ahead. Sing it. I know you are dying to sing this strange thing."

"Thought you would never ask. Ahem. La, la, la."

"Just sing it, Norton." Rick shouted in his best Jackie Gleason imitation.

"Oompah, oompah, oompah, oompah—that's the orchestra."

"Will you sing it!"

Teach joined his hands behind his back and spun his large frame, giving Rick a profile of a fat, English admiral. He sang:

"When I was a boy, I served a term,

As driller's assistant for DeBoni's firm.

I brown-nosed the foremen from first to last,

And I bent down and kissed Chuck DeBoni's ass.

I kissed Charlie's ass so fervently, that now I am a Super for BVD."

"He kissed Charlie's ass so passionately, that now he is a super for BVD." Rick chimed in the chorus.

"Not passionately, you bozo. Fervently."

"Fervent, passionate, what's the difference? This has promise I have to admit, Teach. But cool it. I think that's Church coming round the bend."

There was something different about Barrel-ass. Instead of his usual slouch, he stood erect. He kept close to Church and listened to every word he said. Instead of the usual look of ignorant indifference, his face was screwed up in concentration.

"Oh shit," Rick muttered under his breath. "Church is teaching Barrel-ass the business."

"What's going on," Teach asked.

"I'm showing William the ropes," Church said. "I have to leave for a few days, and I want to give William the chance to take over. Cashman has given it the okay."

"Who's William?" Teach asked.

"I'm William, d-darn it. That's my name, William Brennan." Barrel-ass was clearly making an effort not to curse.

"Sorry, Mr. Brennan, sir." Teach snapped off a salute. "I had thought you were christened Barrel-ass Brennan the third, but I can see I was mistaken. My apologies."

"Well I just as soon you call me Bill."

"Do you know anything about dynamite, Bill?" Rick asked.

"Sure. I've blowed up lots of stuff. I've been doing this job for eight years. You pick up a lot. But Church is showing me how to figure out a shot and stuff."

"This isn't rocket science, boys," Church said. "There's only a few things William needs to know. Mr. Harris will figure out the engineering part of the shot. Dupont teaches the dynamite stuff in just three weeks at their plant, and most of that is not relevant to what we are doing here."

"Now that shipment will be along in ten or fifteen minutes. I need you boys to haul out the old stuff and take an inventory of what we've got. Count the sealed boxes as boxes. If a seal is broken, open the box and count the sticks. We are supposed to have a complete count. Same thing with the caps."

Rick and Teach turned back to the shed as Church and Barrel-Ass climbed back into Church's truck, backed around, and headed back to the job.

"We better get at it. Otherwise we'll have to stack the new stuff outside till we get the inside out and counted. Unlock that padlock."

Rick followed Teach's directions, unlocking the padlock, and opening the magazine door. "Doesn't look like there's too much left here. Let's stack it over there." He pointed to a clear space at the left of the magazine. The two set to work, and in no time had the boxes stacked along side the shed.

"I'll count it and holler out, okay?" Rick said.

"Works for me."

Rick counted the boxes in the small stacks and hollered out the count. After he counted the full boxes, he opened the partials and counted the sticks. They quickly tallied the Hi Pro, Toval, Special Gel, and fertilizer.

There were a few non-standard items to be tallied as well. "Here's two rolls of Prima Cord, one started and two boxes of jackhammer sticks" Rick hollered. "Hey wait. This one's been opened." Rick lifted the top of the box. "Looks like just one stick gone."

"Somebody must have needed to blow his nose," Teach chuckled.

"Yeah, I bet somebody had a stump on the farm they needed to blow."

"How about caps?"

"Looks like one cap missing too."

"I bet that cap went with the jackhammer stick."

"Probably. Hey, is that the dynamite truck?"

There was a grinding of gears as the large cargo van labored up the grade and then lurched around the corner. Teach walked over and waved a turn-around motion at the driver.

The driver backed around and lined up with the magazine door. He jumped down and sauntered over to Teach. "Ain't all yours. Here's your invoice: 100 High Pro, fifty each Special Gel, and Toval, one hundred fifty bags of fertilizer, couple crates of caps, four rolls of prima cord."

The driver jumped up on the truck bed. "I'll hand it down. Let's start a chain going."

They quickly established a rhythm, the driver handed them down, Rick carried, and Teach stacked. It took a couple of hours to get the load settled and do a confirming count.

"All there, I guess." Teach said as he signed the delivery receipt.

The driver took the receipt, climbed up into the cab, and with a wave, ground the truck into gear and lurched off down the access road.

"Shit, worked right through sandwich break." Teach mumbled.

"Let's load back the old stuff, lock up, and drive up to where Côte and Henry are drilling." Rick suggested.

The two quickly restacked the older dynamite in the front of the magazine. Teach retrieved his clipboard while Rick locked up. "Remind me to drop this key off at the office tonight, will ya?"

"Sure. But no big deal. All the padlock keys are the same."

"They are?"

"Yep. After we lost the magazine key a couple of times, and the mainte-nance guys lost the shed key, Calvin suggested we get all the padlocks keyed the same. That way we didn't have to go cutting them open if a key got lost."

"Doesn't seem very secure."

"Nope, convenient, but not secure. But it's also cheaper than buying new locks all the time, and Charlie likes cheaper."

It was about quarter to twelve when Teach and Rick finally got every-thing together, and hopped in the truck and headed up to the ledge. They parked by the compressors just as Côte and Henry and the two chuck ten-ders were shutting down and coming off the rock. Gathering in a shady spot, they all settled down to the business of eating.

Always a fast eater, Rick was through his sandwiches, and nibbling on the *Devil Dog* he had planned for sandwich break. "What do you think about Barrel-ass as a blaster?"

"Shit, if his brains were dynamite, he couldn't blow his nose," Henry growled.

"Now don't say that," Côte said. "The man has some serious experi-ence."

"How's that?" Ding asked.

"Well this happened two years ago," Côte was warming up. "Old Barrel-ass got married. Did very well for himself too."

"He married old Earl Trombley's daughter, didn't he? Pretty thing." Henry chimed in.

"That he did. Mary Trombley. She's about as pretty as Barrel-ass ain't," Côte laughed. "Don't know what she saw in him except maybe a very cushy lay."

"She'd sure-ass want to be on top," Henry chuckled.

"Well, Mary is apparently crazy about old Barrel-ass, but Earl ain't. Least wise, that's what I heard. So, Barrel-ass decides he's got to impress his new father-in-law. Now if you know Earl, you know that the one thing he

likes to do more than anything is fish. And he ain't no dainty fly fisherman. He's a meat fisherman. Goes out and catches till he can't catch no
more."

"Yep, that's true. If you help old Earl catch fish, he'd love you even if
you was a skunk." Henry said.

"Waaalll," Côte drawled, "old Barrel-ass he knows that too. So he
comes up with this plan. He tells old Earl he has a sure-fire way to catch
more fish than he's ever caught before. Not just perch and shit, but rainbow trout. So he rents this cabin on Lake Willoughby. You know where all
them steelhead trout run up from Lake Memphremagog?"

"Yep, Willoughby's got rainbows all right, but you can't hardly catch'm.
Lake's too damn deep."

"That's what Earl said. But Barrel-ass says, 'Trust me, I got a plan.' "
Everyone laughed.

"Sure enough, they get settled and the first night, soon as it gets dark,
Barrel-ass grabs Earl and takes him out in the boat. They putt over to the
deepest part of the lake, right under the big cliff. Old Earl starts to take
out his fishing rod, but Barrel-ass says, 'leave your rod in the boat. Get
your net.'"

"Then Barrel-ass takes this jack hammer stick and pokes a cap into it.
He ties the wires around till it's snug, and splices the cap into a big reel of
wire he's got. He stands up, and whistles the thing around his head a few
times, and lets it fly. They hear it splash way off in the dark. Barrel-ass
attaches one wire to one side of a battery, and sits there holding the other
wire. 'You gotta wait,' he says, 'till it sinks to the bottom.' Old Earl sees
what he's doing and he thinks maybe his son-in-law has a pretty good
idea. 'How long?' he asks. "Bout a minute,' says Barrel-ass. So they sit
there for a minute."

"Then Barrel-ass stands up. He says to Earl, 'Ready?' Earl says, 'Ready.'
Barrel-ass touches the wire to the terminal, and *Boom*! The boat is blowed
clean out of the water, and Barrel-ass and Earl are in the drink."

"What happened?"

"Well, I told ya it were deep there. It were so deep that the dynamite didn't land on the bottom, it just swung down under the boat. It was right underneath the boat when it blowed up."

Everybody roared with laughter. They rolled on the ground holding their sides.

Côte just smiled, "So you see he does have some experience."

"They…hee, hee…they get any fish?"

"Waall, that's a good question. That's the same question the game warden asked when he pulled them out of the water. He'd been sitting right there watching the whole shebang. The boys didn't do no fishin' for a year or so, I'll tell ya."

"Guess that didn't make Barrel-ass too popular with Earl," Henry chuckled.

"You guess right. What I hear is that Earl has shot at him twice since."

"Couldn't have been serious. You couldn't miss that ass if you were trying to hit it." Teach added.

"What ass?" Barrel-ass asked as he plopped down on a log and opened his cooler-sized lunch-bucket.

"I was just telling them about your fishing trip," Côte said. "And how much your father-in-law appreciated it."

"Oh, D-ducky bumps," Barrel-ass swallowed a curse as Church walked up to the group. "I wish you hadn't told everybody that, Côte."

"Ducky bumps?" Teach roared with laughter. "Ducky bumps. We'll have to teach the Duke that one."

"Told what?" Church asked.

"We were just hearing about Bill's fishing experiences," Rick said. "We thought he might be at it again 'cause there was a case of jackhammer sticks with just one missing."

"Is that right?" Church frowned. "You sure? We haven't used any jackhammer sticks since we did the clear cut through the right-of-way. Should be two full boxes."

"There is, minus one stick. One cap missing too." Teach handed over the clipboard and inventory sheet.

"Somebody's been helping themselves," Church said. "I told Charlie we should have separate keys. Well, come on William, we've got work to do."

"You going to the union meeting now that you're management?" Henry asked Barrel-ass.

"Oh, I ain't management. And the chicken and beer is free. I'll be there." He closed his cooler with a sigh, got up, and followed Church back down to his truck.

"You all ought to go," Dodd said. "Big Jim Jensen is going to be there, and he's one hell of a speaker."

"Oh, I don't imagine anybody will miss this," Côte said. "Them union boys is smart holding it on a Thursday. Nobody's got no money left, and a night out with free beer and chicken is a big attraction."

"Damn right," Henry said. "Hold it on a Tuesday, and people still got money for beer and a movie, half won't come. Hold it on a Friday, and everybody just been paid and heading home. Nobody'd come. Thursday's the perfect night."

Rick watched Henry's eyes, and noted that Henry had seen PH walk up behind Teach.

"Hell," Henry continued, "if they could hold a vote before you got your beer and chicken, they'd win on the spot. Be no choice at all, *chicken or chicken-shit.* Oh, speak of the devil. You going to the meeting PH?"

"I just might to see who shows up. Anybody goes to that meeting has put his job on the line." PH growled.

Henry rolled his cigar around in his mouth, bit off a piece of tobacco, and spit it in PH's direction. "Your girlfriend's father spreading cow shit, Squirt? It smells like shit here."

"God, I hope not," Rick said. "He's doing the chicken at the union party. I just as soon he not be spreading shit before he cooks my chicken."

The sound of truck engines starting signaled the end of lunch. They got to their feet and began shuffling back to the job.

"Ducky bumps," Teach said. "Barrel-ass said, 'ducky bumps.' I wonder where in the hell that came out of."

"Big Jim Jensen," Rick mused. "Seems like a pretty heavy-weight dude to be preaching union to a little company like this. Why do you suppose the union is sending their number three guy?"

"Beats me," Teach shrugged. "Maybe they heard about Edgar's chicken barbecue?"

Chapter 14

Big Jim

The remainder of the day's work consisted of odd jobs, picking up stuff, and moving stuff. It was more busy work, than real work. Rick was glad to be done and out at 5:30 on the nose. He had a lot to do. He had go home, get cleaned up, borrow his Dad's car, pick up Kelly and her friend Ginger, who agreed to be the other witness—the maid of honor, she said, get over to Judge Rubenstein's, get through the wedding, bring back the car, and then head off to the union meeting.

For once, everything went pretty much according to plan. His father didn't object to his borrowing the car, and didn't bother to ask why. His mother was already half in the bag, and barely coherent.

Kelly and Ginger were ready when he got to Ginger's house. He figured Kelly's parents were still in the dark. The girls were nicely dressed in pretty summer dresses.

"You girls look nice," Rick said. "Sorry I couldn't put on a suit or any-thing. I have to go to this union picnic tonight."

"You look great, Rick." Kelly started to cry. "Oh…oh. I'm sorry."

"Hey, don't worry. You're doing great. You just gotta be strong. Have you got all the papers?"

"She's strong," Ginger chimed in. "Damn right she's strong." She handed Rick an envelope. "It's all in there."

They parked in Rubenstein's driveway, and Rick went around and opened the door for the two girls. He ushered them up the back steps where Mrs. Rubenstein was waiting. She shooed the girls into the front bedroom, and sent Rick into the parlor where Judge Rubenstein was waiting.

"Ah, the un-indicted co-conspirator." Judge Rubenstein stood by his desk. "Do you have the paperwork?"

Rick handed him the envelope.

"Mmm, blood test. Okay. License, okay. You are going to have to sign here on behalf of Danny. You might make it look a bit like his signature on the license, but not a deliberate forgery, mind you. Inscribe your initials very small next to it."

Rick did as he was told, even spelling Dombroski right.

"You sure that you are not a professional forger, boy?" The judge smiled.

"No sir. Strictly amateur."

"Now, I have this nice picture of Danny," he said pulling it out of the envelope. "I'm going to take all of your pictures against that blank wall, leaving space, and then build a new picture with Danny in it." Photography was one of Judge Rubenstein's hobbies, and he had a fully equipped darkroom in the basement. "Mmm. You need a jacket. Bonnie, do we have one of Thad's jackets here? And a tie? A good one?"

Mrs. Rubenstein appeared like magic with jacket and tie, and in no time had Rick looking like he was ready for the prom. The jacket was just a little large.

The girls came into the room, looking prepped and pretty.

"Now you have to answer for Danny. You are his surrogate—a perfectly legal way to conduct a wedding." The judge motioned for the girls to come forward.

He took them through the whole ceremony. Each place Danny would have responded, Rick said the response. "On behalf of Danny Dombroski, I do."

When the ceremony was complete, all five people hugged as a group. Then the judge had Kelly sign the final papers, next to Rick's initialed rendition of Danny's signature.

Mrs. Rubenstein grouped the three together in front of a blank white wall, with Rick standing on the far left, and an empty space where Danny would have stood.

Judge Rubenstein said, "I know congratulations are not appropriate. We wish you well. I'll mail you the final documents and the picture. Trust me. It will look exactly like Danny was here. It will be spooky. I'm sure you all realize that it will be best for all of us if this event took place with Danny one week ago today. You said that you and Danny were alone long enough to get the job done. We were in town. Rick was around—in fact he was here seeing Thad and his wife off to Woods Hole. That's when we held the wedding, and that's what the documents say. I suggest that you all fix that date in your minds until you are sure that that is exactly the way it happened."

They said goodnight to the Rubensteins, and Rick ushered the girls back to his father's car. He backed carefully out of the driveway and said, "Where to ladies?"

"My house," Ginger said. "My mom and dad are in Boston. We are going to have a little drink and a good cry."

Kelly sat quietly, tears streaming down her face. Rick turned at the end of the block, and headed up the hill to the terrace where Ginger lived. He pulled into her driveway and jumped out, hustling around to open the door.

Kelly stepped out of the car and threw her arms around him, burying her head in his chest. He could feel her sobbing, her chest pressed against him. He felt himself become aroused, and was embarrassed and ashamed. Kelly kissed him full on the mouth. "Thanks Rick," she said. "I wouldn't have minded if it was really, you know, you and me." He knew she must feel his erection.

"Come on, Kelly," Ginger yelled from the doorway.

"I…I've got to go…" Rick stammered.

"I know." Kelly sighed. "I know." She turned and walked slowly up the walk.

Rick was in a daze as he walked back around the car and climbed in the driver's seat. His hormones were raging, yet he knew he shouldn't feel that way. He had just helped out a friend. He tried to focus his mind on something else, but the feel of Kelly's breasts and pelvis pressed against his throbbing penis, would not let go. "Oooh, damn!" he said out loud. He gunned the car, squealing the tires, only to have to jam on the brakes to make the left-turn where the block ended. The car skidded, and came to a stop, just inches from the guardrail.

A rush of adrenaline overcame the testosterone, and Rick sat shaking. Slowly, he backed up, turned, and headed down the hill.

It was already 8:45 by the time he left his father's car at the house, grabbed the motor scooter, and headed off to the boat landing. The cool evening air helped calm him. "Ellen will be there," he thought, and a wave of guilt swept over him. It was like he'd cheated on her. But he hadn't. Not really. Rick shook his head, and caught a June bug square in the teeth. "Blah, pthh," he coughed and sputtered. The turn to Herrick's Cove and the boat landing was just ahead, and he was happy to get off the road.

The party was already in full swing as Rick parked the scooter off behind a tree. No sense taking a chance that some bozo with too many beers in him would back over the bike in the dark. Men were standing in small groups, laughing, talking, and drinking beer. Some were seated at picnic tables eating chicken. Others were in line, either by the keg or the grill, waiting for either beer or chicken.

The boat landing was situated in the Connecticut River flood plain, and consisted of a few picnic tables, a parking area, and a ramp where you could back your pickup and boat trailer down into the water, and launch your boat. The hard-packed dirt roads and paths were a quagmire in the spring, and whenever it rained, but now, were an inch deep in clay dust. A little further down the Herrick's Cove road, there was a handful of derelict cabins. At one time, this had been a popular spot, but the river was so polluted, few of the owners ever used their cabins now.

Mosquitoes swarmed the area in huge clouds, and virtually everyone puffed on a cigar or cigarette in the vain hope that the smoke would keep the voracious insects at bay.

Edgar had set up his barbecue pit to the left of the boat ramp. It was a twelve-foot by four-foot pit, dug just six or eight inches into the hardpack. The whole bed glowed with hot coals. Three feet above the bed, Edgar's grilling rack was set with space for about fifty half chickens at a time. He was well into the third round of chickens. Edgar used his own special barbecue sauce, which was simply oil, vinegar, and black pepper. It gave the cooked birds a tangy-spicy taste that New Englanders love.

"Shee-it, they call that barbecue?" One of Jim Jensen's bodyguards was standing, holding a piece of chicken up by two fingers. "Where I come from, we wouldn't feed this to the niggas."

"Easy Billy Bob," Jim Jensen said. "This here ain't where you come from. It's Ver-mont. They do a bunch of stuff that's different here." He was sipping a beer from a paper cup.

Rick thought Jensen cut a fine figure. He was about six-foot-two inches tall, and probably weighed in at 250, or 260. It wasn't all muscle, but a good bit of it was. The only obvious fat was around his middle, a slightly oversized paunch. Jensen was dressed to the nines in an ice cream suit with a white shirt and open collar. He had a great white mane of hair that swept back from his forehead, and hung down below his collar. His complexion, even in the dying light, was obviously ruddy. Rick knew that Jensen was the number three man in the United Construction Workers Union. He was responsible for most of the east coast. Rick figured that the union must be trying to prove some kind of a point to send one of their top guys up to Vermont, to recruit three or four hundred hard-scrabble farmers who worked construction just to make ends meet. Maybe it was bigger than that. "Maybe this had to do with making all Interstate construction, union," Rick thought.

Rick looked over at the grill and could see that Ellen was busy putting the cooked chickens on paper plates with a dollop of potato salad, a scoop of cranberry sauce, and an ear of corn. Rick frowned as he saw Crackers saunter around the side of the grill and start making conversation with Ellen. "That sonofabitch," Rick muttered. He began working his way through the crowd to get over to the grill and rescue his girl from the leering pan-jockey.

"Hey Crackers," Rick said, coming up behind him. "You bring your wife to this affair? Or if she couldn't come, maybe your girlfriend?" It was pretty common knowledge that during the week, Crackers shacked up with Mary Lou Biset, who worked at the IGA, and then went home to his wife and three kids on Friday night. "Too bad you couldn't bring your kids. They'd of gotten a kick out of this."

Crackers wheeled on him, and raised his fist. Rick was sure he was going to get hit, but Crackers just grinned a perfect, toothy smile. "Better be careful where you drive that little toy scooter of yours, Squirt. Hate to see you go under the wheel." He stalked off over to the beer line, butting in, and grabbing a full cup, while the guys in line shouted obscenities at him.

"Hi Rick," Ellen smiled at him. Rick felt another wave of guilt. "Want some chicken?"

Rick nodded. He took the plate and said, "Thanks Ellen. When you got a second, I'll tell you about the wedding."

Just then, Edgar hollered out, "Ellen, come get these birds before they burn. Damn it, you can talk to your beau some other time. We got work to do here."

Ellen shrugged, smiled, turned, and hurried over to her father. She grabbed the big black roasting pan, and Edgar started tossing cooked birds into it.

Rick wandered over to the beer line. Côte was standing there with Whitey.

"Hey, Squirt," Côte said, "You old enough to drink beer?"

"You the beer sheriff?" Rick countered.

"Just looking out for your virtue, boy," Côte laughed. "Don't want you getting drunk in front of your future father-in-law."

Rick blushed, and looked over his shoulder at the grill. Edgar and Ellen were both busy and paying no attention to him. "I ain't getting drunk. Just want to take the edge off my thirst," he said.

Côte handed him a full cup of beer. "Oooh, this is the right stuff, then. It'll put hair on your wee-wee."

"Did you have any chicken, Whitey?" Rick asked.

"Noo way, boy," Whitey said. "My old lady would break my stones if I ate anybody's chicken but hers. That's one of the penalties of being married to the best cook and the meanest lay in the whole dang country."

"Probably worth it," Côte said.

"'Spect it is," Whitey replied.

The last group was getting their chicken, and Rick could see that the union guys were setting up a makeshift stage. People started to wander over. A bunch of guys made a beeline back to the keg to refill their cups before Jensen started talking.

"Could be a long talk," Henry said, spilling off some foam and topping his cup with the amber brew. "Hate to run dry when that old windbag is blowing."

"Hee, hee. You got that right," old Everett reached out his cup for a fill. "How many times you think they tried this, Henry?"

"Gotta be a half-dozen with DeBoni, don't you think, Everett? Once, up in Montpelier. Once, over in Springfield. Couple times, I heard, down in Massachusetts. They're even organizing up in Granby, I hear."

"Yep, that's what I make it too. They got old Charlie in the cross hairs."

"Old Charlie don't like it much," Côte chuckled. "I wonder if he'll call in some of his relatives to help him out."

"I understand those guys run the union," Henry said. "Be like a gang war wouldn't it?"

"We better get over there. Looks like they're about ready to start." Rick said, topping off his cup. He tossed the remains of his chicken dinner in the trash, and joined the group that was crowding in around the makeshift stage.

Jim Jensen mounted the stage, taking off his white suit jacket as he walked. He tossed the jacket to one of his bodyguards, and strode to the podium. He looked out at the crowd and smiled. Slowly, he unbuttoned his cuffs and rolled up his sleeves, exposing powerful forearms. One look at his huge hands and muscled arms, and you knew. This was a working guy. One of us. Not one of them.

"Hope you boys had enough chicken."

The crowd cheered.

"I want to thank Ed McCormick, and his two lovely daughters."

The wolf whistles brought color to Rick's face. He felt a jealous anger forming.

"Thanks, Ed. My man, Louie here has your check."

Rick looked over at the grill, and saw Edgar wave. He and the girls had the truck mostly loaded. Rick watched Louie walk over and hand Edgar a check. They shook hands.

"You may not have had enough beer yet."

There were hoots and yells of "more beer!"

"And no sense in sending any of the keg back. So help yourselves after I finish talking. But first you gotta pay the piper. You gotta listen to what I have to say."

There were a few laughs, and then the crowd quieted down.

"I hope you don't think that this kind of feed happens every Thursday on a union job. 'Cause it don't. Union dues paid for this feed, and I don't go wasting union dues. 'Cause that's your money, not mine." Jensen paused.

"Right on," somebody yelled from the crowd.

"Your money. It costs you money to be part of a union. Maybe about thirty cents an hour. But that money is your money. It goes for pensions. You all go ask your wives what they think about you having a pension."

"All my wife wants is for me to have insurance, so she can knock me off and live high off the hog!" One of the truck drivers, Toby Morrison, yelled out. The crowd roared.

"Well, she might let you stay around if you was to have a real pension that lasted till you died." Jim Jensen raised his hand. "Ask your wife about medical insurance. Money to pay the doctor if the kid gets sick. Ask her about disability insurance that pays a regular wage every week, just like you was working, but it pays it if you get hurt and can't work. Your wife's going to tell you that these are damn good things to have."

Jensen looked at the crowd, making eye contact with people he picked at random. "These are good things. These are the things that thirty cents an hour pays for, and without the union you couldn't buy those things for two dollars an hour. Still you say, "Damn Jim, where the hell am I going to get thirty cents an hour. My paycheck don't stretch to the next payday as it is. I ain't got no thirty cents to spend on nothing, no matter how good it is."

The crowd was with him. Rick saw men nodding and muttering, "damn right."

"Well, Charlie DeBoni's going give you that thirty cents and more. Charlie's going to pay you more, so you can pay your dues and get that pension, and that insurance, and have even more money left over than when you started."

"You don't know Charlie very well, do you?" Henry yelled out.

Jim Jensen laughed. "Know Charlie? Damn right I know Charlie DeBoni, and he knows me. Me and Charlie have tangled touchholes more than once or twice. I didn't say Charlie was going pay you more because he wanted to. We ain't giving him no choice. Charlie wants to play on this here Interstate, he's going have to pay union wages, and live by union rules."

"Charlie says he'll just shut the fuckin' thing down." Old Clyde spoke up. "And I think he just might do it, too."

"Charlie is an *Eye-talian*. *Eye-talians* tend to get excited, and say whatever comes to mind. But Charlie's going have to look at the dollars he's stuffing in his pockets being a big deal Interstate contractor, compared to what he gets if he goes back to being a goddamn, dinky-assed, sidewalk contractor. And, by the Jesus, we're going to unionize them sidewalk contractors too." Jim smiled. "We know a few *Eye-talians*, too. They like the union. We think our *Eye-talians* can talk a little sense into Charlie if it comes to that."

"Charlie says some of us won't even be allowed into the union," Calvin spoke up. "He says you'll haul in guys from Pennsylvania and Texas, and we won't have no work at all."

"That's bullshit!" Jensen's face flushed with righteous anger. "The union is about saving jobs for you guys. We ain't got nobody who's going to take your jobs. You guys get to keep your jobs, and get a big fuckin' raise."

"That right?" Whitey spoke up, stepping out into the light. His white teeth flashed. "I get to be union too, Mr. Jensen?"

Jim Jensen frowned. He stared at Whitey. "The union's got no place for niggers."

"Hey, Whitey ain't no nigger, he's a mechanic, and a goddamn good one," Calvin shouted.

Whitey waved Calvin down. "So, Mr. Jensen, you be saying that the union comes in, I got no job? That right?" Whitey's voice was dead calm.

"You're like them goddamn niggers in Alabama, with Martin Luther *Coon*, and them others. Causing trouble. The union don't let no niggers take a good white man's job. Them's the rules."

Whitey smiled a cold smile. "Then I don't be expecting that you need my vote." He turned, and walked through the crowd back to the parking lot.

Rick watched him go, from his spot on the edge of the crowd. He saw Whitey stop, and look at the huge Lincoln that Jensen had arrived in. He shook his head, and walked over to his own car, a perfectly kept fifty-eight Oldsmobile, Rocket 88. He opened the door, climbed in, and turned the ignition. The car purred. He turned on his headlights, and Rick thought he saw someone duck into the shadow on the far side of the parking lot. Whitey put the car in gear, and carefully drove through the lot, and down the dirt road back to Route 5.

The crowd was muttering and talking among themselves. Jensen clearly had lost control. "Fuckin niggers," he muttered to himself. "All right, all right. Listen up now. Let me tell you what happens now."

The crowd quieted some, but the feeling of excitement was gone. A couple of men started edging back over towards the keg.

"What happens now is you all go home this weekend, and talk to your wives, and see what the old lady thinks. Then sometime next week, or the week after, we have a meeting and a vote. You vote for the union, you got the union. Period. Charlie's got no choice but to deal with us, or we'll shut him right down. He get shut down he not only doesn't make a ton of money, he has to start paying penalties to the United States Gov'ment. Now you tell me how long Charlie's going to want to do that!"

The crowd started moving towards the beer.

"Good-night, men. Enjoy that beer on the union," Jensen shouted. "Be the last you fuckin' get," he muttered under his breath. But no one heard him. The focus of attention had clearly shifted to the keg.

Rick stood in the shadows, and watched the union men haul down their flag and posters. They left the makeshift stage where it was. Jensen grabbed his jacket, and stormed off to his Lincoln. One of the union men opened the back door for him and he slide in, pulling out a flask as he did. Rick saw him tip the flask to his lips as the door slammed.

Louie, the guy who had given Edgar his check, pulled on a little cap, and went around to the driver's side. The other union goon climbed in the front passenger side. The doors slammed shut.

Rick was just turning away, when an explosion threw him to the ground. He rolled over and saw the Lincoln erupt in a fireball. "Jesus, sweet Jesus," he whispered. Little pieces of Lincoln rained down on him— Lincoln and he didn't know what or who else. Rick tucked up in a ball, and rolled under a picnic table. He heard a clang as a big piece of metal crashed down on the table.

He peered out from under the table. He could see men huddled under tables and behind trees. Old Everett had rolled the keg behind a tree and was hugging it. A huge piece of the Lincoln's bumper was embedded in the tree right where Everett and the keg had been standing. Other cars were burning in the parking lot. A siren sounded in the distance. The State Police barracks was just a mile away. A couple of men got to their feet, ran to their burning cars, and began beating on the flames with their shirts. No one rushed to the Lincoln. There was nothing there but a burning hulk. The acrid smell of burning tires and upholstery, mixed with a smell like barbecued pork.

Slowly, people picked themselves up, and brushed off the dirt. A few more hurried to the parking lot to help put out the little car fires. Côte walked over to his '48 Ford, a rusting hulk, held onto the frame with baling wire and rope. "Dang. Good thing it didn't scratch old Bertha here."

"Scratch it. That fuckin' thing's too ugly to die," Henry said as he inspected his own immaculate '57 Ford Fairlane.

"Don't you go sayin' bad things about Bertha. She's very sensitive."

The sirens got closer, and then two State Police cars came roaring down the dirt road, lights flashing, sirens wailing, and throwing up huge rooster tails of dried clay dust.

The cars screeched to a halt, and a uniformed trooper jumped from each one. They ran towards the burning Lincoln, and then stopped. "Everyone stay put," the taller trooper ordered. "Somebody tell me what happened here?" In the distance, a fire engine's siren wailed.

For a full minute no one said anything. Everyone just stood and stared at the burning hulk. Then one of the trooper's shrugged, "Nothing's going to help that car. Anyone in it?"

Old Everett sidled up to the front, and appointed himself spokesman. "Dang right. That big labor guy, and his goons. All three of'm. *Bloowie*, blown to smithereens."

"Do you mean Jim Jensen? Call this in, Carl!" The shorter trooper motioned to his tall partner.

"I'm on it, George." Carl strutted back to his cruiser, and pulled out the mike to his radio. "Unit 36, to base. We have a car explosion with fatalities here. Witnesses say one of the casualties is Jim Jensen. Requesting a crime-scene team." He listened to the squawking voice of the dispatcher. "Ten-four," he said.

"They're putting a call into headquarters. They said to seal the area till the crime-scene team gets here."

At that moment, Bellows Falls Volunteer Fire Department, Pumper No. 2, came roaring down the dirt road, siren whooping, and lights flashing. It screeched to a stop, and firemen hit the ground running. Before the troopers could stop them, the firemen had doused the Lincoln in foam, and were hauling a hose out one end, while two other firemen dragged a feeder hose down to the river.

"I don't think we need water, Chief!" George yelled.

If the chief heard him, he didn't acknowledge it. The pumps started throbbing, and a brown stream of water gushed from the hose, soaking down the Lincoln, and half the other cars in the lot.

"Shit!" Henry yelled. He leaped in his car, and rolled up the windows, almost getting them shut before the stream crashed into his car. Côte did-n't have the option of closing the windows on Bertha. He threw his square body between the car and hose, and managed to deflect a good portion of the water away, at the expense of getting completely drenched.

Two firemen jumped down from the truck with fire axes, and headed towards the parked cars.

"They come near my car with that axe, I'm shooting the sonsofwhores," Crackers screamed. He was pulling his Winchester out from the window rack of his pickup.

Acting Chief, Elmer Blodget, blew three blasts on a whistle. "Fire's out," he hollered. "Pack up, and let's get the hell out of here."

The firemen began dragging the hoses back to the pumper. George and Carl stood staring at the pool of mud and debris. "Thanks Chief," George said. "I don't know if there were any clues here, but if there was, you sure gave them a bath."

"It was a fire. Our job is to put out the fire. We did." Chief Blodget strode back to the pumper, and climbed up in the passenger's seat. "Let's roll," he hollered.

The huge truck backed around, crunching the fender of a beat-up '54 Chevy pickup. Then it roared off back down the dirt road, siren whooping, and lights flashing.

Teach came up behind Rick. "These guys make the Keystone Kops look competent," he said.

Rick just said, "Wow."

Some of the construction crew were starting to get into their cars, but Carl pulled his cruiser across the road. George hollered out, "Everybody sit down. We will need to talk to each of you before you go. Nobody can leave until we interview them, and the crime-scene crew has a chance to check this out."

There was general grumbling and complaining. Then, Everett hollered out, "There's still some beer in the keg, boys." Everyone began shuffling over to the keg.

Chapter 15

Sneakers

It was nearly midnight before Rick started back to town on his scooter. They had milled around, drinking beer for an hour before the crime-scene team arrived. Then, one-by-one, each of the workers was interviewed by one of the Troopers. Carl interviewed Rick.

After Carl had taken down his name and address he asked, "All right, son, what were you doing here tonight?"

"I work for DeBoni. I wanted to hear what this union stuff was about. That's all." Rick answered.

"Does that make a difference to you? You're a college student, aren't you?"

"Yeah. Well if they vote union I'd have to join. Besides it was a free meal."

"Free beer, do you mean? Did you drink a lot of beer?"

"Nope." Rick didn't volunteer how much he had drunk. He thought, "Wow, if Ellen hadn't of been here I'd of probably had five or six."

"Okay, son. Can you tell me what you saw?"

"About what everybody else saw. Jensen and his guys went and got into the car. They started it up, and *Kaboom*! They were toast."

"Where were you at the time of the explosion?"

"I was standing by that tree, just turning to go over and get my motor scooter, when the blast went off. Blew me right off my feet. I rolled under that table because all kinds of shit was raining down."

"Did you, at any time this evening, see anyone around the car? I mean looking under the hood or otherwise messing with it?"

"Nope. No one."

"How about that Negro who picked a fight with Jensen?"

"Whitey? Shit he didn't pick a fight. If anything, Jensen picked a fight with him. Nope, I saw him leave. He didn't touch their car."

"He could have done it earlier, couldn't he?"

"Yeah. I mean anybody could of done it sometime during the evening. Nobody was paying real close attention to anything but the beer and the food. But it was still daylight. I don't suppose anybody would take a chance and do something like that before it got dark."

"This Whitey knows enough doesn't he? He's some kind of mechanic or something."

"Whitey's the best damn diesel mechanic in New England. But he loves cars. He might blow up Jensen, but he sure as hell wouldn't blow up that Lincoln."

"How about Charley DeBoni? Did you see him around last night? He has made threats against the union hasn't he?"

"No. Charlie doesn't like the union, but I didn't see him. Besides, I don't think he would do that kind of thing. "

"Yeah? Them Italians are all Mafia types. He could have put a contract on Jensen."

"You think so? I thought the Mafia and the union were in bed together. That's what it said in the New York Times."

"You read those radical newspapers? Did you burn your draft card?"

"No sir. I've got it right here. It says IIS. I'm deferred until I graduate."

"Then they'll draft you and send you to 'Nam. Make a man out of you, boy." Carl laughed.

"Who knows? Maybe the war will end first."

"Not likely. All right. Get out of here kid and watch yourself."

"Yes sir." Rick had been trembling uncontrollably by the time the interview was over. He hated that cops did that to him, but he couldn't shake the innate fear. He remembered back one Halloween when he was in high school, and a bunch of them had blown up a mailbox with a homemade bomb. The cops had chased them. They'd split up. He'd run through the playground and was in the clear. He headed down the bank when this deep voice said, "Hold it right there, kid." He'd nearly shit his pants. It was his friend Paul, who had a voice like a bass drum. Paul had laughed himself silly. Rick had had the shakes for hours.

Now, putting along Highway 5, he felt a bit calmer. He passed the setback and started up the last hill before town. The Village Inn sat at the top of the hill overlooking the river. Whitey's wife, Annabelle, was the cook there, and had turned a perennial money loser into the most popular restaurant in the area. As he topped the hill, he saw the town police cruiser slide into the parking lot. Two cops got out, Sneakers Burns, and Chet Chickering. They had their guns drawn. "Oh shit," Rick thought, they're going after Whitey." Whitey's Olds was parked in the lot. He was there picking up his wife.

Without thinking about it, Rick turned into the lot and putted over to the police car. "Hey Chet! Hey Sneakers! What you guys up to? Going to hold Annabelle at gun point and make her cook you a meal?"

"Get out of here, Wallace," Chickering hissed. "This is police stuff. We're going to take that nigger in."

"Come on Chet. That ain't no nigger. That's Whitey. That's the same guy Bob Burke has fixing up his undertaker's car." Bob Burke was a part-time town cop and well liked by everybody.

"Yeah, well the State Police say he's a murdering, radical nigger, and we should use extreme caution."

"Use your head, Chet. You can't go shooting in there. D-d-donnie owns this restaurant. He'll fry your ass if you shoot the place up."

That stopped Chickering and Sneakers for a second, and Rick saw an opening. "Hey let me go in and talk him out. He doesn't even know anybody's after him. He left way before the union guys got blown up. Give me five minutes."

Sneakers said, "Yeah, all right Wallace. Do it quick. Five minutes, and no funny stuff or we'll come hunting your ass."

Chickering put his gigantic 44 Magnum pistol back in his holster. "Hurry up. We ain't got all night."

Rick parked his scooter and hustled up to the kitchen door. It was unlatched, so he tapped and let himself right in. Whitey was sitting at the little table munching on an inch-thick sirloin steak. "Hi Whitey. Hi Annabelle."

"What you doing here, Squirt?" Whitey looked up from his plate. He scowled.

"Hello Rick. How's your Mom," Annabelle said.

"She's great, Annabelle. Listen. Whitey, after you left, somebody blew up Jensen and his guys. They bombed the car."

"That beautiful Lincoln. Oh, no. That's a damn shame. Fine car. Just like Kennedy's car."

"Yeah, well the car and those three guys are in tiny pieces. Trouble is, they think you had something to do with it because you had that little argument with Jensen."

"Ain't got nothing to do with me being black, right?"

"What can I say, Whitey. One minute you're our buddy, Whitey. Next minute you're a nigger."

"Damn. This ain't going to be good."

"Worse than that. Sneakers Burns and Chet Chickering are in the parking lot right now with, their guns drawn, waiting to come in here shooting. I told them I'd get you to come out. I figured that way Annabelle could call Sam Trout, and get a lawyer down to the police station right away."

"Oooh, man. You heard the boy, Momma. Call them attorneys to get my radical nigger ass out of jail. Okay boy, let's walk out together so they don't just shoot me."

Rick opened the door and hollered, "We're coming out guys. Got no guns or nothing."

"Well, get out here," Sneakers hollered. "And keep your hands where we can see'm."

Together, Rick and Whitey walked down the steps and across the lot, hands in the air.

"Howdy, Chet. Howdy, Sneakers." Whitey said, flashing a smile.

"Just get in the car, Whitey. We gotta take you in."

Rick watched them put Whitey in cuffs, and push him into the back-seat. The cruiser squealed its tires as it shot out of the lot and headed back towards town.

"Rick, come here a minute." Annabelle was at the door.

Rick walked back to the kitchen door. Annabelle had a plate of choco-late éclairs in one hand.

"Take these down to the jail, will you Rick? It might make them go a little easier on Whitey. Mr. Trout says he'll have his associate, O'Malley, down there in half an hour. But they can hurt somebody bad in half an hour."

"Yes ma'am," Rick said. "Can you put these in a bag or something? I've got the motor scooter, and it would be tough carrying them like this."

Annabelle found a little box and a bag with handles. Rick tied the bag down on his carrier, kick-started the scooter, and headed into town. It was nearly one o'clock in the morning.

As he putted into town, Rick thought about the two cops. Chet Chickering was certainly not the brightest bulb on the tree. Rick had heard the story about Chickering stopping "The Tycoon," G. William Duque, when he first came to town. Duque had handed him his license. Chickering had stared at it. Then walked behind the Rolls and looked at the license plate, then come back around and said, "How come your license says you live in Philadelphia but you got Pennsylvania plates on this car?" Duque used to tell the story and roar with laughter. Rick had worked for Duque the summer he was sixteen, and he was just setting up his excursion trains. Rick did odd jobs around the roundhouse and sold candy on the train. Duque always had a place for Chickering to make a few extra bucks as a rent-a-cop, or helping out in other ways. That's where Rick really got on a first name basis with Chickering.

Sneakers Burns was a different animal. He'd been a cop in town since as long as Rick could remember. He never said much. Just did his job. He got the nickname Sneakers, because he wore tennis shoes rather than the regulation black wing tips. He said it allowed him to "Sneak up on perps, and nab'm before they knew he was there."

Sneakers was the cop who chased Paul, Rick, Dieter, and Howard that night they blew up the mailbox. Rick didn't think Sneakers had seen who they were, but he always had the feeling that Sneakers knew, and was just waiting for the right moment to slap the cuffs on him. Destroying a mailbox was a Federal offense. Rick sometimes imagined Sneakers making the arrest just as Rick was receiving his college diploma, or maybe during his wedding. He was a quiet guy, but Rick suspected that underneath, Sneakers craved the limelight.

The police station was in a narrow tenement, across from the canal. Rick had never been inside before, and he felt his gut churn. "Just like walking into the dentist," he muttered to himself.

He parked the scooter across the street, grabbed the bag of éclairs, and walked up the steps and through a door that may have once been light blue. "Poor choice of colors," he thought, grimacing at the layers of filth smeared around the knob. The door opened into a long, narrow hallway. There was a glass partition with a window, like a teller's window. Old Marian Crosby sat behind the window. She had been the police dispatcher forever, as far as Rick knew.

"Whatcha want, boy?" Marian grunted.

"Hi. I'm looking for Sneakers and Whitey. Annabelle sent some stuff for him."

"Oh? What's in the bag?"

"Éclairs. Want one?"

"Youbetcherass I want one of Annabelle's éclairs. They're friggin' famous. Maybe I should take the whole dang bag."

"No way, Mizz Crosby. Annabelle said only give'm to Whitey. But I could give you one if you let me go in there."

"All right. It's a deal. But Sneakers is probably going to kick your ass out right quick."

Rick fished in the bag and pulled out an éclair wrapped in tissue. He handed it to Marian, and she stuffed half of it in her face, pointing up the narrow stairs. "Mmnishish good," she mumbled, stuffing the remainder in her mouth.

Rick hustled up the stairs before Marian demanded another. At the top of the stairs the door was open into a narrow, windowless room. Chickering was standing at one end of a table. Whitey was sitting with his back to the wall. Sneakers was seated across from him. Sneakers posed a question. "Tell me Whitey, all you construction boys work with that there dynamite?"

Whitey shook his head. "Nope. I never touched the stuff. Course I don't think there's much to it. Shit, they got Barrel-ass running a dynamite crew and he ain't hardly got the sense to whack his monkey. I expect anybody could figure out how to use the stuff."

Sneakers nodded. He wrote on his pad. "How about wiring it to a car?"

Rick tried to catch Whitey's attention and signal him not to say anything, but Whitey didn't look up. Instead he said, "Nothin' to that. Ground one wire, attach the other one to a spark plug."

"Éclairs anyone?" Rick almost shouted. "Hey Whitey, Annabelle sent down some éclairs. She said your lawyer would be here in just a couple of minutes. Maybe you should talk to him before you talk to these guys."

Sneakers whirled around and glared at Rick. "Get out of here, Wallace. You got no business in here. This is police business."

"Annabelle just sent down some éclairs. If you don't want'm, I'll eat'm myself." He waved the bag and the rich vanilla and chocolate smell wafted into the dingy little room.

"Dang, I want one of them." Chet Chickering was reaching for the bag.

"Here Whitey," Rick tossed the bag to Whitey. "You divvy them up. I got to get home and get some sleep."

There was no resisting the éclairs once you had a whiff. In less than a minute, all four of them were munching éclairs and smiling.

"Dang that wife of yours can cook, Whitey." Chickering was grinning from ear to ear. Even Sneakers was smiling. Rick hoped that O'Malley would get here pretty quick. He didn't think Whitey even considered that these guys might be trying to make a case against him. The thought struck him that Whitey spent all his time working on engines and didn't watch any TV. He'd probably never seen Joe Friday trick a guy into a confession on Dragnet.

Suddenly, a commotion erupted at the bottom of the stair. A high-pitched voice was screaming in a mixture of Italian and English. Rick heard the State Trooper Carl say, "I need to borrow your jail. I need to lock Mr. DeBoni up before he hurts himself."

This was followed by a stream of obscenities in English and Italian. Rick didn't speak Italian, but he had no doubt whatsoever that those words wouldn't be found in your standard tourist dictionary.

He looked at Whitey. Simultaneously they both said, "Charlie."

There was a crashing sound. Marian yelled, "It's upstairs. Sneakers has got a key. Get that crazy sonofabitch out of here."

Charlie kept up a steady stream of invective, as Carl frog-marched him up the stairs. He pushed him through the door into the interrogation room and hollered, "Sit down and be quiet so that I can tell you that you have the right to remain silent."

"Hi Charlie," Whitey said with a smile. "They got you too, huh? Some combination. A nigger, and a dago, the old one-two punch. All we need is a spic, and a Pollack, and maybe a Jew or two."

Charlie sputtered, and then finally sat quiet. "Whitey? What you doing down here? Wallace? Is that your name boy?"

"They think I blew old Jensen to smithereenies," Whitey laughed. "And I wouldn't have minded doing that, but the sonofabitch who blew him up also killed one very fine Lincoln."

"Fuck. The union guy? Blown up?" Charlie turned white as a sheet. "I...I...shit."

"You didn't tell him?" Rick asked Carl.

"Couldn't get a word in edgewise. Minute I knocked on his door he went off like a two-dollar pistol. I hauled him in because I thought he might hurt himself. Never saw anybody turn that color of red before."

"Ol' Charlie do have a temper," Whitey laughed.

"What happened?" Charlie asked, his voice barely audible.

"Can I tell him?" Rick asked Carl. Carl nodded.

Rick gave Charlie the five-minute story from Jensen's opening remarks, through the little tiff with Whitey, to the Fire Department's belated dousing of everything.

"He said that about his Italians?" Charlie asked.

"Yep. That's what he said. He said his Italians could make you see the light."

"Shit."

From downstairs they heard a sonorous voice sweet talking Marian. "Ah, my Maid Marian," he said. "Can you help this poor lad find his worthy client, that dusty gentleman we know by the name, Whitey?"

A moment later, Tom O'Malley poked his head in the door. "That's my man, Whitey," he said. "I need to talk to him right now."

Sneakers nodded, and pointed to the little office next door. Whitey got up and shook hands with O'Malley. He started to say something, but

O'Malley put a finger to his lips. "Not a word," he said. "I expect you've already said things we will wish you hadn't. Come on, let's talk."

"You there, behind the glass. I demand you rectify this miscarriage of justice and release my client at once!" a powerful bass voice boomed from downstairs.

They heard Marian reply, "You got a form 10W BF42?"

"A…a what?"

"Form 10W BF42 release of person in custody form. Can't do anything till we process your 10W BF42."

"Uhh, oh. Where's the form?"

"You got a Form 107 BF19 request for form, form?"

Sneakers hollered, "Marian, for God's sake let the poor man come up here, will you."

"Yes sir. If you want, Mr. Pompous Ass, I'll send him right up."

They heard the tapping of polished wing tips climbing the stair. A somewhat chagrined, but dapper man in a three-piece suit looked in the door. "Charlie," he said, "Are you alright?"

He looked around, and finally decided that the State Trooper must be in charge. He turned to Carl and said, "I must demand the release of my client this instant. What preposterous charges can you have against this saintly man?"

Carl cleared his throat. "Umm, let's see. Resisting arrest; assault and battery on a police officer; foul and abusive language in a public place, and, oh yeah, maybe homicide, three counts."

The lawyer's jaw dropped. He looked over at Charlie. Charlie slowly shook his head. "Let me talk to my client alone, please," the lawyer said.

"I'm out of here," Rick said to no one in particular, and no one paid him the slightest bit of attention. He trotted down the stairs.

"Nice form, Marian," he said. "Your match hands down."

"Hee, hee," she cackled. "Pompous Boston lawyer. Fuck'm."

Rick trotted out to his motor scooter and headed for home. It was 2:30 A.M.

Chapter 16

Crackers

5:30 came real early the next morning, but Rick woke up before the alarm went off. He was groggy and tired, but he gulped down a mug of coffee, slapped together a lunch, and headed off to work. He was running a little late, so he didn't top off the gas tank as he usually did on Friday mornings.

The yard was chaos. Men were standing around in small groups, talking. An unmarked police car was parked by the trailer, and John Cashman was talking to two guys in suits that Rick recognized as being part of the crime-scene team. Rick was surprised to see Whitey's Olds parked in his usual spot. "O'Malley sprung him," Rick thought. "Wonder if Charlie got out too?" He wandered over towards the garage to see if he could catch Whitey and ask him. Halfway across the yard, he heard John Cashman call him.

"Wallace, come over here."

Rick made a left turn, and headed over towards the trailer.

"Wallace, I want you to take these officers up and show them the magazine. Open it up. Let them look around, and do whatever they need to do. Answer any questions you can. Take my pickup."

"Yes sir. I'll get the key."

"Where's the key kept?" the short, paunchy detective asked.

"In the office trailer, on the key board," Rick said.

"Who has access to it?" the detective's cadaverous partner asked.

"Anybody who comes in the trailer. But there's generally somebody there. Me, or Tim, or sometimes Charlie." John said.

"Okay kid, let's go. My name's Redman, Detective Redman. This is Detective Amery," The paunchy detective gestured at his partner. "You're Wallace?"

"Yeah. Rick Wallace."

"You at that shindig last night, Wallace?"

"Yeah, I was there. A trooper named Carl interviewed me."

"Okay. We may want to talk to you too. But first, let's see this dynamite."

Rick went to the office and lifted a key off the board. He noticed that there were only three on the hook instead of the usual five. Then he remembered he had one in his pocket from the day before. He dug it out, and hung it on the board.

He handed the key to Detective Redman, and climbed into the driver's side of the pickup. Avery climbed into the middle, and Redman sat by the door on the passenger side. Rick started the truck, put it in gear, and headed out of the yard. As they turned towards the job, he got a glimpse of Charlie's baby-blue Eldorado screaming into the yard from the highway side.

"Fellow's in a bit of a hurry to get to work, ain't he?" Redman asked.

"That's Charlie," Rick said. "He owns the place. But your guy Carl hauled him into jail last night, so I bet he's still a bit steamed."

"How'd you know that?" Amery asked.

"I was there," Rick replied. Then he gave them a two-minute version of last night's doing at the jailhouse.

The two detectives got a real boot out of Marian's handling of Charlie's attorney. By the time they turned up the road to the magazine, the detectives were treating Rick like a friend.

"Anybody get in here?" Redman asked.

"Yeah. Pretty much. I wouldn't want to drive a regular car in here, but a pickup or jeep, sure."

"Everybody know where it is?" Avery asked.

"I guess so. They don't advertise it or anything. But everybody on the job pretty much knows where everything is, including the magazine."

Rick parked in front of the magazine and they all climbed out. Redman went over and looked at the lock. He yanked on it and looked for scratches around the hasp. "Looks okay," he said. "Good sturdy Master Lock. Top of the line." He unlocked it, and hung the padlock back on the hasp.

Meanwhile, Avery had taken a slow walk around the shed, looking for any attempts to enter it from behind. "Looks clean," he said.

Redman swung open the door. The shed was nearly full, dynamite stacked from floor to ceiling. "It always this full?" he asked.

"We just got a shipment yesterday," Rick answered. "We pulled out all the old stuff and loaded the new stuff in back, then put the old stuff back. We took a complete inventory. Mr. Cashman should have that in the office by now."

"Hmm. Anything look odd to you then?"

"Well, just the one missing jackhammer stick from the box in front, and one cap from the double-oughts. We guessed that maybe somebody had a stump back on the farm they needed to blow."

"That these?" Redman was carefully sliding the small box of jackhammer sticks out of the shed, using just two fingers.

"Yeah, that's the jackhammer sticks. That's the box with one missing. Double-ought caps, ought to be on top, too."

Redman lifted out a box of caps, also using just two fingers. "These?"

"Yeah."

"Better dust'em," Redman said. Amery came over with a small bag of powder and sprinkled it over each box. Redman blew gently and spread the powder around. "Shit," he said. "Nothing but smudges."

"We probably aren't going to find anything, but we got to go through the motions. You touch this stuff Rick?" Redman asked.

Rick held up a gloved hand. "Pretty much always wear gloves on the job. Most everybody does."

Redman opened the box of caps. He took one out and tossed it to Avery. He opened the box of jackhammer sticks, pulled out a stick, and tossed it to Avery as well. "What do you think?"

"Be my guess." Avery said. "Looks like the same tag as we found from the cap wire. The lab may be able to match traces with the stick. Shit, this was really overkill wasn't it?"

"Who else might get a hold of the key?" Avery asked.

"Well, pretty much anybody. All the padlocks use the same key," Rick answered. "Charlie thought that would save some money."

"You mean, anybody who could get any key, could get into the magazine?" Avery was incredulous.

"I guess so. It doesn't make much sense, I know. It's what we call DeBoni logic. Save a penny and lose the whole damn dollar. Heck, I took one of those keys home last night in my pocket and nobody noticed." Rick shrugged. "I guess maybe I shouldn't have told you that, but what the heck, I bet it ain't the first time it's happened."

"Nothing more to see here," Redman said. He had been poking around in the shed while Avery and Rick talked. "Well, at least we got a possible on the dynamite source."

"Yeah, and 300 fucking suspects," Avery added.

"You ever see anybody up here who wasn't supposed to be?" Redman asked. He put the box of jackhammer sticks in the back of the truck. He held on to the box of caps as the three of them climbed into the truck and started back.

Rick thought about that and started to shake his head, but then said "Well the other day I saw PH's truck driving in here after we'd shut down for the night."

"Who's PH?"

"Harris. He's the assistant super in charge of the ledge. I mean, he can go anywhere on the job he wants, and he probably has good reasons to be checking out the dynamite. It's just…" Rick didn't finish the sentence.

"Just what?" Avery asked.

"Well, PH is kind of vocal about the union. I mean, he threatened us if we even went to the meeting. Course, nobody paid any attention to him. Most of the guys think he's a dick-head. That's why guys call him PH, for pecker head. I think he thinks it's short for Patrick Harris."

"How about the other bosses? They all anti-union?" Avery had his notebook out.

"Well Charlie is, for sure. He says he'll shut right down rather than accept the union. Cashman says the union's okay with him. I don't know what the Duke thinks. And the grade foremen don't seem to care one way or another, as far as I can tell."

"How about the men?" Redman asked.

"I don't know for sure, but I think most of them will vote against the union. They like to make a big deal about it to pull PH's chain, and to pull Charlie's chain. Charlie is pretty funny when he's mad. But at the end of the day, I don't think these guys want somebody else telling them what to do. Besides, a lot of them probably wouldn't get jobs if the union were to take over. I mean, a lot of them are just farmers making a living wage, working here 'cause they can. But once the Interstate is done, they'll go back to scratching out a living as farmers. Course, the college kids like me don't care one way or another. We're the bottom of the heap either way."

"What about this Whitey guy?" Avery asked.

"Best diesel mechanic in New England, at least. Maybe the world." Rick answered. "And I got that from Cecil Sommes, the head mechanic at Orleans Trucking. Both of them worked on some diesel locomotives for The Tycoon when I was helping out down at the roundhouse a couple or three years back."

"I take it that didn't cut no ice with the union," Redman said.

"Jensen was pretty vocal about the union not taking blacks. Niggers, he said. Nobody around here ever thought of Whitey as a nigger. Shit, folks around here have hardly ever seen a colored person. Whitey's their friend. And everybody loves his wife Annabelle's cooking."

They pulled into the yard, and the two detectives got out. They stood talking together quietly, and Rick headed over to the office. He hung the key on the board and Cashman looked up. "You take care of those Detectives?"

"They're still here. Outside, talking. But they saw what they wanted. They're taking a box of jackhammer sticks and a box of caps with them to test."

"Mmm. You go help them load that D-9, will you? We won't be blasting for a day or two until they sort some of this stuff out."

Rick left the trailer and sauntered over towards the maintenance shed. There was virtually nothing he could do except get in the way when it came to loading a D-9 on a flatbed truck, but orders were orders.

Donny Aldrich, who usually ran the D-8 down on the fill, was standing by the shed watching Whitey back the rebuilt D-9 out into the yard. Whitey was taking his time, listening to the engine, and feeling how the machine was running as he gently gave it load.

"Whose running the D-8, Donny?" Rick asked.

"Bigun." Donny was referring to Burt *Bigun* Jones, who ran a bunch of the smaller equipment; rollers, sheep's foot, D-4, and the like. *Bigun* referred to the size of his oversized member, which he "tucked in his sock," he bragged, "to keep from tripping on the head."

Whitey backed out into the yard, and slowly pivoted so that the bulldozer was facing the road. "It's a total piece of shit, Donny." Whitey jumped down. "We done everything but put a new engine in it, and it's still a piece of shit."

"Will it out push the 8?" Donny asked.

"Be close. Maybe for a bit. But I expect that we're going to spend more time on it than you are for the next two weeks, or whenever Charlie gets it in his head to bring back the good one." Whitey wiped his hands on a rag. "Good luck," he said.

"Thanks, I guess." Donny climbed up into the seat and spent a few minutes familiarizing himself with the controls. Then he put it in gear, clanked out of the yard, and headed up to the fill area.

Rick looked over at Whitey. "What time did you get out?"

"'Bout 3:30. Annabelle says 'thanks,' and probably wants to give you some food or something."

"Well, I was afraid Sneakers and Chickering would start shooting. Charlie get out the same time as you?"

"Pretty near. They were processing him out when I left."

"Using form 10W BF42?"

Whitey laughed. "Here comes that flatbed."

A huge, red diesel tractor with "Oversized Load" permanently mounted on its front bumper, roared into the yard.

"Goddamnit, Crackers, take it easy with that thing. It ain't no belly pan." Whitey shook his fist at the grinning cowboy behind the wheel.

"What'n'hell is Crackers doing driving that rig?" Rick asked.

"Squat John's in the hospital with kidney stones, or some such shit. They figured they could cut one pan, what with using that old piece-of-shit, dozer. At least, until Donny gets the hang of it. Here comes Chip"

The big D-9 lumbered into the yard. Whitey waved it over to the maintenance shed. "I want to check that thing out a bit before we put it on the road. Might as well change the oil and do some quick maintenance. Why don't you find something else to do for five or six hours?"

Rick flipped Crackers the bird, said, "See ya," to Whitey, and headed over to the office trailer. John sent him off with Everett to pick up scrap lumber along the right-of-way. "You don't need to worry about loading the D-9 if you don't get back in time. We can probably do it without you."

"Guess I know when I'm not needed," Rick laughed to Everett. "Shit, I rather pick up lumber with you any day."

"Dang right. Let's head up on the ledge, and have lunch with them drillers. See what they got to say about last night."

Everett poked along, and got to the ledge just as the air horns on the Euclids blasted the noon shutdown whistle. Rick and Everett grabbed their lunch-buckets, and joined Côte, Henry, and Ding and Dodd.

"Well here comes the man who saved the beer!" Côte hollered. "Old Everett, he knows what's important, by God."

"You ever see the like?" Henry said. "There warn't hardly any little pieces left."

"It was raining Lincoln Continental," Everett chuckled. "I thought sure I was going to take a spare tire in the ass."

"It was awful," Dodd said. "Big Jim was a great guy. Who would of wanted to blow him up?"

"Well, the cops are looking hard at Charlie and Whitey," Rick said. Then he told them about what went on at the police station, and also about the two cops at the magazine early in the morning.

"They're looking at the wrong guys, there," Côte said. "Whitey would never blow up a nice car. And Charlie is a crazy motherfucker, but I can't see him getting his hands dirty."

"I know who I'd bet on," Henry said.

Everyone turned and looked at him.

"Who would you bet on, Henry?" Everett asked.

"PH, that's who. I saw that cocksucker sneaking around in the brush earlier in the evening. I'll bet he's the sonofabitch who done it."

Rick remembered seeing somebody crossing the parking lot when Whitey drove out. "It could've been PH," he muttered.

"What's that, Squirt?" Henry hollered. "Speak up."

"Nothing. I just was thinking that PH sure does hate the union."

"Jesus Christ, speak of the Devil, and up the sonofabitch jumps," Henry said.

PH slammed his door and trudged up the hill to where they were eating lunch.

"Man can't even eat in peace around here," Henry muttered.

"You men talk to the detectives yet?" PH asked.

"They all nodded. "We was interviewed last night at the scene of the crime," Everett said.

"Well, they may want to talk to some of you guys again."

"So let'm talk," Henry growled. "We ain't goin' nowhere."

"Well, watch what you tell'm."

"What's that supposed to mean?" Henry asked.

"Well, they're trying to finger Charlie, and you know he didn't do it. So don't be saying things that make it look like he might've."

"That right? Who you think done it?" Henry's tone was ominous.

"Probably that nigger, Whitey. But I don't know. He might've."

"So now Whitey's a nigger?" Rick asked. "I never heard you *nigger* him before."

"It's what they call'm where I come from."

"Where th'hell you come from?" Everett asked.

"Texas." PH spun on his heel, and strode off down the hill to his pickup.

"*Pubic*, Texas," Côte said. "He's the man from *Pubic*. You can tell, because he's always grabbing his panhandle."

"I think the sonofabitch is worried somebody'll point the finger at him," Henry smiled a malicious smile. "And if I get the chance, I just may wave the flag in his direction. I don't know if the sonofabitch done it, but I do know he's the one guy on this job I wouldn't mind seeing fry for it."

Nobody challenged Henry's view as they packed up and headed back to work. Rick and Everett spent the next four hours cruising the right-of-way, first 2.14 miles north, then 2.14 miles south. From time-to-time, they'd spot a few 2×4's or 2×6's lying off the side of the road. They would jump down, throw them into the back of the truck, and then continue on their way. Everett set a pace that made the job last most of the afternoon."

"Shoot Everett, the way you got this timed, anybody would think you was union," Rick joked.

Everett spat out the window. "Fuck the union," he said. "I been union before. I don't want nothing to do with no union."

They pulled in behind the maintenance shed about 4:30, and unloaded the wood from the pickup onto a stack of used lumber. DeBoni would reuse the wood for concrete forms and the like. Most contractors just burned it because it was too much trouble to reuse it.

As they unloaded, Rick watched Whitey, Chip, and Crackers load the D-9 on the flatbed. He thought about Crackers.

His real name was Marvin Lapierre. He had worked off and on for DeBoni for the past eight years. Mostly, he'd been a truck driver, starting with the old Moss-Sterlings, 6-yard, chain-driven trucks, built in the late thirties and early forties, that Whitey kept working with bailing wire and twine. Later, he had honchoed the fifteen-yard dump trucks built by Autocar. Last year he was promoted to the big belly scrapers, and he was in heaven. He was called "Crackers" because he was nuts—a crazy man, always taking risks with the big rigs he manhandled.

Crackers, toothless though he was, was also known as a ladies man, not that Rick would have looked twice at any of his so-called "ladies." Married, with two or three kids, Crackers always had another woman on the line wherever he worked. "Kind of like a sailor with one in every port," Rick thought. Last year Crackers had sprung for some brand new store-bought teeth and he hadn't stopped smiling since.

You didn't want to get too close to Crackers, especially right after morning sandwich break. His standard morning snack was a raw onion. Most everybody figured he was covering up the smell of some early morning drinking. But nobody ever caught him at it. Charlie was strict about that. Get caught drinking on the job, and you were toast.

During the big moves, Crackers always drove one of the three DeBoni flatbeds. He was the logical choice to take over with Squat John out of action.

Everett and Rick finished up about 5:15. "Enough for one week," Rick said.

"Too dang much, you ask me," Everett replied. "Glad it's Friday."

"Where you live, Everett?" Rick asked.

"Just got a trailer down in the park there," Everett replied. "Winters, I haul it down to North Carolina and park it out on them islands. That's mighty nice."

"Sounds good to me. Well, I got to get rolling. Dang, I promised Ellen's dad that I would load hay tomorrow. Shit! No rest for the wicked."

"He wants to work your ass off to make sure your pecker's too pooped to pop." Everett cackled. "Protect his little Honey from that horny college fuck."

"Probably right," Rick laughed. "Not that she'd let me do anything. But I think it's her mother that's more worried than old Ed. Mora doesn't think I'm good enough for her little princess. She's looking to hitch her to some snooty rich guy. That's why she took her down to Boston last week."

"Got to watch it, Squirt. They all grows up to be just like their Mommas."

"Scary thought, Everett."

Rick jumped on the little Vespa and kick-started it. He putted out of the yard, zipping in front of Crackers who was just easing the loaded low-bed out of the yard. Crackers leaned on the horn, and Rick flipped him the bird.

There was a line of cars, and Rick had to wait before turning onto Route 5. Crackers was right behind him when he turned, and Crackers never even braked, swinging the big rig out onto the highway. Rick gave the scooter the gas, and soon was right up behind the line of slow moving traffic. Crackers kept coming, and when Rick looked over his shoulder, there was the giant diesel tractor right behind him, with Crackers grinning like a banshee, and yelling something he couldn't hear.

Rick gave the little Vespa more gas, and then, suddenly, the rear-end skidded out from under him, and he found himself sliding along the highway, the giant rig right on top of him.

Rick couldn't honestly say exactly what happened. One minute he was up and riding. The next minute he was flat on his back, looking up at the underside of the diesel tractor. Amazingly, the giant wheels hadn't touched him or the scooter.

Crackers' face peered under the truck. "Squirt? Squirt, you all right?"

"Damn, you're a good driver," Rick said weakly. "Never touched me."

Crackers reached under and hauled out the little scooter. "Whatthefuck happened? One minute you was up, then you was gone."

Rick scrambled out from under the truck. "Beats me. It just locked up and went down. Surprised the shit out of me."

"Well, if it was me, I would dump that piece of shit and buy a car." Crackers was visibly shaken.

"I think you're right."

"Need me to radio for help or anything?"

"No, that's okay. I have to get this home. I'll see if it will run. If not, I can head over to the gas station there and call for a ride."

"Yeah, well okay. But shit, be careful. You could get killed."

"Yeah. I will. And Crackers? Thanks."

"Forget it. Gotta go."

Chapter 17

Dad

Rick stood at the side of the road beside his scraped-up motor scooter and watched Crackers pull the big low-bed back into traffic. Slowly, it began to dawn on him how close he had come to being crushed under the wheels of the big rig. He found himself shaking uncontrollably.

Numbly, he kicked the starter on the Vespa. Nothing. He checked to see if it was out of gear, and tried again. Nothing. Then he flipped the switch to access the reserve fuel tank. He gave the starter a kick and the little 250cc engine purred. "Oh man," he groaned, as it dawned on him that he had simply run out of gas. The sound and vibrations of the big rig right on his tail had prevented him from hearing and feeling the engine sputter and die.

He checked over the entire scooter to make sure nothing was hanging loose, and then got on and putted over to the gas station. Fifty-cents worth of gas with a dollop of oil mixed in, and the scooter was as reliable as ever. But Rick's confidence in it was gone. He had had a close glimpse of his own mortality, and realized he didn't want to hang out there on the edge any more. The thought crossed his mind that today was Friday the 13th. "Bad luck? Good luck?" He thought. "I could make a case either way."

"I need a car, and I need it tonight," he said out loud. He began planning his story as he putted back to town.

That night at dinner, he told his story, complete with sound effects. He blamed the scooter, claiming it had locked up. "I've just got to get a car tonight, Dad. Can you help?"

"We have to help him, Dick. We can't have the boy killing himself on that thing. I always hated that motor scooter," Rick's mother said, taking his side.

Rick had to suppress a smile. His mother was always begging him for rides.

"I suppose we have to do it," Rick's dad said. "You have any money?"

"Well, not much," Rick answered. "I haven't made all that much yet. I've only been working for three weeks."

"So you've saved what?" Richard Wallace peered over his glasses.

"Maybe seventy-five, eighty bucks, plus this week's check. It's ninety-five dollars, but I'll need money for cigarettes, gas, lunches, and stuff."

"He means beer," Rick's sister Willa chimed in.

"Shut up, Willa," Rick said. "There's a place between Drewsville and Alstead that has some cheap cars. We could look there. You know, Carney's Cars."

"I hear he's a crook," Rick's father muttered. "But then, they're all crooks. So one's as good as another. Let's get going. I don't want to spend all night at this."

"Can we go too?" Rick's three younger brothers, Moe, Larry, and Curly, chimed up. Their real names were Morris, Laurence, and Charles, but there was no chance that they could avoid the Stooges' nicknames. Rick always suspected his father had named them with the Stooges in mind, but he would never admit it.

Richard Wallace was a man who kept his reasons to himself. He rarely spoke, letting his wife Maureen do all the talking. Rick knew he was a very successful salesman, so he figured his dad must be different with other people.

Rick had always seen his father as a puzzle. What little he knew about him, he had learned from his mother and his grandfather. His father never talked about himself, his past, or his future. To Rick, he just seemed to be there.

Rick's mother fixed herself a drink, and said, "I'll stay here."

"Don't drink all the scotch," Richard said in a serious tone.

The three younger kids had piled into the car and were tooting the horn. "Let's go!" they hollered. "Come on!"

Willa swept out of the room saying, "TK and I are going to the movie."

"You be home by 10:00," Rick's mother shouted.

"Mother! Don't tell me what to do!"

Rick and his father fled the house to escape the inevitable mother-daughter screaming match.

They didn't talk as they drove out to Carney's. Even if Rick and his dad had wanted to talk, it would have been difficult to hold a conversation over the screaming battle that raged in the backseat. Rick's father's occasional "Don't make me stop the car and come back there," had no noticeable effect. Moe was long past the age where he could be intimidated by a threat to stuff him in a mailbox and mail him home.

Carney's was one of a dozen small used car lots that dotted the small towns and hamlets of the area. The big car dealers, D-d-donnie's Chevrolet Cadillac, Ferguson Ford, Eldritch Plymouth Dodge, and Russell Studebaker Nash Rambler Motors, all sold used cars too, but normally they got top dollar for their cars. The little lots dealt in lower-priced cars, usually sporting a good amount of rust, and guaranteed only to get you out of the lot.

"Try to keep it to $300 or so," Rick's dad said as they pulled into Carney's.

"Yes sir," Rick said. He had no idea what the prices would be on these cars, but he figured if his Dad said three hundred, he could probably talk him into spending twice that much.

Actually, it was no contest. One look at the cars in the lot, and Rick zeroed in on a two-tone, royal and robins egg blue, '57 Chevy BelAire. "This one Dad," he said.

It looked immaculate inside and out. He sat in the driver's seat and started the engine. It roared to life, and when he backed off the accelerator, the exhaust rumbled. "Glass packs," he said with delight. "Sounds cool."

Rick's father walked around the car kicking the tires. He opened the trunk, checked the spare, and crawled underneath to look at the frame and wheel wells. Rick checked out the radio. It sounded great.

"Got some rust," his father said.

"They all got some rust," Rick said. "I can patch it with *Bondo*."

"Sticker is $500. Let's talk him down to $300, or $350."

"Aw, Dad. He isn't going to sell it for that. It's too sweet."

Carney was a shrewd man. He let Rick do the sales job and happily compromised $25 on the price to give Rick's dad a small victory. They did the paper work.

"Thanks, Dad. I'll sell the scooter and give you that money," Rick said.

"Just don't kill yourself," his father said.

"Can we ride with you, Rick?" Mo, Larry, and Curly begged.

"Okay, but just home. Then I got to go out."

The three boys piled into the Chevy, with Mo claiming and getting "shotgun" by dint of his being older and stronger than Larry and Curly. "Gun it Rick. Lay some rubber," Mo hollered.

"No way, knuckleheads," Rick said. "Not around Dad."

But Rick did take the dirt road along Cold River, and drove too fast for the road, just to give the kids a thrill. He downshifted the *three-on-the-tree* as he went into each corner, spitting rocks as he gunned it back into the straightaway. "Damn!" he shouted. "This car is sweet."

He dropped his laughing brothers off at the house, and headed out to Sam's Twist Cone. A new car like this had to be shown off. He parked in front of the little white building, which housed a handful of booths on one side, and pinball machines on the other. The center was the kitchen and serving area, and the majority of business was done directly to the parking lot through the little service windows. The only car Rick recognized in the lot was Jack North's '58 Corvette.

"Hey Jackson!" Rick hollered as he opened the door into the booth area. Jack North was sitting in the corner booth sucking down a huge milkshake, with a plate of fries and two cheeseburgers in front of him.

"Ricardo, mi amigo!" North hollered. "What's shakin', bro?"

"New wheels, Jackson. Not that they'll impress you."

"Let me see'm. Don't nobody touch my food or they are dead meat." Jack slid his large body from behind the table and walked up to where he could see out the front window. "*Ahh, leetle '57 Cheby.* You will scoop mucho ass with that machine, mi amigo."

"Yeah, right. But it should be warmer than the scooter on a cold Winooski evening." As they walked back to the seat, Rick gave Jack the quick version of his near fatal accident.

"Too close, my friend." Jack smiled, digging back into his food. "You should quit that dangerous job of yours and come back to work for the Tycoon. We could have some fun." Rick and Jack had bunked together in a caboose when they worked on the Tycoon's excursion train over in Lake Sunapee; the year Rick turned sixteen. Jack, a full year younger, had kept them supplied in beer, and with his mellow voice and facile guitar playing, made sure that lots of young girls were available as well.

"I tell you Jack, since the Tycoon found religion, he's not that much fun to be around. Besides, I never save any money when I'm bunking with you. Non-stop party."

"That's bad?"

"No, not bad. Just doesn't get me through St. Michaels."

"Hey, were you at the union meeting where the guy got blown up?"

"You bet. It was something, man. Let me tell you."

Jack leaned forward, chewing on fries as he listened to Rick's account of the union meeting and investigation. Jack was incredulous when he heard about Whitey being a suspect. "Not Whitey, man. That guy is a frigging genius. You know he just breathed on my 'Vette, and the thing is running like a watch."

"Nigger!" a voice said.

Rick looked around. A narrow-faced, dark-haired man was sitting in the booth behind them. "Turds," he said. "Black turds is all they are. Should hang the sonofabitch."

"Shut up, Gorse, Whitey's no nigger. He's worth ten of you." Jack was on his feet shaking his fist.

Gorse was clearly shaken by Jack's aggressive response. He got to his feet and hurried out. "Nigger-lover!" he yelled as he went out the door.

"Who the hell is that?" Rick asked.

"George Gorse," Jack said, still fuming. "He pushes broom down at Ferguson Ford. Imagine that sonofabitch criticizing Whitey. I think he's Ferguson's cousin or something. Supposed to be sick. Got diabetes or some such thing. Nasty old fart."

"I've been hearing a lot of *nigger* this and *nigger* that," Rick said. This is going to be tough on Whitey and Annabelle no matter what happens."

"I think I'll ask the Tycoon if he has any ideas. He likes Whitey a lot and he's a smart sonofabitch."

"Good idea," Rick said. "What are you up to tonight?"

"Big poker game. I've got Neal Dupris coming up to the parlor car in Chester. Got a bottle of rum in the car and a case of beer. Lined my stomach good with milkshake. I suspect I'm going to win some money. Want to play?"

"Nah, thanks. I got to haul hay in the morning for Edgar. Don't need a hangover."

"Lucky you. Well got to run. Don't be a stranger just 'cause you're a college genius." Jack tossed three bucks on the counter, and headed for the door.

Rick followed him out to the lot and watched him climb into his Corvette. "Sure you don't want to race?" Jack hollered.

"Yeah, right. But I bet I get better mileage than you." Rick laughed. The 'Vette had two four-barrels and was known to suck down a quarter tank in the quarter-mile when Jack opened it up.

"Mileage is for losers, Ricardo." Jack turned over the engine and it rumbled like a lion ready to feast. Rick gave him a wave as he backed around and launched out of the lot, doing 60 by the time he hit the corner.

Rick went back inside. He got a coke, and a dish of fried clams, and sat munching, wishing some of his friends were in town. There were only a handful of guys he hung out with, and Jack was the only one still in the area. Dietrich *Dieter* O'Toole, who also was a senior at St. Michael's, had jumped at an opportunity to study music this summer in Amsterdam. Rick could hardly blame him. Paul had dropped out of Rensselaer, got married, and joined the Air Force. Rick wasn't supposed to know that Paul was huddled in some top-secret listening post in Turkey, but Paul's mother mentioned it every time he saw her. Thad Booth was working as a summer intern at Woods Hole Oceanographic Institute. He sighed. It would be just him and Ellen this summer, he guessed.

"Hi Rick." A soft voice called. "Where's your scooter?"

"Oh, hi Kelly." Rick felt himself blushing. "Traded it in for a car—the little blue Chevy there. Time to get something I can drive all year round."

"Give a girl a ride?" She was dressed in tight white shorts and a yellow top with spaghetti straps that set off her olive skin. She smiled, and her dark eyes sparkled.

"Sure thing." Rick tossed the remains of his supper in the trash. He wiped his suddenly sweaty hands on a napkin, and held the door for her as they stepped out into the parking lot.

Kelly made appreciative sounds as they walked around his car. "Where to Ma'am?" Rick said, snapping to attention and opening the passenger side door.

"Ohh, anywhere. This is nice."

"Nothing fancy," Rick said as he carefully drove over the curb and into the street. He turned south, automatically heading away from Ellen's house. He felt a little surge of guilt as he realized what he had done, and acknowledged what was on his mind.

"Ever drive up by the cemetery above the new high school?" Kelly asked.

"Not in quite a while," Rick said.

"Nice view up there. I wouldn't mind going up there."

"Uh, sure. Okay. You tell your mom and everyone? I mean about the wedding?"

"Yes, and about the baby. They were upset, but they were glad we were married. That meant so much, Rick. I don't know how to thank you."

"Glad to be able to help," Rick mumbled.

They drove slowly through town, and then followed Route 5 South. Across from the old landfill dump, they turned right, and drove slowly up past the turn off to the new regional high school, and into the local Catholic cemetery. "Uh is, uh…" Rick stuttered.

"No, Danny's buried out near his home. There's a little family cemetery out there." Kelly smiled. "But I don't think he'd mind, Rick. He liked you a lot."

"Gee I hardly knew him, Kelly. I mean I liked him okay, but I didn't really, you know, hang around with him or anything."

"I know Rick. But he looked up to you. He said you would be a big success."

There was a spot on the edge of the cemetery that overlooked the Connecticut River Valley. An early June moon hung high in the sky, casting a soft mellow glow on the river. "I forgot how nice it is, up here," Rick said.

"It's beautiful," Kelly said sliding over next to Rick. She took his hand in her two hands and kissed it. "You are beautiful. You are a beautiful person Rick."

Rick thought, "I should get out of here." But he didn't move. He didn't pull his hand away. He turned and looked at Kelly, her hair shining in the moonlight. He felt himself come erect.

Kelly looked up at him. She lifted one hand to his face and let her other hand rest in his lap on his throbbing penis. She smiled and kissed him. He kissed her back. "Back seat," She said.

They made the furious, fumbling love of the inexperienced, and then lay there naked. "Uh, uh, I didn't have a rubber or anything, Kelly."

"I can't get any more pregnant than I am, Rick."

"I like you and everything Kelly, but, but…"

"I know, Rick. You've got Ellen, and you've got college."

"Yeah. I mean I'm not…I couldn't support a family or anything."

"Rick it's okay. I don't want to marry you."

"You don't? Oh. Uh, why?…"

"It's the only way I could say thanks, Rick. I don't have anything else to give. And I thought you deserved thanks."

"Wow." Then Rick laughed.

"What's so funny?" Kelly asked.

"I just had this thought about boy scouts, and why they do good deeds," Rick said.

"Some boy scout," Kelly said. "Take me home Rick. I'm tired."

They didn't talk as he drove her home. He parked, and came around to open the door. As she got out of the car she said, "Careful about that boy scout thing, Rick. You could end up going to bed with a lot of little old ladies." She smiled.

Rick took her hand and squeezed it. "Thanks Kelly."

"Goodnight Rick," Kelly was crying softly. She pulled her hand away and ran into the house.

Rick got back in the car and drove slowly away. He was confused about how he felt. His first real sex hadn't been anything like what he expected. It had been wonderful, but he felt like he had betrayed Ellen. "God, I hope she never finds out," he said out loud.

Rick drove back to Bellows Falls, and then north on Route103. He turned up Darby Hill Road and then on to the access road that led up to the ledge area where Paligrinni was going to begin drilling later that summer. The right-of-way was cleared, but there were only a few pieces of equipment on the site. He parked, and walked out on the ledge. The view was fantastic. He could see north along the Connecticut River, and across to the DeBoni job. Looking northwest, he could see old Route 103 where it wound towards Rockingham and Chester.

"Strange day," he thought. "Nearly killed. New car. Lost my cherry. Shit that's a lot of luck for one day, even if it was Friday the 13th." For some reason he found himself thinking about his father.

He didn't really know his father very well. They had hardly ever been alone together for any length of time except for the two-day drive to Chicago, when his dad had driven him to the seminary. But even locked together for twenty-four hours in the car, they hadn't talked about anything important or personal. Richard Wallace was not a warm, touchy-feely kind of guy. But like tonight, when you needed him, he was there.

Tonight with Kelly made Rick think about his future. What would happen next year when he graduated from college? The army? Vietnam was heating up. They were starting to draft kids in ever increasing numbers. Marriage? What did he want to do?

Rick knew that his father had come to the U.S. from Scotland when he was twelve. Rick's grandfather, also named Richard, had worked in New York City, with Con Edison. Rick knew that he had been in World War I, and was even wounded. The family had come to the U.S., in 1925.

Rick's dad had gone to Columbia. He was a writer, and bummed around with other writers. When most of his writer friends went to France and hung around Europe, Rick's dad had traveled the U.S., working labor jobs, and seeing the country. After a couple of years, he decided to come back to New York, and look for a full-time job. There was a paper industry convention in town, and he had worked as a bar tender at one of the convention affairs. He met a guy named Jim McCarthy who became a life-long friend. McCarthy suggested they head up to Vermont. "Paper companies all over the place, Dick. Just looking for people who want to work their way up."

And that's what happened. Richard and Jim had signed on with a small company that processed and printed various wrapping papers. He started as part-time salesman and full-time pressman. Jim was a full-time salesman. But Richard proved to be so good at selling, that within a year he too was selling full-time. He also got a chance to write a bit—little jingles and phrases that made the various tissue paper wrappings more attractive to the clients. He drew simple line drawings in a Thurberesque style, and added a little catchy phrase; essentially doing the work of a whole ad agency for about $50 a job. Some of his designs were classics in the industry, like the tired looking bloodhound with the phrase, "Give your dogs a rest," that lined the shoeboxes of a leading brand of slippers. Or, "Roses are from the heart," that florists used by the truckload every Valentine's day.

Once in Vermont, Richard was there to stay. He met Maureen at the bank, married her, and kept her pregnant thereafter. "This was probably just as well," Rick thought. He was pretty sure his mother had a wild streak just waiting for a chance to get loose.

But that was it. Rick's father worked on the house out in the country when Rick was young, but since they moved into town he had shown almost no interest in carpentry. Now, he watched TV, smoked, and drank a prodigious amount of scotch every night, washed down with half-a-dozen beers.

Rick's mother blamed the change on Steve, Rick's older brother. His dad had been so proud when Steve was named valedictorian of his graduating class and won a full-boat scholarship to Columbia. He had been crushed when Steve dropped out, joined the emerging drug culture, and moved to San Francisco. But Rick thought the change had really happened before that. Steve might be an excuse, but he wasn't the reason.

Rick thought about Kelly. Why had she made love to him tonight? She was beautiful. She could find another guy if she wanted to, easy. Even pregnant, she should do all right.

Rick had no illusions about himself. He was okay looking, but no stud. He wanted to accept Kelly's gift as just thanks, but he couldn't help but feel she was looking for something more. Was she testing him out to see if he cut it before trying to nab him to father her child? Did he pass muster? "I'm the only guy left in town," he chuckled ruefully. "Maybe she sees me as a last resort."

He pulled out his pocket watch: 12:00. Better be getting home. He stood and stretched. Looking northwest on Route 103, towards Chester, he could see headlights coming fast. He could hear the whine of a car driving at top speed. "Must be doing over a hundred," Rick thought. "Hope he sees the sharp turn ahead." The road had been relocated twenty feet to accommodate the construction, creating a safety zone for Paligrinni's blasting work at the base of the cliff. The result was a sharp right-turn that needed to be negotiated at a relatively sane speed, if a driver wanted to stay on Route 103.

To Rick's horror, the car never slowed. Instead, it rocketed over the low barrier and off the edge into the river valley below.

"Oh, shit. He's dead meat." Rick whispered. There was no way he could get down the ledge to where the car had gone over. He had no choice but to get back in his car, drive carefully back down the access road, and back down Darby Hill Road. The state police barracks was only a mile or so north, a few yards from the intersection of Routes 5 and 103. Rick headed for the barracks, but before he got there, a cruiser went ripping by him with siren howling and lights flashing. Rick stopped, turned around, and headed back to town. As he was turning around, a fire engine roared by, also heading for the scene of the crash. He hadn't recognized the car, and he had no stomach left for disaster. He'd find out what happened soon enough.

There was still a light on when he got home. He was surprised to find his mother sitting up, reading and smoking. "Where you been?" she demanded.

"Just out. Saw Jack. Rode around. Parked up on top of the ledge and looked down on the river for a while."

"You screwing girls in that new car of yours already?"

Rick's jaw dropped. "Uh, uh no," he lied. "I was alone up there. Saw a car go over the bank though. Somebody probably got killed."

"You think I don't know what you and that girl do?" His mother glared at him. "Get her pregnant and you're on your own, mister."

"Aw, I know, Mom. I'm not doing that stuff." Rick started up the stairs. "I'm helping Ellen's dad pick up hay tomorrow. I'll be gone by 6:30. Don't know when I'll be home."

"You mark my words. We got no money to support your little bastards."

Rick fled upstairs.

Chapter 18

Ellen

Rick was out of bed at 5:30 as usual. He boiled water for a cup of instant coffee and headed out the door, anxious to be away before anyone else in the family was up. He stopped for gas at the Motor Mart, and went inside to buy cigarettes.

"Hey Wallace," one of Rick's classmates, Ted Ambrose, was behind the counter. His dad owned the little gas and grocery. "Hear about the accident last night?"

"No, what happened?" Rick didn't see any point in letting people know he'd seen the whole thing.

"That Dupris kid ran his car off the cliff up where 103 and 5 come together. Totally toast. Cops figure he was drunk out of his gourd."

"Same old story, around here isn't it?" Rick said, paying for his cigarettes. "Kid gets drunk and totals the car. Wonder more of them don't die."

"Yeah, I guess," Ambrose said. "Improves the gene pool, I guess." Ambrose was a biology major at Brown. "Tough on his folks, though. I think his old man had plans for him to take over the roofing business. Of course, Neal could hardly manage to take a shit he was so dumb. Probably would have destroyed the business in about a week. But I don't suppose his folks will think like that."

Rick lit a cigarette and started the car. "Shit." he thought to himself, "Dupris was playing poker with Jack last night. Sure as shit Jack got him drunk, fleeced him, then let him drive home. I wonder if the cops will give him any grief over this."

He shook his head over life's complications. The car felt good. It felt right; his kind of car. He smiled as he drove north on Route 5, branching left on 103. There were still fire engines parked where Dupris had gone over the bank. Rick didn't slow down.

There was a spot on 103 where you could see most of Ellen's farm. It covered a hillside with three houses visible: the old main house with its great porches and columns, the small hired man's house, and Ellen's house, a modest Cape Cod, nestled snugly in the valley between a brook and the hill behind. Rick turned down Williams River Road, across the covered bridge, and back up the hill on the other side. He wasn't the first to arrive. There were two other cars in the barnyard, and another pulled in behind him.

"Jump on a wagon, boys," Edgar hollered. "We're starting with the upper meadows. Like to finish that by noon, and get a good start on the lower forty this afternoon."

Ellen was perched on a tractor. Rick climbed up on the yoke, "See my new wheels, Ellen?" he said. "I'll take you up to the big corner for a swim after we get done here."

"Wow, great!" she said.

Rick felt guilty. He climbed up on the wagon with the Savoy brothers and Ellen's sister Lorie. The Savoys owned the next farm over, and everyone around here helped out to make sure they all got their hay in. Edgar was driving a tractor with the baler. The hired man, Ralph Right, drove the third tractor with two Arnold boys from over in Rockingham on the back. They formed a caravan and headed up the road to the access lane to the upper meadows.

Haying is not particularly interesting work. Edgar baled. The two trailers followed him with the youngsters throwing bales up on the wagon.

They filled Ellen's wagon and she headed to the barn with Lorie and Rick riding along to unload. Ralph's wagon moved in, and his crew began loading. So it went all morning. They had the upper meadows picked by 11:45, and broke for lunch. Ellen's mother, Mora, had laid out a giant picnic lunch of fried chicken, baked beans, and potato salad, plus gallons of iced tea and lemonade. They stuffed themselves, and headed to the lower forty where they repeated the process.

By 6:30, they had the lower forty pretty well picked. Edgar called a halt. "Just a half wagon or so in the gully. I'll get that tomorrow. I thank you all. You work pretty damn good. Grab whatever chicken's left when you leave."

Ellen parked the tractor. Rick gave her a lift up to her house, and she grabbed her bathing suit and a towel. "We're going swimming, Mom," she hollered. They didn't wait for an answer. They jumped in Rick's car, and quickly drove out of the yard.

"The big corner?" Rick asked.

"I know a better place," Ellen said. "Head up to Bartonsville."

Rick followed her directions, and they crossed the Williams River at Bartonsville. They turned on a dirt track that paralleled the river, and followed it until it petered out. "We walk from here," Ellen said. "It's just a little ways. It's right behind the Rockingham Country Club. Hardly anyone ever goes there."

They grabbed their suits, towels, and an old blanket and started down the dusty path. The path crossed the railroad tracks and wound down through some ledges to a rocky beach. "Careful, that's poison ivy," Ellen warned. They skirted the thick hedge of three-leaved plants.

"I'll go behind those bushes and change," Ellen said. "No peeking."

Rick spread out the blanket on a spot where the rocks were relatively smooth. Then he grabbed his suit and scuttled behind a bush on the other side of the beach. Quickly, he stripped down and pulled on his suit. He was hot and sweaty and his skin was chaffed from the prickly hay. He was also aroused.

He stepped back on the beach just as Ellen came out from the bushes. Her one-piece suit was cut to reveal, not conceal. Rick rushed into the water to hide his erection. The shock of the cool water made him gasp, as it dampened his sexual urges. Ellen laughed, and ran into the water, splashing him.

They played in the water for half-an-hour, splashing and dunking one another. Rick dove under Ellen's legs and came up behind her. He wrapped his arms around her and she pressed back against him. Without a word they walked out of the water and stood on the shore, arms wrapped around each other. Ellen gave a little shiver.

Rick grabbed her towel and began to dry her carefully, massaging her legs and arms and then thighs and breasts. "Let's take the blanket into the woods," she said.

There was a soft, sheltered spot tucked under a broad pine. It was well away from the trail and the beach. Rick spread the blanket and they lay side-by-side. Ellen kissed him passionately. He felt her hand on his hard organ.

Rick's hands were everywhere, stroking her buttocks and thighs. He slipped the suit off her shoulders, baring her pert, full breasts. Gently he kissed them, his hands working her suit down, over her hips.

"Oh Rick, we shouldn't" she whispered.

"I love you," Rick whispered. "I love you."

If there had been any slight resistance it melted with those words. Suits off, they kissed each other's bodies. Rick put his face between Ellen's legs and ran his tongue between the lips of her vagina. She shuddered and pulled his head up, kissing him on the lips while her hand guided his penis into her. Urgency took command, and he pulled her to him, driving deep, and feeling her hymen split. She gave a little gasp, and Rick held her to him as he came.

"Oh god," she said. "Oh god."

They lay quietly, arms around each other. Ellen cried.

Rick began to talk. "Yesterday, I was a hair's breadth away from death. And I saw Neal Dupris die. I saw his car go over the cliff." He told Ellen about his near-death experience on the scooter, and about his father taking him to buy the car. He told her about meeting Jack, and Jack talking about the card game with Dupris. He didn't tell Ellen about Kelly.

He said, "After Jack left, I just kind of drove around. I was thinking about my Dad. I thought I might just sit up on the ledge over where the bridge will go on 91. I drove up there and just parked. It was nearly midnight, I guess. I heard this car screaming down 103. I saw the headlights come ripping around the corner, and I remember thinking 'I hope he remembers that the road turns sharp right here.' He didn't. He shot like a rocket over the guardrail and down the bank. There was a big whoosh of fire. I couldn't get down from where I was. I had to drive all the way back to Darby Hill Road. By the time I got there, fire trucks and police cars were tearing up the road. So I just went home. I didn't find out it was Dupris until this morning."

"Oh god, so much death." Ellen buried her face in his chest.

He lifted her face, and kissed her again. "I mean it," he said. "I do love you. I don't care if you get pregnant. I want to marry you." As he said it, he realized he meant it. All of the questions he had asked himself the night before on the ledge seemed resolved. It was a reason, a way out.

"My mom would kill me." Ellen whispered, but her body was moving against him. Her hand cupped his testicles, and she stroked his penis bringing it springing back to life. They made love again, more slowly. Dusk was falling.

"I need to get home Rick. Let's wash off."

They raced nude to the water and dove in. After a few minutes of splashing, they climbed out and toweled each other off. "No, not again tonight." Ellen laughed at his erection. She pulled on her panties and shorts and a T-shirt.

Rick dressed too. Hand-in-hand, they climbed the path, knowing their world had just changed forever.

Ellen sat right next to him in the car, her hand on his thigh. They drove slowly. It was 9:30 when they got to her house. "Don't come in, Rick." she said. "My mom will be steamed and it's easier if I face her alone."

Rick was relieved, but felt ashamed for feeling relieved. Ellen reached up and kissed him. "I don't care either," she said. "We'll just get married and get on with our lives."

She jumped out of the car and ran into the house.

Rick backed slowly out of the yard and headed for home.

"What I did on my summer vacation, by Richard Wallace," he said out loud. He laughed. "It will be the most interesting summer essay I've ever written."

It was too early to go home, so he headed north, to Chester. He wondered if Jack had been hassled by the cops.

The Corvette was parked in front of the Pullman-built parlor car that Jack called home. It was tucked on a siding by the old Chester Depot. The rail car sported a sign that said, "If this be rockin', don't be knockin'." But it wasn't rocking. In fact, he could see Jack through the window, playing a soft ballad on his guitar.

"Hey Jackson, want some company?" Rick hollered.

"That you Ricardo? Come in mi amigo. Pull up a beer."

Rick swung up onto the rear platform and opened the screen door. Jack was propped on one of the side bunks, sitting in his skivvies, playing the big Gibson twelve-string. A beer sat on the window ledge.

"In the cooler, man. You know the routine."

Rick opened the cooler and pulled out a can. There was a church key dangling from a string on the wall. He punched open the can.

"You hear about Dupris?" Rick asked.

"Yeah, the asshole. I begged him to stay. 'No fuckin' way,' he says. Jumps in that souped up Mustang convertible of his, and roars out of here like the devil was on his tail." Jack took a sip of beer. "Course, I guess he was." He played a couple of blues chords.

"I saw him go over," Rick said.

"Say what? No way."

Rick told him how he had parked up on the ledge.

"All by yourself, Ricardo, or did you already scoop some tail with that hot car of yours?"

"By myself, asshole. It was just a good place to go and think."

"What I hear is that you were doing your thinking with your prick between Kelly's legs." Jack laughed.

"What? Where did you hear that?"

"*Oooh, a leetle bird told me, mon.* I have my sources." Jack laughed again.

"Well, it's horseshit. I gave her a ride home is all."

"Yeah, yeah. More's the fool you, then. Word's out that she has the hots for you. Nice young widow like that, you could do worse."

"Well, I'm not interested. Ellen and I are going to get married. Maybe even before we go back to school."

"What's Mora think of that? That old bitch doesn't like you much."

"She doesn't know. We just decided tonight."

"Ahhh. I thought I detected the glow of first sex. Tell me, was she a virgin?"

"You think everything is just sex. I mean, we love each other."

"You should've listened to old Cecil. Remember what he always said? 'Don't go buying the cow if you can get milk by the quart.'"

"How much money did you win off Dupris?"

"Oooh, sharp change of subject. Touchy, touchy. $400. The boy's a fool. *Was* a fool, I should say."

"Wonder where he got that kind of money," Rick mused.

"Probably stole it from his old man. The kid was a complete creep."

"You always were one to speak well of the dead, even when you help them get that way. How much did the idiot drink?"

"Most of the bottle of rum and half-a-dozen beers. He couldn't find his fly to take a piss."

"And you let him drive? Damn, Jack. That's practically murder."

"Honest Rick. I begged him to stay. I tried to take his keys. He socked me. Look! Right here. See that bruise. Bastard punched me when I tried to take his keys."

"Cops been around to see you?"

"Nope. I don't think they know where he came from."

"Well, I guess we both have some things we just as soon not get talked around."

"Oooh, blackmail. I didn't know you had it in you Ricardo. You are definitely getting smarter with old age."

"Changing the subject. Did you talk to the Tycoon about Whitey?"

"Yep. He's interested. More interested in Annabelle, I think. He's got a fancy restaurant down in Pennsylvania. He'd like to have her as head cook."

"That would be a pretty good deal for the two of them; Whitey as chief mechanic, and Annabelle as head chef. Should I say something to Whitey?"

"Why don't you wait. Let's see what happens first. Maybe this won't be such a big deal."

Rick tossed his beer can in the wastebasket. "I better be getting back home."

"Stay and have a few."

"Nah. I don't like what drinking with you does to people, Jack."

"Oooh, that's hard, man. Hard."

Rick drove home carefully. Suddenly, he felt very, very tired. He didn't know if it was the haying, the sex, or just the crush of events. He just knew he needed to rest.

Chapter 19

Rest Area

June 2002

"Grampa, Grampa!" Ben's voice brought Rick abruptly back to the present.

"Hey, Ben, what's up? Ready for lunch?"

"No, Grampa. Come on! Come see what I found!"

Rick's knees creaked as he got to his feet. He hoisted the pack and thermos and limped down the hill into the quarry. Ben grabbed his hand and tugged him along over to the rock wall. "Look Grampa, Look!"

Rick bent down and squinted. There, peeking out of a layer of rock was the head of a fish.

"Well, well, Ben. I do believe you've found a real fossil."

"You know what, Grampa?"

"What, Ben?"

"This is a dinosaur fish. My mom showed me one in a book."

"You're right, Ben. It's a dinosaur fish all right. Now we have to figure how to get it out of there." Rick looked at his watch. It was almost noon. "Come, let's eat lunch and we can figure out our strategy."

They found a shady spot and spread out the cloth Willa had packed. Rick handed Ben a sandwich, "Peanut butter and jelly I think. Okay?"

"I like peanut butter and jelly. Can I have a can of pop?"

"You bet, Ben. But don't tell your mom I gave you pop, okay?"

"Oh, I won't. But my dad lets me have some, sometimes."

As they ate, they talked about the fossil. "I think we have to see if we can cut that whole block loose, Ben. It would be easier to split if we can get the whole thing out."

"My mom showed me how to do that. You just look for a crack that's close. Grampa, how did that fish get in that rock?"

Rick scratched his head. "That's a good question, Ben. I don't know for sure, but what I think probably happened was that a big bunch of mud and rocks fell on top of the fish. You know, like an avalanche?"

"And then what?"

"Well, then, I think, more stuff fell on top, and the rocks were pressed together really hard. Then later, when the mountains pushed up here, the rock was twisted on its side. And then later the mountains wore down to what they are now. It took millions and millions of years."

"Yeah, 'cause the dinosaurs all died 65 million years ago, my mom said."

When they finished, they went back over to the wall. Looking closer, they could see that the block containing the fish could probably be worked loose. The ledge here was all "standing on edge," as they used to say in the construction business. It was hard, slate-like rock, with visible thick layers.

Using the hammer, they carefully worked around the edges.

"There, Ben. I think if we can break that one spot loose it will come right out."

"I'll do it Grampa. I know how."

Rick stood back and watched as Ben carefully tapped at the proper spot. He patiently worked the whole area where they wanted it to break, using the pointed side of the rock hammer. "Your mom taught you good, Ben. Keep at it. Give a holler if you get tired, and I'll take a turn."

Rick went back to the pack, and poured himself another cup of coffee. He watched Ben work, and smiled. Ben was a second-generation result of that night on the beach. Tim was the first generation. He'd been born at Mary Fletcher Hospital in Burlington, in March that next year.

Rick reviewed his mosaic. All the pieces were from a single week. Three deaths: Danny, Big Jim, and Neal Dupris, and his first sexual encounters; were they important to the story? What else? What else was important?

The close call on the motor scooter? Maybe. How about the hate? He had never really seen racial hatred in action before. There were people who had shaken Whitey's hand, moments before that were suddenly calling him a *nigger*. George Gorse was like a poison. "Lord knows this family tasted a big enough dose of that poison," Rick thought.

And Ellen. She had been so strong. The two them had struggled to make it, Rick working two jobs, and finishing his degree. Ellen stayed in school until January. It was fifteen years before she was able to go back and finish her degree. She worked five more years to get it, and then? And then their marriage was over. The why of it he never truly understood.

He swirled the cold coffee around in his cup, and tossed it out on the ground. He had no regrets. And certainly, he had no regrets that the marriage ended after twenty years. There really hadn't been anything left. It was an empty husk. He hadn't seen it coming, but once it was there, he knew it was right. They had split peacefully and amicably, and were still friends.

Rick was very much in love with his second wife, Mary Jo. They were two people who met at exactly the right time in each of their lives—perfect companions for the end game.

Rick watched Ben tapping busily at the rock. He let his mind drift back again. "Not enough pieces yet," he thought. " I can see the outline, but I can't see the detail. But things were happening, that's for sure. Things were changing for a lot of people, particularly Whitey."

Chapter 20

Whitey

June 1964

When he got to work on Monday, he could feel how things had changed. An attitude had settled over the job like a fog that just wouldn't burn off. Everyone was uneasy. Jokes were few and far between. People worked, and left immediately at 5:30. Even at lunch, there wasn't much said. Men ate, and then sat and smoked, or snoozed until their half-hour was up. Then they want back to the job, and plodded along, doing what had to be done.

The cops said it was okay to resume blasting, but the dynamite crew had to count every stick of dynamite, and every blasting cap used. Once a week they had to count the magazine, and reconcile the remaining inventory. It was tedious, and Rick thought it was a lot like locking the barn door after the cows were stolen, but he could see the point of it.

Church took Barrel-ass through one shot, and then let Barrel-ass do the next one himself, with Church looking over his shoulder. Barrel-ass's first "solo" shot, was Friday. It was a small shot, and it went without a hitch. Rick watched Barrel-ass emulate Church's style, standing and hollering in both directions, and then squatting to connect the wires to the blasting terminal. He pushed the test circuit, and got a green light. He set the switch that armed the circuit, and raised his two thumbs in the air. In a smooth gesture, he turned over his thumbs and plunged them down on the two terminal buttons. The shot gave a comforting *thump*.

Barrel-ass stood up and raised his hands over his head. An enormous, shit-eating grin split his face. "Call me *Blaster* Bill, boys. You seen it. A perfect shot!"

Sometimes, construction crews let a guy pick his own nickname. That's what happened with Barrel-ass. From then on, nobody called him anything but *Blaster Bill.* Of course, the tone they used didn't exactly reflect a great deal of respect. And they also used the term freely anytime somebody broke wind.

"Did I hear Blaster Bill over there?" Côte would say. "By God, Blaster Bill, that was a good'un. Lot of cordite in that one."

Ever since Danny's accident, Church had become quieter, and quieter. The hollow look in his eyes deepened. The little knowing smile was gone.

Rick knew a kid who was a member of Church's congregation. Wally Jancewitz still went to the services even though he claimed, "I don't believe any of that Jehovah's Witness shit. I just go because my folks would be upset if I didn't, and I don't want to hurt them."

Rick had talked to Wally at the Twist Cone one night. Wally told about the first service after Danny died.

"Mr. Halbert just stood up and told the story about how God sent lightning, and set off the dynamite. He told about Danny flying through the air, and then walking around and talking about angels. He said he thought God had killed Danny as a message to him. God was telling him that he was not doing what the Lord wanted. Tears were running down his face and he said, 'It's my fault. It's like I killed that boy.'"

"It was spooky, man," Wally said, eating a bite of his cone. "People tried to talk Mr. Halbert out of thinking like that, but you could see it wasn't doing any good. His family was crying. He said, 'I got to go somewhere alone and pray. Soon as I get things right on the job, I'll be going. I'm asking you all to help out my family while I'm gone.'"

"They do that?" Rick asked. "The Witnesses all take care of each other like that?"

"Yeah, I guess. Never seen it happen like this before. But when somebody dies, yeah, they all take care of the family. Make sure they don't go hungry and the rent is paid and everything. They're pretty tight."

The day Barrel-ass became Blaster Bill, was Church's last day on the job. He just looked around at everybody and nodded. Then he climbed into his pickup and that was the last time Rick saw him.

"That's what happens when you believe too much," Côte said. "You think you got all the answers and then something doesn't fit. So then you think you ain't got any answers. Your whole world falls apart. I don't know how a good man like that can blame hisself for what was just about as much an accident as anything can be." Côte shook his head.

"Yeah, it ain't like blowing up that Jensen guy. Somebody done that on purpose," Henry bit off a piece of cigar and spit it out on the ground. "Don't see nobody stepping up to take the blame or credit for that, do ya?"

They hadn't seen much of the cops that week. But the next Monday morning, the unmarked car was parked in front of the office trailer when Rick drove into the yard. He found a nice safe place to park the Chevy, and hauled his stuff out of the backseat. He was headed over to the dynamite truck, when John Cashman hollered at him, "Wallace, come over here."

The same two policemen, Detectives Amery and Redman, were standing with Cashman. They both nodded to Rick.

"You know these officers," John said. "They're going to talk to everybody on the job, starting this morning. I want you to chauffer them around and make sure they get to see everything and everybody they want to see."

"Yes sir. Do I use your pickup?"

"No. I asked Whitey to pick us up a jeep. I can't do without my pickup all week or however long this takes. I think he's changing the oil on it. Go get it."

Rick headed over to the maintenance shop. Inside, Whitey and the rest of the mechanics were leaning over the engine of a surplus army jeep. "Tiny little thing, ain't it?" Whitey said. " But it's in top shape. Even Squirt can't probably break it."

"Wow," Rick stared at the olive drab, open jeep, still sporting its army serial numbers and markings. "Is this one of those army surplus jeeps you see advertised in the back of comic books?"

"Well, it's surplus all right," Whitey answered. "But I didn't buy it from no comic book. I bought it from the National Guard for about $900. It's in good shape. I know their motor pool guy, and he does good work."

"You going to paint it DeBoni red?"

"No time now. Besides, I think Charlie's looking to give it to his kid, once we're done with it. Stevie'll probably want it bright yellow with big blue polka dots. I told Charlie, a jeep ain't no car for a sixteen-year-old kid, but he had his mind made up, as usual."

"John says I got to take it now and chauffer the two cops around. Is it set to go?"

"All yours. I'm surprised the cops will ride in a car I worked on. I thought they had me pegged as the mad bomber."

"I guess that's why I'm driving," Rick said. "They figure that you won't blow up a nice kid like me."

"Shee-it, they better not take that for granted," Whitey laughed. "Start her up."

"Uh, uh, maybe you want to start it first?" Rick feigned hesitation.

"Hell, no. I'm going out back for a smoke, quick. You guys better come too."

Rick laughed, and jumped in the jeep. Still, there was just a tiny twinge of doubt when he looked up, stepped on the starter, and saw Whitey with his fingers in his ears. It purred like a kitten. Rick backed out and drove over to John and the two detectives.

Redman and Amery jumped into the jeep, and Rick headed out toward the job. "Who do you want to talk to first?" he asked.

"You," Amery said. "Can you find some shady spot where the noise ain't so loud?"

"Yeah, sure." Rick frowned. "Uh, over by the magazine's probably as quiet as it gets here. Is that okay?"

"That'll do," Redman said from the backseat. "Take it easy. I'm bouncing around like a friggin' ball."

"Oh, sorry." Rick slowed as he turned into the access road to the magazine. They had the place to themselves. Rick figured that Blaster Bill and his crew were up on the ledge plotting the next shot. He pulled the jeep under a sturdy maple that had been spared the axe because it was lucky enough to grow where the road wasn't. "Want some coffee," he asked.

"We brought our own, kid." Amery and Redman each pulled out a thermos and poured themselves a cup.

Rick fished out his thermos, poured a cup, and then lit a cigarette. "Fire away. But I have to tell you I don't know much. I'm just a *dumb college fuck*, remember."

"Just so you're not a smart-ass," Redman grunted. "We got a list of everybody who works on this job. The timekeeper gave us everybody's particulars—name, address, Social Security, and all that shit. You tell us what you know about them as people."

"Okay. But most of them I just know on the job. I'm not real close or anything. I know most of the other college kids from high school. And a couple of people live in town, so maybe I know a little bit more about them. But I don't know anything special or secret about anybody."

"We'll be the judge of that. Who do you know best?" Avery asked. He and Redman both had their notebooks open and pencils poised.

"Whitey, I guess. I mean I've known him for five, or six years. Pretty nearly since he came to town."

"Well, that's a good start. He's a guy we need to know everything about."

Rick looked Amery in the eye. "You guys are barking up the wrong tree with Whitey. He just wouldn't do something like that. Not to a nice car like that Lincoln."

"Listen Wallace, let me tell you about murder. Anybody could do it. Little old ladies do it. Priests do it. Schoolteachers do it. Push anybody and they can murder. We look for three things: motive, means, and opportunity. Your black buddy has got all of those in spades, no pun intended." Avery held up three fingers.

"Motive. The whole fucking crew saw him have a screaming argument with the deceased. That union guy *niggered* him up one side and down the other. That can piss a guy off pretty good.

Avery ticked off a second finger. "Means. This guy Whitey knows everything about cars. Everybody we talk to says he's some kind of a mechanical wonder. The key to the maintenance shed fits that magazine over there."

He ticked off the third finger. "Opportunity. Nobody can say they saw Whitey the whole time at that shindig. Once it got dark it would be a piece of cake to sneak under that Lincoln and wire it up. We ain't got anybody who fits the three as good as your friend Whitey, so he is absolutely suspect number one."

Rick looked at the two officers. " Did you ever think," he asked, "why he would be bringing dynamite to this shindig? I mean, did he know that Jensen was going to lay the *nigger* on him? You think he wired up the car just in case? I mean, I did see Whitey every second after the set-to with Jensen. He just walked to his car, and drove out of the lot. I will swear to that in front of any judge or jury."

"Yeah, well we didn't say we had the case locked up. We have lots of questions we don't know answers to. So let's start. Tell us what you know about Whitey."

"Well, he moved to town about '58, or so. And everybody knew he was here. I mean, he and Annabelle were the first black people to live in this part of Vermont, since probably the Civil War. People would just stop on the street and look at them, they were so amazed."

Rick lit a second cigarette from the end of the first. "I got to know Whitey pretty well about four years ago. I was working for the Tycoon. He was running an excursion train up in New Hampshire, and me and Jack North were working for him, living in a caboose, chasing girls, and having a good old time."

"The Tycoon was running a little steam engine that burned oil, not coal. And something about the oil feed mechanism got fucked up. They couldn't keep a head of steam. The Tycoon's normal steam engine mechanic didn't know anything about oil burners. He couldn't figure out what was wrong. Well, no steam, no rides, no job. So everybody was asking around who might know somebody who could fix this thing. The engineer, old Cecil, pipes up and says, 'There's a mechanic at Freighthaulers Trucking, that's supposed to be some kind of good. I hear they just shut down. Maybe he's available.' Well, the Tycoon himself drives back to Bellows Falls in his Rolls, to pick up this guy and bring him to Sunapee, where we were headquartered that year. And the guy, of course, was Whitey."

"Whitey fixed the thing in about 45 minutes. Nothing to it. But the Tycoon had been called away, and there was no one who could give him a ride home, so we invited him to spend the night in our caboose. He hops over to the station, calls home, and then we all go out for some fast food. I remember him saying, 'Don't none of you guys tell my wife I'm eating this shit. She'll kill me.' Annabelle doesn't like Whitey to eat anybody's food but hers. And if you guys have ever eaten at the Village Inn, you know that she's one damn fine cook."

"So anyway, we settled down for the night. Sipping some beer, and Jack North was playing away on his guitar. Jack's just a natural. He starts playing some Negro spirituals, adding a little blues to it, putting in a few minor chords here and there. Whitey's just sitting there and he says, 'Boy where'd you learn to play like that? Is yo' momma black?'"

"Well, Jack thought that was about as good a compliment as anybody could give him. He laughed, and said, 'She tells me no. But hey, who knows?'"

"I ain't heard nobody play like that since me and Annabelle come north." Whitey sighed. "My Uncle Billy, he played like that, and then some. But I 'spect that by the time you're his age, you'll be a whole lot better than him."

"I asked Whitey where he was from. And that sort of opened the floodgate. He lay back in the corner of his bunk, sipping a cold beer, and gave us his life story. They sort of got a rhythm going, him and Jack. I mean it was pretty cool. It's etched in my memory."

"So, sing it," Redman said.

"Well, I haven't got that knack. But the gist of it is something like this. Whitey was born Emanuel Lincoln Whitefield. He said his nickname was *Manny*, until he got his second teeth. They came in so big and white, his friends started calling him Whitey, and it stuck. Always gives folks a start when they meet the guy. They call Whitey on the telephone, and don't know he's black as the ace of spades."

"Whitey said his dad was killed by the Ku Klux Klan, when he was three or four. They were living in East St. Louis, and there was a lot of Klan activity down there. He lived with his mom, and his big sister, Mayfair and they couldn't do anything with him. He said he was headed for big trouble, running around with gangs and stuff, until he was about fourteen. Then his uncle Billy mustered out of the army, and opened a garage a little north of town."

"Billy had been a mechanic. Helped keep some regular convoy they called the Red Ball Express going in Europe. He said most of the crew was black; drivers, mechanics, everybody. Billy learned everything there was to know about diesels, working twenty hours a day to keep the trucks running."

"Whitey said it didn't take long for Billy's garage to get real popular. Truckers came from all over to have Billy work on their rigs. He was fast. His prices were fair. But most of all, he was damn good. If it could be fixed, Billy fixed it. 'Bout that time, Whitey got into some serious trouble. He got nabbed shoplifting. The storeowner knew Whitey's mother, and talked to her rather than turning Whitey over to the cops. Whitey's mother called in Billy, and to make a long story short, Billy agreed to board Whitey, and teach him the trade."

"Well it turned out, Whitey was just a natural. In a few months, he soaked up everything Billy had to teach, and by the end of the year, Billy was deferring to Whitey on the tough projects. Business boomed. Billy and Whitey got along great. Life was sweet. Then one of the KKK bigwigs bought a truck stop about five miles from Billy's garage. Needless to say, he didn't care for the competition, and they handled it in the usual Klan way. Whitey came back from visiting his mom, and found Billy hanging from the big cottonwood behind the garage. A note pinned to his chest said, 'Here's how you fix a nigger mechanic.'"

"The cops did their usual nothing. Just another nigger dead. Whitey knew better than to try and run the garage himself. But he just couldn't stay in St. Louis. So he grabbed a ride with a trucker he knew, and went down to New Orleans."

"He said he bummed around a bit. Worked in a few garages, and was careful not to show off how much he knew around the white folks. He said he started mixing with some rough company, and is sure he would have ended up in jail if he hadn't happened to deliver a car he had been working on to the back of one of New Orleans' better restaurants. It was Annabelle's father's car. He was the maitre d'. His wife was the cook, and his daughter, Annabelle, worked in the kitchen with her mother. Whitey said it was just like a flash of lightning. He opened the door to bring in the keys, and she was sitting there peeling peaches. He said he just stood there with his jaw bouncing off the floor. She looked up and smiled at him, and he melted into a little puddle."

"Well, Annabelle's daddy and mommy didn't care much for Whitey, but that didn't make no difference to Annabelle. She'd found her man, and she wasn't ever going to let him go. If her folks didn't want him around, well, she was gone too. And they packed a few things in a duffle bag. Stopped at a preacher's house and got married, then got out on the highway and started hitchhiking north. Whitey had to leave his car to settle a debt. They didn't have a clue where they were going."

"A truck driver picked them up. He was hauling shrimp from the Gulf, heading for Boston. He seemed like a nice guy and they talked a little. His name was Tom Murphy, and he worked for Freighthaulers. They had a contract to haul fresh shrimp to Boston's best restaurants. Coming back, he said he hauled lobsters to New Orleans. Whitey and Annabelle didn't have any thought to going all the way to Boston. Well, somewhere in the middle of Tennessee, Murphy's truck broke down. It was hotter than a pistol, and those shrimp were going to cook right in the back of the truck if he couldn't get the thing running. The refrigeration system ran off the truck's electrical system."

"Of course, Murphy was in luck. He had the best mechanic in the south sitting right up there in his cab. Whitey crawled underneath, and in about three minutes, fixed the truck so it ran better than it had ever run. Well, Murphy got so excited he begged Whitey and Annabelle to ride all the way to Boston with him and meet his boss. His boss was Steve Cranze, who owned Freighthaulers. Course, Cranze offered Whitey a job, and Annabelle had no trouble catching on at a restaurant. Later, as Freighthaulers grew, they decided they needed a terminal in southern Vermont. So they built the terminal just south of Bellows Falls, and offered Whitey the job of chief mechanic. He and Annabelle drove up to Bellows Falls, liked it, and took the job. That was in about 1958. Whitey was about twenty-five, or twenty-six."

"Well, you probably know that Steve Cranze got too rich, too fast, and started to stuff some of his profits in his nose. Pretty soon there were no profits, and he was selling off assets and snorting day and night. I think it was 1960 when they went belly up. Meanwhile, Annabelle had taken over as the cook at the Village Inn, and the place was going gangbusters. So, Whitey just set up a little gypsy garage, and did a little work here and there, waiting for something to pop up. That's what he was doing when the Tycoon dragged him up to work on the *choochoo*."

"The Tycoon was impressed with the job Whitey did, and offered him a full-time job as head mechanic. But Whitey didn't care all that much for steam engines. He thanked the Tycoon, and said he'd be happy to work on any diesels that went bad, but he just didn't cotton to steam."

"How did he catch on with DeBoni," Avery asked.

"I guess I had something to do with that," Rick answered. "First time I worked with DeBoni was August, year before last. My friend Dieter and I had just turned eighteen. We took jobs on the hay crew up on Route 103. Man, is that shit work. Shaking rotten hay over freshly planted grass on the banks, so the seeds won't wash away. Dirty, dusty, and not much fun. Anyway, we were loading up the hay wagon from the pile of bales behind the maintenance shed, and we hear Charlie and his head mechanic, some guy named Stew, or something. Charlie was screaming at him. Stew says, 'Can't be fixed.' He throws down his wrench, walks to his car, and drives away. Charlie turns beet red. His best backhoe is sitting there, and it just plain won't run. Charlie hollers out, 'Doesn't anybody know a goddamn mechanic who can fix things?'"

"Well, I didn't know about rhetorical questions, then. So, I pipe up, and says, 'I know somebody who can fix it. He can fix anything.' Charlie growls, 'Who is this wonder mechanic? Get him out here fast.' I said, 'Yes sir,' and ran over to the office and had Tim the timekeeper call Whitey. Whitey comes out. Charlie doesn't even seem to notice that he's a black guy. Whitey says, 'Ten dollars an hour, one hour minimum.' That was pretty high then. I think Charlie was paying his mechanic about eight-fifty. So, Charlie turns pure white. Then he says, 'Okay, but only if you fix it.' Whitey says, 'You're on,' and climbs in the back of the backhoe."

"About then, that Stew guy came back. Somebody had told him that a black guy had taken his job. He hollers out, 'What's that nigger doing in my backhoe?' And Whitey, he pokes his head out of the side-door and says, 'Fixing what you say can't be fixed. Start her up.'"

"Ken Gleason, the backhoe operator, kicks her over, and she starts right up. Purrs like a kitten. 'God Damn,' Gleason says. 'Sounds better than it did new.'"

"This Stew guy just turns around, gets back in his car, and I've never seen him around here since. Charlie hands Whitey a twenty, and says, 'Keep the change.' Then he says, 'You want the head mechanic job, it's yours. But it only pays eight-fifty.' 'Ten dollars, says Whitey.' 'I'll go nine dollars,' Charlie says. 'Ten dollars.' Whitey says. 'Nine-fifty,' Charlie's practically whining now. 'Nine-seventy-five the first month,' Whitey says. 'If I do good, ten-fifty the second month. Then we'll talk.' 'Get to work,' says Charlie. 'Go talk to Tim, and have him put you on the payroll at nine-seventy-five.'"

"So that's how Whitey ended up here at DeBoni. He's probably making as much as the shovel operator now. But Charlie gets his money's worth."

"Any chance that Stew guy would try to get Whitey in trouble?" Redman asked.

"Probably, but like I said, I haven't seen him in a couple of years. I would think I'd have seen him around if he were still in these parts."

"Well, you didn't tell me anything that says that Whitey can't be our *perp*. If I were him, I'd have a big hard-on for guys who sling *nigger* around. Especially after what the Klan did to his father and his uncle."

Rick looked at Avery. He shook his head. "Maybe so, if Whitey didn't have Annabelle. She absolutely won't let Whitey get involved in anything like that. And I've known Whitey a long time. Seen him called *nigger* lots of times. I never saw him lift a finger to hurt anybody, no matter how much they *niggered* him. But even more than that, Whitey just loves automobiles. You've seen that '58 Olds of his. He rescued that. It was a crunched up piece of junk. He's got a picture in his garage. You ought to go take a look. He rebuilt the body. Then he found this little four-cylinder diesel from some European truck, and he just turned that thing into a diesel car. One-of-a-kind. He would never blow up a beautiful piece of iron like Jensen's Lincoln limousine. He couldn't make himself do it."

"Besides, like I told you, I watched him leave after the argument with Jensen. He would have had to do it before. Why would he do that?"

The cops didn't bother to answer. Redman went over to a bush and took a leak. Avery lit a cigarette. He turned to Rick and said, "Find us a better suspect."

They hauled their thermoses over to a small rock formation and sat. Redman held the roster that Tim had given him. "Let's take'm one-by-one."

Rick told them what he knew about each guy on the job. In most cases, it wasn't much. They were a motley conglomeration of farmers, drifters, locals, and full-time construction workers. Full-time, in the sense that that was all they did. They worked eight or nine months of the year for DeBoni, took a three or four-month vacation when the job shut down, and collected unemployment.

Management, the super and two assistant supers, and the grade foremen were mostly permanent employees. The top guys would work on bids in the off-season. The grade foremen would either be laid off, or if there was a right-of-way to be cleared, run the chainsaw crews. Cutting down trees was a winter job.

For most of the crew, Rick might or might not know what part of the state they came from. He might know if they were married or not, and if they fooled around. Those topics would come up at sandwich break and lunch time. For many, he didn't even know their real names, just their nicknames.

"Guess I'm not much help," Rick said.

"Well, you haven't exactly solved the case, kid." Avery answered. "Let's try this. Who wasn't at the shindig?"

"Mmm, let me think. There were a couple of the college kids, Jim, and Frank, who didn't come. I didn't see any of the grade foremen. And Cashman, the Duke, and Charlie. I didn't see PH, either. Far as I know, none of those guys were there.

"It's almost noon. We should go have lunch with some of these guys," Redman said. Who would you start with?"

"Well, I heard Henry say he had a theory. And he and Côte are always good company. Why don't you start up on the ledge with the drillers?" Rick suggested.

"As good as any place," Avery stood up. "Let's move out." He had the natural authority of a master sergeant. They all got to their feet and followed.

Chapter 21

Henry

They climbed back in the jeep, and drove slowly up the northbound lane towards the ledge. Rick looked off to his left into the gravel pit, and could see that Donny and the substitute D-9 were having a lot of trouble pushing the belly scrapers through the fill. He marveled at how pig-headed Charlie could be, even when it cost him far more to avoid the taxes than it would if he paid them.

They parked in the shade, grabbed their lunch-buckets, and walked up the path to the ledge. The crew was just settling down in a small grove of trees that would be in the median when the road was finished.

"Cheese it," Côte hollered. "Here comes Squirt and the cops."

"Interesting company you keep," Henry growled.

"Hey, guys, I just do what the boss man tells me to do." Rick found a log and sat. He half-listened as Avery and Redman carefully interviewed first Côte, then Henry, and Ding and Dodd.

"Tell us a bit about yourself, Côte," Avery said.

"Wall," Côte drawled, "not much to tell." He munched down on a thick sandwich. "I was born up in the Northeast Kingdom. My old man was a Canuck lumberjack. My mother's father was a dirt-poor dirt farmer, trying to scrape a living from the worst soil in the world. Me, I inherited all that. I'm a dirt-poor lumberjack, who has to drill rocks to eat, or eat rocks. I'm still trying to grow shit on that damn poor soil, and it still ain't growin'. Show's you how smart I am."

"Married?" Redman asked.

"Me? Married? You been talking to my old lady, I can tell. Yes, I knocked up some dirt-poor farm girl, and we had a passel of kids. Two of 'em lived. My son Pierre, he's bound and determined to be just as dumb as his old man. Now my daughter, Michele, she's going to do okay." Côte smiled. "She's going to be going to college at Castleton next year. Gonna be a school marm. Be a good'un, too."

"Have you worked for DeBoni long?" Avery asked, keeping the momentum going.

"Let me see." Côte scratched his head. "Henry was here when I came. He'd been here about a month. When was that Henry?"

"Fifty-seven. DeBoni had a 2-mile piece over Manchester way, on Route 7. Ran into a little bit of granite ledge." Henry was watching the cops work the interrogation.

"Let's see then." Côte counted on his fingers. "That'd be about seven years, I guess. Pretty near as long as DeBoni has worked in Vermont. Worked for him some every year. Last three years we've had pretty steady work. We did the little piece on 103. Then we did the interchange on 89, in Montpelier. That was hard rock. A piece over in Springfield. We been here since DeBoni got this job. Me and Henry did the lumbering on the right-of-way last winter."

"What's your opinion on the union?" Redman asked.

"Ooh. The union. You think we might'a blowed up that union guy?"

"Just trying to see what you think."

"Wall, Henry can speak for hisself. Me, I don't care about the union one way or another. But that's just for me. I think they done some good things. Lord knows the owners would be paying us a dime a day if it wasn't for them unions. I just don't like joining things. It means more time.

More people with their hands in my pocket. Hassles that don't mean anything to me."

"Would you vote against it?" Avery asked.

"Ohh, I don't know." Côte took off his helmet and scratched his head. "I might not 'a voted at all. If I did vote, it'd probably have been against. But I can't say I was in one camp or t'other."

"Know anybody who had a real hard-on for the union?" Redman asked.

"A bunch of people. Charlie'd turn red, swell up, and explode if you said *union* anywhere within fifty-miles of the job. PH there's pretty near as bad. Couple of truck drivers got fired off a union job, and cussed it pretty good. I don't know. Lot of these guys figure they wouldn't have a job if the union came in."

"Any threats?"

"None I heard. Just normal bitchin'."

"How about you, Henry?" Avery asked.

"I don't do no bitchin'. I don't say nothing," Henry growled. He chewed a piece off the end of his cigar, and spat it on the ground.

"No, I mean tell us about yourself."

"Ain't nothing to tell. What you see is what you get."

"Where do you live?" Redman asked. He was looking down at his clipboard.

"Probably says right there, don't it? I give all that stuff to the cops at the landing. You figure I lied?"

"We always recheck this stuff. Don't get all indignant. It's just the way the routine goes."

"Fuck your routine. I ain't got time to keep telling you the same stuff over and over again. I need to get back to work."

"Well, we could go down to the barracks and go through this stuff. I thought it would be easier for you guys here. Cashman said we could take all *your* time that we need, and you wouldn't be docked for it."

"Henry G. Baldridge, driller first class, serial number: 0886969. What more you need?"

"Don't be an asshole, Baldridge," Avery snapped. "This stuff is no more fun for us, than it is for you. But somebody blew up that union guy, and we got to find out who."

"Well, it wasn't me. It don't bother me none that he's confetti. But I didn't do it. Me and Côte were together all night, ain't that right, Côte? We drank some beers, ate some chicken, listened to that union guy flap his jaws, and then had the shit scared out of us when he went up in smoke."

Côte nodded.

"Lucky for us old Everett saved that keg when the car blew up. Otherwise we'd of sat their dry until three o'clock in the fucking morning, when your buddies finally got their thumbs out of their assholes, and let us go home."

"What we got says you live up in St. Johnsbury. You're married. You got one daughter who's just got married to some guy who works for DeBoni. That right?" Redman drilled down through the information sheet.

"Yeah. And you know I started just a few weeks before Côte. Been working for DeBoni for seven years. Mostly running the air track, but also clearing trees and brush on the right-of-way.

"You work any with dynamite?"

"Shit. Is the Pope Catholic? I've been on this crew drilling the holes. Course we done some small jobs ourselves, boulders and the like. And shit, I've blasted plenty of stumps. Ain't nobody on this job who don't know something about dynamite. 'Cept maybe some of them *dumb college fucks.*" Henry spit another piece of cigar in Avery's general direction.

Avery ignored the gesture and continued. "Ever take any dynamite home?"

"That'd be telling, wouldn't it? Let me tell you, I bet a couple a cases a year head home in lunch-buckets. This shit is hard to buy, and expensive. Most everybody needs to blow a stump or something from time-to-time."

"Take any of them jackhammer sticks from the magazine?" Redman asked.

"Fuck no! I never even *seen* the magazine. I know where it's supposed to be at, but I never had cause to go there. If I wanted some dynamite, I'd just pick it up when they was loading the shot. Too much fucking work to go steal it from the magazine. When they're loading the shot, it's lying around in heaps. Then too, when a shot goes bad, like it did last week, there's dynamite all over the place. No trick to get dynamite around here."

"You know anybody who hated the union or Jensen bad enough to blow him up?"

"Well, it weren't Ding and Dong here. They loved his ass. I think these two guys is union plants. Like Côte said, Charlie and PH hated the fuckin' union so bad they'd piss all over themselves anybody say *union* when they're takin' a leak. But most of the guys here don't really give a shit one way or the other. They wouldn't be apt to blow a guy up who just bought the beer."

"You guys union plants?" Avery asked Dodd.

"Well, not exactly. I mean, we talked to them guys and we liked the union okay. But we wasn't getting paid by the union or anything. They pretty much told us if we just said good things about the union they'd see that Ding got his card. We was hoping to catch on with Paligrinni when he opens that ledge across the river."

"Sound like plants to me," Henry growled.

"You guys see anybody who was really worked up against the union?" Redman tossed the question at Ding and Dodd.

"Just like Henry and Côte said," Ding fielded the question. "Charlie and PH really hate the union. Some other guys don't like it much. Nobody threatening anybody."

"'Cept PH threatening to fire our asses if we went to the shindig." Dodd added. "But I think it was just talk."

"You got that right," Henry growled. "PH is all mouth, no action. I don't think he's got the guts to blow his nose. Too bad somebody didn't blow his ass up too. That would've been a red letter day."

"A piece of advice," Avery was getting to his feet. "You want the cops to leave you alone, treat us with some respect."

Henry gave him a grin. "Yes sir, Mr. Policeman, sir. You get all the respect you deserve." He stood up. "We better get drilling if we're gonna get a shot off this week."

Rick walked down the hill to the jeep with Avery and Redman.

"Cantankerous cuss, ain't he?" Avery said.

"Yep. That's vintage Henry." Rick answered. "He'd rather pull your chain than give you a straight answer. But I've never seen him do anything nasty. He just likes to rag people."

Rick squired the two cops around for the rest of the day. They talked to a few of the truckers and a couple of foremen. They finished the day down on the fill with the Duke.

Rick introduced the two cops.

The Duke glared at him and said, "Didn't I tell you to keep your ass off my fill? You think I said that and didn't mean it?"

Rick stammered, "Uh, uh, Cashman said for me to take these guys where they want to go. They wanted to go here."

"What can I do for you gentlemen?" Duke turned his attention to the cops.

"We are following up leads, such as they are. Talking to the guys on this job looking for somebody who hated the union or Jensen enough to give him a dynamite ticket to *kingdomcome*." Avery said.

"I didn't know the man," Duke said. "I didn't attend the union meeting. It wouldn't have been proper, me being management."

"You knew about the meeting, of course?" Redman asked.

Duke nodded. "Yes. It was common knowledge. We could hear the damn thing. My wife and I park our doublewide at River View. We could hear the noise all evening. When the bomb went off, we about jumped out of our skins. I was pretty pissed off at first. Thought it was some union stunt. Then when the fire trucks and police cars came roaring by, we figured it was something worse than that."

"Any talk around about disrupting this thing?"

Duke looked at Avery, and smiled. "I don't suppose that it's any surprise to you that Charlie hates the union with a passion. There may've been some words said. I don't recall. But as far as I know, there wasn't no plan to stop the union. Mostly, people were just wringing their hands and whining about how this could fuck up the job."

"How's that?" Redman asked. "Why should the union fuck up the job?"

"Not the union, per se. It'd be the change. If the union came in, there would be all kinds of new work rules, and sure as shit somebody'd do something to piss'm off, and sure as shit the union would pull a job action. It's always like that during the first few months. Sort of trying to show who's in charge. But we ain't got a lot of room for fucking around on this job. We cut it pretty close to win it as it is. And what with Charlie fucking it up every chance he gets, we'll be lucky to get out of it with our ass."

"So, you're saying that this union thing could have been real bad news for DeBoni." Avery made a note on his pad. "So bad, somebody might of done something about it?"

"I don't think so. If anybody was to do something, it should have been me. I really burned my bridge with Charlie over his sending the goddamn D-9 up to Granby. We need that damn dozer here. We're way behind on the fill, and we can't start the bridge footings until we hit the quarter mark."

"Burned your bridge?"

"Yeah, I got a bit hot under the collar and called him a 'stupid fuckin' Wop, who didn't have the brains to be a sidewalk contractor.' Not one of my smartest moves. Particularly 'cause he'll be needing another super if he gets the piece up by Springfield. That would've probably been my job. Now he'll probably give it to Harris. That, or move John up there, and give this job to Harris. Maybe if I blew up the union guy, Charlie would forget what I called him. But shit. I don't give a fuck. He *is* a stupid Wop. His old man, who was a sidewalk contractor, could run this job better than Charlie."

"This Harris guy. He the one they call PH? He the type to do it?" Redman raised one eyebrow. He'd heard Harris mentioned once or twice before.

"Shit, no reason to. He's got the fucking job unless he runs over Charlie's foot or something. Nah. Probably some dumb laborer here who figure's he'll get canned if the union takes over. And he's probably right. These *dumb college fucks*, like Squirt here, and the drunks and bums Charlie hires to do odd jobs, will all be toast if the union comes in."

"So you didn't go over to the union shindig." Avery asked.

"No. My wife'll tell you. I just sat there cussin'm out."

"Yeah, well wives are apt to say what you want'm to say." Avery observed.

"Not my wife. She'll nail my hide to the wall if she gets the chance. She's never forgiven me for our boy Grant getting killed down in Maine. I wasn't anywhere near there, but she figures it was my fault anyway." Duke stared into space and muttered something.

"What's that?" Avery asked.

"I said it ain't fucking hardly worth it. Anything more you need to know?"

Avery and Redman looked at each other and shrugged. "I guess not."

"Christ on a crutch, boy, what the hell are you doing?" Duke was storming across the fill, hollering at the top of his lungs at Mike Hennessy, who had hadn't been paying attention, and created a puddle in the middle of the fill with his fire hose. Rick felt a bit sorry for him. Mike was a shirt-tail cousin, and Rick knew that he could slip off into a daydream at any time— a dangerous habit out on the fill with the big belly scrapers roaring by.

"That's it for today, Wallace," Redman said. "We'll probably be back at the end of the week, or early next week. Depends."

They climbed back in the jeep, and Rick drove slowly off the fill, back to the yard. Avery leaned in to talk to Redman in the backseat. "Any ideas, Horse?"

"Shit, no. Still looks like the nigger to me. But it ain't exactly an airtight case."

"How about this Harris guy?" Avery asked.

"We talked to him once. He had a pretty good alibi if I remember. Fuckin' somebody's wife or girlfriend, I forget which. Didn't want to name the chick unless he had to. Said it would cause some mighty hard feelings."

"Probably piss off his wife some, too," Rick chimed in.

Avery winced. "Wallace. You didn't hear nothing. You got that?"

"Hear what?" Rick laughed. "Deaf as a post. Running that fucking drill will do that to you, you know."

The cops didn't say anything more. Rick parked the jeep by the office trailer, and said, "Any time you gentlemen need a chauffer, I'm your man."

Redman and Avery just waved at him. They were deep in conversation as they walked to their unmarked car.

Rick climbed the stairs to the office trailer, looking to drop off the keys, and take off early. He stopped on the top step as he heard Charlie shout, "I don't give a shit about your problems, John. I pay you to run the job. Don't come telling me you're running late, goddamn it. If I have to pay a fuckin' late penalty, it will come out of your paycheck."

John's voice rumbled in the background.

"Whadda fuck you say?" Charlie screamed.

"I said, 'take the job and shove it up your Dago ass, you sonofabitch. I quit.'"

Rick jumped clear, and John Cashman, one of the mildest mannered men he'd ever met, exploded through the door, jumped in his pickup, and roared out of the yard.

Two seconds later, Charlie burst through the door screaming in Italian. Rick didn't have a clue what he was saying, but he was sure Berlitz didn't teach those words.

"Charlie?" It was Tim, the timekeeper, speaking very softly.

"Whadda ya want?"

"Your father is on the line."

"My father? My fuckin' father? Whad'hell that old goombah want? Shit, I don't wanna talk to my father."

"You want I should say you left?"

"Yeah. No. Shit. I'll talk to him." Charlie went back into the trailer.

Rick crept back up the stairs and opened the door. Charlie was standing by the desk talking Italian into the phone. Rick hung the keys on the board, gave Tim a little wave, and ran like hell.

Just as he got to his car, Whitey was coming out of the maintenance shed. "Hey Wallace, what's going on over there?

"I think Cashman just quit," Rick said.

"Ahh, shit. Again? It takes a lot to get John mad, but Charlie can do it. That's the second time he's quit this month. One of these days, he ain't coming back."

"This could be the time," Rick said. "Charlie was blaming him for the job running late, after Charlie sent all the good equipment up to Granby. Apparently, they're going to get hit with some late penalties."

"Mmm. Probably 'cause Paligrinni can't start till they lay the footings for the bridge."

"Could be. Duke was cussing about that too. I guess they're really behind."

"You get some new wheels, boy? How come you be buying a car, and not coming to see old Whitey?"

"No time, Whitey." Rick told him about the accident on the scooter. "Sonofabitch just locked right up on me. I thought I was road kill."

Whitey looked at him. "Boy. You just ran out of gas, is all. That truck making all that noise, you just didn't hear or feel it. Scooter can't run without gas."

"Yeah. I know. I figured it out. But still, I needed a car. I just didn't want to ride that damned thing any more."

"What'd you pay?"

"Five hundred."

"Five, fuckin' hundred? Man you got skinned. Three-fifty, tops. Look't that rust."

"Yeah, that's what my dad said. But I wanted it."

"So daddy footed the loan. Which he'll never see a dime of. Boy, I'm ashamed of you. You be a regular Freddie the Freeloader."

Rick hung his head.

"But bring it 'round the garage. We'll patch her up some. Let me check out the engine. That little six should last 500,000 miles. It don't hardly have to work at all. Provided that is, you remember to put some oil in from time-to-time."

Rick brightened. "Thanks Whitey. You're the best." He tossed his lunch-bucket in the back of the car. Then a thought came to him.

"Whitey?" Whitey was heading back into the shed.

"Yeah, boy."

"You getting hassled in town?"

"There be some assholes that are talking nigger. You know how it goes."

"Yeah, that guy Gorse is acting like he's Ku Klux Klan. I asked Jack to talk to the Tycoon and see if he had anything going. I think he'd move both you and Annabelle to one of his parks in Pennsylvania in a heartbeat."

"Well, probably. He's a good guy. But I don't want to work on no *choo-choos*. And Annabelle, she ain't going to leave D-d-donnie in the lurch. Man depends on her."

"Yeah, well D-d-donnie's got one foot in the grave. No telling what will happen if he croaks."

"That's true. But Annabelle ain't going to add to his troubles, I can tell you that. She'll stay right here till he's dead and buried. Then when them shit-ass nephews of D-d-donnie's take over, it'll be different. I 'spect they'll run the whole friggin' empire into the ground in about a week."

"Maybe he'll leave it all to the church, or something."

"Don't matter. The nephews'll take it to court. By the time it's settled, it'll be just scrap. But I thank you for thinking of me, boy."

"Yeah, well I think you should keep your options open. It could get ugly, Whitey. It could get *real* ugly."

"I seen *ugly*, boy. You remember what I told you about my uncle? I understands ugly."

"Them cops still think you're the prime suspect."

"Them cops don't think. They just ain't got any other answer. But they ain't got no evidence against me. That's what O'Malley said. He said, 'don't sweat it, Whitey. They's just blowing smoke. They'd get laughed out of court.'"

Rick nodded. "That's probably true. I guess the assholes will be a bigger problem than the cops."

"They usually is. Course where I comes from, you can't tell one from t'other. They's all the same kind of redneck."

There was screaming and shouting over by the office trailer, and Whitey and Rick walked over to the edge of the building and peered around the corner. Charlie was screaming at Tim in Italian. Tim just stood quietly and let him scream. Finally throwing his arms in the air, Charlie stalked down the stairs and over to his car. He yelled something at Tim, then climbed in, slammed the door, started the engine, and roared out of the yard sending up a rooster tail of dust.

"Let's go see what's up," Rick said.

"You go," Whitey shook his head. "I gotta clean up. You can tell me later."

Rick trotted over to the office trailer. Tim was standing on the top step.

"What was that all about, Tim?" Rick asked.

Tim shrugged. "Damned if I know. I can't speak Italian. I sure hope John comes back, though. I just got a call from Bob Strong, the state inspector. His crew is going to be over here Monday, and go over the job with a fine toothcomb. They're worried we're fudging the compaction tests. They're worried we ain't going to get the footings set in time for Paligrinni to start. Could be big trouble."

Rick walked back to his car. Bob Strong was a good friend of his family. In fact, it was Strong who got him on with DeBoni back a couple of years ago, when he turned eighteen. He chuckled, thinking about the graduation party he'd had at his house when Betty McCary had decked Strong with a left hook. Strong was just about Rick's height, 5'8", or so. McCary, who graduated with Rick, was 6'3", and built like the proverbial brick shithouse. Strong was dancing with her, and his head came right to her boob. Strong had had a couple, and couldn't resist giving it a little nip. Next thing he knew, he was sprawled out on the floor with a shiner.

Rick was still chuckling, as he drove out of the yard and headed home.

Chapter 22

The Tycoon

Driving home, Rick spotted John Cashman's truck at the Twist Cone. On impulse, he pulled into the lot. He could see Cashman sitting by himself, in the farthest booth, his back to the door. Rick hesitated, and then shrugged his shoulders and went in. He asked Libby, the counter clerk, for a Coke. He paid her, and walked over to Cashman.

"Hi, Mr. Cashman." He stood awkwardly by the edge of the table.

Cashman looked up. "Uh, oh. Wallace. You want something?"

"Uh, no sir. I was just wondering if you had really quit."

"Oh you heard that, did you? I sure ought to quit. That crazy man is running this company right into the ground. I shouldn't give a shit. It's his company. But I can't help it. I just can't stand to see the waste."

"Uh, well, I hope you don't quit, Mr. Cashman. If you quit we might get PH for a super, and if you don't mind me saying so, I don't think he can handle it."

"What the hell do you know about it, boy?"

"Uh, I've just been around him enough. The men hate him. I don't think he really knows what he's doing."

"You want to work, you better keep those opinions to yourself. Besides, Charlie'd probably give it to Duke. He's a good head."

"Well, Mr. Duke didn't think so. He said he chewed Charlie a new asshole over the D-9 fiasco, and now he's on Charlie's shit list. At least, that's what he told the cops."

"Oh." Cashman suddenly got where Rick was getting his information. "You spent a lot of time with them cops, didn't you."

"All day. They're still pretty clueless. Still think Whitey probably did it. But shit, everybody knows he didn't."

"Mmm, yeah. Anything else, boy?"

"Well, Tim said Bob Strong and his crew were going to give the job a complete inspection on Monday. Said they were worried that we'd been fudging the compaction tests and stuff like that."

"Aw, shit. Strong knows me better than that. I'll give that sonofabitch a call. He can come test. But he ain't going to find any fudged tests. He'll probably see we're a couple of weeks behind, though. That's what Charlie's fuming about. We could get fined $10,000 a day. Especially if Paligrinni pushes for it. It's a Guinea war. If we don't have them footings in by the second week of July, we're in a heap of shit." Cashman held his head. "Oh crap! I can't quit this week. Hell, I'm calling Granby and ordering Crackers and Chip to bring back my goddamn dozer. Charlie can go fuck himself."

Cashman got out of his seat, and fumbled for coins. Rick offered the two quarters he had as change. Cashman took them and went over to the wall phone.

"See ya, Mr. Cashman. I got to get home."

Cashman paid him no mind, digging in his pants for his address book. He was dialing as Rick went out the door. As he walked to his car, Jack North's Corvette pulled in alongside Rick's Chevy. Jack shut down the engine.

"Ricardo, mi amigo!"

"Jackson, you old salty dog."

"Smile when you say that hombre. What's shaking?"

"Just heading home. Been squiring those two cops around. Abbott and Costello, or Laurel and Hardy, or whatever their names are."

"And all I ever did, was shoot a deputy down!" Jack crooned.

"Come around to the house. Let me clean up and we can go do something."

"I'd follow you, but I'd run right over you. See ya there." Jack's Corvette roared. He backed around, and with a little chirp of rubber, launched it onto the main drag.

"Shit," Rick thought. "He'll go to Brattleboro and back before I park in the driveway."

Actually, the Corvette was parked in Rick's driveway, and Larry and Curly were climbing in and out of it. Jack had a soft spot for Rick's little brothers. Rick could hear Jack's guitar from the front room.

He parked in front of the house and went in the front door. Jack was in the front living room playing for Rick's mom and dad. They both thought the sun rose and set on Jack, and loved to listen to him play. Jack, of course, loved being loved.

Rick wasn't jealous. His parent's regard for Jack had made it possible for him to accompany Jack on some pretty wild, crazy adventures, including the summer they spent in Sunapee, living in a caboose. In fact, Rick figured he would have led a pretty sedate life except for his adventures with Jack. Jack, on the other hand, lived a life that seemed like one adventure after another. Some of those adventures became songs.

"Did I ever tell you of the time,
I got pendiculis pubis—the crabs, yeah!
It was down Westminster way.
She told me it was her first time.
I guess she meant, first time today!"

"Oh, Jack you're terrible." Rick's mother said, lighting a cigarette.

"Itch some?" Rick's father asked, chuckling.

"The Stooges are wrecking your car, Jack," Rick said.

Jack just waved at him.

Rick went into the kitchen and got a beer. Then he headed upstairs to take a quick bath. When he came back down, fifteen minutes later, Jack was still playing, sipping a scotch in between numbers. His folks were laughing.

"Those two cops still think that Whitey is the prime suspect," Rick said. He filled in his folks and Jack, on his day of chauffeuring the cops from interview to interview.

"Oooh, ooh. I meant to tell you." Jack said.

"Tell me what?"

"I talked to the Tycoon about Whitey, and the first thing he said was, 'That wasn't supposed to happen.' I about shit."

"What do you think he meant by that?"

"I don't know. But the thought that came to me in that second was, 'This guy knows more than he should.'"

"What the hell would the Tycoon care about union stuff? That doesn't make any sense."

"Yeah. Well he's anxious to do something for Whitey and Annabelle."

"Maybe we should go talk to him. Whitey says he doesn't want to be a choo-choo mechanic, and he says Annabelle won't walk out on D-d-don-nie. Maybe the Tycoon's got some ideas that will encourage Whitey. Is he around?"

"Oh yeah. Him and the Christians are having a prayer meeting right about now. Should be done in a half-hour or so. Let's go grab a burger and then head up to the yard."

"Don't go mixing with those Holy Rollers," Rick's mom said.

"Don't worry. We'll stay well clear of them. The Tycoon himself is more Christian that I can stand in one conversation." Jack laughed. "Damn, it never ceases to amaze me how much one man can change."

Rick and Jack shooed the kids out of the Corvette, and headed out to the Twist Cone to grab a burger. They talked about the Tycoon, G. William Duque, scion of the Pennsylvania Duque clan, founders of Duque Farms, the country's largest producer of berries, apples, pears, peaches, and apricots. G. William had inherited the farms and added large-scale production of top-of-the-line jams, jellies, and pie fillings. He was a master promoter, and managed to link his hobby, railroads, and his business in a truly innovative way. The farms and orchards were spread out over three states. Production was centralized in Rickets Glen, a tiny town about 150 miles west of Scranton, in the heart of the Appalachian Mountains. The Tycoon linked all of his farms to his production center in a hub and spoke, rail system. He purchased several short-line railroads, and using these right-of-ways with strategic leased track rights, he had the world's only express fruit railroad. He advertised that the average time from the tree or bush to the jar, was less than 48 hours. And people literally ate it up. The Duque fruit empire was conservatively estimated at nearly a billion dollars.

Once he set it up, the empire pretty much ran itself. That left the Tycoon with a lot of time on his hands, and a passion for railroads. First, he created some theme parks that linked two or three farms in five-to-ten-mile rail loops. Each farm was a stop, complete with a turn of-the-century station, ticket-office, restaurant, newsstand, and gift shop. While he used modern diesels for his berry and fruit transport, he resurrected old steam engines to give visitors to his parks a thrilling ride, with a taste of the old west. Excursion trains had four passenger cars, a dining car, and a caboose. The dining cars and station restaurants featured Duque pies and tarts. The Tycoon scoured the country for recipes, and often as not, the cooks who created them.

Each little park complex was a stand-alone business that also promoted the Duque lines of jams, jellies, and pie fillings. They made money hand-over-fist. What could be more American than berry pie and steam trains?

In addition to being a genius, the Tycoon was a wild man. He caroused, spent money freely, played huge practical jokes, and generally had a great time. Anybody who was around him for more than a couple of hours, heard him tell some poor long-distance operator, "Ma'am, that's *Duque*, as in fuck, not *duke*, as in puke. Do you think we could sell any fruit with name that rhymed with puke?"

Sometime in the middle 1950's, he got it into his mind that he wanted an all steam-operated railroad. About that time, the Rutland Railroad in Vermont went bankrupt, due to a prolonged strike. The Rutland had miles of track through some of the most scenic country in the world, and the track provided a border-to-border link with virtually no competition. Whoever owned the Rutland, could set his own freight prices to destinations within the state.

Buying a railroad out of bankruptcy is not a simple manner. The Tycoon was a shrewd negotiator and larcenous to boot. If he couldn't steal the thing, he really didn't want it that bad. But to steal it, he had to be patient. So he decided to get himself a presence in the area, and bide his time. He bought an old Boston & Maine roundhouse (they had also gone bankrupt and been liquidated). He began accumulating interesting steam engines as they became available around the country. Most engines he bought at scrap prices. Some he bought for less than scrap.

He put a crew to work rehabilitating the engines and an assortment of Pullman sleeper, parlor, and dining cars, and cabooses from all the famous railroads in the country. Nothing in his operation had even a whiff of freight. Jack got involved because his father was close friends with Tom Caine, an out-of-work Rutland Railroad engineer and steam enthusiast. Tom became the Tycoon's number one man, and he in turn hired on all of his cronies. Jack, at fifteen, was ranked as a crony. Jack, in turn, brought in Rick, and one or two other guys they hung out with. Not everyone was allowed to hang around the roundhouse. Lots of parents expected that wicked things were happening there. And, of course, they were. But while the crew had a lot of fun, they were also pretty discreet. Rick's parents never gave it a thought because Jack was there. Rick got the first of many hangovers sleeping-over in the caboose. Jack had a taste for some poisonous alcoholic combinations.

The summer Rick was sixteen; the Tycoon rented a short piece of track in Sunapee, N.H., and ran a short-line excursion. Jack worked as a fireman, or brakeman. Rick sold *Duque Mini Very-Berry Pies* on the train. It was the summer of pure debauchery every sixteen-year-old dreams of. The only reason Rick didn't lose his virginity, was his inability to hold his liquor. He always passed out before the action got hot. If he could believe even 10 percent of the stories everyone told, everybody else had a "fucking" good time.

After that summer, Rick got involved in other things, and in summer jobs where he didn't spend more than he earned every week. He was Jack's friend, so he was always welcome at the roundhouse or wherever else the crew was assembling.

The Tycoon bided his time. He leased a small piece of a Rutland line, and ran some excursions. Then, when the right-of-ways were about to be sold back to adjacent property holders for a penny a linear-foot; the Tycoon made his move, and snapped up the full line from Massachusetts to Derby Line. Rick didn't know what he paid, but it was considerably less than a penny a linear-foot. Rumor said it was ten dollars a linear-mile.

Just this past year, two events came together to change the nature of the Tycoon's enterprise. One was an itinerant preacher who called himself Theobold Magus. He approached the Tycoon and asked if he could rent his meadow and set up a tent and hold a revival. The Tycoon's first reaction was to say, "No fuckin' way, Jose!" Then he thought about it, and considered that most of the people attending the revival would probably spring for a ticket on the train. So, after some thought, he agreed for one weekend only. Magus then asked if there were an empty boxcar or some such place he and his group could bunk until the meeting. Again, the Tycoon's instincts were to turn him away, but he had a dozen empty, unrefurbished Pullman cars, sitting on a siding. So, he said the crew was welcome to use them for the next few days. But he warned Magus they were not to count on them, because the cars were due to be shuttled over to the roundhouse for refurbishment pretty soon. The Tycoon didn't think to ask how many followers Magus had. He had forty-seven. Now he has one hundred forty-seven, and they are still using those Pullmans, plus some of the old crew-cars they used to bunk the rail crews when they were building the railroads.

The other event happened before Magus even held his revival. The Tycoon was walking along, laughing it up with Tom Caine, and some of his cohorts. He was chewing on a fat cigar, and Caine, in his usual slow drawl, told a risqué joke that the Tycoon found hilarious. He roared with laughter, and inhaled his cigar. It lodged in his throat, and he dropped like a stone.

The Tycoon was a notorious practical joker, so Caine and the others thought nothing of it. In fact they kept walking. Theobold Magus was standing a few feet away. He rushed over, grabbed him around the gut from behind, and lifted him up. The Tycoon spat out the cigar and gasped for breath. Magus said, "I think the Lord has spoken."

People say that the conversion happened right then, and there, but Jack said it actually took quite a while. What the rescue did, was give Magus the Tycoon's ear. From that point on, Magus talked to the Tycoon every chance he got, and it wasn't long before he hit on a happy blend of Christianity, and larceny, that appealed to the Tycoon's nature. According to Jack, Magnus showed Duque the secret of the "Jesus hook," a strategy that untold numbers of traveling evangelists have used with great success. Reduced to its simplest terms, the *mark* is distracted, and drawn into a trusting relationship by using Jesus as the hook. Once a trust relationship has been built, the *preacher* finds it an easy matter to siphon cash and other gifts from the trusting true believer.

All the time Magus was showing the Tycoon how to use the technique; he was working it on him. He helped himself to the Tycoon's facilities, and to considerable cash. He held revival meetings every weekend. It wasn't long before regular tourists started shying away, because there was always one of Magus's followers handing out a religious tract, or asking for a donation. The steam trains rapidly became a *Christian* theme park, of sorts.

Tom Caine, and most of the old-timers, moved their headquarters to Ludlow, and focused on reintroducing freight to Vermont. They made no pretense about using steam. They went straight for the most cost-effective diesels they could find. And the Tycoon supported them. He lost interest in developing the world's largest steam exhibition. He kept the displays simple, and spent a lot of time with Magus and his crew, entertaining important *Christians* from around the country. He pretty much let Caine and his boys run the freight show they wanted to run. And, as far as Rick knew, they ran it well.

Rick and Jack finished their burgers, and motored out to the little rail yard the Tycoon had built in a meadow north of town. The Tycoon had his own deluxe Pullman, where he bunked when he was in town. In the old days, you always had to be careful when you knocked. The Tycoon frequently entertained ladies in his quarters, and none of those ladies was his wife. Melanie Duque despised trains of any kind. Now, rumor had it, sometimes Magus would have the Tycoon pray with a sweet young heiress, but these private sessions happened elsewhere, at a camp that Magus ran in Canada.

"Ahh, the Christians are all preparing for the lions," Jack said as they pulled into the yard. They could hear hymns being sung in the station house, which was now more church, than depot. "Wonder if the Tycoon is with them?"

"Guess we'll have to knock, and find out," Rick said.

They swung up onto the rear platform of the car, which was formerly part of the Presidential train Harry Truman rode when he was barnstorming the country in his campaign against Dewey. Jack knocked. "GW, are you decent?" he hollered.

"Why, Jack, my boy. Come in. And who is this? Richard? I haven't seen you in a long time, Richard. You shouldn't be a stranger here. Your friends miss you." The Tycoon was dressed in striped pajamas and a plain dressing gown. He wore simple, floppy slippers.

"I've been reading the *Good Book*," he said.

"Hi, Mr. Duque," Rick said, feeling uncomfortable. This man seemed nothing like the man he knew as the Tycoon. "Are you ill?"

"No, no Rick. Not in body. But I have been ill in my soul. And now I am trying to get well. Would you boys like some fruit juice, or Kool-Aid? Perhaps some iced tea?"

"No, we're fine, aren't we Rick?" Jack was pacing the long, narrow room. "We came to talk to you about Whitey."

"And Annabelle," Rick added.

"Oh my, yes. They are two of God's special children. We mustn't let anything happen to them." The Tycoon squeezed his bible.

"It's not bad, yet," Rick said. "But there are people in town saying some pretty nasty things. I know this isn't Little Rock, or Selma, but I'm afraid some of these woodchucks will get liquored up, and somebody like Gorse will get them excited, and then who knows what will happen?"

"Well, I would be most happy to give Whitey and Annabelle a job. Good jobs, safe in Pennsylvania. I've offered many times."

"Trouble is," Jack said. "Whitey don't do *choochoos*, and Annabelle won't abandon D-d-donnie when the man is practically on his death bed."

"We can handle the choo-choo part." For a second, the Tycoon sounded like his old self. "I've got a fleet of trucks that need to be kept in repair. Every berry farm and orchard has a lot of diesel equipment. We could find plenty for Whitey to do."

"How do we get Annabelle to leave D-d-donnie?" Rick asked.

"Perhaps I should ask Donald to tell her to go," the Tycoon said. "He is ill. Perhaps I can talk to him about Jesus, as well. We should visit him tonight."

They agreed that there was no time like the present. The Tycoon called D-d-donnie, and he agreed to talk to them. As the Tycoon got dressed in the master-bedroom, Jack said, "Shouldn't we ask him about what he said earlier? You know, about how it wasn't supposed to happen to Whitey?"

Rick agreed. When the Tycoon came out, Rick asked, "Did you know the union guy who was killed?"

"I met him. Yes, I met him. That very same day." The Tycoon looked distressed. "He stopped here and wanted to talk about us using union help on the rail crews. Of course, we are a non-union shop. He was a most dreadful man. He suggested that he knew people in Pennsylvania who would organize my factories and farms if I didn't play along, and make the railroad *union*, at least for the rail crews."

"What did you do?" Jack asked.

"I sent him to Thomas. He handles everything to do with the railroad. I told this Jensen that it would be Thomas's decision, and I would stand behind whatever Thomas wanted to do. I was very firm."

"You said something about it not being supposed to happen to Whitey. What did you mean?" Jack asked.

"Well, the strangest thing. I walked out with Jensen to his car. It was a magnificent 1961 Lincoln Continental. Theobold was there looking at the car. He said to Mr. Jensen, 'This is the same car President Kennedy died in. It may not bode well for you.'"

"Wow. What did Jensen say?"

"He took the Lord's name in vain, and used an obscenity. Then he asked me who this weirdo was. When I told him that Theobold Magus was a man of God, he laughed, and swore again. He said, 'Your man of God better keep his goddamn nose out of my affairs, or he'll be talking to God, face-to-face, real quick.' Then he drove away."

"Wow. Did Magus have anything to say to that?"

"He did. Theobold said, 'He brings God's wrath down on his own house,' Then he said, 'on his car, too.' But I didn't hear him say anything about it hurting Whitey. I can't imagine why God would want to do that."

Chapter 23

D-d-donnie

"J-j-jesus? D-d-do I w-want to know about J-j-jesus?" D-d-donnie was sitting propped up in a bed, in his front parlor. There was a table on either side of his bed. On one, there were dozens of jars, bottles, and tubes of medicines: some prescription, and others, over-the-counter patent medicines. The other table supported a stack of financial reports. "Y-y-you came over h-here to t-t-talk about J-j-jesus?" He was incredulous.

"No. No." The Tycoon waved his hands. "We came to talk about Whitey and Annabelle. But I thought afterwards you and I might talk about Jesus."

"Wh-wh-what about A-a-annabelle?"

"Perhaps you should explain," the Tycoon turned to Rick and Jack.

"Tell'm Rick," Jack said.

Rick carefully explained the whole situation that put Whitey under suspicion for blowing up Jim Jensen. Then he told about Gorse stirring up trouble in town.

"G-g-gorse, that w-w-weenie w-w-whacker." D-d-donnie was sputtering mad. "That l-little s-sonofabitch is only g-good for p-pushing a b-broom in h-his c-cousin's g-garage."

Rick explained how the Tycoon was more than pleased to give both Annabelle and Whitey jobs in Pennsylvania, but that Annabelle would never leave her job because she was so loyal to him. But that maybe if he insisted, she would reconsider.

"R-right now?"

"No. But we need to be able to get them out of town quickly if trouble starts. Maybe it won't happen. But it wouldn't take much. You know how there have been all those lynchings down south. That could happen right here in Bellows Falls."

"Ok-k-kay. I'll t-t-talk to h-her. Y-y-you're a g-g-good boy, W-w-wallace. I w-w-wish m-my shit-ass n-nephews were s-so good. N-now g-go. I'm t-t-tired."

"About Jesus," the Tycoon said.

"St-st-stop with the J-j-jesus," D-d-donnie shouted. "I'm a J-j-jew!"

"Oh." The Tycoon was nonplussed. He followed Rick and Jack out the door as D-d-donnie's nurse bustled around trying to calm him down.

They had driven over in the Tycoon's 1923 Rolls Royce limousine. It had an open chauffeur's cab, and a closed passenger compartment. Rick had acted as chauffeur on the trip to D-d-donnie's house. Now Jack took the wheel, saying, "You keep him company on the way back. F-f-fuck J-j-jesus. I'm a J-j-jew!" "Jack laughed at his own parody of D-d-donnie's farewell.

Rick climbed into the plush passenger's cabin. It had a bar, a radiotelephone, and a small refrigerator. At one time, the Tycoon would have offered Rick a beer, or perhaps a glass of Champaign. Now, he said, "Some iced tea?"

Rick passed. He wondered to himself how he could get the Tycoon talking about Jensen's visit to the rail yard. Something there didn't seem quite right. But the Tycoon had other thoughts on his mind.

"Tell me about this Donald. Did you know he was a Jew?"

Rick nodded. "I guess so. His last name is Eckberg. I guess that's Jewish. It's never been a big deal around here. We have a few Jewish families in town. Most of them go to the synagogue in Claremont. But I guess a couple belong down in Keene."

"How did he get so wealthy? I don't see the Eckberg name on anything? Doesn't seem like the kind of place that would normally attract Jews. I deal with many Jews in my business. We supply several kosher producers. But usually you expect to find them in the big cities. Places where there is a lot of commerce."

Rick shrugged. "I don't know too much. Just what people say. The story I hear, is that he showed up in Bellows Falls right about the turn-of-the-century. He was a kid, maybe fourteen, all alone. He got a cart, and pushed it around town collecting rags. The paper companies were always looking for rags to add to their paper. You know it gives the paper more strength. D-d-donnie sold the rags to the paper companies. Nobody else was doing it, so he had a corner on the market. He stuttered. People felt sorry for him. I don't know. I guess he made some money at it."

"Fortunes have been started on less." The Tycoon sipped his iced tea. "Obviously he must have branched out. Doesn't seem to be much of a business in rags today."

"Yeah, well he still does that. Everything D-d-donnie starts, he keeps doing. He hires teenagers, kids with nothing. They collect rags in Bellows Falls and Brattleboro, I think. I don't know who they sell to. But you're right. A local blacksmith was injured and had to sell his shop. D-d-donnie bought it. Paid the blacksmith's apprentice to run it. Even paid the blacksmith to sit out front and talk to customers. People in town really liked the guy, I guess. So they did okay. But where he made his dough, was betting on General Motors. He turned his blacksmith shop into the town's first filling station and repair shop. He got the Cadillac dealership for all of Vermont. And, at the same time, he made a deal with Standard Petroleum to handle all of their gasoline and oil products in New England. You could say he put one over on Rockefeller."

"All of New England?" the Tycoon was incredulous. "That can't be."

"Well, that's what they say. I guess old Rockefeller figured out he'd been snookered pretty quick, and he and D-d-donnie did some negotiating. In the end, D-d-donnie kept the franchise for a few counties around here, and he gets a penny a gallon on everything else sold in New England."

"Whew! That's a lot of money."

"But he's always been just a regular guy. And he really cares about this town. When something goes wrong or a business is in trouble, he's usually there to buy it up for a price that's more than it's worth. Then he sets somebody up to run it. The Village Inn is like that. Must have been five owners went belly-up before D-d-donnie finally bought it. Then he finds Annabelle, and like magic it's the most popular restaurant in the state."

"Who are these nephews?"

"D-d-donnie never married. At least if he did, nobody knows about it. But after he'd been in town about fifteen years, these two women show up and say they are his sisters. He welcomes them with open arms. They settle down and live off D-d-donnie's money. Pretty soon, they get married to local people. One married an Irish guy, Jimmy O'Reilly. The other one marries a Polish guy, Stan Karpinski. They have kids. Sons. D-d-donnie gives'm all jobs. The kids are pretty useless. The two families, O'Reilly, and Karpinski, are always squabbling. Most everybody predicts that once D-d-donnie goes, the family businesses will go down the drain, fast."

"Mmmm. I suspect there will be opportunities here." The Tycoon sank back into the lush upholstery.

Rick considered how to broach the subject of Jensen's visit. But the Rolls came to an abrupt stop. The side door opened, and Jack, standing like a chauffer said, "We have arrived, sir."

"Oh, thanks, Jack. I'll see you boys some other time. It's time for my evening prayers." The Tycoon stepped down, and walked slowly towards the station. Theobold Magus emerged from the shadows, and took him by the elbow. Together, they went into the depot.

"That's one spooky guy," Jack said.

"Spooky, is right." Rick and Jack climbed into the Corvette. "Wait a second, Jack. Pop the hood." He had just had the recurring nightmare image of Jensen's car exploding.

"Why? What's wrong?"

"Probably nothing, but let's look."

Jack popped the hood release, and they both went around to look at the engine. Jack lifted the hood. Rick peered into the shadows. "I don't see anything. Wait. What the hell is that?"

"Let me get a flashlight." In fifteen seconds, Jack was back, shining a flashlight into the compartment. There, tied around a sparkplug wire, on the massive V-8, was a red ribbon.

"Whatinhell?"

They carefully examined the rest of the engine compartment. Rick took the light, and crawled under the low-slung sports car, shining the light in every nook and cranny he could see. "Nothing," he said.

"Fuuuuck," Jack groaned. "I hate this. What do you think it means?"

"It means somebody's fuckin' with our heads."

"Who? Who would want to scare us?"

"Well, it wasn't the Tycoon, because he was with us." Rick dusted himself off. "The car is here. Magus is here. He gets my vote."

"We should go haul that guy out and beat the shit out of him." Jack was getting red in the face. A sure sign his blood pressure was up.

"We would just piss off the Tycoon. I don't think Magus would tell us anything. I don't think the sonofabitch knows how to tell the truth. He'd just *Jesus us* this, and *God's message us*, that. Can you start that thing without us getting in?"

"Yeah, but we'll be so close it wouldn't make any difference." Jack jumped in and started the engine. It roared to life and settled into a throaty idle.

Rick shuddered. Then climbed into the passenger seat. "Let's get out of here."

"Where to?" Jack backed around, and then launched the car over the railroad crossing, accelerating all the way to the intersection with Route 5. There were no oncoming lights, so he never even slowed as he came to the stop sign. The tires squealed as they hit the blacktop, and they were racing back towards town.

"Anybody over at the roundhouse?" Rick was hanging onto the chicken bar, petrified, but loving every minute of it.

"Beats me. Probably not."

"Let's go over there and regroup. I need time to think."

Jack backed off the accelerator as they neared the top of the hill, and downshifted. They were doing a sedate 30 mph when they passed the town cruiser with Sneakers Burns at the wheel. Jack gave him a wave. Jack turned down Canal Street, and took the scenic route through the old depot, past Lewiston Paper, the company where Rick's dad worked, and past the chicken processing plant. Canal Street emerged right where Route 103 crossed the Connecticut River to New Hampshire. The roundhouse was on the New Hampshire side, built almost into the base of Fall Mountain, and looking as if it had been abandoned for centuries. In the days of steam, hot cinders from the engines in the rail yard regularly set Fall Mountain on fire. More recently, that task had fallen to local boy scouts. The mountain was just beginning to recover from the latest fire, just three years ago.

Jack parked out of sight, between the office and a storage shed. He unlocked the office door, and he and Rick went inside. "Hallooo, anybody here?" Jack hollered. His voice echoed back. "All out drinking somewhere. Probably all up in Rutland. Tom found a damn good little *yard-dog* engine up there, and I'm sure they all went up to look."

"Let's use Caine's office," Jack said. "You can't see the lights from the road." He turned on the desk lamp, and plopped down in the wooden swivel stationmaster's chair, behind the solid oak roll-top desk. Rick turned a straight chair around, and straddled it, resting his arms on the back.

"Besides," Jack chuckled, "this office has the added benefit of a well-stocked bar." He popped open the bottom drawer, and pulled out a fifth of Canadian Club. "Want a little taste?"

"Any beer around?" Rick asked.

"Check the Coke machine. Cecil usually keeps a few bottles in there."

Rick went out into the mechanic's shop, and opened the top of the Coke cooler. He slid a longneck Schaefer off the rack, popped the top, and went back to his perch. He took a long sip. "What're you thinking?"

Jack was sipping a shot of Canadian neat. "Actually," he said, "I was thinking about Dupris' funeral. They asked me to sing, you know."

"No, I didn't. What did you sing?"

"Oh, *Amazing Grace*. Some other hymn. They did the Mass in English, you know. I guess it isn't supposed to be yet, but I guess some of the churches are experimenting. You know, the music has really gone to hell. There was some great stuff in Latin, but nobody's written any good English stuff, yet. But you know, the curate there. What's his name? Pritchell? He's kind of a modern guy. He asked people to come up and talk about Neal, and of course people were shy. I think that Pritchell had a thing for Neal. Couple of people came up and said bullshit about what a wonderful boy he was. Pure crap. When everybody else had said what they wanted to say, I hauled my guitar up and said, 'You all know Neal, and he was my friend. You all love him. You say good things about him. But let me tell you, Neal wasn't a saint. He was a guy who loved fun.' I could see some people nodding. I said, 'He was a guy who liked a little taste of the *dew*, from time-to-time.' More nodding, some of it pretty vigorous. 'Fact is, he liked a bit too much, from time-to-time, and that's why we are holding this little party for him. But he wouldn't want us here weeping. He'd like us to remember him like he was, and have a little fun. I'd like to play a song he liked. A song that sort of summed up his philosophy, I think. It's Irish. You know the good think about Irish tunes, is you can sing'm as a jig, or you can sing'm as a dirge, and they still work. I'll kind of sing this somewhere in between.'"

Jack leaned back, and sang *a cappella*, in his clear, tenor voice.

"What more diversion can a man desire,
Than to woo a girl, by an open fire,
A Kerry pippin to crack and crunch.
And on the table, a jug of punch?
Tooralooraloo, tooralooralie,
tooralooraloo, tooralooralie.
A Kerry pippin to crack and crunch,
And on the table, a jug of punch."

"I started with the second verse. I figured this audience was only good for about three verses. Monsignor Flaherty was sitting on the side, and I thought he was going to have a stroke on the spot. I looked at him, still playing at a moderate pace. I picked it up to a fast jig. I said, 'The Irish know that the difference between a jig and a dirge, is just God's whim. One day he plays you a jig, and the next day, a dirge. It's just the way life is.' And didn't the Monsignor smile? So, I played at a jig tempo."

Jack laughed. "They were eating it up. Some of them were singing along with the chorus."

"Ye learned doctors and all your art,
cannot cure a depression on the heart.
But even a cripple forgets his hunch,
When he's curled alongside of a jug of punch."

"For the last verse, I slowed way down to a dirge tempo, and sang real quietly:"

"And, when I'm dead, and I'm in my grave,
No fancy tombstone will I ever crave.
Just lay me down in my native peat.
With a jug of punch by my head and feet."

"They all joined in the chorus. Even the Monsignor, I think"

"Tooralooraloo, tooralooralie,
tooralooraloo, tooralooralie.
Just lay me down in my native peat.
With a jug of punch by my head and feet."

Jack took a swallow of whiskey. "There wasn't a dry eye in the place."

"I bet not," Rick laughed. "You are a ballsy ham. Couldn't resist an audience when you should've been on your knees, asking, no, *begging* forgiveness, for making sure Neal had a jug or two that night."

Jack waved, "Fuck it. Wasn't that night, it would have been some other night. The boy was a lush. I think I did him up proud. It's a better sendoff than he deserved."

"What did his folks think?"

"Came up and wrung my hand, and thanked me for being such a good pal to their boy. They said it was beautiful, and they would treasure it always. They asked if I would record it on a tape for them."

"Let's talk about this *Whitey* thing," Rick said. "This is screwy. I don't get it at all. Can you make sense out of it?"

Jack poured another two-finger shot. "Way I see it, Whitey is just an innocent bystander. Whoever did the deed, is happier than shit that Whitey appeared to take the blame. Even if they liked Whitey, they probably couldn't do anything without looking guilty themselves. So, Whitey is pretty much fucked."

"Yeah, but let's look at the characters. Jensen was a thug. But he was an important thug. He didn't come up here just for that DeBoni revival meeting. Already, we know he was making some other stops too, like at the Tycoon's. He might have left behind a whole slew of people pissed enough to blow him up."

"Yeah, but how many of them would know how, or where to get dynamite?"

"Yeah," Rick said dejectedly. "And not just *any* dynamite. The cops say the dynamite and the cap can be traced directly to DeBoni's magazine."

"I wonder if that's true, or if they just say that shit," Jack knocked back his drink. "I mean, how would we know?"

"It doesn't make sense for it to be just *any* old DeBoni working stiff. Shit, Jensen was feeding them free chicken, and beer. They could always vote against the union if they didn't want it. Makes more sense that it was

Charlie. But you'd think he'd hire professionals, and they wouldn't use his dynamite."

"I'm still wondering about that Magus guy," Jack said. "He's a sneaky fucker. He's Jesus this, and Jesus that, but you know he's stealing with both hands. I just can't figure why he'd give a shit."

"Yeah, I'm with you. I'm figuring it was probably one of DeBoni's supers. Probably, PH, 'cause he's the biggest asshole, or, it was Magus. But I can't for the life of me figure out why they'd do something that drastic. I mean, blowing somebody up is pretty serious shit."

"You said a mouthful, Brother." Jack finished his glass of whiskey. "I'll drive you home. We can stop at a couple of bars and see if there is any serious trouble brewing."

Rick finished his beer, and tossed it to Jack, who dunked it in the wastebasket. "Sounds like a plan. Probably should stop at The *Brow*."

Drinking was the number one recreational hobby in Bellows Falls, and the town had plenty of places to get sloshed. People tend to stay with their own kind, and each bar had its own special clientele. O'Brian's, was the Irish pub. Ronzelli, handled both the Polish and Italian crowd, but on different nights. Both bars served mainly the guys who worked in the town's two remaining working paper mills.

The Barn, under the Hotel Windom, was the fashion spot where couples went to drink sociably. World War I, and World War II veterans, drank at the Legion. Korean War veterans, and guys who really got into the shit in World War II, seemed to avoid the Legion. Catholic professionals, doctors, and lawyers, and management types, drank at the K of C. Protestant professionals were mostly Masons, and drank at the Masonic Lodge. Of course, there were Moose, and Elks, and Italian-Americans, and Polish-Americans, Sons of Erin, and half a dozen other social clubs, where small, close-knit groups got together, got soused, and talked about the "old country." Rick figured that all his father needed was a *Scottish-American Club*, and he'd never come home. He had a momentary image of his father, deep in his cups, singing old Harry Lauder songs in his high nasal voice that sounded like a half-in-the-bag, bagpipe. He shuddered.

The *Brow*, was where farmers from the outlying towns drank when they came to town. The proprietor was Caliph Brower, who had run a marginal dairy farm for forty years out in Westminster. Then, Kearn Hatten, the school for problem kids, had to expand, and offered Brower more money for his land than he had earned in all forty years combined. He took it, and bought a bar just off the square, on Westminster Street. It was right next to Firestone Hardware, which carried a lot of tractor parts, and other specialized farm hardware. The farmers, or *woodchucks*, as the *townies* called them, had never had their own drinking spot. They took to The Brow, like a duck to water.

While Rick had been by The Brow a thousand times, he had never been inside. He knew he would not be welcome, and frankly, there was nothing in The Brow he was interested in. But Jack, particularly Jack with his guitar, was welcome everywhere. And Jack's repertoire ranged from blues to bluegrass, and from folk to country and everywhere in between. You never had to ask him to play twice.

"Pretty good crowd for a Monday," Jack said, as he lifted his guitar from the jump-seat. They had to park down past the Post Office.

"I wonder what brings all those boys into town?" Rick mused.

"Baseball game, I think. I think the Legion team is running some kind of tournament, and Saxon River and Grafton both sent teams."

"So, they're either celebrating, or crying in their beer," Rick said.

But they weren't doing either. They were talking. They were making angry little speeches about "that kind," and "them going back to where they came from."

The room was filled with smoke, and Rick lit up as much in self-defense as for want of a cigarette. Jack didn't smoke, and Rick usually didn't smoke around him. .

"Join the cancer crowd," Jack said.

Rick didn't answer. He squinted through the smoke, trying to make out who was there. They were mostly young, in their twenties, big, raw-boned farm boys, who had been doing a man's job since they were seven, or eight years old. A thin, hatchet-faced man, with dark hair, was sitting among the hefty, blond farmers. "Gorse is here," Rick said.

"Whatchadrinkin' boys?" Caliph Brower was standing over them.

"Beer," Jack said. "What's got on draft?"

"Ballentine and Gansett," Brower said. "'Bout you?"

Rick waved. "Nothing, thanks."

"Shit. Got a Budweiser?" Jack asked.

"You got a buck?" Brower countered.

Jack threw a five on the table.

"I'd let ya play for draft beer," Brower said. "But the bottled stuff costs me too much money."

"They don't look like they're much in the mood for music," Rick said. "What's going on?"

"Oh, that little weasel, Gorse, has the boys riled about the nigger who blew up the union guy. Shit, most of these guys never even seen a nigger. But now they think they got to save their women folk from the *black hoard*."

Brower went to get Jack's beer. Just then, the three Allard boys got up and started for the door.

"Where you guys going?" somebody hollered.

"Haying tomorrow. Can't spend the night drinking, and worrying about niggers. You boys take care of it." The three Allards headed out the front door.

Losing three guys let the air out of the crowd. Pretty soon, others were making their excuses, and heading out. Gorse was getting agitated.

"Bunch of you guys don't care if them black turds ruin your women," he snarled.

"I see him out my way, I'll run a fork through'm," Grant Driscoll said. But he don't come on my property, so I guess I don't got no call to get excited." He and his brother and their hired man got up and headed for the door.

"You drinking any more, Gorse?" Brower yelled.

"Gimme another," Gorse whined.

"You ain't gonna have one of yer diabetes things, are ya?"

Gorse was nodding, slumping down in his chair.

"Shit. Better call the ambulance. That sonofabitch is always forgetting that drinking knocks him for shit. His diabetes don't care for alcohol, at all." Brower went over to the phone and dialed.

"That's all for tonight, I guess," Rick said. "Damn, I have to get some sleep, too. Probably going to have to actually work tomorrow. None of this chauffeuring stuff."

Jack left half a beer on the table.

"Not tonight," he said as they got in the car. "But it could happen. It really could happen."

"'Fraid so," Rick answered. He wondered what the hell he, a twenty-year-old boy, could do about it. He felt like a lone reed, trying to hold back a wave.

Chapter 24

Strong

It was a hot and sticky night. Rick couldn't sleep, so he took his pillow out onto the porch roof and smoked. He wondered if Jack had made up the story about the funeral. You could never tell with Jack. Damn, but he wanted it to be true. I guess that proved that Jack was pure entertainer.

He thought about the whole deal with the explosion, and Whitey being the prime suspect. Something was screwy, but he just didn't know what. He wondered if he should call Avery or Redman, and tell them about Jensen threatening the Tycoon. He figured they'd just blow him off. But shit, if they didn't know, and it was important and he didn't tell, then what?

Birds were chirping. Rick shook himself awake. "Probably about 5:15, or so," he thought. It was still hot and sticky. He got up, and crawled back in through the window, glad he had the room to himself now, and didn't have to put up with complaints from his older brother, Steve. He pulled on his work clothes, and went downstairs to make coffee and a lunch. By six, he was out the door.

He stopped for a couple of buck's worth of gas. Looking at his wallet, he realized this Chevy was costing him about five times what the scooter cost to run. He might have to cut back on his cigarettes. He shuddered.

He didn't know how he could get through a day of construction without cigarettes.

Driving to the job, he could see that the day was going to be overcast, one of those endless days without the sun when you lose track of time.

The yard was already busy. He parked, and headed over to the dynamite truck. Blaster Bill was leaning against the truck.

"What's up Bill? Lot of activity this morning." Rick tossed his lunch-bucket in the truck.

"Big inspection coming. State guy, Strong and his crew, are going to be here on Monday. Everybody's scared shitless he's going to shut the job down." Bill munched on a doughnut and slurped some coffee. "You're not on this crew today. Cashman said Ding and Dong quit, and you're back working for Henry."

"Okay," Rick said, and grabbed back his lunch-bucket. "Just me? I'm doing both Henry and Côte?"

"Nah. I think that Hennessy kid is taking care of Côte. The Duke threw him off the fill 'cause he made a puddle or something."

Rick went back to his car and drove carefully up the right-of-way. He crossed over to the southbound lane, and followed a dirt track around to the abandoned quarry where the drillers were parking. Côte's beat-up '48 Ford coup, and Henry's pristine '57 Fairlane, were both parked in the shade. Rick pulled his Chevy in next to Henry's car, and noted that his was the same year. "Not bad," he said out loud. Grabbing his lunch-bucket, he hiked up over the hill to where the compressors were parked. He slid his bucket in under the compressor, and poured himself a half-cup of coffee. He was glad to be back on the drilling crew.

"Well, here's fucking *Dick Tracy*. Where's the cops, Squirt?" Henry growled. He was unwrapping his first cigar of the day.

"Hey, Henry. You chase off Ding and Dodd?"

"Nah. Them guys was union plants. The union sent'm somewhere else. You know this other *dumb college fuck* that's coming up here?"

"Yeah, Mike Hennessy. He's my shirttail cousin by marriage or something. He's okay. A bit spaced out, but he'll work hard."

"Not too concerned with getting to work on time, is he?" Côte said. He tossed the remainder of his coffee on the ground. "Going to be a coffee day. Hot, and dark."

"Like you like your women," Henry growled.

"Oh, I like my women any way I can get'm. Course, I don't get many. Not near enough." Côte laughed. "Any way but fat." He wiggled his square butt and sang, "I don't want her, you can have her, she's too fat for me. She weighs two hundred and ninety-three. That's way...oh, lookie here. Here's our new boy."

Mike Hennessy came trudging over the hill, hauling a picnic-hamper-sized lunch-bucket. Mike was about six-foot-one, well built, and had a perpetually perplexed look on his face, as if life was always one step ahead of him.

"Hi," he said. He put his lunch-bucket under the compressor. "What do I do?"

"Well, you come with me," Côte said. "I'll show you. That's some lunch-pail you got there. You get a little hungry, do ya?"

"Come on, Dick Tracy. This ain't a fuckin' police job. Let's throw some steel." Henry relit his cigar, grabbed his grade-stake, and hiked up the hill. Rick followed along, pulling on his gloves.

About ten minutes later, Mike came over and asked, "What time is it?"

Rick looked at his watch. It was exactly 7:10. "Bit passed seven. You forget your watch?"

"Lost it. Damn, this day is dragging." Hennessy went back and stood by Côte.

Five minutes later, Rick was walking over to bring Côte a sharpened bit, and he heard Mike asking Côte what time it was. Côte was reaching for his watch, and Rick hollered out, "Nearly 8:00." Côte pulled out his watch, gave it a double take, and looked up at Rick. Rick raised an eyebrow and grinned.

Côte said, "Seems about right."

Rick passed the word on to Henry. Every time Mike asked the time, they added another half-hour to forty-five minutes. By eight o'clock, they were telling Mike it was five minutes to sandwich break. "We're working through," Henry growled. "They got way behind and want us to work through. Grab a sandwich on the run if you want."

The day was heavy, hot, and stayed gray. Mike had eaten two of his sandwiches, and consumed about a gallon of water before 9:00 A.M. He had no feel for how long it should take to drill a hole. They were positioned so they couldn't see any of the trucks or belly pans. "What time is it?" He asked for about the fifteenth time.

"Nearly noon," Rick said, looking at his watch. "This next bit of time will drag. Always does right before lunch."

Mike asked two or three more times before ten. At ten, Côte said, "Quick lunch now. They won't be shutting down. Trying to make-up time."

The crew went down and poured a cup of coffee. Henry ate half a sandwich. Côte had a little fruit pie. Rick had a Devil Dog. Mike ate two more sandwiches and a huge piece of cake, washed down with a quart of pop. "You guys don't eat much," he commented.

"Yeah, trying to hold down my weight," Rick said.

"Too damn hot," Henry groused.

"Saving it for dinner," Côte said. "Running short this week and got to make my pennies last."

They were back at work at 10:10. Mike kept asking the time, and they kept advancing the day. "You know this doesn't drag near as much as standing down on the fill," Mike commented. It was eleven A.M. Henry had just told Mike it was "pretty near three."

They drilled another hole, and repositioned the drill. Rick checked his watch. Almost noon. He pulled off his gloves, "About enough for one day, don't you think?"

"I don't know," Côte said. "Give me a bite to eat, and I can probably put in another full day. Whaddya think, big fella?"

"Nah, I want to go home," Mike said. "This is harder work than running the hose, and I'm tired."

"That so?" Henry laughed. They could hear the air horns as the Euclids shut down for lunch. About that time, the sun peeked through the overcast for the first time. "They might only pay you for half-a-day if you leave now." He laughed.

"What the?…" Mike looked up at the sun and then at Rick, Côte, and Henry, who were laughing and slapping their legs. "You…you…shit. What time is it? Is it only noon? Damn you guys."

"I think I'm going to call you *Quick Time!*" Côte laughed. "Does a full day's work in just half-a-day. That ain't too smart. They still just pay you for the time you work, not how much you get done. You'd never make in the union, Quick Time."

"I even ate all my lunch," Mike groaned. "Jeez Louise. You are mean bastards." Then he laughed. "Teach me to lose my watch, I guess."

Rick was still chuckling when he found a place in the shade to sit. He knew that Mike would plot and scheme till he got even, but damn, that was a good joke. There weren't many people who would fall for that joke, only a *dumb college fuck*. Of course, Mike wasn't exactly a *dumb college fuck*. He had dropped out of Keene Teacher's College, and enlisted in the Navy. He was due to report pretty soon.

"What's all the hullabaloo down on the fill?" Henry asked, as he parked his carcass under a tree up near the top of the ledge. From there he could look down the valley, and get a pretty good view of the entire job.

"Big inspection," Mike said. "State guy, Bob Strong is bringing his crew out on Monday. They're going to test sample the fill."

"How come?" Côte asked. "I thought they tested that all the time."

"They do," Mike answered. "But the reason I got shit-canned down there was I ran the water too long in one spot. It dug a hole, and there was wood in the hole."

"Wood? How much wood? We talking a stick, or a tree? And how the fuck did there get to be wood in the fill?" Henry chewed down on his cigar.

Mike shrugged. "I don't know. The Duke looked in the puddle I made, and saw a stick. He pulled on it and it was connected to a 2×4. I think they're going to bulldoze the whole fill to find out if that's all."

"Shit. They don't want to do that." Henry stood up. "Squirt, tie two pieces of steel on the side of the compressor. We'll go down there and show'm how to test."

Rick and Henry had his rig off the hill and hooked up to the compressor, ready to roll by 12:30. They were stowing the rest of the gear to one side, when PH drove up to drop off their fresh water jugs.

"What the hell are you doing?" He screamed at Henry.

"What the fuck do you care?" Henry grinned and spat a wad of cigar end at PH's feet. "I'm taking this down to the fill to bore test. I hear they found wood."

"Who the fuck told you to do that?"

"Nobody. I just figured it was a whole fuck of a lot cheaper than scraping off the entire top to see if there was more wood down there."

"You don't go anywhere less I tell you. You hear me? That's fuckin' Duke's problem. I got ledge to blast."

At that moment, John Cashman drove up. He jumped out. "Ah, I see you thought of it before I could ask," he said to PH. "Take her down, Henry. Duke's setting up a grid."

PH hooked his thumbs in his belt and pushed out his chest. "Yep, that's how we do it in Texas. I told these boys it took first priority."

Henry almost swallowed his cigar. His face turned red, and he was about to scream a profanity, when he caught John's eye. He smiled. "Yes, sir. Our man PH, he knows his shit." Henry gunned the air track and the big compressor wagon lurched, almost knocking PH down. "Clear the way," Henry hollered. "Coming through. PH said 'Do it!' We gotta get it done."

They wound their way slowly off the hill and down across the fill. Henry drove, walking behind the air track, and sometimes riding on the wagon-tongue. Rick walked behind, feeling like a pioneer crossing the Great Plains. His job was to make sure the thick air-hose didn't get fouled under the compressor.

When they came off the hill, they could see a group standing around, out on the leading edge of the fill. A small dozer had pushed back a mound of fill. As they got closer, the Duke separated himself from the pack, and waved them over to the south corner. Henry found a level spot, and parked the compressor. They unhitched, and Henry moved the drill over to where the Duke was pointing. Rick untied the two pieces of steel, grabbed his grease pot, and followed, staggering under the load.

"I don't know how that fucking wood got in there," the Duke was clearly upset. "Somebody must be coming in here at night, and digging holes and burying it. Then covering up good, so it looks the same. It's fucking sabotage, is what it is!"

"Don't suppose it was the same someone who called in Strong, do ya?" Henry asked as he positioned the boom.

"I don't know what to suppose. I can't figure out who would do it. Them other companies are winning more than their share. Why would they sabotage us?"

"Maybe it wasn't a company. Maybe it was the union." Henry suggested. He ran the drill straight down with little resistance. "Pretty much layer of gravel, layer of crushed rock, another layer of gravel, so far. No wood."

Rick hoisted up the next steel, and screwed it on. Henry ran it down too. "Same thing," he said. Rick put on the third steel.

"Should be about six to eight-feet more to bedrock," Duke said.

Henry ran the steel down. At six feet, it hit rock. "Right on the nuts." he said.

"Here's the grid," Duke said. "Drill every six feet, side-to-side. Back six feet, and then do it again, with the holes midway to the first row. Just like that, back and forth."

"Okay," Henry brought up the steel, and Rick unscrewed it.

"Mr. Duke?" Rick said.

"Yeah. What?"

"Wouldn't it help if you had one of Strong's guys out here? I mean, you may have to do this all over again, Monday."

Duke looked at Rick. "I don't want the State inspector thinking I'm salting my fill with goddamn wood. I..." Duke stopped. "You're right. I'll send somebody down to call him. Keep drilling Henry."

"You're pretty ballsy. What made you think of that?" Henry asked.

"Strong is a family friend. I know he wouldn't take *God's* word that the fill was okay, if it had been called into question. In fact, he'd wonder what the fuck we were doing drilling these holes. He's a pretty suspicious guy."

Sure enough, they had drilled four holes, when Strong himself drove out on the fill in a green pickup, emblazoned with the Vermont State Seal. First thing he did, was point Henry back to where they had drilled the first hole. He marked off three feet, and had Henry drill the same pattern, but three feet over. The results were the same.

With no solid rock resistance, the drilling went fast, and Rick was kept hopping, greasing steel, putting it on, and taking it off. While he worked, he watched Strong talking with Duke and John. Charlie was also out on the fill. He was clearly agitated. Duke showed Strong the wood they found. He was waving his arms, and they were shouting at one another. From the hand motions, it looked like Strong was suggesting peeling back a layer or two of fill.

Henry shut down the drill. "Wood," he hollered. They were about thirty feet from the front edge of the fill, and about dead center. Strong came running over, closely followed by Duke, Charlie, and John. Henry ran the drill back up the boom. They were on the first steel. "About eight-feet deep," he said. Splinters were clinging to the drill bit. No question, it was wood.

"Drill me a circle 'round this," Strong said. " Move out two feet. If you're still hitting wood, two feet more."

Henry backed the air track up a bit, and repositioned the boom. He ran the drill down, and hit wood at the same depth. He ran it back up, backed off another two feet, and drilled again. This time, it ran straight down without hitting resistance.

"Fuckin' piece of plywood, ain't it?" Henry observed. He moved the drill over and drilled two feet from the first hole. Again, he hit wood. Two feet more, and he hit nothing.

"Get a backhoe here and let's dig this," Strong ordered in his raspy voice. "We got to get it out. You go back and keep drilling the grid."

By the time Ken Harrow got his backhoe out on the fill, and had scooped out enough dirt to expose the plywood, Henry and Rick had finished drilling the grid with no more hits. Ken snagged the plywood with the end of the bucket, and tossed it up on the fill. "Half-a-sheet." he hollered.

Strong pointed him to where they first hit wood. Ken maneuvered the backhoe over, and scooped out the hole. Two 2×4's, and a small stump were tossed up on the fill.

Henry and Rick walked over to Strong, and the other bosses.. "Didn't hit nothing else," Henry said.

"Doesn't mean there isn't more of it. Itty-bitty pieces like this, you could have missed, " Strong said. "Still, they ain't much of a risk. All these pieces at about the same depth?"

"I'd say so." Henry said. "About eight feet, give or take a foot."

"Two-days fill," Duke said. "That means if they weren't buried too deep, they was probably buried over the weekend."

"We got the call, Monday," Strong said. "Said you guys were burying all kinds of trash. Wouldn't give a name. Said he was worried 'cause it could ruin the road and the bridge."

"You know me better than that, Bob. I don't bury nothing but good fill."

"I do know you, Duke. I know you piss some people off, from time-to-time. Who hates you enough to sabotage your job?"

"I don't know, Bob. I'm racking my brains, but I've hardly even yelled at anybody. Well, except for a couple of college kids. Like, Wallace here."

Strong looked over at Rick, "This your work, Rick?"

"No way, man. I just thread the steel. Besides, who would dig a hole like that if they weren't getting paid for it? My guess is, that it's somebody who can use a bulldozer."

"Makes sense," John Cashman chimed in. "If it weren't pretty smooth, Duke would've noticed the disturbance."

"Last I knew, they weren't letting us dumb college fucks anywhere near a bulldozer." Rick looked at Charlie.

"Damn, right. Damn, right. You guys bust enough stuff as it is. Strong, what are you doing about this? Somebody's sabotaging my job. This is going to cost me a lot of down-time, and down-time is money."

Bob Strong glared at Charlie. "Be glad I don't make you dig the whole fuckin' thing up, Charlie. I could, y'know. Maybe I even should."

Charlie turned white as a sheet. "Uh, no offense, Bob. I…"

"But, I won't. I think we got it all. And if we don't, it sure isn't anything big that'll rot and leave a cavity, and cause something to collapse. But I want you to post a guard. If you don't, we're going to do this same thing every Monday morning. You got that?"

"You coming back Monday?" Cashman asked.

"No need. This is what that yahoo wanted me to see. I've seen it. Let's see if we can figure out who's behind it." Strong scratched his head, tilting his white helmet forward. "How about the union, Charlie. Think they could've done it because you blew up their boy?"

"Goddamnit. I didn't blow up that sonofabitch. I wish I had. But somebody else did me that favor. I ever find out who, I'll shake his hand. That man was a damn pirate. Threatened me with the fuckin' Mafia. Me. Can you believe that? You think it was the union?"

"I don't know," Strong said. "It's just, the union would think of something like this, and they can be nasty enough. But I don't know what they got to gain here. If *you* lose money, how do they make money?"

"I go out of business, a union company gets this job. Could be. Sonsofwhores."

"Seems far fetched to me. You fire anybody Charlie?"

"Hell no. I should fire the whole lot of 'm. Look at that. We're three weeks behind!"

"You want I should call the cops in?" Strong looked at John.

"Not if you can help it. Them cops have cost us a good week so far. Charlie's sending our best dozer up to Granby, cost us the other two."

Charlie's face got red. He started to say something, and then turned and walked back to the truck he had driven up on the job.

"Get back up on the hill, boys," John Cashman said to Henry. "And thanks for thinking of this. We at least got one problem solved."

Bob Strong headed for his pickup. He stopped and turned. "I will probably run an extra test or two from time-to-time. And I won't be giving you any warning." He climbed in his truck and headed off the fill.

Chapter 25

Mora

As Rick was leaving the job that night, he saw Avery and Redman by the office, getting into their car. Rick hesitated for a moment, and then stopped. He walked over.

"Uh, Officer Redman, you got a second?" he asked.

"Oh, it's you, Wallace. What do you want, kid?"

"Uh, it's probably nothing, and you're probably going to tell me to mind my own business, but the other day something happened that might be important. I don't know that it is, but it might be."

"Spit it out kid. I want to get home to my old lady. She's baking a ham tonight. Ham and potato salad are my summer favorites."

"Yeah, well. You know the Tycoon?"

"You mean Mr. Duque? Yeah, we know him."

"Well, I was talking to him the other day, and he said Jensen stopped and threatened him. Said he had to make the rail crews union, or the union would shut down the Tycoon's fruit factories."

"Yeah, so?"

"Well, I just thought that if Jensen was making stops and threatening people, there might be other people who wanted to kill him, you know? I mean, it makes as much sense as Whitey."

"Hmm, maybe. We'll look into it. See ya around."

"Yeah, right. Sorry I wasted your time." Rick turned and started back to his car.

"Hey, kid! Come back here. We do look into the stuff you tell us, ain't that right Avery? Hell, we chased down the guy whose job Whitey took."

Rick looked puzzled. "What guy?"

"You're the one that told us. When Whitey fixed the backhoe out on Route 103."

"Oh. Oh, yeah. Stew, something or other. I don't even remember what he looked like. You found him?"

"Yeah, we got his name from your timekeeper, and I thought I recognized it. Stewart Ferguson. We busted him a couple of years ago for running a chop shop in his brother's car dealership.

"Ferguson Ford? No shit. That's where Gorse works. The guy who's agitating against Whitey."

"Yeah, well this Ferguson did a little time. He's out now. Nobody knows where he is. They haven't seen him at Ferguson Ford, and they don't want to see him. He cost them big-time."

"Huh. Who would have thought? But, you don't know where he is, huh?"

Avery handed over a picture. "You see him, let us know."

Rick took the picture and stared at it. "Wow, put a beard on that guy, and he's Theobold Magus, the preacher who's holed up with the Tycoon."

"You sure about that?" Redman sounded excited.

"Yeah, and I didn't tell you. But when Jensen threatened the Tycoon, this Magus guy looked at Jensen's car, and said that it was just like the one Kennedy got shot in. He suggested Jensen might be in for some big trouble."

"Now, that sounds serious. Why didn't you say anything?"

"I just figured, you know, the dynamite came from here. How would this preacher guy get our dynamite?"

"Could be from his cousin who works here." Avery said.

"His cousin?"

"Yeah, that guy Harris you guys call PH. He's a cousin of some kind."

"They tell you that somebody tried to sabotage the job here?" Rick asked.

"Yeah. Cashman said not to worry about it. He had it under control and was going to post a guard."

"Wonder if there is any connection?" Rick mused.

"Don't know. But we'll ask this Magus guy when we talk to him. And I think we'll do that sooner, rather than later."

"Shit. There goes my ham and potato-salad dinner," Redman groused.

Rick's head was spinning as he drove home. Maybe Whitey was off scot-free. Maybe the Tycoon would be rescued from that blood-sucking Magus. He'd hunt up Jack, except he was taking Ellen to the movies. Maybe he'd catch Jack, tomorrow.

"We're all too hot to eat," his mother hollered as he came through the door. "Fix yourself whatever you want." She and his father were sitting in the living room, drinking Tom Collins cocktails. They were snacking on cheese and crackers.

"Okay by me," Rick said, grabbing a beer and heading up for a bath. He never minded missing a meal at home. There probably wasn't a worse cook in town than his mother.

After his bath, he rummaged in the refrigerator. There, among the layers of mold and unidentifiable leftovers, was a new package of hot dogs. He grabbed two, and tossed them in a pot to boil. He cracked another beer, and stood in the doorway to the living room while he waited for his dogs to cook.

"You know that crazy preacher up in the Tycoon's rail yard? He's Floyd Ferguson's brother, Stewart. Used to work for DeBoni. Did some time for running a stolen car operation out of Ferguson Ford's body shop."

"Those Ferguson's are all scum," Rick's mother said with conviction. "Look at all they give poor George to do. Just pushes broom."

"You know George Gorse?"

"He was in my high school class. We even went out for a while." His mother smiled. "He can be real sweet."

"Huh," Rick said. "Not the Gorse I know. He's out there trying to talk the woodchucks into lynching Whitey."

"Well, he has a thing against the Negroes. He lived in Texas for a year or two, and I guess things are different down there."

Rick's hotdogs were boiling. He shut off the stove, and grabbed a couple of slices of bread, some mustard, and some relish from the refrigerator. At least, the relish was supposed to be green. "Probably getting my share of penicillin," he muttered. "I'm off to take Ellen to the movies. See you later." He left without waiting for an answer.

Driving out to Ellen's farm, Rick could feel himself getting excited. Maybe Ellen would rather park somewhere than see the movie. He wondered vaguely whether she had had her period yet.

He thought about his mother, and her teenage relationship with Gorse. "Ugh," he said out loud. "Imagine having that sonofabitch for a father." He wondered what his mother could have ever seen in the guy. They were like polar opposites. His mother was a fun-loving liberal. Gorse was a mean-minded bigot. He didn't get it.

He turned onto Ellen's road, and there she was, sitting by the side of the road. She waved at him.

"Hey, hi there, Miss. Would you like a ride?" Rick grinned at her. But Ellen wasn't grinning. In fact, she was crying. "Oh. What's the matter, Hon? What's wrong?"

Ellen climbed into the front seat beside him. "Back up," she sobbed. "I don't want my mother to see me."

Rick did as he was told, and then took the other fork heading for Springfield. Ellen slid over by him, and clutched his arm. "What's going on?" Rick asked.

Ellen said nothing for a while. Then she pointed to a side lane that went up over the hill, into one of the remote fields. Rick carefully turned onto the track, and followed it up and into a small stand of trees, on the top of the ridge. When he was sure they couldn't be seen from the road, he stopped and turned off the car. He took Ellen into his arms and held her, saying nothing, waiting for her to tell him the problem in her own time and in her own way.

"Sh-sh-she says I can't see you anymore." Ellen sobbed. "She says I have to go out with this g-guy from Harvard. She says y-you're not good enough."

Rick hugged her tightly. "She's right about that, Ellen. I'm not good enough for you. You deserve the best. All I've got is love." Rick chuckled. "That sounds like a teeny-bopper song, doesn't it? All I've got is love, dah, dah, dah, dah, dah."

"Rick be serious," Ellen wailed. "She means it. And wait till she finds out I missed my period."

"You what?"

"Well, I'm late. It's only a couple of days. Maybe it's nothing."

"But you don't think it's nothing."

"No. I'm as regular as a clock. I think I'm pregnant." Ellen tried to pull away, but Rick hugged her fiercely.

"Good," he said.

"Oh, how can you say good? It changes my whole life."

"Yeah, It makes it, *our* life. Don't you see? We have to get married, quick. Then, your mother can't do anything."

"But Rick, we're still in college. We don't have any money. How would we live?"

"I'll get a job. I'll get two jobs. We'll survive."

"Y-you'd do that for me?"

"I'd do that for us! And, for little junior, too!" He patted Ellen's tummy. "Hmm, I get horny just thinking about it. It'll be beautiful! You're beautiful!" He ran his hand over her stomach, slipping it into her shorts. In a moment they were touching and stroking each other. He took her by the hand, led her out of the front door, and into the back of the car. They made passionate love, and then lay naked in each other's arms.

They watched the moon rise through the back window. "Beats going to a movie," Rick said.

"Rick we've got to tell her. She'll be furious." Ellen found her clothes on the floor, and began dressing.

"Yeah, I suppose so," Rick said. "To tell you the truth, she scares me shitless." He found his underwear on the floor, pulled them on, and then groped around for his shorts and shirt.

"You? You don't have to live with her. She's been trying to run my life my whole life."

"Yeah, why does she do that? Do all mothers do that with their daughters?"

"Some, I guess. But my mom is a special case. She's just weird."

"Well, if we have a girl, I don't want you running her life. She gets to be her own person, okay?"

"Hah. Fat chance. I'll take her to all the social affairs, and hook her up with a doctor or a lawyer." Ellen laughed. "But maybe I'm not even pregnant."

"I think you are." Rick took her hands in his. "I think you are, and I think it's a boy. The next one will be the girl."

"What are you, a witch doctor? I need to go see a real doctor and be sure."

"Tell me when and where. I'll be there."

"No, this I have to do myself."

Ellen snuggled up close to him, as Rick backed the car around and eased his way down the dirt track to the road. They said nothing as they drove back to Ellen's house. As they got close, she said, "You could let me off, and I could walk home from here."

Rick was tempted. He dreaded facing Mora, but he said, "No let's drive right up. If she's there in the kitchen, we'll tell her." He continued on and pulled into the yard.

"Lights are off," Ellen said. "Maybe she went out, or to bed."

"Maybe. I'll walk you to the door."

He came around, opened her door, and took her hand. They walked slowly to the house. They stopped at the stoop, and embraced. Suddenly, they were blinded by the glare, as the outdoor spotlights came on, all at once.

"Get in this house!" Mora screamed. "Get in this minute! You get out of here, Rick Wallace, and stay away. We don't want you here."

Rick was stunned by the outburst. Ellen was trembling, violently. He put his arm around her, and held her close. They didn't move from the step.

"Did you hear me, you Catholic trash? I said, get out of my yard or I'll call the police." Myra throw open the door. She was in her robe and slippers. Her hair was wild, and her eyes red.

Rick and Ellen held each other and didn't move.

"Get out! Get Out! I'll get Edgar's gun!"

"Mora," Rick said. "Mora we have something to tell you."

"I don't want to hear anything you have to say! Leave my daughter alone. Get your hands off her."

"Mother." Ellen spoke quietly. "Mother, we're getting married."

"You are, like hell! Over my dead body! You are not throwing away your life on this piece of Papist shit!"

"Mom, I'm probably pregnant!" Ellen stamped her foot. "We love each other, and we're getting married and that's it." Rick had never seen her so forceful.

Neither, apparently, had Mora. She was speechless. She looked from one to the other, and wailed, "Oh, God. Where did I go wrong?"

"What'nthehell is going on out here with all this racket?" Edgar was standing there in his T-shirt and undershorts. "Mora will you leave these kids alone so I can get some sleep?"

"She's pregnant. That bastard has been *fucking* her. They're going to get married. All my plans, wasted. Oooh, God." Mora collapsed in a kitchen chair, weeping.

"Oh, damn. Get in here, you two. Let's figure out what's going on." Edgar waved them into the kitchen, and Rick and Ellen meekly followed orders. "Sit," he said. And they sat.

"All right, you, daughter. What's this about being pregnant?"

"Daddy," Ellen began to cry. "D-daddy, I'm not sure. But my p-period is l-late. So, probably."

"I take it you two know what causes that?" Edgar glared at Rick.

"Y-yes sir. B-but we're in l-love. We're going to get married."

"Dirty, filthy, scum!" Mora raged.

"Now, Mora." Edgar held up his hand. "It's only pure luck, that *you* weren't knocked up at thirteen, with all the fellas you took for a roll in the hay. When I first went to work for your dad, every farm kid in the county told me that I should catch you in the milk parlor. They said you had the best milk-maiden's hands in town."

"Oh, you…you…shit! You horrible, horrible, shit!" Mora fled from the room, screaming.

Rick and Ellen sat there, stunned. Edgar turned back to them. "All right. You don't have to get married if you don't want to. You can have the baby taken care of one way or another, if you don't feel you're ready for this."

"Daddy, no!" Ellen was aghast.

"Just telling you your options. We aren't going to get out the shotgun. How about you, Rick. You have any second thoughts?"

"N-no, sir. It's what I want. I want this child."

"It's going to be tough," Edgar warned. "We got no money to support you. Don't suppose your folks do either, Rick."

"No, sir. But we can do it. I can work while I'm finishing school. My folks will still pay for school, I think."

"You tell them yet?" Edgar asked.

"Not yet. Tonight, I guess, if they're up."

"Okay by me. Next thing. You should just get married, *quick*. Don't plan any big thing. If you get it done, your mother will get over it.

Especially, when she has a grandkid to hold. But if you give her time to plan, she'll do her best to screw it up."

Rick and Ellen looked at each other. They nodded.

"Get it done, and you can use the little house until you're ready to head north." Edgar was talking about the small hired hand's house, down where the farm bordered the railroad track.

"Ralph quit yesterday." Edgar said, anticipating their question. "Going down south to Massachusetts, to live with this sister."

Edgar stood, and looked at Rick, "Now get the hell out of here, son. I got cows to milk at 5 A.M. Ellen, get off to bed. Make a doctor's appointment, tomorrow."

Rick and Ellen stood. He held her hands, and looked into her eyes.

"Now! Damn it! Now!" Edgar snapped.

Rick laughed, and said, "See you tomorrow."

He felt like he was walking on air as he skipped to the car, jumped in, and backed out of the yard. He thought he heard Mora screaming as he drove away, but he didn't stop. He had to work tomorrow as well, plus, he had a whole lot of new responsibilities.

As he drove home, the enormity of the life-change swept over him. "Damn," he said. "A father. Me. Damn." He began to make mental lists of all the things he had to do, and do quickly.

There was a light on in the front room. His mother was sitting up, smoking and reading. A glass of red wine sat at her elbow. "Good movie?" she said.

"Uh-didn't go." Rick said. He sat on the arm of an easy chair.

"His mother looked up, "She pregnant?"

"How-how did you know?"

"You think I'm some kind of a *stupe*? Anybody could see that starting a few weeks ago you were up to something new."

"We don't know for sure. I think she's going to make a doctor's appointment tomorrow."

"You tell her folks?"

"Yeah, tonight."

"How'd Mora take it? No, don't tell me. She had a *shit fit*, right?"

"Wow, did she. But, Edgar was okay. He pretty much shut her up. He told us we could live in the little house till we headed back to college."

"Rick. You don't have to get married." His mother took a drag on her cigarette and crushed it out in the overfilled ashtray. "You're young. You've got your whole life ahead of you. You don't have to tie yourself down, now."

"Mom, I want to. I can feel the energy of this. It gives me purpose. I was just hanging around school, drinking, thinking of ways to avoid going into the army. Now, I got to make something of myself."

"It'll be hard, Rick. We'll pay for your school, and maybe help out on rent. But you're pretty much on your own."

"I know, Mom. I know. It's scary, but it makes me feel, I don't know, like a man, I guess."

"Sleep on it. It's not too late to change your mind. You can be sure that Mora will be doing her damnedest to get Ellen to change her mind."

"I'll sleep on it. But I'm pretty sure I won't change my mind." Rick kissed his mother, and headed for the stairs. "You should sleep," he said.

"Sleep enough in the grave," she answered, and lit another cigarette.

Chapter 26

Mom

Time dragged by at an agonizingly slow pace. Rick had a lot on his mind. He and Ellen had to make an appointment for blood tests, and apply for a marriage license. He wanted to do that, even if Ellen wasn't pregnant. He talked to Ellen everyday, but she wouldn't let him come to the house.

That next weekend was July 4th, but Ellen wouldn't see Rick. She said that she and her mother were "working things out." Rick didn't know what that meant, but it frightened him. Ellen scheduled her pregnancy test for the following week. She didn't know if she would get the results before the weekend.

The job was in chaos. One thing after another went wrong. Guys were taking turns working as night watchmen, getting double time, but Rick figured most of them just found a good spot, and went to sleep.

Everyone knew that they were behind schedule, but still, nothing ever seemed to get done on time. Blaster Bill screwed up a shot, and they had to redrill it, losing two days. The hill they were carving for fill, suddenly turned to clay. They worked two days to scrape out the clay layer, and get back to the fill gravel they wanted. The clay would be useful elsewhere, so they stockpiled it. The whole exercise cost them two-and-a- half days.

Bob Strong was back to check once, and Henry and Rick hauled the air track down on the fill and drilled random test holes. They all checked out.

Over the fourth, two DeBoni truck drivers got in a fight at the Springfield firework's display. They were tossed in jail, and Charlie had to bail them out. One of the drivers skipped town immediately, leaving them a driver short. Squat John's kidney problem turned into kidney failure, and the flatbed driver died. That meant Crackers was snagged to transport equipment every couple of days, and that meant one belly pan was not in regular use.

Friday noon, July 11th, they were sitting under a tree, eating lunch. Côte summed up the situation. "You know," he said, "it's like the life-blood has drained out of this company. It looks like it's a company, but it's really just a corpse. Got no blood. No energy. Folks are just walking through the motions. They don't give a shit about doing a job right. They just want their paycheck and want to go home."

"That right?" Henry asked. "How about you?"

"Me too. I just want to go home and rub bellies with my old lady. How about you Squirt. You rubbing any bellies?"

Rick grinned. "Maybe one, or two."

Henry said, "Only belly he rubs is his own." He made an obscene jacking off gesture.

"Oh, don't pick on the boy, Henry. He found a good toy, and he wants to play with it. Hell, we all do that from time-to-time." He sang, "Hands in his pockets, big smile on the boy, wishing he could suck it, playing with his toy. Oh whack it, smack it, slam it in the door, cuff your old dumb brother, till you can't cuff him no more."

"You make that up?" Henry asked. "You ought be in Nashville."

"Speaking of pulling his pud," Côte gestured down the hill. PH was walking up, hands in his pockets, jiggling his change.

"Must have brass balls," Henry said. "I can hear them clanking."

As he came up to the group, PH pulled his hands out of his pockets, and his truck keys clattered to the ground. He didn't seem to notice, so Rick hollered, "Dropped your keys, Mr. Harris."

PH looked at him strangely, and then down on the ground. "Oh," he said, and picked them up. "We about got this redo drilled?" he asked Henry.

"It'll be done tonight, if we don't have some other kind of disaster."

"Yeah, well see that it is. And after this one, we're doubling up. Twice the size grid we've been doing. We are way the fuck behind."

"Ain't particularly smart," Henry opined. "Gives you a lot more chances to fuck up, and Blaster Bill still ain't quite got the hang of this. If he knew what he was doing, we wouldn't be drilling this one, twice."

"I'll design the shot." PH said.

"Well, that gives me a fuck of a lot of confidence," Henry snarled. "You know enough about dynamite to blow your nose?"

"Shut the fuck up, Baldridge. This is my ledge, and I'll blow the fucker the way I want. I don't need no advice from some two-bit farmer making extra pocket-money, by drilling holes in the rock."

"You're the man, PH." Henry smiled. There wasn't any humor or cama-raderie in the smile. It was more the kind of smile a dentist makes before he drills your tooth, Rick thought.

"See that you don't forget that." PH turned and walked down the hill, jingling his keys in his pocket.

"Admirable restraint, Henry," Côte said. "I thought you might just cold-cock the sonofabitch."

"Mr. P. fucking H., will get his soon enough," Henry growled. "I can wait."

The afternoon dragged on. Rick's cousin, now named *Quick Time*, seemed to be in a daze. Côte had to tap him with his grade-stake every time he wanted a new piece of steel mounted. Rick made a stupid mistake, and Henry backed the air track over a steel drill-shaft, bending it. Henry chewed his ass out royally. It was that kind of day.

It was 4:30 before Tim, the timekeeper came around with checks. "What took ya so goddamn long?" Henry growled.

"Shit, soon as I hand over the checks, guys are running for their cars. If I handed them out at noon, there wouldn't be nobody here." Tim headed back to his truck. "Remember, quitting time is 5:30, you guys," he hollered back over his shoulder.

"Wouldn't dare leave now," Côte yelled. "We'd be trampled in the rush."

Tim laughed.

"That's it. Last hole." Henry ran the drill up to the top of the boom, and Rick removed the steel. Henry ran the hammer back down, and picked up the last steel. "Might as well park this down in the old quarry. Blaster Bill will be shooting first thing, Monday morning."

Rick hauled the air-hoses clear, while Henry maneuvered the air track down to the compressor and hooked it up. "Wonder why they didn't just shoot this today," Rick said.

"They sent Blaster Bill off to Dupont dynamite school. The short course." Henry said. "Probably like pissing in the wind. Bill ain't too sharp."

While Henry and Côte pulled the compressors across the southbound right-of-way and down the path to where they had parked their cars, Rick and his cousin carried the steel over to the next section of ledge. "Long week, huh." Rick said.

"Damn, it was like a year. I almost wish you guys had kept up telling me that time was flashing by." Mike Hennessy grinned. "But this is it. I'm done. Going to Maine for a week, and then I report to Portsmouth Naval Base."

"Well, you're well trained for those long, boring days at sea," Rick said.

"Shit. Got to be more exciting than this."

Rick wished him well, and headed for his car. Henry and Côte were long gone. As he drove out of the quarry and headed back through the job, it was clear that Tim was right. There wasn't a soul left, except for

Everett. He was sitting on the hood of his pickup, sipping a cold beer. Rick stopped.

"Don't know enough to go home?" he hollered.

"I'm the watchman this weekend. Old Charlie's paying me to sit here and drink beer. Ain't nothing wrong with that." Everett grinned a gap-toothed grin. "Might make enough this year to take me down to *Floreeda*, this winter, instead of North Carolina. Stay warmer. Cold ain't no good for an old man's bones."

Rick waved, and headed on. He thought that Tim would be finding the cancelled checks from Everett's overtime pay sometime next March, if he was still only cashing his checks when he needed the money. On the other hand, maybe it was Everett taking the risk. This company might not still be in business when he got around to cashing his checks. Rick made a point of stopping and depositing his check at the Vermont National. With maybe a kid coming, he knew he had better start saving. He and Ellen sure weren't going to have the dough to go to Florida, this winter. They might not have the dough to buy an orange, *or* a grapefruit.

"Why the big frown?" his mother said, as he came in the kitchen door.

"Oh, nothing. Just thinking about how we'll make ends meet this year. It's pretty scary."

"I told you that you don't have to do this. It's too much to take on, at your age."

"Yeah, and I told you I was going to do it, and I am. But it's still scary. I mean, I got to grow up sometime. Look at Mike Hennessy. He's going into the Navy, next week."

"I hope they don't let him steer the ship," Rick's mother laughed. "They'll end up at the North Pole. Mike has the attention span of a two-year-old."

"I'm going to get Ellen. Maybe we can talk about the wedding and stuff, later."

"Well, there's not much to say, is there? You won't be expecting us to be there."

"No. We'll do it small and private. Hopefully, Judge Rubenstein will do it for us."

"Rubio, my Rubio." Rick's mother smiled. "Where fore art thou, Rubio? We did plays together you know. I had such a crush on him. He's so smart."

"When was that?" Rick asked.

"When you were little. I was a star. We had quite a group."

"Did Dad act?"

"Pffffph. Your father? Are you kidding? I tried to get him to write a play for the group, but he was busy building in those days. No time for frivolity. I love frivolity. Now, all he wants to do is drink beer, and watch TV. I had to practically break his arm to get him to take us to Maine this year."

"Maine? What's Maine?" Rick asked, getting a beer out of the refrigerator.

"We've rented a place on an island in Maine. We are all going. We're even taking TK. Willa would never go, unless we brought TK. But I want him there, too. That girl better be careful, or I'll steal TK right away from her."

"Right, Mom. He really would rather have a middle-aged woman, than a beautiful, young girl. Get serious."

"Don't make fun of your mother. I am serious. I know things Willa could never know. A mature woman makes a fine mistress. Read your Ben Franklin."

"You are as nutty as a fruitcake," Rick laughed. "Imagine the headlines. 'Old lady absconds with teenage daughter's boyfriend.'"

"Don't you call me an old lady." Rick's mother grabbed the broom, and swung it at him. He dodged, and ran through the dining room and up the stairs. He could hear his mother screaming something about being young and beautiful, as he closed the bathroom door and ran the tub.

Rick called Ellen before he left. She told him to pick her up at the end of the road. "My mother doesn't particularly want to see you," she said.

"Okay. Long as you want to see me."

"Yeah. I want to see you, Rick. I need to see you. I'm going crazy. Come quick."

Rick was out the door on the run. He jumped into his car, and tore out of the driveway, squealing to a stop at the stop sign at the end of his street, just as the town cruiser drove slowly by. Chickering was at the wheel, and gave him a hard look. Rick waved, and drove slowly through town, waiting until he hit the town line before he put the pedal to the floor.

He was at the end of Ellen's road in less than ten minutes. Even so, she was sitting there at the end of the road, head down, weeping.

"Ellen, Ellen are you alright?"

"No, I'm not all right. I'm pregnant."

"Yeah? Well, we thought you would be."

"Well, thinking, and being, are different. Do you know what kind of hell my mother is putting me through?"

"Baby, baby, come on. Get in the car. Let's get out of here. We got so much to do. So much to plan."

Ellen let herself be led into the car. Rick got back behind the wheel, and Ellen leaned against him. "She wants me to get an abortion, Rick."

"No way, Baby. We're getting married. That's my son, too."

"Oh, Rick, I'm so scared. She told me all kinds of horrible things about the baby being deformed and stuff. I'm so scared."

"Don't believe a word of it. She's angry. She's trying to hurt me, by hurting you. But you are of age. You don't need her *say so*. Ellen, you're an adult. I'm an adult. We can do this. We don't have to ask anybody."

"She's not going to pay for my college. She said, 'Education is wasted on a slut.'"

"Jesus. That woman has a mean mouth."

"Rick, will it be okay? Can we do this? You won't leave me, will you?"

"Never, Ellen. In my mind, we're already married, and marriage is forever."

"What do we need to do?"

"Well, here's the list I've got so far. First, we need to stop and see Judge Rubenstein, and ask if he'll perform the ceremony. We can do that tonight. Tomorrow, we should go see Doc Yeager, and have him do the blood tests. It will take about a week to get them back. When we get the tests, we can see Mrs. Cheney down at the Town Clerk's office, and get our license. Of course, it will then immediately be known, far-and-wide. Telling Mrs. Cheney is better than posting bans in the Church, or taking out an ad in the Bellows Falls Times. We can't afford a real honeymoon, but I'm thinking we can head up to Burlington and Winooski for the weekend, and find an apartment and maybe jobs. And you should check in at Mary Fletcher."

"You have been thinking. Oh, now I'm getting excited. Who will we have at our wedding?"

"Well, I think we should do it real small. You, and me. Do we need anybody else?"

"Of course, silly. We have to have witnesses. You need a best man, and I need a maid-of-honor. They'll be our witnesses. Who will you get?"

"Jeez, I don't know. Dieter is in Holland. Paul is in Turkey. I think Jack is still sweet on you. It would be cruel to ask him. Maybe Thad will be back. "

"Okay. All my friends are gone, too. I'd ask Lorie, but she has to live with Mom for a few more years. Mom would put her through hell. Maybe I'll ask Kelly. She's a friend, and I know she's around. She'd understand, too. I mean, she's pregnant, so she wouldn't, you know, think I was weird, or a slut, or anything."

"Uh, uh, Kelly?" Rick felt real uncomfortable with the thought of having the only other woman he'd ever made love to being his wife's maid-of-honor. "Uh, okay, I guess, if you can't think of anybody you'd rather have."

"Why? What's wrong with Kelly? Don't you like her?"

"Uh, sure. I like her, okay. No, Kelly's fine. I was just thinking after all she's been through, she might not want to. But ask her if you want."

They drove in silence for a few minutes.

"Before we see Judge Rubenstein, I'd like to introduce you to my grandfather."

"You have a grandfather in town? I didn't know that."

"Yeah, Tommy Mac—that's for McGuire. He's my mother's dad. They don't get along. That is, my mom doesn't acknowledge that Tommy Mac is alive. It's weird. Something to do with him abandoning her when she was little."

"Oh. Is he nice?"

"Yeah, he's great. It's just one of those weird things about my mom, that I'll never understand. Maybe all mothers are weird."

"Mine sure is. She had her heart set on me getting involved with that *creepo* from Harvard. That's what she dragged me to Boston for. I didn't tell you 'cause I didn't want to worry you. Man, was this guy stuck on himself."

"Probably worth a gazillion dollars. You could have lived high-off-the-hog."

"High-with-the-hog you mean. He was an insufferable pig, who thought his poop didn't smell. Oooh, it makes me mad just to think about him."

"Mine does."

"Does what?"

"Smell. Pretty ripe, actually. I've been known to stink everybody right out of the house. Why I remember…"

"Oh, Rick, you can be such a jerk."

They were laughing as they pulled up in front of Tommy Mac's place. Tommy was sitting on the porch, rocking and smiling. He waved to Rick as he got out of the car. "Don't get up Grampa. We'll come up."

When they got to the porch, Tommy was standing and smiling. "Well, now, the day I don't get up for a lovely *colleen*, will be the day they plant me. Introduce me to this vision of beauty, Rick."

"Grampa, meet my soon-to-be-wife, Ellen McCormick. We're just going over to see the Judge, and arrange for the wedding."

"A lucky man, you are Rick. So you're not of the Catholic persuasion, Ellen? Good. My wife was not, as well. I'm a firm believer that Catholics have way too much certainty about their position, and it's far better to leaven that with a little solid Protestantism." Then he whispered, "Don't go telling them down at the Sons of Erin I said that. They'll think I'm an *Orangeman*."

Ellen smiled, charmed by Tommy's immediate acceptance of her. He took her hands in his hands, and looked into her eyes. "So, you'll be expecting a little-one sometime shorter than nine months."

Ellen gasped. "How…how did you know?"

Tommy laughed. "Well, I'd like to tell you it was a special gift we Irish have. But truth be known, most of the people who go to see the Judge for a quick wedding, are in a family way. It's the nature of things. And don't you be embarrassed, lassie. It's the most natural thing in the world to make love to the man you love. It's what keeps the world going round, and gives Uncle Sam fodder for his cannons."

"I think it's going to be a boy," Rick said. "I don't know why I think that, but I do."

"Aye, I think you're right," Tommy cocked his head, and looked at Ellen out of one eye. "A boy it is."

"Maybe we'll name him Tommy," Rick said.

"Now, I'm flattered, boy, but I would be wishing, if it fits your want, to name the lad, *Timothy*. That was my boy's name. Timothy Patrick McGuire, poor wee lad. Taken by the fever before he saw his first birthday. I've always felt his spirit was around looking for a new home."

"I like Timothy," Ellen said. "I have an Uncle Tim, too. He's my Mom's brother, and my favorite uncle."

"I didn't know you had a son, Gramps. That means my mother had a brother," Rick said. "She's never mentioned him. Not even on Memorial Day, when she puts flowers on *Momma's* grave."

"Aye, well, she never knew him. He was first-born, and didn't live the year. And she never had a mother around to talk of him. I suppose she knows. But maybe she's forgotten." Tommy Mac looked sad, and frail. "She's good at forgetting people, my Maureen is."

They stood silently for a few moments. Then Tommy Mac gave another great sigh. "Come here lass, and give your new grandfather a great hug. Then you'd better be off to do your arranging."

Ellen put her arms around the old man, and hugged him close. Tommy gestured, and Rick came over and joined the hug. "God's speed, kids. Don't take any crap from anybody. You'll do just fine. Now, get out of here, and let an old man go to bed."

Rick and Ellen held hands and walked slowly up the street to Judge Rubenstein's house. His wife, Bonnie, was out, but the Judge was expecting them, and showed them into the parlor. "Not often I get to marry off the same guy twice in the same summer, Rick."

"What?" Ellen was taken aback by the off-hand remark.

"Oops. Sorry, I figured you knew that Rick stood in for Danny, him being indisposed at the time." Judge Rubenstein didn't look at all embarrassed by the slip of confidence.

"Rick?"

"Come on, Ellen. You were the one who asked me to help Kelly out. Somebody had to act as surrogate, so that she and Danny could be officially married. I was the guy who was there."

"Well, why didn't you tell me?" Ellen was distressed.

"Didn't think of it. Didn't seem that important. Why do you care?"

"It's...it's...I don't know. It just seems wrong. I don't know. It bothers me."

Rick put his arms around her. "Come on, Babe. It was just like being in a play. Judge, tell her. Please?"

"A pure formality. A live person must answer the questions and sign the documents for the marriage to be legal. Rick brought her here, so he was handy. Plus, we didn't want too many people knowing about this. I expect that's why Rick didn't say anything to you. The fewer people who know, the less chance somebody will complain, and we'll all have to go through some legal mumbo-jumbo to get back to the same result."

"Oh, I guess it's all right. But I'm sure not having Kelly as my bridesmaid."

"Okay with me." Rick breathed a sigh of relief. "She was your idea. I think you ought to ask Lorie. She'll do anything for you."

"To be a witness, the bridesmaid has to be eighteen or older," the Judge said.

"Lorie's too young, then. I'll get somebody. Maybe Janet, my friend from the U. She just lives down in Brattleboro."

They talked with the Judge, and set the wedding date. It would be 7:30 P.M., on Thursday, July 31st. Rick would get Friday off, and they would take a three-day honeymoon in Burlington. The Judge's stepson, Thad, would still be working at Woods Hole, so Rick would have to scout up someone else for best man.

As they were leaving, Ellen excused herself to use the bathroom. Judge Rubenstein took Rick aside, and said, "I thought perhaps you hadn't told her. Women are funny about things like this. It didn't mean anything to you, but it does to Ellen. I figured if we put it on the table now, it couldn't come back and cause you problems later."

"It's okay Judge. I should have told her. I'm just glad she's not going to have Kelly in the wedding. That would be too weird."

"I'm tired, Rick," Ellen said when she rejoined them. "Take me home. When does Doc Yeager have office hours?"

"Eleven A.M., on Saturday. I'll pick you up at ten. I don't think we are supposed to eat anything. We'll go out for lunch after, okay?"

"Sure. Okay. I just throw it up in the morning anyway."

They walked back to the car, and drove in silence most of the way home. Finally, Rick said, "Ellen, I'm sorry I didn't tell you about standing in for Danny at Kelly's wedding. I mean, I really didn't think it was important."

"Men are complete idiots," Ellen said. "Of course it's important. And when you didn't tell me, that's like you were hiding something. That's even more important."

"Me? Hiding something? Jeez, Ellen. Like I said, I wouldn't have been involved at all, if you hadn't told me to help her out. I mean, you knew I arranged for the marriage thing. I told you that, didn't I?"

"Yeah. You just didn't tell me *you* said all the vows. It's like you've already been married once."

"I was just a stand-in. Don't you understand? I just played the part. Somebody had to do it. Jeez!"

"As long as you didn't stand in anywhere else. All right, forget it. I'm tired. Goodnight." Ellen gave Rick a peck, and jumped out of the car.

Rick was swept with the dual feelings of guilt and relief, as he watched her close the door. He backed slowly out of the barnyard, and drove home.

It was just after nine o'clock, when he got back to town. Driving down Atkinson Street towards home, he passed the Super Duper grocery store. Just beyond the store, he saw Kelly, staggering down the street, struggling to carry two huge bags of groceries. He wanted to pass by, but he couldn't. He stopped, reached over, opened the front door, and said, "Can I give you a ride, Mrs. Dombroski?"

"Oh, Rick. You're a lifesaver. Thanks." Kelly looked helpless.

Rick got out, and opened the back door. He took each bag, and set it on the floor. Then he held the front door while Kelly climbed in. As soon as he got in the car, she slid right over next to him.

"Uh, where to, ma'am?" Rick gripped the wheel with both hands.

"I'm not going to bite, Rick. I just rented a little apartment over on Hadley Street." She reached over and squeezed his leg. "I'll show it to you."

This felt like very dangerous water to Rick, but he didn't see how he could do anything but give her a ride home, and help her carry in her groceries. He cleared his throat. "Ah, ah, Ellen and I just saw Judge Rubenstein."

"Oooh, Ellen's got one in the hamper, too! Cool. You devil, you." Kelly was laughing at him.

"Yeah. Some devil. Ellen went nuts when she heard I stood in for Danny. I guess I forgot to tell her. I mean, it didn't mean anything, did it?"

"You dope. You don't know anything about women, do you? Of course it meant something. It meant something to me. It means something to Ellen. For a smart guy, you sure can be stupid." Kelly pointed to a driveway. "Right here. You can pull all the way around back."

Rick helped her out of the car, and got the two bags of groceries. Kelly sprinted up the stairs to open the apartment door. Rick staggered up the stairs and into a tiny kitchen. He put the bags on the table. "Uh, uh, there you go," he said, turning to leave.

"Not so fast. I have to give you the cook's tour. It's little. It won't take a second." Kelly grabbed his hand and dragged him through the kitchen door, into a tiny living room. It had a small couch, a chair, and a second-hand television set. "My sitting room," she said, gesturing. "All a woman could desire, except a man."

"And now, the piece de résistance." She dragged him through the door into a small room that contained only a double bed. "The Queen's boudoir." She shrugged off her summer shift, and stood in just her panties. "And of course, the Queen."

She pulled Rick down on top of her. "Would you please pleasure the Queen, Sir Knight?" She kissed him passionately, her hand sliding into his shorts and stroking his erect penis. "I see you stand ready."

Rick told himself he had to escape this woman's clutches, but he found his hands slipping inside her panties and stroking her firm buttocks. She grabbed his hand and guided it between her legs, and he rolled his finger over her tiny clitoris. She moaned. "Kiss me there, Rick, kiss me there."

He slid down, drawing down her panties, and pressed his face into the warm, wetness between her thighs. He found himself licking, and sucking, as she writhed with pleasure. He slipped out of his shorts, and slid into her. He came, almost at once, but she wouldn't let him go. She thrust, and bucked, and writhed, clutching him fiercely. And then, suddenly, she relaxed. "Ellen as good as that, Rick?" Kelly laughed.

Rick sat up. He was awash with shame. How could he do this? He had just arranged for his wedding. The woman he loved was pregnant with his child. How could he be *fucking* some other woman? What kind of a low-life was he? He fumbled for his clothes, and got dressed.

Kelly stretched out naked on the bed. She ran her hands over her breasts, and down across her stomach. "Doesn't show yet, does it? Thanks, Rick. It felt good to be treated like a woman. I've missed it so much. Ellen's a lucky girl. You two should move next-door, and I'll keep you company when she's too tired."

"No!" he said it more forcefully than he wanted to. "I mean, Kelly, I can't do this with you anymore. It's wrong. I love Ellen. I need to be faithful to her. She'd die if she found out. She'd hate me, and…and she'd be right. This was a terrible thing for me to do."

"I didn't think you were so terrible, Sweetie. I thought you were pretty good. A little quick, maybe, but you've got a natural tongue." Kelly sat up, and grabbed a bathrobe. "Run on home, Rick. Thanks for the lift. Thanks for both lifts."

Rick stumbled out the door and into his car. He backed out of the driveway, and drove aimlessly for a while. He was in Saxton River, when he finally stopped, turned around, and drove home.

He could see that his mother was still up reading, sitting in the front room. He dreaded talking to her, but there was no way to sneak by, and go upstairs, without her seeing him.

"That you, Rick?" His mother's voice was husky from too many cigarettes, and more than a little red wine.

"Yeah, Mom."

"Come in here. Tell me what you were up to. Did you set the wedding date?"

Rick slumped into a chair. He started to form a lie, and then without warning, the truth gushed from his mouth. "Mom, I was unfaithful. We spent all evening planning the wedding, and I screwed another girl on my way home. What kind of a rotten shit am I?"

"Tell me about it," his mother said, her voice calm.

Rick quickly recounted how he had offered Kelly a ride home, and ended up in her bed. "But I knew it would happen, Mom. I mean, I knew if I stopped, it was going to happen, but I stopped anyway."

"You *stupe*," his mother said. "You think that was your fault? Ha. Men. They always think that they're in charge. Let me tell you buster, no man is ever in charge when it comes to sex."

"What do you mean? I mean, I could have just passed her by, couldn't I?"

"That's what your *big head* told you. But she already had a lock on your *little head*. And with men, the *big head* always follows the *little head*." His mother lit another cigarette. "Doesn't matter how smart you are. Aaron Rubenstein, the Judge, is just the same as Happy O'Connor, the garbage man. A woman, any woman, can lead them into bed in a heartbeat. That's how we've run the world all these years."

"Huh? Women run the world?"

"Get used to it, buster. You guys do all the heavy lifting; we make the decisions, and use a little sex to get you to do the right thing. Good thing, too. Men in general aren't very smart. Not that a lot of these broads are very bright. Look at that Jackie Kennedy, letting Jack go to Dallas. She ought be horsewhipped."

Rick had no idea where his mother was going with that line of talk, but he knew whenever she got going on Jack Kennedy, it could last all night.

"What can I do, Mom?"

"Well, first thing, you can forget it. Don't go letting your Catholic guilt drive you to confessing to Ellen. She'll make the rest of your life miserable if she knows. I would. Any woman would. There are times to tell the truth, but this isn't one of them. So forget it ever happened."

"That seems, I don't know, so dishonest."

"Of course, it's dishonest. Marriage is dishonest. You go telling your spouse the truth, and in no time there is no marriage. You think I tell your father everything?"

"You don't? Does he tell you?"

"Hah. No way. Of course, I find out. But he never says a word. He was *porking* that numbskull secretary of his, Dorothy, for a year. He never told me. I knew, of course. Everybody in town knew, because Dorothy has the brains of a retarded hamster. She's bragging about it down at the Barn, about every other night. And look at that. Dorothy is butt-ugly. She's got six fingers on one hand, and still he can't keep his prick in his pants. Maybe she gives a mean hand-job, I don't know."

"Didn't you get mad at him?"

"For being dumb, yes. But not, for not telling me. If he tells me, I've got to do something about it. If he doesn't, I can pretend it didn't happen, and get even some other way. That's the way *good* marriages work."

"Doesn't sound very romantic."

"Romance has nothing to do with it. You can be lovey-dovey, and make babies. Lord knows I've made enough. Six of you rotten, ungrateful, brats. Isn't that enough romance for you?"

"I just mean…oh, I don't know. I guess, I'm always hoping the next thing will be better than what I've got. I have this dream of me and Ellen, setting off on our own, and really making it big. Me, writing the great American novel. You know, fantasy stuff."

"You can forget the writing stuff when you've got a house full of kids. When do you ever see your father write? He used to write the most beautiful poetry. Hah! Now it's 'Your dogs deserve a rest,' tucked into every box of Blood Hound slippers. Real Pulitzer Prize stuff."

"I'm not going to just work at some job I hate, like Dad. I mean, why live?"

"Oh, he doesn't hate it as much as he likes to whine about it. It keeps him in beer and scotch, and that's all he really gives a shit about. But believe me, *Bub*, you'll be doing the nine-to-five, if you expect to feed your little brat, and keep Ellen in expensive clothes. I know she loves expensive clothes."

"Don't call him a little brat. We're going to name him Tim. Your father said you had an older brother named Tim, who died before you were born."

"Tim's a nice name." His mother picked up her book, and took a sip of wine.

Rick got up, and started up the stairs. His mother said, "The other thing you have to do is keep away from that slut, Kelly. She's looking to get her hooks into you."

Chapter 27

Jack

Rick was up at his usual 5:30 A.M. He made a pot of coffee, and took a cup out on the front porch. The Rutland Herald was on the top step, and Snuffy, Dieter's dog, was lying on top of it. Snuffy spent a lot of time at Rick's house, now that there were no kids at home at the O'Tooles.

"Hey, Snuff, big night?" Rick gave the dog's ear a scratch, and was rewarded with a couple of tired tail thumps. Snuffy was the ruling *cocksman* among the canine set in town. If there was a bitch in heat last night, you knew Snuffy got to her. Rick noticed more and more dogs in town looked like the wire-haired, part-Airedale, part-who-knows-what. He figured in another ten years, every dog in town would be carrying Snuffy's genes.

Rick sat on the stoop, opened the paper, lit a cigarette, and sipped his coffee. There was no news worth noting. Never was in Bellows Falls. "God, I'm sick of this town," he thought. "How can people live their whole lives here? How could my father have moved from New York City to here, and then just stay?"

He thought about whether he should confess to Ellen. The guilt gnawed at him, and made him want to spill his guts. But he knew Ellen would be horribly hurt, and probably so enraged that she would give in to her mother, and get an abortion. He had to keep it quiet. The danger was, that somebody else would tell. Maybe even Kelly. Then, if he hadn't told Ellen, his sin would be even greater. Still, the end result couldn't be worse.

"How do you keep all your women satisfied, Snuff?" Rick scratched the dog's ear again. Snuffy was too tired to even wag. He just grinned at Rick, closed his eyes, and sighed. "Yeah, I know. Some guys got it, and some don't."

It was just six A.M., but Rick couldn't bear the thought of hanging around the house until nine, or nine-thirty. He went back into the house, and grabbed his keys and wallet. He jumped in his car, and headed out of town, driving north, towards Ellen's house. He didn't know where he was going, or what he was going to do for the next three-and-a-half hours. His fishing stuff was in the trunk. Maybe he'd stop at the job, and climb down around where the bridge abutments were being poured. He could fish upstream from there. There were some big trout in the Williams.

He turned on Route 5, and headed down to the entrance road to DeBoni's office. "I better be a little careful," he thought. "Everett might have his 30-30 deer rifle in the back of his car. Don't want to surprise him, and have him take a shot at me."

Rick slowed by the turn-off to the yard, and was surprised to see Whitey's Olds parked next to the maintenance shed. He turned in and parked. "You there, Whitey?" he called softly.

"Yeah. I'm here." Whitey's voice was choked with emotion.

Rick opened the side door, and looked in. Whitey was standing next to the little olive drab jeep. But the jeep was twisted, and bent. Whitey was crying.

"Jeez, what happened?"

"I told Charlie," Whitey sobbed. "I told him a jeep was no car for a crazy sixteen-year-old boy. My Uncle Billy, he said them jeeps killed more officers in the war than the Germans did."

"Oh, shit, who was driving? Was he hurt?"

"It was Charlie's kid, and he's dead."

"Stevie? Oh, no. Poor Charlie. Shit, how did it happen?"

"Stevie was racing around. Probably had some beer in the car. Cop chased him. He took a corner too sharp, and it rolled. That's what they do. They roll. Center of gravity is too high, and the wheelbase is too narrow. Billy said that's what happened to them officers. They'd get some cracker private to drive them, and he'd drive like the *Revenuers* was after him. Sure as shit, he'd turn it over, and kill the officer, and more-often-than-not, hisself."

"Wow. I don't know how Charlie will be able to survive this. He loved that kid a lot. He was always braggin' about him."

"Yeah. He was an okay kid, too. He liked to hang around and see how things worked. I thought he might actually have it in him to be a mechanic."

Whitey lifted the shattered windshield, and let it fall with a clank. "I won't be able to stay here, Squirt. Every time Charlie looks at me, the two of us will bust out bawlin'. I'll have to move on to something else."

"Don't do anything too quick, Whitey. You know the Tycoon would love to have you and Annabelle."

"What are you doing here, Squirt? This is Saturday. You should be tucked in your bed."

"Aw, I never can sleep late, Whitey. Just the way I'm made. I got to pick up Ellen at ten, so we can get our blood tests. We're going to get married end of July."

"Well, that's nice. You know Annabelle's gonna want to bake the wedding cake."

"No shindig. Just a quiet wedding, with Judge Rubenstein doing the honors. Ellen's mother is having a shit-fit about it."

"She got one in the oven, then?"

"Yeah. Not much of a secret, is it?"

"I always wished me and Annabelle could have had a couple. Then I look at this." He gestured at the mangled jeep. "Then I don't know. Awful lot of heartbreak in kids. Lord knows I was heartbreak enough for my momma."

"Whitey, could I ask you something? Something personal? I mean, if you don't want to answer, that's okay."

"Ask away."

"Are you always faithful to Annabelle?"

"Shee-it. I am. And not just Texas faithful, either. That woman would know if I so much as took a little peek at some strange pussy, and she'd cut my balls right off."

"What's Texas faithful?"

"Old cowboy term, I guess. Oil riggers use it, too. For that matter, truckers and sailors do the same damn thing. They just don't count it as cheating, if they have some fun with a professional whore. They only count it, if they's fuckin' the neighbor, or something. You planning on cheating already?"

"No, no." Rick said, too quickly. "I just hear the guys talk, and wondered, you know, if everybody was fucking around."

"Well, maybe everybody but me. And I ain't taking no chances with that woman. I don't even think about it. Now, get out of here. I got to see if I can salvage something of this jeep, and maybe DeBoni can sell it, get a few bucks back. I'm sure Charlie isn't going to want it around here."

Rick left Whitey banging on the little jeep. He got his fishing gear out of the trunk, and hiked up the road towards the fill. He figured it would take him a good twenty minutes to get down to the river. It was 7:30. He'd be fishing by 8:00, and could fish forty-five minutes to an hour, and still be in plenty of time at Ellen's. As he walked, he tried to imagine what it was like to be told your son was dead. He couldn't imagine it.

As he approached the fill, Rick heard loud voices arguing. He slowed, and cautiously walked up to where he could see out over the fill. Everett was parked square in the middle. He was standing by his truck, and waving his arms and hollering. Rick couldn't quite make out who he was hollering at. Thinking he might need help, Rick broke into a trot.

As he got closer, he could see that it was PH. He was on foot, but his truck was probably parked up the hill. He was also waving his arms, and hollering at Everett.

"What's the big to-do?" Rick hollered as got closer, yelling so that they'd know he was there, and wouldn't be surprised.

They both turned. "What the fuck are you doing here?" PH screamed. "Who told you, you could be on this job on Saturday?"

Rick was stunned. "What's the big deal? I'm just cutting through to the river. Thought I'd see if I could raise a trout."

"This site is off limits," Everett hollered. "Damn it Squirt, don't you have no common sense. If I didn't see it was you, I might'a shot ya." He held up his 30-30.

"Well, I did think of that. That's why I didn't sneak around. I figured if you saw it was me, you might ask questions first, and shoot later. Did you guys hear that Charlie's kid was killed last night?"

"We heard." PH stuffed his hands in his pockets, and jiggled his keys. "Tough luck for that family. If you're going fishing, you best get moving."

"Yes sir," Rick walked past them to a trail that led off the northwest side of the fill, and down through the wetlands to the river. He trotted down the hill, and through the swamp, leaping from grass tuft, to grass tuft. He managed to make it to the river, only getting one foot wet. It didn't matter. He'd be wading wet, anyway.

Rick had just switched from worms to flies. He had just a few in his little fly case. He selected a Royal Coachman, and tied it on. There was a dark swirl of water near the opposite shore. He made two false casts, than laid out a near perfect cast, just upstream of the swirl. He was congratulating himself on the cast, when the fish struck. Lifting his rod-tip, he set the hook and played the ten-inch rainbow for a couple of minutes, before coasting him into the shallows. Rick had always killed what he caught, but when he lifted the pretty little fish, he had second thoughts. "Damn, what am I going to do with a fish? I give it to Mora, and she'll throw it in my face." He slipped the hook from the trout's lip, and slid it back into the water. The fish swam slowly away. For some reason, releasing the fish made Rick feel really good.

He fished for another half-hour, or so, and then pulled in his line and nipped off the fly. He broke down his rod, and started walking slowly back. He was halfway through the swamp, when he heard Everett's 30-30, bark.

"Shit," he said, slipping into the mud. He waded as quickly as he could to the edge of the swamp, and then ran up the path. He was out of breath when he got to the top, and stood there panting. Everett was standing by his pickup, squinting down the barrel of his rifle, which was pointed back up the slope towards the ledge area. The gun barked again.

"Damn, missed." Everett hollered. He jacked out the spent cartridge, and levered another into the chamber.

"What you shootin' at, Everett," Rick hollered.

"Woodchuck. Missed the bastard twice."

"Whew. Thought you mighta been shootin' at PH," Rick laughed.

"I wouldn't a missed that sonofabitch," Everett said, with no humor in his voice.

"Shit. I thought maybe PH was your kid, the way you two were so lovey-dovey up here," Rick teased.

"You suggestin' I'm related to that cocksucker? You say things like that, I just might take a shot at you."

"Take it easy. I was just funnin' a bit."

"Nothing funny about it. Well, I better get up the hill. I got some cleaning to do."

"Thought you missed?"

"Missed the woodchuck. Hit me a nice doe, though. She'll taste good tonight." Everett climbed into his pickup, drove around in a tight circle, and then headed back up the hill towards the ledge.

"*Government beef.*" Rick grunted, and trudged across the fill. He glanced at his watch. "Almost nine," he said. "Still plenty of time." When he got to the yard, he noticed that Whitey's car was gone. There was no one around at all. He tossed his fishing gear in the car, and walked over to the maintenance shed. He saw the padlock was in place. "Damn. Too bad I didn't keep one of those keys," he said. Then he shrugged, and walked back to his car.

As he drove out of the yard, he saw PH's pickup coming down off the file. It turned into the yard. Rick thought about stopping, and then shrugged and kept going. "None of my business," he said, out loud. He thought about the little trout, and smiled. Amazing how not killing that fish made him fee so good. Then he thought about Stevie DeBoni, and the smile vanished. "So much death," he said.

Rick stopped, and turned into the driveway of the hired man's house, at the foot of the hill, on the river side of Edgar's property. Ed had said that the hired man was gone, and that he and Ellen could use the house until they went back to school. He walked around. It was a cute little house. If he remembered correctly, there was one bedroom down, and a dormitory-like room, up. He wondered if it needed some cleaning, and made a mental note to ask Ellen.

He stood on the front lawn and looked south. The railroad ran along the east side, and beyond that, the river. There was a great swimming hole below the trestle where the tracks crossed the river. As he looked down that way, he thought he saw someone at the edge of the woods. Probably some other local, hunting up *government beef*, or maybe somebody going fishing, he thought. He checked his watch: 9:45. He guessed he could chance arriving a couple minutes early.

Ellen was already sitting at the end of her road. She had a small suitcase. Rick stopped and helped her into the car. He put the suitcase in the back seat, without comment. Then they continued on to Alden Hill Road, which led down to Highway 5.

"You moving in with me?" He asked, trying to sound hopeful, even while he was figuring out how he could get his mother to go along.

"No. I called Janet. She invited me to stay with her in Brattleboro, until the wedding. I thought it was a good idea. My mother is driving me nuts. It sure isn't fair to Lori, though. She's going to have a rough time."

"Your Mom know?"

"My dad does. He'll tell her, if she ever talks to him again. She is still furious over those terrible things he said about her." Ellen giggled.

They rode in silence for a while. Then Ellen moved over next to him, and squeezed Rick's arm. "Janet's working in a jewelry store. We can buy our rings. She said she'd give us a good price."

"Sounds good to me. When do you want to do it?"

"Right after we see Dr. Yaeger. Okay?"

Rick agreed. They were early at Doc Yaeger's, but for once, that worked out. He came in early. "Short rounds at the hospital," he said. "Come on in"

The blood test took only a couple of minutes. Doc Yaeger packed up the samples to send to the lab. "You should hear by Friday. Soon enough for you?"

"Yes sir. Send it to my house. Ellen will be out of town until the wedding." Rick wrote his address on the return mailer.

"I can give you the name of a good obstetrician in Burlington, if you'd like. Her name is Marie Wright, and she's one of the first women in obstetrics in Vermont, and she's a crackerjack." Yaeger smiled. "She's also probably the busiest doc at Mary Fletcher, so it won't hurt if I give her a call."

Ellen was very pleased with the offer. Later, as they were driving to Brattleboro, she said, "Everyone has just been so nice. I thought people would shun me, and point at me, like I was a whore or something. But nobody except my mother, seems to think we did anything wrong."

"I remember Tommy Mac once saying, 'The first kid can come anytime. After that, it usually takes nine months.'" Rick said. "It makes me think that practically everybody makes love before they are married. The Church points its finger and says it's a sin, but nobody believes it, because it feels so right. And heck, it isn't like it doesn't happen. Four of the fifty-five girls in my high school graduating class were pregnant at graduation. That's more than seven percent!"

"And that doesn't count the five, or six, who had D and C's up at the hospital," Ellen added. "My friend Joanne was a candy-striper up there, and she says it was like a parade. I know everybody does it. But that doesn't stop tongues from wagging. And a lot of people take pleasure from putting somebody down. I know that's what Mom is afraid of. That people will talk, and point the finger, and that it will make her look bad."

Janet worked at Baker's Jewelry, and she was working today. Rick parked, and he and Ellen strolled into the store, holding hands. "Ah, I spy a pair of love-birds," Janet waved from behind the cash register. "What can I interest you in. Perhaps a huge diamond engagement ring?"

"Too late for that," Rick said to the perky dark-haired girl. "I think Ellen here wants to buy me a large, iron manacle and chain."

"Hi, Janet," Ellen said. "Thanks for taking in this poor unwanted waif."

"Speaking of which, where's your suitcase?"

"I left it in the car. I didn't know if you would want it cluttering up the store."

"Nonsense. Go get it, Rick. Ellen and I have plotting to do."

Rick went out to the car, and got the suitcase. By the time he had returned, the girls had picked out the rings. "I don't really need a ring," Rick protested.

"Like hell, mister. Ellen can't have you out there with all the hungry women chasing after you, and you loving every minute of it, because they think you are still single. The ring says 'hands off. This hunk is taken!'"

"Right. The only time hungry women might even notice me is if my arms are full of hot cheeseburgers."

But the argument was settled. Janet sized the rings, and then put them on lay-away. Rick gave her a twenty-dollar deposit, and promised to bring the rest the following Friday when he got paid. "I should have the blood tests then," he told Ellen. "Say, and couldn't we get our license right here in Brattleboro, and not alert the whole town?"

They agreed on that plan. Ellen told Rick she'd check at the town clerk's office to see if that was okay, and would call him sometime during the week.

Seeing that the two women were roundly ignoring him, Rick said his goodbyes and fled.

Rick was a little surprised at how relieved he felt to be free of the women, and thoughts of the wedding. He turned onto Interstate 91, and put the gas pedal to the floor. In no time, he was whizzing towards Bellows Falls at seventy. The little Chevy shimmied at speeds above sixty-five, so Rick backed off a little. Two minutes later, a State Trooper roared by doing eighty or more. A few miles down the road, the trooper had a car pulled over, and was writing a ticket. "Wow. Sometimes it pays to drive a junker," Rick said out loud.

The Interstate ended in Westminster, at Kern Hatten Road. The ten-mile section bypassing Bellows Falls was under construction. Already, merchants in Bellows Falls were losing business to Brattleboro. Rick figured that as soon as 91 got there, the local stores would be losing business to Springfield as well. Bypassing the town, preserved historical Bellows Falls, but it also sounded the town's death-knell. Rick speculated that in another ten years, or so, there would be few, if any, merchants left. As Rick entered the town, driving by the tenements that lined Westminster St., he wondered if this town was really worth preserving.

It was 6:00, when Rick got home. "Jack called, and said he'd meet you at Twist Cone around 7:00." Rick's mother told him. "How did things go with the doctor?"

Rick brought his mother up to date on the latest developments. "I need to talk Jack into being my best man," Rick said. "You know he was always sweet on Ellen. I hate to ask him."

"Don't worry about it," his mother said. "Jack's a free spirit. He has no intention of settling down. He'll be happy for you."

Rick decided he'd grab a plate of fried clams at the Twist Cone, and headed out early. He was sitting at a table, his back to the door, munching on the nut-sweet full bodied clams that Twist Cone did so well, when someone said, "Yuck. How can you eat those things."

Rick turned, and let out a groan. "Hi, Kelly. I like them." He turned back to his clams, but Kelly plunked herself down across from him. She was dressed in a T-shirt with no bra, and skin-tight, short-shorts. Rick could see her nipples through the thin cloth, and despite his best efforts to ignore her, he felt himself become aroused.

"Oh, Rick, don't you like me?" Kelly pouted, and batted her eyes at him.

"I like you, Kelly. I like you *too* much. I just can't see you. I can't do that to Ellen."

"But how about me? I have needs, Rick. And I can make you very happy." Kelly slid her hand under the table and up Rick's leg. Her fingertips touched his erect penis.

"Please, Kelly. Please?" Rick wanted desperately to escape, but his erection was so obvious he was afraid to get up. A throaty roar signaled the arrival of a motorcycle.

"Oooh, he's so hot!" Kelly withdrew her hand, and was gazing out the window.

"Who?" Rick asked, both relieved, and a trifle offended that he was no longer the center of attention.

"Rocky Santee. Don't you think he's the most?"

"Santee? That thug? Gimme a break, Kelly. You don't really go for that guy, do you?"

"Oooh. He's like a wild animal. He makes me all tingly inside." Kelly hugged herself. "But he'd never look at me. He'd think I'm damaged goods."

Rick looked over his shoulder. Santee stood tall, beside his Harley. He was dressed in jeans and a T-shirt that looked painted on his muscular body. He was admiring himself in his side mirror, combing his greasy, black hair, back in its customary ducktail.

Rick thought, in fairness, that Santee was an alright-looking guy, if you liked hoodlums. He was just under six-feet tall, well built, and had the high cheekbones of his Indian heritage. To Rick, he looked like trouble. Most of the cops in Vermont and New Hampshire would have agreed with that assessment.

"I'll never understand why women like that kind of guy," Rick said. "He treats'm like dirt, and they lap it up."

"You wouldn't understand, Rick." Kelly watched as Santee got back on his Harley, kick-started it, did a small wheelie, and roared out of the parking lot. "He's dangerous and exciting. And every girl alive thinks she can tame the beast."

Just then, Kelly's friend Ginger, walked in. She greeted Rick, and then said, "Did you see *The Rock*? Oooh, isn't he sooo cool?" The two girls left, chattering away about how marvelous Rocky Santee was. As Rick watched them leave, he saw Jack roar into the lot in his Corvette. The girls waved at Jack, and he waved back. He was grinning as he came through the door.

"Ricardo. Still wowing the local ladies, I see."

"Not me, Jackson. Those airheads are swooning over Rocky Santee. He just stopped and preened himself in the parking lot."

"Ain't that something?" Jack laughed, and ordered a double-cheeseburger, fries, and a large shake. Rick dumped the remains of his dinner in the trash, and sat back in the booth with his feet up on the seat, sipping his Coke.

Jack stayed at the counter talking to the girl, until his cheeseburger was done. Then he carried it over to Rick's table. He sat down, took a huge bite, and a sip from his chocolate milkshake, and sighed. "Damn, I was hungry. Haven't eaten since noon yesterday."

"Not counting all the hors d'oeuvres you gobbled with your drinks last night, right?"

"Ow. You wound me, Ricardo. I may have had a chicken wing or two, but nothing substantial, I assure you."

"I can see you are wasting away, Jack." Rick laughed, as he eyed Jack's substantial bulk. "A mere shadow of your former self."

"Serious news," Jack talked between bites. "Cops were out at the depot the other day, looking for Theobold Fucking Magus. Know anything about that?"

"Yeah. I know they figured out he used to work for DeBoni, and also used to run a chop shop in Ferguson Ford's body shop. His real name is Stewart Ferguson. He did some time. Did they arrest him?"

"No. Couldn't find him. He vanished. All his people are still there, praying up a storm. But old Theobold has ascended into heaven, or something. Actually, I think he's hiding out somewhere. All them Christians disappear from time-to-time, for three or four hours. Then they're back weeping and rolling."

"What's the Tycoon think of all this?"

"He's plenty upset. He told the cops he knew Theobold had done time. Theobold had told him. Told him he found Jesus in prison, and was a changed man."

"Found a new scam, it looks to me." Rick said.

"Well, the Tycoon still has faith in his man," Jack said, finishing up his French fries. "So what else is shaking?"

"I'm getting married, Jack. Me and Ellen. In a couple of weeks."

"Really. You're really doing it? Man. I can't believe it. What's her old lady say?"

"Mora's not too pleased, as you might imagine. Edgar's okay with it, though. Ellen's pregnant."

"Well, I figured that. You know what causes that, I expect?"

"That's what Edgar said."

"Funny guy. Hard-nosed farmer, but a real good man."

"Yeah."

"Jack, I know you were always sweet on Ellen. But..."

"Don't say another word. She's your woman, Rick. She always has been. For me, she was a fantasy. Somebody to dream about."

"Would you be my best man?"

"Damn straight. Wouldn't let you do this without me. Let me buy you a shake."

"Actually, I could really use a beer."

"Come on, then. I got a stash up in Chester. Come on up. Plan on spending the night. You're going to be too drunk to drive."

Rick grabbed a dime, and plugged it into the pay phone. He dialed home, and told his mother he was staying over with Jack.

"Good idea," she said. "I don't want you ending up like the Dupris kid, or DeBoni's kid, either. By the way, that Kelly slut called here earlier. You are going to have to do something about her, Rick. She's bad news."

"Yeah, I will Mom." Rick hung up, wondering just what he was going to do about Kelly. He and Jack went out to their respective cars. "Race you to Chester," Jack challenged.

"Yeah, right. Some race. Forget it. Just keep the beer cold."

Jack was sitting on the back platform of his Pullman parlor car home, when Rick pulled into the old Chester Depot yard. He waved a beer at Rick. "Glad you could get here this week. Damn, that car of yours is slow."

"It runs. And it's cheap." Rick took a beer, and sat on the platform next to Jack. "These are nice digs, Jack. You've sure come up in the world since we camped in that old caboose over in Sunapee."

"Not quite up to the Tycoon's, but pretty comfy. It could use hot and cold running broads, though."

"Caine living here, too?"

"Nah, he's got one like this up in Proctorville. He wants to stay as far from them Christians as he can get. His relationship with the Tycoon is strictly business, now. Have I ever given you the tour?"

He opened the screen door, and ushered Rick into the car. The front was a sitting room with two sofas and two chairs. It looked just like it had the last time Rick was here. There were clothes strewn about, and it seemed like a half-dozen guitars and banjos, propped up against the walls or lying on the furniture. "I could use a maid," Jack laughed.

The back of the car had two stateroom bedrooms, each with a toilet and shower. "Have to have it pumped every couple of weeks. In the old days, they'd just dump on the tracks."

"No kitchen?" Rick asked.

"Nope. Just a refrigerator. All I need. Keeps the beer cold. I eat over at the Diner most of the time."

Rick kicked some clothes onto the floor, and settled in a chair. Jack went over to a cabinet and pulled out three different liquor bottles. "Gonna mix you my famous Singapore Sling, or Zombie, or whatever the hell it's called."

"Beer's fine," Rick said.

"No way, man. You're getting married. You need to get plastered. It's an obligation." He handed Rick a tall, frosty glass, filled to the brim with a foaming liquid.

Rick took a tentative sip. "Mmm. Not bad. Maybe, even good."

"Fucking great, is what you mean. It's my secret brew—vodka, brandy, and an ingredient so secret, that if I tell ya, I'd have to kill ya." Jack had mixed himself one as well, and he pushed some stuff off a sofa and sat down, automatically picking up a guitar.

"I'm glad you'll be my best man, Jack. I was worried that you would be pissed-off. I mean, I know I've been going with Ellen for years, but still, marriage is different."

"Yeah. I won't be fantasizing about sleeping with my best friend's girl friend any more. Now, I'll fantasize about sleeping with his wife." Jack struck a discordant chord.

"What are you going to do, Jack?" Rick sipped his drink, enjoying the glow.

"Do? Do I have to do? "Do lak I do, lak I do." Jack crooned a Roger Miller parody. "Did I tell you I have a gig at Bromley? Old man Pabst himself hired me. Going to sing every Friday and Saturday night in the

lounge, from eight to midnight, starting December 1. Pays $200 a week-
end, plus a free season's pass."

"That's great, Jack. Could be a big start. Got anything cooking before
December?"

"Couple nights at the Weston Inn. Got a maybe down in Putney for a
couple nights. I can play here in Chester any time I want. But it's an old
crowd." Jack ran the chords for *When You and I Were Young, Maggie*.
"Have to bone-up on my geezer music. Plus the chick action is a little too
Geritol for my taste."

"Ever think of really making a push to go big-time? I mean, you are
great. When you play, the guitar is alive. It talks. Remember how Whitey
asked if your momma was a black lady?"

Jack laughed. "Funny thing. He wasn't so far from the truth. She ain't
black, but she's where whatever talent I've got, started."

"Really? I didn't know your mother was musical." Rick pictured Jack's
mother standing in her housecoat, cigarette in her lips, a large, unkempt
woman, who rarely ever said anything.

"You sure didn't think it was my father, did you? Man, the only thing
he can play is the odds. Sonofabitch can't even fart on tempo." Jack played
a couple soft chords. "I know Momma doesn't look like much now, but I
got pictures of her when she was young. She was beautiful. She played the
piano, and sang near the army base, down there in Biloxi. My father
picked her up one night, and fed her a snow job. The man's a regular
Sergeant Bilko. Shit, I think Phil Silvers modeled *Bilko* on him. She married him. That was about the last time he even talked to her. He did buy
her that old upright piano that's in our living room. Some nights, when
she thought there was nobody home, she used to play it and sing. I'd hide
sometimes, just so I could listen to her. I never let on. I know she didn't
want nobody to know."

"Man, that's sad." Rick was slurring his words.

"You know, your mother is something like that, too. Different, but still
the person you see, isn't the real person. She keeps that hidden."

Rick pondered that thought. His mother? A secret person underneath? It was too much for his already alcohol-fogged brain.

"My father won my first guitar, this little *Gibson* here, in a poker game. He came home, tossed it to me, and said, 'Here. Don't say I never gave ya nothing.' That was it. Man though, I thought I'd died and gone to heaven. I was about twelve. Already, I was drinking every afternoon. I was fucked up. But I got that guitar, and the minute I touched it, I knew. I tuned it to that old piano. Figured it out from a book that was in the guitar case. And I started to play. It probably saved my life."

"How come you never went the whole way? You know, learn to read music and stuff?" Rick was really feeling the booze now. His face was flushed, and he kept dropping his cigarette.

"You know, I could do that. But then, I would be playing somebody else's music. This way, *I* hear it. I figure it out, but I figure it out *my* way. And when I play it, I play it *my way*. If I ever learned to read music, it would be like putting on a pair of handcuffs. I'd be a prisoner to it."

Chapter 28

BVD

The last thing Rick heard was the opening lick to a New Orleans blues number.

He woke up with a start. The sun was streaming through the window, and his mouth tasted like he'd been chewing the roadbed. Jack was snoring softly on the sofa. Rick didn't want to move, but he had to piss.

"Arghhh." He screamed. His head felt like it had been split with an axe. His stomach churned. He staggered down to the toilet, barely making it before he vomited his guts out. Or at least that's how he felt, kneeling, head practically in the shit-stained bowl, heaving until there was nothing to heave, and then dry-heaving, bringing up the last little traces of rancid bile, that burned his throat and mouth.

He flushed, and staggered to the little sink. He was shocked that he didn't look as bad as he felt. Just pale. Eyes bloodshot. He ran water and splashed it on his face. He stripped off his clothes, got in the tiny shower, and turned on the water full blast. It was ice cold, but he didn't care. He stood and shivered, and let it run into his mouth, spitting and swallowing, alternately.

After a few minutes, he got out and looked for a towel, finally settling for a slightly used hand-towel. He bent to put on his shorts, and nearly fainted. His head throbbed. He groped in the medicine cabinet, and found a bottle of aspirin. Shaking out three, he gobbled them all at once, but couldn't work up enough saliva to swallow. He cupped his hand under the faucet, and slurped some water, finally getting the aspirin down.

Pulling on his shirt, he staggered back out into the car. Jack was still sleeping peacefully. The clock said: 7:00. Rick staggered out to his car, and managed to drive to the Chester Diner. He ordered a cup of coffee, surprised that the waitress didn't see anything odd in his appearance. He scalded his mouth on the first swallow, and gulped some water. He forced himself to go slow, sipping carefully. He had a second cup before he started home. His headache had settled to a thundering roar.

He drove home carefully, even the sound of his tires on the pavement, too loud for his fractured brain. He parked in the driveway, and staggered in through the kitchen door. His mother was standing in the kitchen, eating a piece of toast. She looked at him and said, "Serves you right, you *stupe*."

Rick managed to get up the stairs, and collapsed on his bed. It was four in the afternoon before he dared open his eyes. He got up, scrounged a bowl of soup, and then went back to his room. He lay on his bed feeling crappy, unable to read, unable to even think. Finally, he fell asleep again. The next morning, he felt wobbly, but a little closer to human.

Bad as he felt, when Rick got to the job the next morning, he seemed to be the most alive guy there. Everyone had heard about Stevie's death. Faces were long. Guys avoided even looking at each other, afraid to show their emotions.

Côte and Henry were both silent. They moved their rigs into position, and began drilling the next shot on the expanded grid that PH had laid out. The hammering rock drills were way too loud for Rick's sensitive skull, but he grit his teeth. Drilling was going slowly. He hiked down to the water-cooler between every added steel, and swallowed cup after cup, of water. When Teach arrived with the dynamite truck, Rick asked Henry if it was okay if he helped carry dynamite out on the shot.

"What's the matter? I'm not giving you enough work?"

"Henry, I'm suffering the worst hangover in my life. I thought if I worked up a good sweat, I'd get rid of some of the poison."

"That right?" Henry laughed. "Well, shit. We're going slow here. But you come running when I holler."

Rick trotted down the hill and called out to Teach, "I'll give you a hand."

"Well, you do that." Teach hollered back. "This ain't no union job. We let drillers work like laborers, here."

For the next four hours, Rick hauled fifty-pound boxes of dynamite up the hill, and distributed around the shot. About once every ten minutes, he had to run over and help Henry add, or remove a piece of steel. Once, he took a five-minute break to sharpen a drill bit. But the strategy worked. He felt a hell of a lot better by lunchtime.

Blaster Bill had the shot wired by lunch. Henry and Côte moved their rigs across the southbound right-of-way, and down into the little quarry where they parked their cars. Teach came over and said, "Blaster Bill says to tell you he's a shooting at high noon."

"He said that, did he?" Henry muttered.

"Actually, I said it. Bill's not quite that articulate," Teach laughed.

They grabbed their lunch-buckets, and found a shady spot, well protected from the blast. Bill dragged his wire over, but it didn't reach down into the quarry. He set his blasting-box up on the top.

"Kind of exposed, ain't ya, Bill?" Côte hollered.

"Should be fine. Should be fine." Bill hollered back. "All clear!" He hollered down towards the fill.

The air horns sounded as the Euclids shut down. The silence screamed.

Bill held his thumbs up, and then plunged them down on the buttons of the blaster-box. There was a thump, then a bang. "Ow," Bill yelled.

Rick and Teach rushed up the hill. Bill was holding his gut. "Piece of fly-rock," he wheezed. "I'll be okay. Skipped off the ledge, and caught me right in the gut."

"You ought to get that looked at," Teach said.

"No way, fuck. I'm okay. Don't say nothing to nobody." Bill was adamant.

"Okay, man. You're the boss." Teach and Rick walked back down to finish their lunch.

"Not everybody who can fuck up the same shot, twice," Henry growled. He pulled out a fresh cigar, and bit off the tip. He lit it, and began chewing on the end.

"This job is sure like that, though. I can't think when I've seen a job with so many fuck-ups. We seem to be jinxed." Côte stood up. "Jinxed, or sabotaged. One, or the other. Now, I expect old Charlie won't be in for a while. I don't know if that's good, or bad. But it makes a fella wonder whether the company will last till payday. Be nice if they told us something, once in a while. They treat us like mushrooms. Keep us in the dark, and feed us shit."

Almost on cue, PH pulled up in his pickup. "Meeting down on the fill at 4:00. Get some work done before that, you fuck-offs." He headed up the hill to talk to Bill, who was sitting on his blasting-box, eating a sandwich. It was pretty clear to everyone down below, that PH was giving Bill a royal ass-chewing.

"Damn, you'd think it was him hit with the fly-rock," Teach said.

"He'll get hit with more than that, one of these days," Henry growled, spitting a piece of tobacco. "Sonofabitch is going to get blown to smithereens if he don't watch it. It's kind of an unwritten law that you don't holler at the guy who sets off the dynamite."

"You think Bill's got that kind of meanness in him?" Côte asked.

"Maybe not Bill. But a few of us around here do." Henry grabbed his lunch-bucket and carried it over to his car.

The drilling crews fired up their compressors, and began the trek back to the ledge. The dynamite crew wandered back over to the shot, and began picking up scraps and wire.

The day wore on. From this spot on the ledge, Rick could see down across the fill. It looked like they were only working two belly pans. Even at that, the old D-9 couldn't keep up. Despite John's best efforts, Charlie hadn't let him bring back the new D-9. It was taking longer to push one pan through to get a load of fill, than it took the other pan to deliver and be back waiting for a load. "Too much waiting around," Rick thought. "No rhythm on this job."

About three in the afternoon, he heard a cheer. He looked down on the fill, and there was Chip coming across, on the new D-9. "Damn," Rick said. "Old John finally had his way." As he watched, the D-9 went out into the middle of the fill and parked. He saw Chip jump down, and saunter over to talk to the Duke.

"Things are happening," Rick yelled at Henry.

Henry was watching, too. He just grunted. Then he hollered, "Holy shit. It's BVD."

A huge Cadillac limousine worked its way across the fill. John Cashman's pickup followed. "That magnificent old Guinea has come to take charge, 'cause his little boy couldn't do the job." Henry was positively chortling.

"Maybe, because his grandson is dead," Côte said.

"Yeah. Maybe. We better get down there. People are starting to assemble." A steady stream of trucks, pickups, and personal cars were coming in from all directions, and forming a circle down on the fill.

The drilling crew shut down, and drove their cars down to the fill. They were among the last to arrive, and found themselves on the outside of the circle. They stood on the bumpers of their cars. The mechanics were also late, and Whitey came over and climbed up on Rick's bumper. "Don't mind if I join you, do ya Squirt?"

"Always welcome, Whitey. I figure if the bumper breaks off you're the right guy to have around to fix it."

"Yeah, I'm some kind of fixer, I am. Sure wish I had fixed the governor on that jeep, so that Stevie couldn't unfix it. Worse thing is, I taught him how to do it."

Chip's D-9 was in the center of the circle. Chip was sitting in the seat. The door of the limousine opened, and a short, thin man, in a three-piece suit, stepped out. The workers were dead silent. The man had wispy, white hair. He walked from his car to the bulldozer. Chip jumped up and reached down, giving the old man a hand up onto the tread. He thanked Chip, and turned to face the assembled men.

A cheer broke out spontaneously. "Bee Vee Dee! Bee Vee Dee!" the men shouted. The old man held up his hands for quiet.

"Thank you."

Rick had worried that he might not be able to hear the old man, but his voice carried in that strong, flat way, men make themselves heard, when machine noise is deafening. Rick had also expected an Italian accent, but Benito sounded more like Boston, than Naples or Rome.

"This is a sad day for the DeBoni family. Our boy, our bambino, Stevie, is dead. No one is to blame. He was a good boy, but like most boys, he took chances. When you take chances, sometimes you lose. Stevie lost." Benito wiped his eyes with a white handkerchief.

"I'm going to ask you men to do something for me. But first, we have some business we have to settle." Benito took off his jacket and handed it to Chip. He rolled up his sleeves.

"This union thing. We got to end this one way, or another. I was told that Jensen said he would get his Italians to fix us, if we didn't go union. Well, I know his Italians. I know Raymond, in Rhode Island. I know John, on Long Island. I know Joe, in New York City. I know Salvatore, in New Jersey. I know all these people, and I know they like the unions. The unions help them make a lot of money."

"I called Raymond. We grew up in the same town in Italy. We came to this country about the same time. Raymond still talks like a *goomba*. But maybe that's good for his business. I said, 'Raymond my friend, the union is telling me that you are going to do harm to my business if my men don't vote the union. Is that true?'"

"Raymond says to me, 'Benito, no. All we ask is you giva your guys da vote. That's alla we ask.' So I says to him, 'Okay, Raymond. I will give them the vote.'"

"So that's what we are going to do next. John is going to pass out some paper and pencils. The paper says, *Union Yes*, or, *Union No*. You just circle the one you want. While John is passing out the slips, let me tell you, if you vote *yes*, you get the union. I don't care which one. They'll work that out. We finish this job. After that, I don't know. You vote *no*, we don't have a union. We probably win one or two more pieces of Interstate 91. We keep going. You get work for maybe five, or six-more years. Maybe more. We keep trying. We hope for some luck."

"The union *yes*, means I got to pay you another fifty cents an hour. Some of you may think, 'Hey, look at Benito. He's got a big Cadillac Limo. He can afford a lousy fifty cents.'" As Benito talked, John Cashman passed out slips of paper and a pencil. Behind him, Tim the timekeeper held out a hat, and workers put their slips in the hat.

"You think, fifty cents, that's not so much. But we got four-hundred people on this job, and the job in Granby. Fifty cents is $200 per hour. We're working fifty hours a week. That's $10,000 a week. We work maybe thirty-five weeks a year. That's $350,000. A job is maybe two-and-a-half, three-years. That's a million bucks. Fifty cents an hour is a million bucks a job. If we add a million bucks to our bid, maybe we don't win the next job. Guys like Paligrinni got lots more equipment than us. They can bid lower, push us out. Then they jack up their prices. They bring in their guys from out-of-state. Who hires you guys?"

Benito looked around. "You got them all collected Tim? You go do a count. Take one of the truck-drivers with you, so everybody knows this is on the up-and-up. I'll ask these guys the favor."

The little nattily dressed man, standing on the tread of the bulldozer, looked out over the group of rough, dirty, construction workers.

"You men," he said in a voice that was both quiet, and loud, "you men are my family. I come to this country in 1936, and I leave behind fifty generations of DeBonis. Barons, peasants, kings, thieves, even a Pope. He may have been one of the thieves. But that was Italy. I am an American. My family in America is my boys, and their wives. Except for my Mario, who is too busy fucking every girl he meets to find a wife. Their children, my grandchildren, these are my close family. But you, the men who work for me, and who work with me and my boy Charlie, you are family, too."

"Family comes together when there is tragedy. Losing my little Stevie, is a tragedy that rips out an old man's heart. I want you all to come to the funeral. It's going to be on Wednesday afternoon. It will be at the church in Bellows Falls. St. Charles. I want you to drive some of the big trucks with our name on the side, so that everybody knows this tragedy happened to a DeBoni. To *our* family. I give you all the half-day, with pay. I know most of you can't afford to give up a half-day's pay."

"You come. Then when the funeral is done, you bring my grandson back here. I bought a little piece of land from McCormick, up by where the rest area will be, on the southbound lane. I got the Town of Rockingham to issue me a graveyard permit. The Monsignor promised to send his curate out to bless the land. After the funeral, we will bury Stevie here. He would like that. He always wanted to be part of the "big job," he called it."

He looked over the men. "Will you come?" he asked.

They roared their replies, "Yes. Hell, yes. Damn straight! Try and keep us away!"

Benito smiled. "Tim, you guys got a vote?"

"Yes sir, Mr. DeBoni." Tim came forward with his clipboard in one hand, and the hat full of voting slips in the other.

"Jump up here, and tell them the count."

Tim grabbed Chip's hand, and scrambled up on the track. He turned and faced the crowd. "For the union," he shouted, "Eight votes. Against the union, "two-hundred seventy-five votes."

The men went wild, cheering and screaming. It was like they had won a lottery. Rick heard somebody growl, "Who are those sonsofabitches that voted union?" But it was drowned out in the rejoicing.

"Thank you." Benito held up his hand. "Thank you, men. You really are family. I got some more announcements."

Gradually, the crowd quieted.

"Charlie isn't going to be able to run things for a while. His heart is broke. He needs a rest. We give him a rest."

"You run it, Benito!" someone in the crowd yelled.

"No, no." Benito held up his hand again. "I'm an old man. I know what I can't do. I'm asking John to step up to be managing director of the company. That will mean some other changes. But John will tell you about those."

Benito looked out over the men again. Tears came to his eyes, and suddenly he looked again like a little old man. "Thank you boys. I love you."

"Bee Vee Dee! Bee Vee Dee! Bee Vee Dee! Bee Vee Dee!" The chant became a roar that echoed through the valley. A large man in a three-piece suit, who Rick figured must be a bodyguard, rushed over and helped Benito climb down. The giant supported the old man, as he made his way back to the car. The Cadillac backed around and drove slowly off the fill.

John Cashman shuffled forward and climbed up on the bulldozer. He looked over the group. "We're behind on this job. It's not your fault, but you have to catch up. We'll work an extra half-hour every day through the fall, as long as light permits. And starting this weekend, Saturday work is available for some of you willing to put in the extra time. I know a lot of you live quite a ways away, and need to get home. But those who can, we may have work for you at overtime rates."

John looked over the group. "Duke will be job superintendent. He'll have to run the fill, and the bridge footings, too. But he will have overall responsibility for this job. I'll be managing the bids on three, or four new jobs, and with luck, we'll be starting at least one of them in the fall. That means there will be opportunities for promotions for those of you who give a shit about them. But it also means we should have work for at least a few more years."

Rick looked around. Most of the men had given John their complete attention. Only PH seemed to be distracted. He didn't look at all happy.

"I want Everett, Chip, Whitey, and Tim to join me and Duke, as pall-bearers. Henry, you and Côte take charge of getting the grave ready. We need to be able to drive right in there. We'll use the dynamite wagon as our hearse. Ken, see if you can get the small backhoe up there. Clyde, after the burial, I'd like you to use the Grade-All to make the place look pretty. PH, find us some good fill. We'll want crushed stone around the casket. Then a couple of feet of regular fill, and the best topsoil you can find on top. Baldridge and Côte, I know you guys know something about monu-ments. See if you can make something appropriate. We'll need to start now. I can't pay you overtime for the grave work."

The spirit of the job changed. Where just a couple hours before, every-body was looking to get out as fast as they could, now people were hang-ing around, looking for ways to help. A contingent headed up to the gravesite. Sam, one of the grade foremen offered to stake it out, and mark the spot for the grave. Ken and Crackers headed out to the job in Springfield that was just being finished. Crackers would ferry back the small backhoe, and Ken would drive the Grade-All, which had its own truck-body.

Rick followed Henry back to the quarry, while Côte set off to collect a small compressor and a couple of jackhammers. They parked, and Henry began surveying the walls. "Pretty good stone," he said. We can pop out a slab that will look damn nice on Stevie's grave."

When Cote arrived, he and Henry checked over the stone carefully, and finally settled on a six-foot face, that sat on the south end. They hooked both air-hammers up to the small compressor, and side-by-side, they drilled a row of five-foot holes, exactly two feet back from the edge. "Go get us a half-dozen jackhammer sticks, and eighteen caps, zero delay,"

Henry shouted. He tossed Rick the key to the magazine. "Bring the small blaster-box, too. And a small roll of wire."

Rick marveled that Henry had a magazine key. Then he thought, he must be the only guy on the job who didn't have his own magazine key. "Great security," he muttered. By the time he got back with the dynamite and caps, Henry and Côte had finished drilling the rock.

"Start moving stuff out of here," Henry ordered.

Rick and Côte moved the compressor and the cars, up onto the right-of-way, and then hiked back down to the quarry. Henry had the shot loaded and wired. "This works right, we'll pop that slab right out, and Côte can get to work carving it."

There was no time to ask questions. They rolled the wire back down the woodland trail, until they were about 150 feet from the quarry. Henry placed the blaster-box behind a massive maple, and connected the wires. "Here goes," he said, and pushed the button. There was a bang. Rick rolled up the wire, as they walked back to the quarry. A near perfect block of stone, had broken away from the ledge, and lay flat on the quarry floor.

"Dang, you're good," Côte said. "Let's see if we can turn it over."

Together, using drill steel as levers, the three of them turned the stone. The face was smooth, with a flat finish.

"You mark it out for me, will you Henry?" Côte asked.

"You do it, Squirt. You're the *college fuck*."

"What'll I say?" Rick asked, taking the red marker crayon from Henry.

"His name. Stephan DeBoni. His dates. Probably, 1948 to 1964. And then, something about him." Henry spat out the end of his cigar. "It ain't complicated."

"Say, 'A good boy.'" Côte said.

"How about 'A good man?'" Rick asked. "Steve would like to be thought of as a man."

"Yeah, good."

As Rick wrote out the information, trying to space it nicely on the stone, he asked, "How come you guys know about this stuff?"

"We both worked up in Barry, right after the War," Henry said. "I worked out in the quarry doing about what you do. Côte worked in the monument shop. He was learning to carve them gravestones."

"Jeez, how come you guys didn't stay there. I bet granite work pays better than this job."

"Don't be so sure," Henry grunted. "They was cheap fucks. But I left, 'cause the foreman was an asshole, and I decked him one day when he called me a sonofabitch. Côte left because he can't spell."

"Can't spell? That sounds interesting."

"Well, it's true," Côte said. "I was never too good at spelling. And, I dropped out of school in the 7th grade. And, I didn't learn nothing but shooting in the army. So I ain't going to win no spelling bees."

"Ain't gonna win no popularity contests in New Hampshire, either."

"Hey, come on guys. Tell me the story. This sounds good."

"Well, it was like this," Côte said. "They had a rush order for a monument, to put up in a park over in New Hampshire, someplace. Crawford Notch, or Norford's Crotch, or someplace like that. I don't remember the town."

"It was Gorham," Henry said.

"Okay, if you say so. Anyway, they ordered this monument for this local bigwig. He was editor of the newspaper. One of those newspapers that's always calling everybody a Communist, and hates Jews and black people. You know, like the one in Manchester. They're all alike over there in New Hampshire. They'd back Hitler, if he was running for president. They must love that kind of shit."

"Anyway, this editor, his name was James A. Fariter, died, and left a lot of money to the town to build some sort of a park or something. So the town fathers figured they better put up a monument in the park dedicated to the guy. They ordered this thing. They had a name for it. Looked like a big pecker."

"An obelisk?" Rick asked.

"Yeah. That's it, I think. Anyway, it comes into the shop all polished and pretty. And I'm supposed to carve the guy's name on it. And I do. A really fine job. Very pretty." Côte sat back on his haunches. "They bundled it up, shipped it off, put it up in the park, and planned a big unveiling ceremony. Nobody had really looked at it. So there they is. The band's playing. The mayor makes a speech about the "Winds of Change," and how this fella knew the directions the wind was blowing, or something. Should of carved it on a weather vane, rather than that *obeleski* thing. Then, they pull the cord, and unveil the monument. And they noticed that I forgot the *i*. It said: James A. Farter, The Wind of Change."

Rick rolled in the dirt holding his sides. "Damn, Côte I think you got it right. Hee, hee, hee, hee, haw."

"Well, I'll finish this tomorrow. What do you think, so far." Côte brushed the dust off where he had been chiseling as he told his story.

"Damn, that's perfect, Côte. You're a real artist."

"So, they didn't want me no more at the quarry. I don't know why." Côte laughed. "But it's okay. I don't think I had the stuff to carve them fancy angels, and things. So, I'd have been doing names and numbers for the rest of my life."

"And, spellin' 'em wrong," Henry added.

It was getting dusk when they left the job. It was the latest Rick had ever worked, but he felt great. Things seemed to be getting better after summer's pretty dismal start.

He called Ellen when he got home, and told her about the strange doings. She was in much better spirits than she had been at home. Rick felt even better when he hung up. Ellen was out of Mora's clutches for a while. Janet was helping her organize for the wedding and the future.

Meanwhile, the house was in turmoil. The family was already bringing stuff together for the great Maine excursion. The front living room was piled with clothes, books, and paraphernalia. Rick's mom, and sister Willa, ran an almost continuous battle, screaming at each other, slamming doors, and otherwise trying in vain to intimidate one another. The

Stooges: Moe, Larry, and Curly, battled over who would bring what. Curly was dead set on bringing Snuffy.

Rick's father sat and drank scotch, and paid no attention to the commotion. Rick fled to his room, wondering if he should camp out on the job until they left. It was Rick's mother who precipitated the state of perpetual crisis, as she always did when the family ventured even a few miles from home, together in the same car. Rick figured she probably was deathly afraid of leaving Bellows Falls, although he couldn't fathom a reason why that might be so. She translated her fear into an endless series of battles, perhaps hoping that one would be serious enough so that she could say, "I'm not going." It had happened in the past. Rick prayed it wouldn't happen this time.

The whole family was on to her game, and refused to be baited into a fatal fight. The exception was Willa, who battled her at every step. But Rick's mother could never let Willa win a fight, so Willa's feisty attitude pretty much guaranteed the trip would happen.

Sometime around ten, the battle subsided for the day, and Rick dropped off to sleep.

Although Rick got to the job early the next day, he found that he was among the last to arrive. Drivers were cleaning and polishing their trucks. "What's up?" Rick asked Simon, one of the Autocar drivers.

"Gettin' a jump," he said. "I'll just have to run a rag over her tomorrow before we head into town."

Whitey had a backlog of drivers who wanted some little thing fixed on their truck, before they took it out on the highway. He seemed to be more than willing to accommodate the drivers, but Rick noticed that he wasn't smiling.

Teach had the dynamite wagon backed into the maintenance shed. "Loafing all day?" Rick asked him.

"Hell, no. If this piece of crap is going to be the hearse, we need to do some major prettying up. You want to ride along with me tomorrow?"

The idea of riding with a coffin, spooked Rick a bit, but he agreed. He headed up to the old quarry to park. Côte was working over his slab. "Come over here, Squirt, and make sure I spelled everything right. Didn't call him Stevie Big Bone, or something like that."

"Yeah, that's his Uncle Mario." Rick surveyed Côte's work. "Damn nice, Côte. You're a real artist. I like the little mark." Côte had cut a little circumflex under the inscription.

"Oh, I don't know. I just chiseled a bit here, and there. You better get up the hill. Henry needs to take his rig over to the gravesite. We got to blast a little bit to get our little buddy in the ground."

"Where ya been?" Henry growled when Rick got to the ledge area.

"Dang, Henry. It's not even 7:00 A.M., yet," Rick protested.

"You heard John. We gotta make up for lost time." Henry had the air track connected to the compressor. "Mind the fuckin' hoses, and let's get this thing over to the grave."

Rick snaked the hoses off to one side, and Henry dragged the air compressor over the ridge, to the southbound right-of-way. There, they headed north a few hundred yards, to where the rest area was staked out. Henry unhooked the air track, leaving the compressor in the right-of-way, and ran the drill back through the rest area, up a hill, and into the woods beyond. Ken already had the small backhoe in there. He was pulling some stumps where one of the men had cut down the small trees in the area. They had left a gorgeous maple, easily a hundred-and-fifty-years old, that shaded the area.

Ken and Henry palavered. Then Ken moved the backhoe over, and scrapped away the topsoil where the grave would go. He hit ledge at about four feet.

"Leave the dirt," Henry shouted. He waited until Ken had backed the shovel away, and then moved in and set the drill. "I'll just be using this one steel," he told Rick. You get somebody to bring us a box of jackhammer sticks and caps. No, make that Special Gel. We can break the sticks. We'll only need five, or six."

"Any delays?" Rick asked.

"No. Double-oughts will do fine. Get moving."

Rick trudged through the woods back to the quarry. He was pleased to find Everett there with his pickup, dropping off the water-cooler. He told Everett what he needed, and Everett said he'd take care of it. "I'll bring a blasting machine, too," he said driving off in a cloud of dust.

Côte was back working on the fill. He had a new chucktender, a kid named Garrison, who was related to one of the truck-drivers. Rick headed back to the gravesite. When he got there, PH was standing there, hollering at Henry. Henry didn't even look at him. But when PH reached over and grabbed Henry's shoulder, Henry swung around, grade-stake high. He barely missed PH's head with the deadly swing.

"Damn. Don't sneak up and grab me, you stupid sonofabitch," Henry hollered. "I damn near kilt ya."

PH was white as a sheet. He simply turned and walked back to his truck.

When PH was out of sight, Henry let out a guffaw. "Dumb sonofabitch," he chortled. "I knew he was there all the time. Just thought he needed the piss scared out of him. Did he piss his pants, or what?"

"Well, I didn't see the stain," Rick said, "but he turned about as white as that dust. You did scare the bejeebers out of him."

"Where's the dynamite?"

"Everett's bringing it. Said he'd be here in ten minutes."

"Be about right. Almost done here. Pretty short holes. Nice white quartz, here. It'll make a damn pretty vault."

They just finished, when Everett drove up with the dynamite. He and Henry set the charges, and Everett pushed the button. There was a little "whump." Henry signaled Ken, "All yours, he hollered." He and Rick went back to the compressor, hooked it up, and headed back to the ledge they were supposed to be drilling. They were set up and drilling, by 8:30.

The day was uneventful. They drilled a lot of holes. At the end of the day, they walked back over to the gravesite. Ken had scooped out a perfect grave. There were neat piles of crushed rock, regular fill, and loam, by one side of the grave. Côte's handy work was lying off to one side, chain in place, to swing it onto the grave. Chip had made a nice, firm road, for the hearse and mourner's cars to follow. The mourners would park down below, where the parking lot would be, when the rest area was complete. Chip had cut a gentle road up the hill for the hearse. There was space for the hearse to park at the edge of the woods. The pallbearers could carry the casket from there.

They all agreed that if you had to be buried, this was as good as you could get. About 6:15, Father Pritchell showed up with a bucket of holy water. He walked around the plot saying prayers, and sprinkling water in every direction. The men stood silently and watched. "There you go," the priest said. "As holy as the catacombs underneath the Vatican. It doesn't get any holier than this."

They watched Father Pritchell leave, and then headed for their cars. It was 7:45, by the time they headed home.

Things were much the same on Tuesday night at home with preparations for the Maine trip in high gear. Rick called Ellen and they agreed that he'd meet her at the store on Friday night, and pay for the rings. The town office stayed open Friday night. They could get the marriage license and join Janet and her boyfriend for a burger and a movie.

Rick fled to his room. They would be working tomorrow, so he had to wear work clothes. But he picked through the stack of clean work clothes, and found jeans and a work shirt that hadn't been stained with grease beyond his mother's laundering abilities. He also cleaned his work boots, and put a little polish on them.

He got to the job even earlier on Wednesday. Still, he wasn't the first, by far. He noticed that the old Moss-Sterling dump trucks were lined up, washed, and ready to go. The trucks dated back to the late thirties and early forties. They had a chain-drive. They were among the first pieces of equipment Benito had purchased and had a kind of nostalgic value that would add to ceremony.

Teach had the dynamite wagon completely spiffed up. Someone had painted the DeBoni logo on the side-panels. "Even got you a seat," Teach hollered. He held up a wooden crate. "Don't want you to get your duds dirty."

"Very pretty," Rick said. "Shows what you can do. When PH sees that, he'll make you keep it shiny all the time."

To say they worked that morning would be an exaggeration. But they did drill some holes. Everyone did his level best to stay out of the dust, and to avoid getting grease on himself. They pretty much succeeded. Right after lunch, they all headed down to the yard.

John Cashman organized driving teams. They were taking the dynamite wagon, the three Moss Sterlings, four Autocars, and the lowboy, with Chip's D-9 aboard. There would be five company pickups plus the two mechanics' trucks. Every vehicle held two men. The rest of the men took their personal vehicles. John told them to park along Green Street, all facing north. He told Teach and Calvin, who was driving one of the Moss-Sterlings, to drive up Cherry Hill and into the parking lot behind St. Charles School. The dynamite truck would serve as hearse for the trip back to the job. Calvin's Moss-Sterling would serve as a flower truck.

The pallbearers doubled up for the drive. Everyone else was on their own for the trip to town. Teach drove a steady thirty-five miles per hour. "Dead boys," he said. "Seems you and me, Squirt, all we do is ferry around dead boys."

St. Charles sits high atop Cherry Hill, towering over Green Street. A flight of stairs that is a real penance to climb, provides access from Green Street for those afoot. Drivers park in the schoolyard behind the Church. That's where Teach parked. Rick and Teach stood by the wagon and waited. Ten minutes later, Shaughnessy's hearse pulled up along side them. Michael Shaughnessy was driving the hearse himself. Rick's grandfather, Tommy Mac, was beside him. He gave Rick a wave.

"Unusual for a hearse," the mortician said. "But I suppose it has carried its share of dead. It's an army ambulance isn't it?"

"Yes sir," Teach smiled. "I'm sure you're right. If it saw duty, it saw death. What's the procedure here? As you might guess, we're pretty new at this."

"Well, I haven't done all that many exchanges, myself," Shaughnessy said. "Here's the routine. You guys go in and get seats. We'll bring the casket to the front door where I'm told there will be pallbearers. We'll use our cart and place the casket in the aisle. Then I'm done. I'm sending Tommy Mac with you to help with the actual burial. He knows the ropes, so to speak. It wouldn't do to drop the boy. Sit up front on the right. You'll have plenty of time from the end of the funeral service to slip out through the sacristy and bring the ambulance down to the front door. Ah, I see the family pulling up to the front door now. Once they are inside, I'll bring the hearse around."

Teach and Rick walked down to the front door of the church. Five Cadillac limousines were taking turns disgorging people. There were women in black veils, and men in dark suits. Rick recognized Benito and Charlie from the first limousine. He assumed the women were their wives. The second limousine had both Mario and Antonio, Antonio's wife, and their two sons. Mario was escorting a gorgeous blonde with too much makeup, and a very short black skirt.

The family entered through the main front door, and Rick and Teach stayed out of the way, going in a side door and down the right-hand aisle. At the end of the aisle, there was a small altar and a statue of St. Joseph. Teach was gazing around like a hick in the big city.

"First time inside a church?" Rick asked, giving Teach a little dig in the ribs.

"Pretty near." Teach chuckled. I'm not much of one for this religious stuff. How about you?"

"I was," Rick answered. "Even spent a year in the seminary. Not any more. But I spent a lot of early mornings serving mass in this place. I know every crack and fleck of peeling paint."

The church was classic turn-of-the-century Roman Catholic. It had a high, sharply pitched ceiling, painted in ornate designs. Large stained-glass windows were evenly spaced along both the north and south sides. There was a huge circular stained-glass window above the choir loft.

The main altar was a monstrosity of ornately carved marble. It sat atop four steps, and rose in multiple tiers. Behind the altar, a wide panel of ornately carved wood rose from the floor to just below the small circular window depicting the sacred heart of Jesus.

The pews were all oak. The left side was a mirror image of the side where Teach and Rick were seated. There was another small altar with a statue of the Blessed Virgin Mary. All three altars were all behind a marble and brass altar rail that split the sanctuary from the church proper. A high, cylindrical, ornately carved pulpit bridged the altar rail. The sanctuary was filled with floral arrangements, and the sweet smell of flowers was nearly overpowering.

The church filled rapidly. The family members were seated on either side of the main aisle in the first four rows. Rick was surprised to see that Monsignor Flaherty himself would be saying the funeral mass. He had a full complement of assistants with Father Pritchell and two priests that must have been part of the DeBoni entourage.

All the tall candles were lit on the high ledges of the altar, and six candles in stands were lit at the edge of the sanctuary, where the coffin would sit during the mass. This would be a solemn high requiem mass. The giant pipe organ, which sat at the back of the choir loft, thundered the opening processional. Escorted by three priests, and preceded by an altar boy bearing a cross, the Monsignor walked solemnly down the aisle to meet the coffin at the door.

At the back of the church, the Monsignor faced the coffin and sprinkled holy water to the left and to the right, intoning: "*Asperges me.*" Tom Kaiser, in his high, reedy voice, led the small choir in the response: "*Domine hyssopo et mundabor lavabis me et super niven dealbabor.*"

Rick craned his neck to see. The coffin was on the little trolley. The pallbearers, dressed in clean work clothes, were arranged around the coffin. John and Duke were at the head; Whitey was behind John on the left, and Everett was behind the Duke, on the right; Chip and Tim were positioned at the foot.

When they reached the altar rail, the six men lifted the box, and Tommy Mac, standing discreetly at the side, moved over and lifted the trolley up into the sanctuary. The pallbearers set the coffin back down on the trolley, and stepped away. They took positions on either side of the sanctuary, standing with their hands folded.

For the first time, Rick could actually see the coffin. It was a simple, but elegant, traditional coffin. The handles were thick, new rope. The box was wood, highly polished, but natural in color. It was either maple or light oak, Rick couldn't be sure which. Sometimes the coffins were open for this part of the ceremony, but the lid was shut on Stevie's box.

The mass started. The Monsignor croaked, "*Requiem aeternam dona eis,*" and Tom Kaiser picked up the verse. Kaiser's nasal tones were burned into Rick's memory, and he dreaded the *Kyrie* and *Dies Irae* that still lay ahead.

The Mass progressed at its normal pace. The *Kyrie* was every bit as painful as Rick expected it to be. Teach leaned over and whispered, "Is the goal to make us all wish we were the one's who was dead?"

"Pretty much when Tom's singing," Rick whispered back. "He's coming to the *Dies Irae*. That's his *piece d résistance.*"

"*Dies Irae, dies illa*" Kaiser whined.

"It means: *this day of wrath,* Rick whispered. "Pretty much sums up Tom's singing, doesn't it?"

Kaiser croaked, "*Tuba mirum spargens sonum.*"

"Something about the trumpet's awful sound," Rick muttered. "What can I say."

Finally, Kaiser got to the last verse, "*Lacrimosa dies illa.*"

"Day of tears," Teach said before Rick could translate. "I had a little Latin, too, you know. Part of a classical education."

"Yeah, but did you get the next line about sparing me this one, o Lord?"

Teach chuckled. "*Dona eis requiem.* Give them rest. Give us all a rest."

The Monsignor went to the pulpit, and read the epistle and the gospel. Rick was surprised when the Monsignor stayed in the pulpit to give the homily. Rick had expected the homily to be given by one of the young priests from Boston, who might know the DeBoni family better.

The Monsignor looked old. He closed the thin gospel book they used for funerals. He stood and looked out over the assembled DeBoni clan.

"Three times this summer men have come to me," he said. His voice still carried the church without benefit of microphone. "Three times they have asked the same question. The question is, 'Why do old men live and young men die?' What can I tell them? What could I tell Mr. Dombroski, whose son Danny was killed in an accidental explosion? What could I tell Mr. Dupris, whose son died in a fatal car crash? What can I now tell Charles and Benito DeBoni, whose son and grandson also died in a car crash?"

"These men look to me to tell them God's plan. This plan, that plucks from the earth, people who have not yet had time to give back. People just on the edge of life."

"Often, I counsel mothers and fathers who have just lost an infant. I counsel them that the child is in heaven, spared the toils and troubles of this world, a special favor from God. I don't know if they believe me. I know they want to believe me. They want to take comfort that the death is meaningful, not senseless. That from it, some good will come, if not to them, at least to the soul of the infant."

"But a young man or woman on the edge of life, is different. They have survived the trials of childhood. They have gotten through the turmoil of adolescence, or at least are nearly through. They look and see only a future of promise. Work. Family. The fruits of life. And in an instant, they are gone. And with them, all the hope, the joy, the love we have invested in them is gone, too. They are our future, and they are gone."

"These old men ask me this tough question. I hear the question. I could say, as so many times we must, 'It is a mystery.' I used to say that. But now, I too am old. I feel the grave calling to me fondly, and I do not fight the call. What I say to these men is, 'I do not know. But someday in the near future, I will see God, face-to-face, and it is the first thing I will ask Him.' And they nod. The old men understand. I suspect that God gets this question a lot. And I suspect, He has an answer that makes sense. But I do not know what it is."

"I say to you, let each of you hold in your hearts what you loved of young Stephan DeBoni. And let each of you also hold the question dear. And when it is your time, ask the only One who can answer. God bless you."

As the Monsignor turned and began his slow walk down the pulpit stairs, a rich baritone voice filled the church with a powerful "Ave Maria." It was John Salvatore, singing a cappella. His voice was a town treasure.

Rick didn't know whether John knew the DeBonis, or had been recruited to sing. John had been in Rick's class in high school, one of five superb singers in a class of just 104. The others, Kathleen, the soprano, Rachel, the alto, Jonathan, the tenor, and Paul, the mellow bass, were all superb, but John was in a class by himself. He had a voice Perry Como or Dean Martin would have killed for. Yet, he was completely casual about his talent. Rick remembered once, when he was helping direct these mas-terful voices in the senior musical, he had said to John, "Salvatore when you sing, women swoon, and men weep." John had laughed and said, "It's the garlic."

Now, his voice filled every space in the church, as he crooned "Ave Maria's," sweet plea. The magic of his voice lubricated the rusty valves of tear ducts, that hadn't cried in half-a-century. Rick was weeping unabashedly. He looked over at Teach, and saw tears streaming down his face, as well. Rick could see John, Whitey, and Chip, from where he was sitting, and all three were wiping tears from their eyes.

Somehow, Salvatore's voice transformed the entire service. Even Tom Kaiser sounded decent as he finished off the ceremony with the *Libera Mei*. Teach and Rick slipped out through the side door into the sacristy, and from there out into the parking lot. They climbed into the old jeep ambulance, and drove it carefully down the sidewalk, positioning it in front of the church. Rick jumped out, and opened the back doors.

Tommy Mac was there. "Be just a minute now, Rick." He swung the two heavy doors open and latched them.

When they reached the church door, the six pallbearers lifted the coffin up to shoulder height, and then walked carefully down the stone steps. They slid it into the ambulance. "Take good care of him, guys," John Cashman said. "A gentle ride. As gentle as possible, anyway. Teach, circle around the church and down Cherry Hill. You can see the trucks lined up there. Go to the head of the line."

Rick helped his grandfather into the dynamite wagon and gave him the crate to sit on. He introduced Tommy Mac to Teach, and then squeezed himself in between the coffin and the wall. "Row, Charon, let's get this boy across the river."

"First Latin, and now Greek. I don't know about you, Squirt. I don't think you're ever going to make Super at DeBoni." Teach put the jeep in gear and carefully circled around behind the church. Calvin's Moss-Sterling was parked at the sacristy door. Men were loading the flowers into the small dump body. Teach turned right at the exit, and headed straight down the steepest part of Cherry Hill.

"Easy there. This thing is sliding my way, and there ain't no room for it to slide."

"I was going to suggest we take the gentler route round by School Street," Tommy Mac chuckled. "We don't want the boy all scrunched up at one end of the coffin."

" Too late, now," Teach hollered. "Bythejesus, we'll make her." He eased the wagon around the corner at the foot of the hill, and proceeded slowly along Green Street. Behind them, the five Cadillac limousines carefully snaked their way down the steep hill, squealing around the corner.

"I think you set a precedent," Tommy Mac said, looking behind him. "Hope they don't bring that old dump-truck down that hill. I'm not sure its brakes would hold."

They didn't have to worry. Calvin was not at all swayed by the direction taken by the ambulance and limousines. As soon as the wreaths and bouquets were loaded into the old Sterling, he headed down the gentler hill, past the high school, turned on School Street, and came around the long way.

When the ambulance, limousines, and flower-truck were all assembled, Teach began the slow trek back to the job-site. As the flower truck passed the lead truck parked on Green Street, the big trucks fell in behind, creating a procession that was more than a mile long. Sneakers had the town cruiser up at the junction of Green Street and Rockingham Street. He waved them through, holding traffic from the square at a standstill. Chickering was at the intersection of Atkinson Street and Rockingham, and he, likewise held traffic back as the entourage moved slowly by.

The whole town turned out. It was like a somber circus parade. Drivers waved to the kids on the side of the street. Chip was sitting high on his D-9, on the back of the flatbed. He grinned his chipmunk smile, and doffed his baseball cap, spitting a stream of *Day's Work* tobacco juice onto any car that dared to try passing the procession.

A state trooper pulled in front of the red ambulance, and led the parade out of town, lights flashing. The long chain of trucks, pickups, and cars, inched its way along the river, past the Village Inn, and headed north on Route 5.

"Tell me, Gramps," Rick said to his grandfather, "is Mr. Shaughnessy upset that he didn't get the whole funeral?"

"Not Michael. He takes his work seriously. If the family wanted to set the corpse aflame on a barge in the river, Michael would do his best to get the permits. Besides, Mr. DeBoni paid him well, I think."

"A Viking funeral. That would be something," Teach said.

"We had one, once, you should know," Tommy Mac laughed. "A fella name of Ericsson, wouldn't you think? They put him in a long-boat, up at the boat-landing, and set the whole thing afire."

"Really? I never heard about that," Teach said. "When did that all happen?"

"Oh, not too long after the first War. Unfortunately, the boat sank, put out the flames, and they had to fish the corpse out of the drink. It wasn't Shaughnessy's finest hour. Michael's father about had a heart attack on the spot. That's why Michael is such a stickler for details, sending me up to make sure you louts don't drop the poor boy on his head."

"Did you see the Viking funeral, Gramps?"

"Nah. I was in Maine at the time. But I heard plenty about it."

The trooper stopped, and blocked traffic on Route 5, so that the entourage could make the turn into the job-site. Teach carefully negotiated the turn, and inched his way up the hill and onto the fill. He proceed as carefully as possible, lurching here and there, as the old jeep worked its way up the northbound right-of-way. At the top of the hill, they crossed to the southbound right-of-way, and turned into the rest area. The men had done a good job smoothing out the parking area, and building a gravel road up the hill, and back into the woods to the gravesite. Teach drove to the prepared space at the edge of the woods, and turned into the brush, leaving the back doors clear for unloading the coffin.

Tommy Mac jumped out, spry as ever. He had three coils of new rope in his hand. He walked over to the gravesite and looked in. "A fine, solid resting place for the boy," he said. He laid the three ropes, spaced across the grave.

The limousines, pickups, trucks, and cars all found places to park, and the crowd slowly climbed the hill and found places to stand around the grave. The pallbearers went over to the ambulance, and prepared to move the coffin. Tommy Mac grabbed six, beefy workers, and made sure each of them had hold of a rope. Only then, did he signal the pallbearers to bring over the coffin.

Walking carefully along opposite sides of the grave, the pallbearers centered the coffin over the grave, and gently lowered it onto the ropes. The rope handlers strained to hold the coffin still, and the pallbearers each stepped back and assisted one of the rope handlers.

The Monsignor hadn't come out to the grave. Father Pritchard, and the two priests from Boston went through the graveside ritual. Charlie, looking as if he hadn't slept in a week, hobbled forward, and threw a handful of dirt onto the coffin. Tommy Mac gave the nod, and the men lowered the coffin into the ground.

By hand, the men carefully shoveled crushed rock in and around the coffin. They laid a soft layer of dirt over the top. Benito himself signaled Clyde to drive the Grade All in, and finish filling the grave. Under Clyde's gentle hand, the Grade All carefully filled the grave, packed it, and smoothed the landscape. Using the small chain, they lifted the stone Côte had carved, and placed it flat over the grave.

Benito came up and stood before the stone. "A good man." He sighed. "A boy, still but man enough to die. Thank you, boys. You did a nice job. My Stevie will like this place."

One-by-one, the men brought bouquets and wreaths from the Moss-Sterling, and laid it on the grave. A few crossed themselves. Most just stood silently for a minute, and then walked slowly back to their cars.

Benito put his arm around Charlie, and led him back to the limousine. The women were already in the car. "He'll always be close, Charlie. He'll always be close," the old man murmured.

"Monsignor Flaherty asked the right question, didn't he?" Rick said to his grandfather.

Tommy Mac looked down on the neat gravesite. "Aye," he said. "A question I ask myself every day. After the people leave, you boys will want to move that stone off, until the ground settles."

They walked through the woods to the quarry where Rick left his car. They drove home in silence, not needing to say a word. Rick could feel his grandfather's love hugging him, and he hoped his grandfather could feel him hugging back.

"We're getting married a week from tomorrow," Rick told his grandfather as he let him out of the car.

"Ahh, take care of that girl, Rick. And take care of my little Tim." He gave Rick's hand a squeeze.

When he got home, his mother said, "D-d-donnie died today. Funeral's on Friday, at Shaughnessy's. He's being buried at Oak Hill. Bet those sisters of his can't wait to get their hands on his dough."

Rick thought of the tough old man giving the Tycoon hell from his deathbed. "Old men die too, I guess," he said.

Chapter 29

Santee

The rest of the week went quickly. There was a visible energy on the job, that hadn't existed before. The Duke assumed day-to-day management of the job, and he was a much more visible presence than John Cashman had been. He gave orders, and expected them to be carried out. And generally, they were. Duke wasn't a man to cross. His temper was legendary, but he was respected for being both smart and fair.

While Saturday work was now available, neither Henry nor Côte had planned for it this week. So, there was no opportunity for Rick to earn the extra overtime pay. He was more than a little sorry, because he had damn little money saved, and huge responsibilities looming in the very near future.

Friday, at the end of the work shift, he stopped in at the office and asked to take Friday and Saturday off, the following week.

"Married? You're getting married? By the jumping Jesus, Wallace, what in name of all that's holy are you getting married for?" Duke stood, hands on hips, staring straight at Rick, and making him wish he could melt through the trailer floor.

"Uh, uh, well, for one thing, she's pregnant. But I mean it's okay. I love her and everything. I mean we were going to get married, anyway."

"I wouldn't think you could afford not to work."

"Yes sir, I mean no sir. I can't. So, I was wondering if maybe I could do a night watchman shift, or something to make up the missed day."

"Give me that schedule, Tim." Duke grabbed the clipboard. "Officially we're scrubbing the night watchman job after Tuesday night, providing nothing else happens. I'm making sure everyone knows that. You got that?"

"Uh, yes sir." Rick was glum. A short paycheck was not going to help.

"That's officially. Unofficially, I'd like you to take the Wednesday night shift. Lie low. If you see anything, you'll have a radio to call in the state police. But don't say anything to nobody. Got that?"

"Yes, sir. Great. That'll be great."

"Think you can work Thursday on no sleep, and get married too?"

"Yes, sir. Yes, I can. I don't need much sleep."

"I can see why. You're spending all your free-time in bed." Duke laughed. "Get out of here. And keep the night watchman thing quiet."

That night, Rick met Ellen at the jewelry store where Janet worked. He paid for the rings, and then he and Ellen hurried over to the town office to get their marriage license. Later, they joined Janet and her boyfriend for a burger and a movie. Ellen had everything planned for Thursday night, including what Rick would wear. She had reserved a motel for them in Rutland, right next to Sewards, an ice-cream shop infamous for its "Pig's Dinner" banana-split (eat one and get the second one free) and an ice cream frappe they called the "Awful, Awful." It was the unofficial halfway stop between Bellows Falls and Burlington. "We'll be too tired to drive all the way to Burlington," Ellen said.

"Sounds great to me. I wouldn't mind if you booked it in Chester. There's things I'd rather be doing than driving." Rick ducked as Ellen swatted at his head.

It was after midnight when Rick got home, but the house was in total chaos. The Stooges were racing upstairs and down, carrying stray articles of clothing, books, games, and drawing stuff. Willa and her mother were screaming at each other at the top of their voices.

"Can't say I'll be sorry to see you leave," Rick said to his father.

His father laughed. "Come outside. I've got something for you."

Rick followed his father outside. His father handed him an envelope. Rick opened it. There was a check for $500.

"Wow, Dad, thanks." Rick wanted to hug his father, but held back. It wasn't a hugging family. "Thanks a million, Dad. We really need this to put a deposit on an apartment and stuff."

"I know. But use some of it for a little fun, too." His father flicked his cigarette out into the night, and went back inside and up to bed, oblivious to the bedlam.

Rick went upstairs too, and crawled out on the porch roof. He lay there propped against the house wall, smoking until the noise gradually subsided. Willa and the Stooges wandered off to their beds.

Rick came back in and went downstairs. His mother was sitting in the front living room, smoking and drinking wine. "You'll have fun, Mom," he said.

"I'm not going." His mother stared up at him. "What are you laughing at?"

"Mom, you say that every trip, even when we're just going to Aunt Libby's farm. You're going, and you'll have a great time. You'll get all the lobster you can eat."

"We'll see in the morning. If I don't feel like it, I'm not going."

"Dad gave me a check."

"Yeah, I know. I told him to."

"Thanks. We really need it. We'll make it, and this will really help."

"Oh, Rick, I wish you weren't getting married and could have some time for fun."

"This is what I want, Mom. Really."

"But you're turning me into a grandmother."

"I can just see you. You'll be just like Grandma Wallace, walking around saying, "Ooh, the poor little wee bairn.""

"Stop it. That's not funny." But his mother laughed. "You know they buried D-d-donnie today," his mother changed the subject.

"Yeah, I guess. It's a Jewish thing, isn't it? A quick burial."

"Yep, have to be buried before sundown on the day before the Sabbath. But he wouldn't let them plant him in the Jewish cemetery in Claremont. I heard he said, 'P-p-put me in Oak Hill. It's g-g-g-good enough for the Unit-t-tarians, it's g-g-good enough for m-me.' You know he and Shepherd Farmer were always good friends. D-d-donnie used to say, 'I l-like Unit-t-tarians b-because they d-don't th-think they've g-g-got all the answers.'"

"As good a place as any, I guess," Rick said, yawning.

"They'll be necking on his grave," His mother said. "We always used to go to Oak Hill to neck."

Rick said goodnight, and went upstairs, trying to imagine his mother necking in a cemetery. He couldn't make the image work.

Rick was up at 5:30, but he didn't beat the hoard by much. The Stooges were laughing and hollering, and running around. TK showed up on the doorstep at 5:45, with a small knapsack.

"Got enough undies in there, TK?" Rick said.

"Let me see, twelve pair," TK replied. "January, February, March…"

"Oh, changing more often than usual," Rick tossed back.

"Don't change," TK replied. "Just put the new ones on top."

Rick laughed. "Looks like it'll be tough to find a spot for that." He pointed at the sagging Plymouth station wagon. It was loaded to the gunwales with additional suitcases and coolers tied to the rack on top."

"Maybe I better help with the packing," TK laughed. "They seem to be using the pylon strategy; whatever it is, just pile it on."

As Rick watched the car get loaded, the image that came to mind was a cartoon with furious activity represented by a ball of dust with little number signs, question marks, ampersands, and other comic-book cursing, sticking out of the cloud. The ball of dust rolls back-and-forth from the house to the car, and a giant pile of stuff is loaded onto the top of the car. Then, TK the giant, comes and compresses it, and fits it into the car. And finally, like magic, it was done. Everyone had a last pee, and they were loaded and ready to go. Rick walked down to the driveway.

"Thanks again, Dad, Mom. Have fun all you crazy people."

"I'm not going," Rick's mother said. Curly, sitting up front between his father and mother covered his ears.

Rick's father just smiled and backed the car out of the driveway. Rick heard Larry say, "Are we there yet?"

Laughing, he walked back to the porch and sat on the step. Seven-thirty in the morning, and already it was hot. He watched Snuffy come slowly down the street from the terrace. Snuffy was walking like he was pretty sore, not unusual after a night of love.

Snuffy looked at him. "They all went to Maine, Snuff." Rick shrugged. Snuffy paused, and then continued on towards his house the next block over. "I can see who counts with you, Snuff." Rick called after him. Snuffy kept walking.

Rick went in and made a cup of coffee. As he came back out on the porch, Jack drove up in his Corvette. He jumped out, and hauled his guitar, banjo, and a small suitcase up the steps. Rick took the banjo from him and raised one eyebrow.

"Putting the car in at Whitey's. He's going to tune it. Said he needs it for a day or two. I thought you wouldn't mind if I bunked with you."

"No problem, Jackorino. My house is your house, you know that."

Jack set his stuff inside the door. Opened his guitar case and took the twelve-string Gibson out on the porch. He sat down and began tuning.

"When you need to be at Whitey's?"

"Oh, nine, or so. They all gone?"

"Yep. Headed out to Maine. You should have seen that car. Looked like the Okies heading for California."

"Okies?"

"Yeah, you know. *The Grapes of Wrath.*"

"Didn't see that movie."

"It's a book, Jack. Well, it's a movie, too. But it's a book by Steinbeck. About the dust bowl. You know, back in the thirties."

"Ahh." Jack plucked a few strings, and sang:

> *"Thousands of folks back east they say,*
> *are leaving home most every day,*
> *beating their hot old dusty way, to the California line.*
> *Across the desert sands they roll.*
> *They're getting out of that old dust bowl.*
> *They think they're going to a sugar bowl. But this is what they find.*
> *The po-lice at the port of entry say,*
> *You're number fourteen thousand for today.*
> *If you ain't got the doh, re, mi boy, If you ain't got the doh, re, mi,*
> *You better go back to beautiful Texas,*
> *Oklahoma, Georgia, Kansas, Tennessee.*
> *California is a Garden of Eden (It's true!)*
> *A paradise to live in or see.*
> *But believe it or not,*
> *You won't find it so hot,*
> *If you ain't got the doh, re, mi."*

"Woody Guthrie," Jack said, playing a few more licks. "Needs a fiddle, though."

"Damn Jack, if they ever set Einstein to music, you'd be a friggin' nuclear scientist."

Jack laughed, and switched to a rock and roll beat. He crooned:

> *"E equals M C squared, oh baby,*
> *E equals M C squared.*
> *You got an ass that's critical mass*
> *I got a notion for a nuclear explosion*
> *E equals MC squared."*

Rick threw up his hands, and laughed. "I give up, Dr. Einstein. That's cool, relatively speaking."

Jack put his guitar back in its case. "What's the plan, mi amigo. How are we going to celebrate your last free days?"

"Fuck me, Jack after that last drink you gave me, I'm afraid to drink with you. I know why it's a secret recipe. Everyone who ever drank it died."

"Oh, you pussy. You just didn't let it settle long enough. Can't go getting up at the crack of dawn after you drink the nectar of the gods."

"Yeah, Bacchus and Pluto, and old Satan himself. Some gods."

"What time is it? Eight-fifteen? We can head over any time. Whitey's usually up and working early."

Jack shucked his guitar inside the front door, and strolled back out to his Corvette. "Want a head start?"

"Nah," Rick hollered getting in his Chevy. "I know where it is. I'll see you there."

Jack roared off in a cloud of blue smoke. Rick followed at a leisurely pace. Whitey lived out towards Westminster, up a dirt road just beyond the old town dump. Now that the landfill had been closed, this was becoming very desirable property. Rick wondered if George Gorse had his eyes set on snapping up the property cheap after driving Whitey out of town. It fit what Rick had learned of Gorse's reputation. "Sonofabitch," he muttered, turning into the drive. Whitey's house was a small, traditional white-clapboarded farmhouse. What had once been a dairy barn was converted into a three-stall garage, with clearance enough for a semi-tractor. Whitey had one grease-pit, and two lifts installed. Jack's Corvette was already on one of the lifts.

"Don't you worry about it, son," Whitey was saying as he gave Rick a wave. "I'll fix your little baby up so you'll think it just came off the show-room floor."

"Think you can tune it to get twenty miles per gallon?" Rick asked as he walked into the barn.

"Twenty gallons per mile, is more like it with them two four-barrels," Whitey snorted. "Hey, Squirt. Leave your buggy here, too. I'll tune it up for your wedding voyage. My little gift to you."

"Shit, that means walking to town," Jack grumbled.

"I'll give ya a lift, man. I gotta get some parts." Whitey chuckled. "Course, a little *shank's mare* might take a pound or two off that monumental gut of yours."

"Whadaya mean? I'm in shape." Jack sounded offended.

"Damn right," Rick chimed in. "Pear-shaped."

"Oooh, that hurts. You really know how to hurt a guy."

"This is going to be my last week at DeBoni," Whitey said. "I just can't work there with Charlie's kid getting killed. I know I shouldn't, but I feel responsible."

"Wow. That'll leave old man Benito in the lurch, won't it?" Rick asked.

"Nah. I got a guy, Jim Evans, used to work for me at Freighthaulers. Knows everything about as good as I do. He'll take the job."

"What are you going to do, Whitey?" Rick asked.

"Don't rightly know. Work gypsy here for a while, anyway. Depends a bit on what happens to Annabelle, what with D-d-donnie turning up d-d-dead."

"What do you think will happen to the restaurant?"

"Beats me. We'll find out Tuesday, I guess. Got a call from Sam Trout. Says he wants us at the reading of the will."

"Tuesday? That's pretty early. I didn't think they'd read the will until after the week or whatever when the guys in his synagogue pray for him."

"I don't know nothing about that," Whitey scratched his head. "But I think those two sisters are pushing to get this done fast, so they can start spending the big bucks."

"That I can believe. Bet those shit-ass nephews are out pricing Lamborghinis and Ferraris. Hey, maybe he'll leave it all to you, Whitey." Jack laughed.

"More likely, they want to collect on my parts bill, so they can divide up the $47 bucks I owe, too." Whitey grinned. "Come on. I'll run you in and drop you in the square."

Jack and Rick piled into Whitey's pristine '58 Olds. The diesel turned over and purred like a kitten. "Now that's an engine, gentleman." Whitey flashed his teeth. "None of that expensive gasoline. Just pure diesel fuel. So cheap, they practically pay you to take it. Heck you can run the oil from your furnace if you want and beat the tax."

"Great, if you're pushing a load of dirt," Jack sneered. "But how's it off the line?"

Whitey didn't answer, just put the pedal to the metal, and the car launched like a rocket. It was doing sixty by the end of the driveway, and Whitey had to brake sharply to make the turn onto Route 5. "Rocket-88, gentleman." He laughed.

"It was downhill," Jack said through gritted teeth, hanging onto the chicken bar for dear life.

"Maybe I can find one these here diesels for your 'Vette. I do, I'll just drop it in."

"No way, man. That would be a sacrilege."

"I suppose it would," Whitey sighed. "The god of stupidity would send you to hell for doing something half-way smart."

Whitey dropped them off at the Coffee Shop, saying both cars would be done by 3:00 on Sunday. He headed off to the auto parts dealer.

"Shit. We're on foot, man. For nearly two days. What the hell are we going to do? I'm bored already."

"Stop whining, Jack. Let's get some beer and hooch, and head back to my place. We can hang around a while, then go looking for trouble." Rick dug in his wallet and gave Jack a ten-dollar bill. "If you can buy the booze, I got to go to the bank."

Jack was a full year younger than Rick, but even though he wasn't quite twenty, he had no trouble buying at the State Liquor Store. His size and natural gift for gab carried the day. He bought a fifth of cheap whiskey and another of rum.

Rick was glad the Vermont National had Saturday morning banking hours. He deposited the check his father had given him, and met Jack in front of the bank. They stopped at a corner grocery store on the way home, and bought a couple of six-packs of beer and some sandwich makings.

"Leave the stuff on the dining room table," Rick said. "Before we put anything away, I'm cleaning the refrigerator."

"Ah, the slime monster, I know it well." Jack cracked a beer and went back on the porch to play his guitar.

Rick found some garbage bags, and began systematically sniffing everything in the refrigerator, throwing most of it away. When it was empty, he scoured it with Clorox and then baking soda. As he cleaned, he considered that if the refrigerator bothered him, he could clean it any time. Then he rejected the idea. If you took the initiative and did a job, it was yours for life. Only Willa had the gumption to take on housework that needed to be done without regard for the consequences.

Satisfied, he stored the salvaged food plus the beer and the sandwich makings they had purchased. He too, cracked a beer and went out and sat on the porch, listening to Jack play.

It was a hot day, and the two friends sucked up beer for a while, and then made a sandwich for lunch. After lunch, they switched to hard liquor, and Rick fell asleep in a living room chair about mid-afternoon. When he woke up, it was after eight, and in the shadow of Fall Mountain it was already getting dark. Jack was snoring on the sofa.

"Hey Jackson, you dead?" Rick hollered loud enough to pierce the veil of sleep.

"Hmm, hum, nope. Just resting." Jack turned over.

"Come on. Get up. Man, I can't believe a whole Saturday went by and we did nothing. You'd think we were old men."

"It's them afternoon cocktails," Jack stretched and grinned. "They rob you of your vital energy."

"Let's hoof it up to the Twist Cone, and get something to eat. I'm starved."

"Alright, alright. Gotta piss." Jack staggered through the kitchen to the back bathroom.

"Sound like a race horse, back there." Rick got up and headed upstairs to change his shirt and comb his hair. When he came back down, Jack was neat and presentable.

"Let's go Cisco," Jack slipped his guitar case behind the sofa.

"Si, Pancho." Rick found his wallet and they headed out the door.

They walked slowly, and the streetlights were on by the time they reached Twist Cone at the north end of town. There were a few high school kids around, but no one they knew. They ordered burgers and fries and found a booth.

"This is about as wasted a day as I remember," Jack muttered between bites.

"You got that, Jackson." Rick replied. "Probably be the story of my life from here on, except of course for the drinking. Doubt if I'll see much of that."

They finished and just sat, staring out at the night. Rick smoked. Jack bought a second order of fries, and munched them slowly. It was nearly ten when they were startled out of their lethargy by the rumbling and backfiring of a motorcycle.

"That hog's got some problems," Jack muttered. "Who the hell is it?"

Rick craned his neck. "Rocky Santee and a couple of goons. Who else?" He lit another cigarette.

Rocky and the other two motorcyclists talked and joked out in the parking lot for a few minutes. Rick didn't really know either of the other two. He thought one was from North Walpole, and the other maybe from Springfield, but he wasn't sure. "Add all their IQ's together and you get a negative number," he joked.

"Yeah, I think these guys make the Three Stooges look like Nobel laureates," Jack answered.

"Don't you be talking down the Stooges," Rick chuckled. "Them's my brothers."

Santee came through the door. "Hey Dora, half a Coke, okay?"

"Sure Rocky. It's on the house."

"Thanks, Dora." Santee turned and pulled a pint from his pocket, he topped off the half-cup of Coke with whiskey. "Whatcha looking at, freaks?" He challenged.

"Nothing, Rocky. Just looks like you got the best Coke in the house." Jack chuckled.

"Yeah, well to hell wid this shit. I'm gonna score some *grass*, man."

"Around here?" Rick laughed. "I think the only grass in Bellows Falls is lawn clippings."

"A lot you know, fuckface. But this stuff's in North Walpole. Over the bridge."

"That, I can believe," Jack said. "Some real low life's over there."

"You guys want some? Cost you five bucks an ounce. I get another ten bucks, we can buy a kilo. Share it up."

Rick started to say no, but Jack jumped in. "Sure, why the hell not. I don't smoke the stuff, but there are always broads looking for a little doobie."

Rick laughed. "If it's a little doobie you're their man."

"Hey, watch it man. You'll hurt my feelings. "

"You guys in?" Santee was antsy. "Show me the green."

"Hell, we'll come along," Jack said. "Got nothing else to do."

"Let's go then. We'll leave the bikes here." Santee led the way out the door.

It didn't feel right to Rick, but he shrugged and followed Santee. They walked in a small group, Santee and Rick side-by-side, Jack with one of the goons on either side of him.

The streets were empty as they turned and walked across the Arch Bridge. Halfway across the bridge Santee spun and threw a punch that landed square on Rick's lower lip. He felt his lip split and a front tooth loosen.

Santee stood and danced in front of him, hands up, getting ready to punch again. "Come on you muthafuck. You niggalover. Fight you chickenshit."

Rick kept his arms at his sides. "I'm not fighting you, Rocky. Why would I fight you? Why did you hit me?"

Santee raged, "Fight, you nigger lover. Let that fuckin' nigger fuck our white girls. I'll kill you." Finally, frustrated that Rick wouldn't strike back, Santee grabbed him by the front of his shirt and dragged him over to the rail. He pushed Rick out, leaning him over the edge.

Santee spit. Rick watched the spittle spiral down to the dark swirling water of the Connecticut River, forty feet below. "See how long it took that spit to hit, muthafucker? How long you think it'll take you?"

"The same amount of time," Rick said quietly.

"What? You stupid shit. A big fat piece of turd like you is gonna go a lot faster."

"You'd think so, wouldn't you? But that isn't how it works. Gravity works on everything the same, Rocky. You, me, spit, whatever. Galileo proved it around 1600." Rick stared down at the water and wondered if he was going to find out if it was really true.

Rocky pulled him back onto the bridge. "Huh? Well, what about that nigger? How come you're helping that nigger fuck all our white girls?"

"You mean Whitey? Who said Whitey ever fucked anybody but Annabelle?"

"Gorse. He says pretty soon every kid in town will be chocolate."

"You know Annabelle, don't you Rocky?"

"Da black lady what cooks at the Village Inn. Sure. She this nigger's woman?"

"You bet your ass. And if Whitey even *thinks* about thinking about any other woman, white, black, or green, Annabelle will cut his nuts off, and serve them to him as Rocky Mountain oysters."

Rocky laughed. "I bet she could do it too. She's one tough lady."

"She is. But shit, Rocky. Whitey's a good guy. You want your hog to run right, run it down to Whitey's place. He's a fucking genius with motors."

"Yeah? My machine is running a little ragged. He do that for me?"

"You bet. If I ask him." Rick thought furiously. "Hey Rocky, you want to drive truck? The big ones? The semis?"

"Yeah, man. But nobody will hire you unless you're already a truck-driver."

"Whitey's your guy. He knows every trucking company in the country. They're begging him to work on their diesels. He asks, they'll give you a job. But he won't ask for you unless he thinks you can do the job."

"Hey, you fuck. I'd be a great truck-driver."

"Go see him tomorrow. I'll call him. Tell him to expect you. But you got to stop listening to that asshole, Gorse. Man doesn't know shit."

They were standing talking calmly now in the middle of the road, in the middle of the Arch Bridge. A car started across the bridge, and they moved over onto the sidewalk again.

"Besides," Santee said. "It's fucks like you that get all the good girls."

"Huh?" Rick shook his head. "Me? What girls I get besides Ellen? I'm marrying her this week."

"I seen you cozy with that Kelly chick. I seen you just a week or so ago."

Rick laughed, and then stopped as Santee brought up his hands and said, "You laughing at me, muthafuck?"

"No, no Rocky. Honest. It's just, you know who we were talking about? *You.* Kelly's got the hots for you."

"You shittin' me, man? That classy broad?"

"Absolutely. Course, you know she's pregnant. She married Danny Dombroski, and he got blown up."

"That mean she can't fuck?"

"No, not at all. She can fuck all she wants for quite a while. And I think, you know, she really misses it."

"Shit, but she's gonna have a kid."

"Yeah, but the Feds will pay to raise the kid. You know, Social Security. The kid will get a monthly check till he's eighteen."

"Huh?" Rocky scratched his head. "Well, I ain't gonna pound ya, Wallace. But watch yourself, muthafuck." Rocky and his two thugs swaggered off the bridge, turning back towards the Twist Cone. At the edge of the bridge, Rocky turned and yelled back, "Call that Whitey guy for me. Okay?"

"Okay. First thing tomorrow," Rick hollered back, his voice cracking. "Oh, shit, Jackson. I may have peed my pants," he whispered.

"You and me both, Son." Jack put his arm around Rick, and led him off the bridge. They headed back to Rick's house, taking a short cut through the square.

Rick's knees were shaky. He felt like he might collapse at any second. "Jack," he asked, "why did we go with him? I mean you and me, we don't do pot. Why the fuck did we go walking across the Arch Bridge with the meanest thug in the goddamn state?"

"Asking myself the same question, Rick. I don't know. Bored, I guess. Bored, *and* stupid. That's all I can figure."

"You know, it's like I dreamt it all before-hand. I knew what was going to happen, but I couldn't stop it from happening. Shit." Rick touched his tooth and winced. Hope I don't lose this."

"Don't wiggle it. Leave it alone. Sometimes they heal up by themselves."

"Thank you, doctor Jack. Oh, yeah, and thanks for jumping right in and fighting for my life."

"Are you nuts? They'd have killed me. Besides, you were handling it. You were magnificent. I nearly shit my drawers when Santee said, 'How long you t'ink it take you to hit da water.' Then you say, 'Well, according to Newton's second law, and figuring the rate of free fall at thirty-two feet per second, I calculate that, allowing for the differences in aerodynamic structure, wind resistance, and other *extrania*, it would take approximately the same amount of time.'"

Rick laughed. "Ow. I didn't say that."

"Pretty close. Something about Galileo, I think. I mean, how in the world did you come up with that answer?"

"Don't know. It's just when somebody asks me a question, I know the answer to, I can't help but raise my hand. Compulsive brown-nose, I think."

"You should have seen Santee's face. It was like, duh! He was so amazed, he forgot why he was pounding the shit out of you."

"He ain't stupid, Jack. Undereducated, sure. But he's a pretty shrewd cookie, I think. Soon as he caught on that Whitey could help him, his whole attitude changed."

"That was brilliant, too. You got Whitey to fix his bike, which Whitey can do in a heartbeat, and you got Whitey giving him a reference or something. Damn, you think fast on your feet."

"I tell you, I wasn't thinking at all. It was like it was all scripted out. I just read the lines." They turned the corner to Rick's street. "You know when we were out at Whitey's, I got to thinking that maybe that creep Gorse has his eye on Whitey's property. You think?"

"Could be, could be. I gotta change and get a drink in me. Damn, I'm still shaking."

"You? Fuck, I can hardly stand."

The two staggered into the house. Jack headed for the back bathroom, and Rick headed upstairs. Fifteen-minutes later, they were both back in the living room, cleaned up, and sipping drinks.

"Ow, shit. That stings." The liquor felt like fire on Rick's split lip.

"Drink more. It'll numb it." Jack was gulping a huge rum and Coke. "Besides, the alcohol will keep it from getting infected."

"You are a wealth of medical knowledge, my friend." Rick winced, and took another big gulp. In fact, he could feel the alcohol gradually deadening the pain.

"You calling Whitey tonight?"

"Nah. Too late. They'll be up early tomorrow. Annabelle's got baking to do for the Sunday church crowd. Usually, Whitey takes her over to the restaurant about 5:00. He'll be home sipping coffee by quarter to six."

"You know you sicced that animal onto Kelly, don't you?" Jack was on his third drink and finally calming down.

Rick was well into drink two. He answered, "Only told him the truth. I wanted to say, 'If you weren't so busy looking at yourself in the fucking mirror, Santee, you'd have seen the chick drooling over ya.'"

"Really? She's got the hots for Santee? Damn that doesn't make much sense, does it? Course you never can figure why women pick one guy over another. Look at Ellen picking you."

Rick heard those words as he drifted off. When he opened his eyes, it was already getting light. Jack was sacked out on the sofa. Rick touched his lip with his fingers and winced. He wiggled his front tooth with his tongue, and winced again. "Shit. I was hoping it was a dream," he said out loud. It didn't wake Jack.

Rick went to the kitchen and made coffee. It was nearly six, so he grabbed the phone, and dialed Whitey's number.

"You're either real anxious or got a wrong number," Whitey answered.

"Got the right number, Whitey. This is Rick." He quickly filled Whitey in on the past night's doings. "Can you help Santee?" he asked.

"Yeah, yeah. Bike's no problem. Take about two minutes. I think Fred Henderson over Peterborough could use a trainee driver. You know Peterborough Trucking? He was telling me the other day how tough it is to find guys he can trust. I ain't sending this Santee over unless I think he'll give Fred a full day's work, for a full day's pay."

"You be the judge," Rick said. "I think he'll probably be okay. He's a tough guy, but that ain't all bad in that line of work. Say, Whitey, do you think this Gorse creep has his eye on your property?"

"If he does, he's shit-out-of-luck. I got a standing offer for thirty-five big ones. That's seven times what I paid. I doubt that little maggot could come up with anything close. Well, well, what have we here? I hear a motorcycle coming up my drive. Could be your thug. I'll see you this afternoon."

Jack was still asleep, so Rick took his coffee out on the front porch. The paperboy was pushing his cart up the street. Rick went down and collected the two Sunday papers, giving the paperboy the two dollars his mother had left. He had strict orders to save her the Sunday New York Times crossword puzzle.

It suited Rick's mood to sit on the porch, smoking, drinking coffee, and reading the Sunday papers. A little after ten, Jack staggered out to join him, nursing a Coca Cola. "You quit the party a little early," Jack grunted.

"What can I say? I was literally beat." Rick touched his lip. "Does this look bad?"

"Not too bad. A little swollen and purple. It'll be okay by Thursday, I think. You call Whitey?"

"Yep, and just in the nick of time. Santee drove up while we were on the phone."

"Huh. That punk's an early riser?"

"Seems to be. You up for some bacon and eggs? I'm cooking."

"Yeah, I guess. Nothing runny." Jack grimaced. "Couldn't take runny this morning."

Rick cooked, and they ate in silence, reading the paper. Rick cleared the dishes and washed them. Then he said, "Hey, why don't we grab a couple of beers each, and hike over to Whitey's, by way of Gageville. You know. Follow the Old Covered Bridge Road, and cut up over the hill. Come down behind the new school and the cemetery. We can drop right down on him."

"We could toss a line in the Saxton's," Jack said. "We could, if we had our fishin' stuff."

"Yeah, mine all went to Maine with the Stooges."

"Mine's in Chester."

Neither had anything better to do, so they dug around for an old knapsack, stuffed a six-pack in it, and hiked out to Gageville. It wasn't a long walk, maybe a mile-and-a-half. Rick was in his stride, but Jack was lagging. "Not so fast. This is more walking than I do in a week."

"We're committed now." They hiked across the steel trestle bridge that spanned the Saxton's where the old covered bridge had once stood. It had been one of a half-dozen covered bridges burned by vandals a couple of years earlier. No one was ever caught for it, but both Rick and Jack figured that Conrad Briton, the president of the school board's son, nicknamed *The Torch*, had something to do with it.

They stayed on Old Covered Bridge Road until a dirt track shot off over Bald Hill. They followed the old logging road up to a strange area of sand dunes and trails. Kids had raced cars, shot their twenty-two's, and parked up here for two generations. They stopped and rested, looking over the carcasses of old jalopies. "Regular demolition derby up here," Rick said.

"Yep. Old Chimp Morrison must have left five or six of those, himself." Jack said. "That boy rolled more metal than a steel mill, and never got so much as a scratch."

"What's he doing? You know?"

"Yeah. Last I heard he was stealing cars in Boston. Insurance scam. Owners pay him to steal them, and dump them in the harbor."

"Cream rises to the top, I always say." Rick laughed. "BF boy makes good in grab and sink scam. I can see the headlines now."

Jack looked back the way they had come. They could see the gash where I-91 was being built. "You know," he said. "This road is going to change our world. We won't be just exporting our best fledgling gangsters to Boston. We'll be getting the scum off the sewers from New York, New

Jersey, you name it. It's going to get ugly here. Look at last night. Already we expect to be able to buy a kilo of pot."

"Afraid you're right, Jack." Rick swallowed the last of his beer, and pitched the bottle against a rock. "What are you going to do?"

"Don't know. Hit the road, maybe. Travel around. Play and sing. You can get a gig almost anywhere if you aren't greedy. Come Thursday, when you and Ellen get married, there ain't going to be much left for me to do in this town." Jack finished his beer and tossed the bottle into the collection of broken glass. "I'll leave it for some kid to use as a target."

Rick hefted the much lighter knapsack, and they started down the hill to Whitey's. It was only another mile or so, and the dirt road down was well used. As they walked into the yard, Whitey was running a rag over Rick's Chevy. It gleamed in the afternoon sun.

"Wow. It never looked that good before, Whitey." Rick hollered as they came across the yard.

"Wait till you hear it run. Purrs like a kitten." Whitey flashed his teeth. "Your beast is roaring and ready to go too, Jack."

The Corvette sat like a crouched panther in the shade of Whitey's big maple.

"Santee show up?" Rick asked.

"Yep. Nice fella once he gets over hisself. We tuned that Harley up just perfect. It rumbles that ol' *potatopotatopotato*. Boy was right pleased with it. Got him hooked up with Fred, too. I think I got me a new best buddy."

"That's a relief. I can't use many more of these." Rick pointed at his fat lip.

"That's a beaut. Your new wife is going to love it." Whitey chuckled. "You know, you may have been onto something with that land grab thing. Santee said Gorse is trying to buy up Bald Hill and the whole area up here. Looking to put in some kind of a dirt track for racing. My driveway is the best access road you can find. Plus, you know I'd give the boy some grief with the town council over a dirt track. Especially so close to our new high school."

"Santee done doing his dirty work?"

"Oh, yeah. He said the farm boys abandoned Gorse a couple of weeks ago. Didn't see nothing in it for them. That's when he started recruiting the hoods. Santee said Gorse bought them some hooch and pot. Promised they could run the track. And talked up this nigger thing. Now Rocky say, 'Any fuck what touch my friend Whitey, answer to me.'"

"Hey, Whitey, you go over and fix Ho Chi Minh's car, and we can end the war." Jack laughed. "Tune up, not out. Maybe I won't have to worry about the draft."

Whitey wouldn't take money from either Jack or Rick. He said Rick's was a present and he got more than enough value winning over Santee. Jack wished him well, and headed out saying, "I got to run this beast for a while. I'll see ya sometime, Rick. Maybe tomorrow night."

Whitey looked over at Rick. "What you hanging around, for boy? You got no place to go?"

Rick smiled. "No, I got places to go and promises to keep, Whitey. I'm just thinking about Santee. Do you think he's okay? I mean, can you trust him?"

Whitey pulled at his chin. "Trust him? Trust him to probably do a good enough job for Fred. Do I need to trust him more than that?"

"No, not you, I guess. It's just, well I kind of fixed him up with this girl, and I'm worried that maybe I didn't do her any favors."

"Let's have a cold one, and you can tell me about it, boy."

Rick sipped the cold beer and told Whitey the whole story about Kelly. He hadn't meant to. He had intended to tell him about letting Santee know about Kelly, but before he was done, he told the whole sordid tale, from arranging her marriage to cheating on Ellen. Whitey just listened.

When Rick was done talking, Whitey got up and opened another two bottles of beer. He handed one to Rick.

"Here's what I think," Whitey said. "It's over and done. Santee and this Kelly girl will either do all right, or they won't. It ain't your worry. Kelly is doing what comes natural to a woman, and that's finding a mate to protect her baby. You was the first one she grabbed at. But you're taken. Now, she's grabbing for Santee. And, I tell you, she could probably do worse."

"You just got to get over it, boy. I think you're still half hoping you'll get a little more of that *poontang*. But now, you has to pay attention to your one and only. And I mean, only. Get that, Squirt? But don't you go blabbing to her about your adventures. Ain't no woman wants to hear that."

Rick hung his head. "I hear you ,Whitey. You're right, as usual."

They sat quietly for a minute. Then Rick said, "Whitey, as long as we're talking all serious here, can I ask you a question?"

"You can ask, boy. Doesn't mean I'll answer."

"Well, I see you putting up with a whole lot of shit. That Jensen guy calling you a nigger. Gorse trying to get the town worked up to burn you out, and maybe hang you, I don't know. And the cop said it. He said if he was you, he would be plenty pissed at somebody like Jensen laying the *nigger* on him in public. How do you do it? How come you're not just filled with hate and ready to kill?"

Whitey stood up. He hitched his thumbs in the back of his belt and stood facing Rick, balancing on his toes. Rick saw his left shoulder dip, and then his right-hand flashed out with a straight razor that was lightly touching Rick's throat.

"What you call a nigger with a straight razor, honky?" Whitey's voice was low and mean.

"Suh-s-sir," Rick whispered, afraid to swallow.

Instantly, the razor disappeared. "And what do you call me, Squirt?"

"I guess I always called you my friend," Rick said, his voice a little unsure.

"Well, what you think is better? Is it better somebody calls you *sir*, 'cause he's afraid you'll slit his throat, or is it better he calls you *friend*, and means it?"

"It ain't that I ain't got some hate. I got anger for my papa. I can't hardly even remember him, but I know those fuckers murdered him 'cause he was black, and he was there. No other reason. And I got a ton of anger for

Billy. When I found him hanging in that tree, I swore I would kill every one of those motherfuckers if it took me my whole life. Oh, I got hate enough."

Whitey paced. "Squirt, you don't know. You just don't know. You know how many black people was killed by the Klan in St. Louis? Thousands. You ever hear about Tulsa, Oklahoma? Town went on the rampage, burned out black folk who never done them a lick a harm, and murdered may 300, or 400 men, women, and children. Little babies, Squirt. Little babies."

Whitey picked up his beer and drank. Then he sat down and put his feet up. "I was carrying all that hate, Squirt. I went down to New Orleans and I was hanging out with some guys and we were planning. We were going to start a revolution. We were going to start murdering right back. Then, Squirt, I got Annabelle. And I realized right then and there, that I had all the important stuff. What I need some ignorant white man's respect when I got the best woman in the world loving me? And Annabelle, she introduced me to the Doctor King. You know that man, Squirt?"

"I've heard about him," Rick said. "I don't know a lot about him. Just that he's organizing some sit-ins and stuff down south."

"He's a beautiful man, Squirt. He says that if we want the world to change, why we just got to change it, but we don't never have to raise our fists in anger. And damn, ain't he doing it?"

"He's making some powerful enemies, Whitey."

"And some powerful friends, Squirt. But mostly he just be making a difference. Annabelle had me take her down to Boston to hear him preach. Man, can that man preach. I can't remember his exact words. But what he said, Squirt, was that killing ain't never been stopped by more killing. Never. He said, only love stops killing. He says Jesus didn't tell you to love your Momma or your friends. He know you love those people. Jesus tell you to love your enemies. To turn the other cheek when they hits you. And Dr. King he says you love your enemies and it ain't long before they can't hate you. They stop being your enemies. It's just not human nature to give back hate for love. "

"So yeah, Squirt. I got some anger, but mostly, I just shakes my head in wonder at how dumb some people can be. But like with Rocky, there, a little good, beats out using the razor damn near every time. Just the same, though, a razor can be a useful tool. So I keep it handy, just in case love don't work fast enough, and some redneck is getting ready to hurt some-body I care about, somebody like Annabelle."

"Thanks, Whitey. I hope the hell I've found a woman who is half the woman Annabelle is. And I hope I can be half the kind of man you are. You're the best. "

"You'll do all right. Squirt. Just don't think too much."

Rick headed home and called Ellen. She and Janet were still in Boston. They had made a run to outfit themselves for the wedding. Rick decided he too better start thinking about the wedding.

He went upstairs and hunted through his closet looking for the clothes Ellen told him he would wear, and stuff he might want to move out to the little house. He came across a suit jacket that belonged to his older brother, Steve. He tried it on, but it was too long in the sleeve, and too tight around the chest. The thought struck him that his mother had put Steve in the same black hole she had consigned Tommy Mac. Steve went from family superstar, to just about nothing, in no time at all. Rick won-dered if the same fate awaited him after he got married.

He poked around, and then hit the sack early. But sleep was elusive. "How do you plan the rest of your life?" he thought, and stared at the ceil-ing until sleep took him by surprise.

Chapter 30

Magus

The renewed energy carried over to Monday. The job hummed. They finished drilling the last of the northbound ledge in the morning, and moved the rigs down to begin working their way through the southbound ledge. It was good to have the full panoramic view of the job again.

The dynamite crew joined the drillers at lunch. Everett was working with the dynamite crew, filling in until they could hire another weak-minded, strong-body, to haul and lift. Everett immediately gravitated to the softer chores, driving and working with Blaster Bill, while Teach was back hauling fifty-pound boxes of explosive. But Teach didn't seem to mind. "By the Jesus," he said. "We keep up this good work, we'll be out of work by mid August."

"What the fuck do you care?" Henry asked. "You'll be in your cushy classroom by then, anyway. I heard John won the stretch above Springfield. We'll probably start clearing up there before the end of the summer."

"Hey, Everett," Rick asked between bites of his sandwich, "you been around since God made the earth. How come you don't have a nickname?"

"Hee, hee, Squirt. I've had a few, I have." Everett poured a cup of coffee and slurped it. "When I was your age, I was called *The Hammer*."

"That's 'cause he was always pounding his pud," Henry joked, making an obscene gesture.

"Your ass. I was a mean sonofabitch. That's in them days. Then, back shortly after I started with DeBoni, they called me *Flyer*, for a while."

Côte laughed. "I heard about that. You sent that poor little fella they hired right out of Randolph, for a bit of a ride."

"Dumb fuck," Everett coughed and spat. "We was putting a roof on a maintenance shed and it was windy. This little feller just got his degree from Randolph, and a brand spanking new grade-foreman thought he was a big boss. He's telling me this and that, and how to do simple shit. I was trying to slide one of those big tin panels in place on the roof, and the wind was giving me all kinds of problems. It was pretty scary, I'll tell ya. So, I hollers, 'Grab hold of this, kid.' He grabs it, and lifts it up flat into the wind and I let go. Kid didn't. He sailed off the roof like an *aereoplane*. And crashed and burned like one, too. Hee, hee."

"Kill him?" Rick asked, not seeing what was funny here.

"No, busted him up some. They said I was flying him like a kite. That's why they called me *Flyer*, I guess. Probably would've called the kid *Kite*, if he had come back. But last I knew he was selling shoes over in Bennington. Figured it was safer just to look up skirts, I guess."

"Mostly, though, I just try to avoid getting a nickname. It just gets ya noticed."

"Hell, yes," Henry added. "Then, they'd want the old fart to work."

"I heard they used call you *The Dip*," Côte said. "This old fart can pick a pocket with the best of"em. Ain't that so?"

"It's true. I learned it working in carnies when I was just a kid. They used to send us out to work the crowd. We could keep half of what we brought back. Course, took most of us about a minute to figure there wasn't much sense in bringing any of it back. Ain't this your watch, Teach?" Everett handed Teach his pocket watch and grinned.

"I knew you did that," Teach laughed. "It felt so good, I didn't want you to stop."

They were finishing lunch when PH came by. "Let's get moving. We gotta shoot that today. You think this is a fucking picnic?"

"No, it's lunch, mister. You don't fuck with lunch." Henry bit of a piece of cigar and spat it in PH's direction. "Course, you're enough to ruin anybody's appetite. I think I'll go puke."

PH glared at Henry, and then stormed off. Everyone got up and headed back to work. The dynamite crew headed back to the end of the north-bound lane, and the drillers to the leading edge of the southbound lane. Rick heard Everett say, "Someday somebody'll give that cocksucker his. Earn a damn good nickname."

It was 5:15 when they shot, losing just fifteen minutes of productive time. The drillers walked back and looked at the shot. "Fucking lucky," Henry said. "Big shot like that is mighty risky."

"Glad we're done with it," Côte said. "Lot better to be working the new ledge. This is going to be a purty road, ain't it?"

Rick stared back down the valley and smiled. The fill was starting to take shape. The first footings were in for the bridge. Paligrinni had drilling crews working the ledge across the way. You could capture what it was going to look like. "Damn right it will be pretty. We do good work."

Rick stopped at Polaski's Market on the way home, and picked up a few things. There was no sign of Jack, so he cooked himself up a little steak on the grill, and tossed it in a big Kaiser roll. The steak sandwich, some potato chips, and a little salad did the trick. He ate it on the front porch, sipping a cold beer.

After eating, he called Ellen. She was so excited about her trip to Boston that Rick didn't bother to tell her about the fight on the bridge with Santee. He wrote down all her last minute instructions. There was nothing he really had to do. Mostly, it was Ellen babbling her way through all her thoughts about getting married. Rick was glad she wasn't having any second thoughts. He told Ellen he was doing guard duty on

Wednesday night, so he could have Friday off. She was going home on Tuesday night to pick up some stuff while her mother was visiting in Massachusetts.

"Well, I guess I'll talk to you at the wedding," Rick said.

"Just be sure you say, 'I do.'" Ellen laughed. "I don't care if you say anything else."

The call put Rick was in a good mood. Jack showed up about 8:00, and they sat on the porch and drank beer.

"Is that who I think it is?" Rick asked pointing to the end of the street.

"Looks like *The Torch* to me," Jack said. "Must be a hot time somewhere tonight."

"Hey, Torch, what's up?" Jack hollered.

Conrad Briton, alias *The Torch*, came up onto the porch. "Just the guys I was looking for. Ya got another one of them beers?"

"Help self, Torch," Rick said. They waited while Briton went to the kitchen and got a beer. "Didn't leave any matches lying around, did I?" Rick joked.

Briton came back sipping a beer. He plunked down on the porch and lit a cigarette, flicking his lighter on and off a half-dozen times. "Shouda been there last night."

"Been where?" Jack asked.

"Down by the old paper company."

"Why? What was shaking?" Rick knew that no matter how hard he pushed, Conrad would have to deliver his tale with full dramatic effects.

"Big doings. Gorse was trying to get a mob together to go burn out the nigger." Conrad flicked his lighter a couple more times.

"Who was there?" Rick asked, suddenly concerned.

"Every low-life in town," Conrad smiled. "And me, of course. Gorse had a keg of beer and a half-dozen bottles of whiskey. He was really pouring the fuel on the fire."

"Cops break it up?" Rick had seen Whitey at work, so he knew he hadn't been burned out the night before.

"Better than cops." Conrad took a full swallow of beer. "Rocky Santee."

"*Brrum, bumblum, bumblum, bumblum.*" The Torch loved to make engine sounds. "That old Harley of his has never sounded better. He walks it down the hill on its back wheel, and then spins it with a power slide. He lifts it back up on its stand, and walks over to Gorse."

Conrad was standing now, acting it out.

"Gorse says, 'Hi, Rocky. We's burning out that nigger tonight.' Santee just looks at him. 'Ya with us, Rocky?' Gorse shouts. 'Cause we're doing it with or without ya.'"

"Rocky turns and looks at the crowd. There's maybe twenty-five punks there all liquored up. He says, 'Any of you muthafucka's lays a finger on my man Whitey, and you is dead. I personally am going to see to it. Got that?'"

"Well, they are all shucking and jiving and saying, 'Hey, man. We ain't gonna hurt nobody. We just be drinking this cocksucker's whiskey.'"

"Then Rocky turns, and he picks the keg out of the big garbage can. The can was filled with ice to keep the beer cold. Then he grabs Gorse by the crotch and the throat, and turns him upside down and stuffs him in the can. You can hear him gargling in the water and ice. I figure he's gonna drown. But Rocky picks up the whole can, Gorse and all, and throws it over the bank down to the river. Then he gets on his Harley and *brooa-rooom*, he does a wheelie all the way up to the square, and he's gone."

"Great story, Torch. That's worth another beer." Rick went in and brought out three fresh brews. "So did Gorse drown?"

"Nah, some guys pulled him out. They drank his whiskey and most of the beer, and went home. I'm guessing you won't hear Gorse talking nigger again any time soon."

Rick gave Jack a high-five. "Guess this fat lip worked for the best. Who would have thought it?"

Jack filled the Torch in on the doings the night before, elaborating on the way Rick buffaloed Santee with science and kindness.

"Not quite all true," Rick said. "But close enough. Maybe we're done with that crap, once and for all."

"The cops still haven't tagged anybody for the bomb," Jack reminded him. "Till they do, Whitey will be a suspect."

"I think they are looking for Magus now, though." Rick mused. "I don't know they can prove it, but I think they've moved him up to number one suspect."

They talked for a while, and then Rick left Conrad and Jack on the porch, and hit the sack. The next morning, he noticed that sometime during the night, the Torch had lived up to his name. There was a pile of several hundred burned matches. It made Rick shudder.

Tuesday was a pretty ordinary day at work. The talk was about Whitey taking the afternoon off to go to the reading of D-d-donnie's will. Guys had Whitey inheriting a billion dollars. Word had also leaked that this was Whitey's last week, and naturally the road crew put the two things together.

"You think that nigger gave that old Jew blow-jobs?" PH snarled.

"Knowing Whitey, I'd guess ring-jobs," Côte answered. "Man gives a mean ring-job. You see what he done for my little beauty?" Côte was talking about his decrepit '48 Ford.

"I'd give you a ream-job, you cocksucker," Henry said under his breath as PH walked away.

Rick didn't find out what actually happened until Wednesday morning. He had packed a sleeping bag and some snacks in his trunk to tide him over Wednesday night. He got to the job around six in the morning. Whitey's car was already there. Whitey was sitting in the maintenance shed sorting through the tool chest, setting his tools in a separate carryall.

"Hey, Whitey, what happened? Are you a billionaire?"

"Sit down, Rick. Grab a cup of coffee. This was the strangest thing that ever happened to me in my life, and I've had a few strange ones."

Rick did as he was told. He lit a cigarette and sipped the hot, black brew. "Tell away." He knew there was no sense trying to hurry Whitey.

"Went home about noon. Picked up Annabelle on the way. We got cleaned up, and got down to Lawyer Trout's office about 2:00. We wasn't the first or the last. They showed us into this room with a huge, polished oak table. Big enough to seat twenty people. D-d-donnie's two sisters and their husbands was already sitting down. They was on opposite sides of the table. Muriel O'Reilly and Jimmy on one side. Ruth Karpinski and Stan on the other. Their sons, I forget who belongs to who, but all of them, Michael, Jimmy, Little Stan, and Donald, are all sitting there joking around. They sit us down at the far end. Pretty soon other people who work at businesses that D-d-donnie owns come in. Jack Murphy, who runs the Chevy dealership. Maurice, who runs the Cadillac side. Sammy Goodwin, who's running the rags, Henry Orbit, the guy doing the oil business. Couple of others I don't know. And two rabbis. Rabbi Levy from Claremont, and Rabbi Wasserman from Keene. And, oh yeah, Shepherd Farmer, the Unitarian preacher was there."

"When we're all sitting down, Sam Trout himself comes in. He looks like he was already governor. He's dressed to the nines in a three-piece suit, dark hair, steely-gray at the temples, and a smile that's pretty near as good as mine." Whitey grinned.

"Sam stands up there and thanks us all for coming. He apologizes for how quick this is after the burial. He says something about it being wrong to read the will before the mourning period is over, but that the family has insisted. He hopes the rabbis will forgive this impropriety. They nod and smile. Everyone nods and smiles."

"Then, Sam says he's going to read the will just as Donny put it down. These are Donny's words. He says, 'I want to stutter when I read this, because that's how my friend D-d-donnie talked. But I won't. If I slip, please forgive me.'"

"He reads, 'I Donald Eckberg, being of sound mind, do this fourteenth day of May, 1964, set forth my last will and testament.' He stops. 'As you can see,' he says, 'this is a very recent will. There have been other wills, but they have all been superseded by this will. Sometimes when people don't like the way the last will reads, they try to get it thrown out and have an earlier will instated. I helped D-d-donnie write all of his wills. This is by far the most generous he has been to any of you. At D-d-donnie's instructions we destroyed all prior wills. I do not believe that any copies of prior wills exist. This is it.'"

"He reads through some legal mumbo-jumbo, then he gets to the bequeathing. 'To my sisters, Muriel O'Reilly, and Ruth Karpinski, I leave each the deeds to their homes in Florida, their Cadillacs, with the promise of a new Cadillac each year, when they return their old Cadillacs in good condition, and a sum of $500,000 each.' The two ladies throw their hands up in front of their mouths. Sam keeps reading. 'You girls have lived off me for forty years. Your husbands have stolen millions of dollars from me. I have the proof of this. The money I leave each of you is enough, provided you don't let those crooks Jimmy and Stan get their hands on it. Join the other old Jewish ladies in Florida, and have a nice time.'"

"There was some commotion here. The old ladies fainted, and had to be revived, and their husbands huffed and muttered. Once they all get settled, Sam gets them all upset again. He reads, 'For each of my shit-ass nephews, Michael, James, Stanley, and Donald, I have given you employment for all your working lives. Each of you has proven to be useless as an employee, and dishonest to boot. I have evidence showing that you have each stolen thousands of dollars, and would have stolen more, had I given you the chance. So, now I give you what I had when I came to this town. I had $14. 95. To be generous, I conclude that in today's money, that's worth 100 times more. So, I bequeath to each of you, $1,495.00. Take it and do as I did. Make your own fortune.'"

"Well, let me tell you there was some screaming and hollering and yelling about I'll sue, and all manner of profanities."

"When Lawyer Trout got them quieted down, he says, 'You better listen to this,' and reads from the will. 'Over the past several decades, I have carefully collected evidence of every illegal act performed by my relatives. Mostly, they stole from me. Sometimes, they stole from other people and

I had to make sure that the people they stole from did not suffer. I have given to my lawyers, to be held in a safe place, incontestable evidence of three felonies committed by Jimmy O'Reilly, the elder, and seven, by Jimmy O'Reilly, the younger; six felonies by Stanley Karpinski, the elder, and four, by Stanley, the younger, who is not the sharpest knife in the drawer. I have evidence of three cases of *grand theft auto*, by Michael, plus other felonies too numerous to mention here. I have evidence of felonious assault committed by Donald, and a documented case of statutory rape. This evidence is sufficient to send each and every male relative to a long vacation in Windsor State Penitentiary. In the event that any of my relatives take action to overturn this will, or in any way hamper the distribution of assets set forth herein, I instruct my attorneys to turn all evidence over to the Windham County Attorney, and those matters that represent federal crimes, of which there are eleven, to the U.S. Attorney, and to spare no expense in assuring that these felons are brought to justice.'"

"'If you are thinking about statute of limitations,' Sam says, 'there are quite a number of these crimes that are still prosecutable.'"

"Well, there was all kinds of commotion and screaming, and all the family stormed out. Annabelle and me and the rest of them folks just sat there with our jaws on the floor. It was amazing. Then Sam reads the rest of the will, which basically gives each business to the guy running it, along with some working capital. He gives the two rabbis control of the income stream from Standard Oil, but he does it under a trust that Sam runs and gets a management fee from. He sets up a chair in Religious Thought, for Shepherd Farmer, at Vermont College in Woodstock. The old man is so pleased, he grins from ear-to-ear."

"What about you guys, Whitey?" Rick is on the edge of his chair.

"Well, that's what I was thinking, too. Then Sam says, 'Annabelle, I'm not going to leave you the Village Inn. It's not worthy of your talents. Instead, I have purchased a piece of property at the intersection of Interstate 91 and Interstate 89 in White River Junction. I bequeath this land to you and to your husband Whitey. And I bequeath a construction fund of $500,000, to build a fine restaurant and a diesel service operation. I'm sure you two will make me proud.'"

"Holy shit, Whitey. That's fantastic. It couldn't happen to better people. Damn. That is fantastic."

"It is, isn't it." Whitey was quiet. "That old man was quality people. We never asked for nothing, but still he reached out and did this for us. We're going to call it *D-d-donnie's Dine and Diesel*. What do you think?"

"I think, great. Oh, man. What a fantastic deal. There are going to be a lot of people who hate it that you got this lucky, Whitey, but believe me, you and Annabelle deserve it. You got to invite me to the inaugural dinner. Me and Ellen that is."

"Rick, you've been a hell of a good friend. You can eat with us any day, and every day. And you know I mean that."

"I do, Whitey, but I'd look like a balloon after about a week of Annabelle's cooking."

The other mechanics began to wander in, hollering at Whitey to leave them a few tools. "I can't help it all the good stuff is mine," Whitey said. "You guys get old Charlie to buy you some tools. Can't fix stuff without tools."

Rick left them laughing and joking, and headed up to the ledge.

Word had gotten out that Rick was going to get married Thursday night, so he had to endure an endless series of crude and tasteless jokes. At lunch, Côte had to tell him about his neighbor, *Friendless Freddy*.

"Ol' Friendless was not good for much. He was a mooch and shiftless. Couldn't get a day's work out of that man. So you can imagine we was all pretty surprised when old Friendless caught himself a wife. She was from up in the Northeast Kingdom, and probably hadn't seen many men other than loggers and poachers. She warn't bad to look at, mind ya. Kinda plain, but pleasant." Côte took a sip of his coffee, and leaned back.

"Well, couple of things happened. First, ol' Friendless decided he just had to run some pigs. He got about a dozen, and had them wallowing out there in a mud-hole on the corner of his property. Then, by God, didn't he get his ol' lady pregnant? About a year latter, the pigs was pretty big and the kid was maybe three-months old. Friendless' wife handed him the baby while she was doing the laundry or something. Old Friendless, he walked out to look at his pigs, and didn't he drop the baby right into the slew. Well, a big old sow just gobbled that baby right up. Just like that."

"Jesus, Côte, that's pretty gruesome," Rick said.

"Worse than that for ol' Friendless. His ol' lady just shut him right off."

"She what? Shut him off?"

"You bet. She's says, 'Goddamn it, Friendless I ain't lying on my back and grinding my hips and letting you stick that filthy thing in me just to make fodder for your pigs.'"

Côte let out a hoot. "Ain't gonna make no fodder for your pigs. So ya see, Squirt. You gotta be careful. Them women is always looking for an excuse not to give ya a good piece of ass from time-to-time."

Rick shook his head. Sometimes construction humor just passed him right by.

Rick shared Whitey's good luck with everyone, and almost to a man they whooped and hollered and said, "Damn, if ever a man deserved it, Whitey does." The exception was PH. He said, "Fuckin' nigger. Well at least he'll go be worthless someplace else."

Rick bit back his anger. No sense losing his job.

At quitting time, Rick went down to the office and waited for the Duke, shooting the shit with Tim, the timekeeper. Tim was grinning about Whitey's news. "Dang, we will be up that way in a year or two. I'm planning on getting a permanent meal ticket at Annabelle's restaurant."

"Hate to lose him," the Duke said coming in the door. "But a man gets a chance like that, he's got to jump on it." He looked at Rick, "Okay, Wallace, here's the deal. You head out like you were going home. Wait maybe two hours, then come back through the right-of-way from Arden Hill Road. Park out of sight. Find a perch up on the ledge, and watch down on the fill. If they do anything, it will probably be to the footings. Here's a radio. It's a direct link to the State Police barracks up the top of the hill. They say they'll have a couple of guys on call all night. They can be here in three or four minutes. Don't, and I repeat, do not take any chances, or try to apprehend anybody. I don't want another kid getting killed on my job."

"Yes, sir. It okay if a buddy of mine keeps me company?"

"Yeah, alright. But don't go getting drunk or fucking around on the equipment. Do the job. That's all I ask. If anybody shows up, it'll be along about midnight, I guess. I don't know that anybody will, but I figure tonight's the night, if it's going to happen. Everybody knows we shut down the watch. So, if it's an inside job, it'll happen tonight."

Rick drove back to town. Jack wasn't at the house, so he left a note on the dining room table, and a map showing where he would be. Then he grabbed a sandwich, a six-pack of beer, added that to the snacks he had in the trunk, and headed back to the job.

It was about 7:30, when he made his way slowly along the right-of-way. The job was deserted. He parked in the old quarry, and lugged his cooler and the radio up to the top of the ledge. He found a nice sheltered spot where he could see down across the fill, and settled down. He was just popping his second beer, when he heard a crash behind him. He dropped the beer and charged back along the path. Jack was trying to extricate himself from a raspberry bush. "Damn. I tripped."

"Great job, Daniel Boone. You made me drop my beer."

"No sweat, I brought some more. Help me get the fuck out of this."

With Rick's help, Jack finally got free. He followed Rick up to his vantage spot. "Not bad. You think you'll be able to see down there when it gets pitch dark?" It was already dusk.

"I think so. It's pretty open. And I think there's a moon tonight. Won't be any doings for a while. Did you bring anything to eat?"

"Eat? You want to eat? Maybe you should catch a squirrel and toast it on a fire or something. Yeah, there's some chips and stuff in the bag. You hear about Whitey?"

"You bet. He gave me the whole story this morning." Rick proceeded to retell Whitey's account of the will reading.

They sat for a while, sipping beer, and talking. "Wish I'd brought my guitar," Jack said. "This is frigging boring."

"We'd make great spies if you were whooping and singing," Rick said. "Why don't we take shifts? It's about 11:00, now. I'll go to 1:00, and you can go 1:00 to 3:00, and then I'll go the last shift."

"Makes sense. You bring a sleeping bag?"

"Yep, over there. Find someplace soft, and get some rest."

Jack disappeared into the brush. Rick stood up, and moved to the crest of the hill. In the moonlight, he could see most of the features down on the fill. He leaned against a maple and watched.

Nothing moved. Rick shifted. He was drowsy. He checked his watch: 12:15. Another forty-five minutes. He scanned the fill, and then did a double take. Something was moving down there.

"Could be a deer," he muttered to himself. He moved out into the open and strained his eyes to see. "Something. I think it might be somebody." He brought the radio up, ready to key the transmit button.

Suddenly, he heard a crunch behind him. He half-turned, and saw the grade-stake flash in the moonlight. He raised his arm in reflex. That, and the fact that this grade-stake had a knot right in the center, saved him from serious injury. He took the blow across his raised shoulder, and the stick snapped. Still, the force threw him to the ground. He rolled, trying desperately to get away.

At that second, a dark mass flew from the brush and crashed into the attacker. Jack, who had been pretty useless in the fight with Santee, was an instant hero. He flattened the attacker on the ground and pinned him. "Get a belt or something. Tie him up," he panted.

Rick pulled his belt loose with his good arm, and looped it around the attacker's feet. He jerked it tight, and Jack concentrated on his arms. He rolled the attacker over and brought his arms up behind him. "Get *my* belt," he gasped for breath.

Rick undid Jack's buckle, and pulled it clear. He had some feeling in his left arm now. He helped Jack tie the attacker's wrists, and then pull the two belts together to bend him double. "There, fuck. That'll hold him."

"Shit, I gotta call the cops." Rick thumbed the *mike*, and called the State Police. "This is the watchman at DeBoni's. We got vandals on the fill, and an attacker on the hill."

"On our way, sir." the voice responded.

Rick and Jack watched as the cops came with full sirens. There were two cruisers. They could see the vandals running back across the river and up the tracks. By the time the cruisers were on the fill, they were gone. Jack had a flashlight and signaled the troopers from the hill. After a bit, one of the cruisers inched its way up to the base of the ledge. A trooper climbed up to where they were holding the attacker.

"Who you got there?" He asked shining his flashlight on the trussed-up figure on the ground.

"Beats me, didn't look." Rick said. He walked over and turned the attacker over. "Sonofabitch. It's PH. Well what do you know?"

"Get off me, you fucking vandals," PH screamed. "Officer, these punks were trespassing. I tried to apprehend them. Sonsofbitches mugged me."

"What a crock of shit," Rick bellowed. "Look at this. Bastard beat me with a grade-stake. I think the fucker's in cahoots with those creeps down on the fill."

The trooper's radio crackled. He picked it up and spoke. He listened a bit, then said, "Ten-four." He took out his handcuffs, and snapped them on PH. Then he undid the belts and hauled PH to his feet. "The others got away. Ran up the tracks. We probably won't get them. Apparently they dropped a homemade dynamite bomb, though. I'll take this person in. We'll have somebody here all night. You guys come up to the barracks and give us a statement, will you?"

He led PH down the trail to the cruiser. PH was hollering and complaining how he was just doing his job.

"Thanks, Jackson. Nice tackle."

"Nothing any bona fide hero wouldn't have done. Too bad you're not a fair maiden. I could use a little *maiden head*."

"My hero. Brave and crude." Rick laughed. "Ouch, this shoulder really hurts. Let's go to the barracks."

The two headed back to the quarry. "Hey, where's the 'Vette?" Rick asked.

"You think I'm dumb enough to bring a 'Vette in here? I borrowed the truck from the railroad. Told Caine I was going fishing."

Jack followed Rick, and they drove down through the right-of-way. A trooper down on the fill stopped them. "Any damage done?" Rick asked.

"No sir, we got here in time," the trooper replied. "Course if we'd been a little quieter, we might have actually caught somebody, but the lieutenant does like his siren."

"Any idea who they are?"

"Ideas, but no proof. We'll scour around here. Maybe they dropped something besides the dynamite." He waved Rick and Jack through, and they drove over to the State Police barracks.

Barracks is actually a bit of an exaggeration. The building was a little two-bedroom bungalow. The living room had been turned into a dispatcher's office. The two bedrooms served as interrogation rooms. PH was being questioned in one room. Jack and Rick were shown into the other. Redman was seated at the table.

"This is Detective Redman," Rick said to Jack. "He's been investigating the Jensen bombing."

"You must love this case, kid," Redman said to Rick. "You keep showing up like a bad penny. What the hell are you doing here tonight?"

"We were…ah, I mean, I was hired by the Duke to be watchman tonight. Jack was helping me out. Good thing for me, too. Is Avery questioning PH?"

"Yeah. Don't worry about what Avery is doing. Tell me your story. You first, big guy. You Jack?"

"Yep, that's me. Jack North. Railroader, folksinger, and all around hero."

"I don't need no smart stuff. Just tell me the story."

Jack quickly told the story from his perspective. He had been sleeping when a sound woke him up. It sounded to Jack like somebody had stumbled on the trail. It took him a minute or two to get out of the sleeping bag. "Too bad, too. I was just a second or two, too late, to stop that sonofabitch from whacking Rick, here. But I got him before he could strike again. Tackled him and flattened him right out. Then we tied him up with our belts, while Rick called the cops on the walkie-talkie. Course, you guys came sirens wailing, so the creeps down on the fill got away, easy. But our guy didn't get away."

"Yeah, yeah. Pretty unlikely we'd have sneaked up on them anyway. Not unless we had sent some guys in on the tracks. That's what I suggested, but the lieutenant knew best. How about you, Wallace? Anything to add?"

"Pretty much the same. I had seen some movement down on the fill. Thought first it might be a deer. I came out of the shadow of the tree, trying to see better. I heard PH, spun, and got my arm up just in time. Goddamn glad it wasn't Henry swinging that grade-stake. I saw him take the head off a goose, once."

"What was this PH guy doing up there? You know?"

"Nope. He yelled he was looking for vandals. I think he's in cahoots. Shouldn't have been anybody there but Jack and me. I suspect he was supposed to keep watch while those creeps did their work."

There was some noise in the outer area, and Rick recognized the Duke's voice. "Harris? What the hell was Harris doing there?"

"Duke will tell you that I was the night watchman," Rick said.

"You guys go get yourself some coffee or something. Don't leave yet. I need to talk to this Duke guy. Then I need to see what Avery got out of this Harris character. I'll tell you, though, we've had our eye on him for some time. He just hasn't done anything until now that we can point to and say, 'he did it.'"

As Jack and Rick came out of the interrogation room, they ran into both the Duke and John Cashman. "Heard you got whacked," the Duke said. "You okay?"

"Yeah, just a bruise. Won't be able to lie on that side for a while."

"Have to do it standing up, huh?" Duke chuckled. "See Tim first thing, and draw your pay for the week. We'll put something extra in for the hazardous duty. Then take the rest of the week off. Who's this guy?"

Rick introduced Jack to John Cashman and the Duke. "Good big guy," Cashman said. "You want to work?"

"Nah, thanks," Jack answered. "Too hard on the hands. Need to keep'm nice for playing the guitar."

"What he means is, that the work's too hard, period. Our Jack would rather work the railroad, which means hardly at all." Rick poked Jack in the ribs. "Ain't that right, Jackson?"

"Oh, Ricardo, you do me wrong. I'm a hard working guy. Just this stuff is not my style."

"Well, if you ain't interested in working hard, we ain't interested in you," the Duke said. "Come on John, let's see what Harris has got himself into."

Jack and Rick hung around the kitchen drinking coffee and pop from the fridge. The sun was coming up by the time Redman came to get them.

"Okay. Just one question. Did Harris recognize you?"

"I don't know," Rick answered. "He didn't say my name or anything."

"Shit. Too bad. We'll have to let him go. His story hangs together. He had been told that there wouldn't be a watchman. Cashman says he's the kind of guy who might take it on himself to check out the job."

"Only if he could make sure Charlie knew about it," Rick said. "He's not the kind of guy who would do a good deed when no one was watching."

"Yeah. You're probably right. But that ain't proof. So he walks. We'll keep watching him though."

"Any ideas about the vandals?" Rick yawned.

"Ideas, plenty. No proof. We're pretty sure that Magus guy has a hand in it."

"They're probably camping up the river a ways," Rick offered. "Lots of good places to camp on the Williams. Pretty remote. Especially now that the trail in from Route 5 is cut by the job."

"You could be right. We may organize a sweep, sometime. Haven't got the manpower for it right now."

Rick and Jack went out to their cars. "Well, we can head down to the Miss Bellows Falls, and grab some breakfast," Rick suggested. "Then, I got go back and get my check. But I can catch some z's before the wedding. You staying at the house?"

"Nah. Let's head to Chester and grab breakfast there. It's not much farther. Then I'll bunk out at the old parlor car."

After a leisurely drive to Chester, and a huge breakfast of eggs, bacon, hash-browns, and toast, Rick headed back and picked up his check. He was pleased that Duke had Tim add an additional $100 to it. "Damn, getting whacked pays pretty good," Rick said to Tim.

"If you want, we'll set you up and you can sell whacks to the crew for five dollars a pop."

"No, thanks. Some of those guys are a little better at it than PH. Think I'll pass. Got to go get my beauty sleep so I'll be ready for my bride."

"Have a good wedding. See ya on Monday. Course you won't be good for shit. All fucked out, I imagine."

"God, I hope so," Rick said over his shoulder as he headed back to his car.

Rick headed back to the house. He luxuriated in a long, hot bath, and took a nap. It was about four in the afternoon when he woke up. Suddenly, he had to hurry. He raced down to the square and got a haircut. Back home, he dressed in his dark slacks and light-blue sports coat. He threw a few changes of clothes and a toothbrush into his soft-sided suitcase. He backed the car out of the driveway, and then remembered the rings and the marriage license. He rushed back and hunted through the house until he found them. As he was leaving, he thought about locking up. It wasn't something you usually did in Bellows Falls, but there wouldn't be anybody here for quite a while. He hunted through the junk drawer and found a key. Suddenly obsessive compulsive, he checked all the burners and faucets before he locked up. He was glad he did. The water was trickling into the tub and the stopper was set. A few more hours, and it would have been a disaster.

Finally, he was out the door at ten to seven. The wedding was at seven-thirty, and he still had plenty of time. Driving slowly, he got to Judge Rubenstein's house at the same time as Ellen and Janet. Jack's Corvette was already parked in front. Rick saw his grandfather on the porch two doors down. He waved, and walked down. "Wish me luck, Gramps," he hollered.

"May the wind be at your back, and the road rise up to meet you, Rick. Take care of that lovely girl."

"I will, Gramps. Gotta run. You want to come to the wedding?"

"Nah. It's not for an old man, Rick. Just bring young Ellen around when you get back from your honeymoon."

"You got it, Gramps. You're number one on our list."

Janet had hustled Ellen in the door, making sure that Rick and Ellen didn't talk before the wedding. Rick snorted at the superstition, and then retrieved Ellen's suitcase from Janet's car and locked it in the trunk with his own. They looked good together there.

The judge and his wife had the living room set up nicely as a wedding chapel. Mrs. Rubenstein played the piano, and she was at the keyboard. Jack was standing, talking to Judge Rubenstein. "Ah, Ricardo. Didn't slip out of town, I see. Did you bring the license and the rings?"

Rick produced the requested items. He was pleased to see that Jack was dressed up in a dark suit. "Jackson you look more like the groom than I do."

"That's because, if there was any justice in this world, I *would be* the groom. But alas, there is not."

"Ready? Are you ready?" Mrs. Rubenstein was getting anxious. "You girls ready?" she called.

"We're ready." Janet said.

Mrs. Rubenstein struck up the Wedding March from Mendelssohn. Janet and Ellen came slowly into the room. Ellen had the bouquet Rick had ordered at the last minute. Janet was wearing a corsage. Ellen was dressed in simple, but elegant summer dress. She wore a small lace veil.

The ceremony was simple and traditional. They said their vows, and put rings on each other's fingers. Judge Rubenstein said, "By the powers vested in me by the State of Vermont, I now pronounce you man and wife. You may kiss the bride."

Rick looked deep into Ellen's eyes. At that moment he felt the happiest he had ever felt. He kissed her gently. "More later," he whispered. She laughed.

Then they were running to the car. Jack was on the porch playing the banjo. Rick recognized *So long, it's been good to know you.*

Finally, they were off. It was already 8:30, and they needed to get to Rutland.

As soon as they got out of town, they stopped at a pull-off, and Rick shed his jacket and tie. Just after they passed the Route 5 turn off from 103, Rick heard the thundering roar of a motorcycle. He looked in the rear-view mirror, and could see it was Rocky Santee roaring up behind him.

"Oh, shit, trouble," Rick said. Santee roared alongside. He looked over at Rick, and grinned. He gave him a thumbs-up sign, and raced by.

"Isn't that Kelly on that back of Rocky's motorcycle?" Ellen said.

"Looks like it to me," Rick replied. "Damned if I know what girls see in a thug like that."

"You wouldn't," Ellen said. Then smiled, and snuggled up next to him.

Rick thought about asking her what she meant by that. Then he thought better of it. But for the rest of his life he would always wonder.

Rick and Ellen had a honeymoon weekend where everything went right—better than right. It was idyllic. From the first night beneath sheets together in the little motel next door to Sewards, to the slow, Sunday drive home, it was sheer bliss.

Not only did they have a marvelous time together, but they found an apartment half-way between Burlington and Winooski. They made arrangements with Dr. Wright for Ellen's routine prenatal care, and they each found jobs for the first semester. At the end of the drive home, they found the little hired man's house well stocked with homemade bread, and groceries, a homecoming present from Ellen's sister, Lori.

"Does it get any better than this, Rick?" Ellen asked. "We're home. We're safe. We're snuggled in with good food. How can we be anything but happy?"

"I'm happy," Rick whispered. "Very happy."

The ancient bed was lumpy, but they didn't mind. And although they were in bed by ten, it was well after midnight when they fell asleep.

Rick was disoriented when he awoke, but Ellen's soft snores clued him in. He slipped out of bed, and dressed in his work clothes in the dark. He gave Ellen a peck, wandered out to the kitchen, and put the coffee on. When it was hot, he poured a cup and wandered out on the stoop for a smoke. Edgar was waiting for him.

"Hi, Edgar. Want some coffee?"

"Nope. Just had some." Edgar lit a cigarette. "Good honeymoon?"

"The best." Rick filled Edgar in on their luck with the apartment and jobs. "Ellen even had a first visit with a doctor. Woman doctor. Seems real nice."

"Hmmph." Edgar grumbled. "Not much on doctors, man or woman, but I guess it's the right thing to do. Tell Ellen her mother would really be happy if she came up today. I think Mora is ready to bury the hatchet. She's a smart woman, and knows better than to beat a dead horse."

"Great. I know that's been eating on Ellen."

"We'll be cutting the first corn this weekend. You lend a hand?"

"You bet, Ed. Gotta pay the rent, somehow."

"No rent. But you live on a farm, you work on the farm. Just the way it is. Keeps people from overstaying their welcome, I'll tell you."

Rick laughed. "We'll be moving up to Burlington on Labor Day. Can I borrow your stake-body truck and move up some furniture a few days before that?"

"Probably, if we get the corn all in. Gotta go. Them cows are dragging their tits on the ground." Edgar gave a wave and headed up the hill to the main barnyard.

Rick went back in the house and packed a lunch. He gave Ellen a little shake. She opened her eyes. Rick told her what her father had said about visiting Mora. Ellen smiled a knowing grin. "I knew she'd come around. She'll be wanting to throw a big party and claim you were her best idea." Ellen rolled over and snuggled back under the quilt. "See you tonight," she muttered and was asleep almost instantly.

Rick envied Ellen's ability to lie abed, and thought maybe that being pregnant had something to do with it. He took one long look across the fields, and at the mist rising off the river. "Going to get a swim in, tonight," he said out loud, as he climbed in the car and headed off to the job.

If Rick thought the ribbing was rough on Wednesday, it was ten-times rougher on Monday.

"Looks a bit peaked, don't you think?" Côte said. "Don't imagine he was too weak to fuck this weekend, do ya?"

"'Bout near fucked to death, I'd say," Henry spat a piece of tobacco. "That woman just used him up, and left an empty husk." He spat again. "Ain't gonna be worth nothing today, for sure."

"She a virgin?" Basil Garrison, Côte's new chucktender, asked.

"If she was, there's been another *immaculate deception*," Teach chuckled.

Monday they finished drilling a shot and about five o'clock, they shut down for the blast. It went off without a hitch. PH was there for just a few minutes, and then gone. He seemed very nervous and avoided Rick. That was okay with Rick. He commented on how nervous PH seemed, to Côte.

"Well, he does. He's been jingling his change and his keys till you think he's going to come in his pants. He doesn't stop and talk or give orders. He just sort of flits around. I think maybe John and the Duke don't really believe his story about checking out for vandals. They just haven't got any proof that he was up to something else. I don't think Mr. Pecker Head has a long-term career with DeBoni."

"I don't think Mr. Pecker fucking Head's got much of a long term, period," Henry snorted, spitting a wad of tobacco on the ground. "If somebody else don't do it to him soon, I'm probably gonna take the sonofabitch down."

"Henry, he ain't worth the trouble," Côte cautioned. "Can you imagine spending time in jail because you hurt *that* sonofabitch?"

"You gotta get caught, to go to jail," Henry said, throwing his gear in his car.

Rick was anxious to get home, but tried not to show it. Nonetheless, he got a few comments about rushing home for a quickie, and accusations of already being pussy-whipped. "All in all," he thought, as he raced home, "no worse than I expected, and maybe even a little softer than these guys at their worst. Don't think their hearts were in it."

Ellen was sitting on the stoop, cutting snap beans as he drove up. "Come on," he said, "forget the beans for a while. Let's go for a swim."

They changed into their suits, grabbed towels, and headed off across the field, heading for the swimming hole, underneath the trestle. The path paralleled the railroad tracks. As they neared the trestle, they could see a man standing in the middle of it, his arms spread.

"Magus," whispered Rick. "Wait a second. Let's see what he's up to."

Ellen grabbed Rick's arm, "Rick a train!" she shouted.

Rick looked up the track. A rail car was barreling towards them. Rick shouted, "Magus, a train!" He and Ellen leaped into the ditch as the car rushed past, tilting wildly as it raced around the corner and out onto the trestle.

Rick stood up. The car was disappearing in the distance. The trestle was empty. "Ellen, run back and phone fire and rescue. I'll see if I can help."

Ellen raced back towards the house. Rick climbed the bank, and walked along the track out onto the trestle. He looked down on the river. There, fifty feet below the rail-bed, the Williams River raced over rocks under the trestle, and widened into a large pool. In the pool, there were a dozen people dressed in white robes. As Rick watched, they carried the body from the pool, and laid it gently on a stretcher. They picked up the stretcher and began climbing the hill to the tracks.

Rick shouted, "Wait. Stay right there. We've called fire and rescue."

One of the twelve turned, and looked up at Rick. "Tell them the Magus has gone to God," he said. Then he turned and the followed the stretcher-bearers up the path.

In the distance, Rick could hear sirens. "They're almost here," he shouted. But they paid no attention to him. They reached the tracks, and then turned and walked in solemn procession towards Bellows Falls

A fire truck lurched its way down the farm road to the edge of the field. A state police cruiser was right behind it. Firemen carrying medical kits scrambled out of the truck and headed for the trestle at a run. Rick could see Ellen starting back across the field.

"Where's the body?" the first fireman, Elliot Studley, asked, as he met Rick in the middle of the bridge.

"They took it." Rick answered.

"Took it? Who?" Studley was joined by Mark Enfield, the captain of the volunteer group from Rockingham.

Rick explained about the group below the trestle, in the water. "I think it's some of those Christians who are camped out in the rail yard. I don't know any of them, but these people were clearly some kind of religious weirdoes."

"Don't that beat all?" Studley said setting his kit down on the track.

The state trooper, Jack Farnsworth, puffed his way onto the bridge. "What's going on?" he asked.

Rick gave his version of the story again.

"Magus? Shit. That means I have to call Avery and Redman. Anything to do with Magus, they have to be called." He unhooked his walkie-talkie, and walked back towards his car.

Ellen came across the trestle and stood next to Rick. "Boy, you sure made that call fast. These guys were here in no time." Rick said, giving her a squeeze.

"Somebody else had already called," Ellen said. "The fire and rescue dispatcher said somebody called about the runaway rail car, and somebody called about a guy getting knocked off the trestle."

"Huh? They must've called before it happened." Rick scratched his head. "I didn't see anybody else down here, and the closest phone is our house."

Avery and Redman must have been in the area. Rick looked back across the field, and saw their unmarked cruiser working its way down the farm road. He watched them park and clamber up the bank. They came across the trestle. Avery didn't look too happy about the height. When he got to the group standing in the middle, he gestured for them to move across the bridge. "I don't care to stand on the edge of this thing," he said, unapologetic about his fear.

Redman gave Rick the eye. "You again? Every time trouble happens, there you are. I'm starting to think you're causing all this havoc."

"Ellen and I were just coming down for a swim," Rick protested. He proceeded to tell his version of the story again.

"Where the hell did they go?" Avery asked.

"Down the tracks. Towards town." Rick pointed. As he did, there was a *whoosh* and a spear of flame shot up into the sky, followed by a huge puff of black smoke.

"Whathefuck?" Studley yelled. The two firemen raced back to the fire engine for their fire gear. Avery, Redman, and Farnsworth ran clumsily along the tracks in the direction of the flames.

Rick and Ellen followed at a slower pace. The two firemen lumbered by them a few minutes later.

Rick and Ellen didn't try to keep up. They just followed the tracks. A half-mile down the tracks, there was a short siding. The fire was in the river beyond the siding. They followed the path down to the river. At the river's edge, the two firemen, Avery, Redman, and Farnsworth were standing, watching the roaring fire that engulfed the small island in the middle of the river.

"Nothing we can do to that," Mark Enfield said. "Don't look like a danger to the woods. Might as well let it burn itself out."

"Looks like a funeral pyre," Rick said pointing at the blazing stack of wood in the middle of the island. "I bet they put the torch to Magus's body."

"Yeah, well he must be made of gasoline, then," Avery commented. "Lot of accelerant feeding that fire."

"You got that," Studley chuckled. "I'd say twenty gallons, at least."

"Well, I guess that suspect is toast," Redman said.

"Probably what he wants you to believe," Rick commented. "Looks fishy to me."

"How so?" Avery asked. "Pretty clear cut. Runaway rail car knocks Magus off the trestle while he's preaching. His people give him a royal send off. Could happen that way."

"Yeah, well rail cars don't just run away." Rick ticked the points off on his fingers. "Those air brakes are designed to lock the second the air connection is broken. So that's fishy. It's fishy that somebody called fire and rescue before it happened. The closest phone is our house. Where else could somebody call from? And, it's fishy that they had a stretcher all set to carry a body, and even more fishy that this funeral pyre and twenty gallons of gas were all set up. Not something most people carry around."

Avery sighed. "When you put it that way, I guess there are some questions. Shit, I was hoping we could put one thing to bed, at least."

"You still want to swim?" Rick asked Ellen.

"No! That place gives me the creeps, now."

"Let's go home and eat, then." Rick and Ellen started up the path. "I know one thing we can put to bed," Rick chuckled.

Ellen punched his arm.

Chapter 30

PH

The story of the runaway rail car, the diving and dying preacher, and his funeral pyre was all over the job the next day. Rick was able to add details, spiced with his skepticism. But Rick's skepticism was met with plenty of skepticism as well.

"Why would some guy fake his death out in the middle of the god-damn woods, Wallace." PH had overheard Rick expounding on his theory. "Don't make sense. If you were going to fake your death, you have to do it where people would notice. If you hadn't come along, nobody would have heard about this at all."

"Not true. The fire and rescue had been called. I figure one of those Christians was going to stay and tell the story. When I showed up, he figured he didn't have to."

"Cops think he's dead, I hear," Everett put in his two cents. " Heard they found some bones and stuff in the ashes. Figure it was human."

"I'm surprised they could even tell that," Rick said. "Man, that fire was rip-roaring. Studley said he thought they must have used twenty gallons of gas."

"Bones don't burn no good," Côte offered. "You know when they cremate a guy? What you get ain't ashes, so much as ground up bones. They put the bones in a drum with some big rocks, and roll it around until the bones are broken into itty-bitty pieces. And them crematoriums is hot, let me tell you, but they still don't burn the bones."

"How you know that, Côte?" Henry asked.

"Working in the tombstone shop. You get all kinds of funeral directors come in and talk. They don't like cremation, much. Cuts into their profits."

"I guess. Ain't much sense buying a fancy casket, and then burning it up." Henry mused. "Then again, I guess it don't make much sense burying it either."

"What do you think, Henry? We ought to flush'm down the toilet?" Teach prodded.

"What the fuck difference it make? They're dead. They don't give a shit." Henry bit off the end of a new cigar, and spat it on the ground. He made a production of lighting the cigar.

"I want you guys to keep drilling here." PH interrupted their lunchtime conversation. "We're going to take the rest of the ledge in this shot. Then we'll be done with it on this job. Except for some boulders and little shit here, and there."

"Pretty risky," Henry spat another piece of tobacco on the ground. "Shot get too big, and I've seen them blow funny. Lot's of opportunity for cracks and stuff to fuck-up the delays. Two shots would be safer."

"When I want your opinion, I'll ask for it." PH spun and walked quickly back to his truck.

"You better run, you fucker," Henry muttered. "What's the hurry, I wonder? We just got the Springfield job, but we won't start clearing for a couple of weeks yet. Wonder if the stupid bastard thinks the Duke will lay us off?"

Côte shrugged. "Doesn't make much difference, Henry. We drill here. We drill there. We spend a couple of weeks polishing the compressors. All the same to me."

The crews returned to their drills, and the day proceeded like most every day on road construction, slow, hot, dusty, and dull.

That night, Rick and Ellen had dinner with Ellen's folks. Mora was all smiles, and planning a giant send-off party the last weekend of the month. As Edgar had suggested, Mora knew when to cut her losses. From that day forward, she was solidly in support of everything Rick and Ellen did, and was already getting excited about becoming a grandmother.

It was still early when they said their goodbyes, and headed down the hill, so Rick and Ellen decided to take a quick run to Chester to pick up a few groceries. They grabbed what they needed, and at Ellen's urging, Rick bought pipe tobacco instead of cigarettes. He had started smoking a pipe when he was thirteen or fourteen. He and Dieter had taken up the pipe to ward off mosquitoes and black flies when they were fishing. But road construction was always cigarette time for Rick. Still, he acknowledged, they couldn't really afford cigarettes on their tight budget. Besides, Ellen let him buy a couple of six-packs of beer.

As long as they were in Chester, they decided to see if Jack was hanging around his parlor car. The Corvette was parked in the depot lot. As they got out of the car, they could hear him playing the guitar. Rick hollered, "You decent, Jackson? I'm bringing a lady in."

"Just average, Ricardo, just average. But I do what I can. Come on in, you old married couple. See how the single people live it up."

The car was the usual chaos of clothes, instruments, and bottles. Jack was perched on the sofa, a tall glass at his side. He was picking through a series of chords, varying the rhythm. He looked up at Rick and Ellen as they came through the door. "I can tell by your shit-eating smiles, that the novelty ain't worn off yet," he laughed.

"True, true," Rick smiled. "So tell me, did your boys catch that runaway freight car?"

"Damn right they did. Cecil ran the little switcher back up the line from the yard to the flats, just below where the tracks cross under Route 5. You can see about a mile of track there. When the car came into sigh, he got that little engine moving at about the same speed, and let the car kiss it. Said it was as gentle as a baby's fart. Then he just eased it along to the yard."

"How'd he get word about the runaway?"

"Somebody called Tom Caine's office. Tom put it over the radio. Funniest thing. When Cecil got to the yard, there must've been fifty of them Christians milling around. They cheered him, and swarmed all over the switch engine and the freight car. Treated Cecil like a big hero. You know he never had much truck with that crowd."

"How'd it happen? Anybody know?"

"Tom Caine figures it's got to be sabotage of some kind. Uncouplings happen once in a while. But shit, the airbrakes almost always work unless they are manually set not to lock. He doesn't think it was an accident."

"We saw the thing, you know. We were at the trestle when it supposedly knocked off Magus. Personally, I think it was a set-up."

"Hmm. Could be. You know the Christians have all disappeared? Every last one of them. Cops came looking for them this morning, and there wasn't a soul in their place. All their stuff is gone. Vanished."

"Well that breaks my heart," Rick said. "What's the Tycoon think of that?"

"Word is, he's moving back to his Philadelphia mansion, and shutting down the whole excursion train thing. Tom said the lawyers want to talk to him. He thinks they're going to offer to sell him the freight business. He's pretty excited about that."

"You know what Ginsburg said about the Sugar River line. 'Short-line railroads are a very sweet business.'"

"True enough. But I think for Tom, it's more than the money. He buys this out, he *is* the Rutland Railroad. It's like winning the strike twenty years later, and having them give you the company."

"Well, we got to run. Work tomorrow, you know. Can't be late. I'm a responsible family man now."

"Yeah, yeah. I can see it's really the bedroom that's calling. Don't blush there, Ellen, you look as anxious as Rick does." Jack chortled.

Ellen threw a dirty sock at Jack, as they headed out the door and hurried back to their snug abode.

Thursday night after work, Rick and Ellen drove into Bellows Falls. Rick wanted to check out the house before his parents got back from Maine. He also needed to pick up some clothes, and start sorting through stuff they would move to Burlington.

The house was hot and musty, and they opened all the doors to let it air out. Ellen picked up the Bellows Falls Times on the front porch, and brought it in. She scanned the front page. "Look at this Rick. I can't believe it. The Bellows Falls Times has a scoop!"

Rick hurried over to the dining table where Ellen had spread out the paper. There on the front page, were two photographs under a headline, "Preacher Dies in Bizarre Accident." Both pictures were taken from the riverbed looking up at the trestle. The first picture showed Magus standing on the lip of the trestle, arms spread, obviously preaching to the masses below. The second, showed a body hurtling through space. The rail car was visible on the trestle. "Holy shit," he said. "Tell me this wasn't a set-up."

"Looks pretty real to me," Ellen said, hugging herself, to ward off a shiver.

"Yeah, but why would they have a camera? How come they take the picture at just the right moment? And look at that. The boxcar door is open."

"What's that mean? You see them open all the time." Ellen looked confused.

Rick shrugged. "You're right. It's just, if you were going to throw a body out of the car, you would have the door open."

"But where else would Magus be? He couldn't just disappear."

"I know. It's a puzzle. That car is going awful fast for somebody to jump on. That would have been pretty dangerous. I don't know. I just don't think that guy in the sky is Magus. The whole thing looks like it was set-up as a movie stunt."

"You're just too suspicious. Do you have the stuff you want? I want to get a twist cone and head home."

Rick nodded. He grabbed the paper, and stuffed it in the bag with his clothes. They closed and locked the doors again, and headed back to the farm.

Friday, the talk on the job was all about the pictures. At lunch, Rick was expounding on his theory of why the whole thing was bogus. Teach and Everett had joined Rick, Henry, Côte, and Garrison, who had earned the nickname, *Big Fart*, by demonstrating an uncanny ability to break wind at will.

"Doesn't make sense that they'd have that camera and catch those great shots unless they were staging it," Rick said.

"I don't know," Teach frowned. "Might have been taking pictures of Magus for the Church bulletin or something. Just got lucky on the drop-shot."

"Yeah? Then how come they got twenty gallons of gasoline to toast him with? Tell me that, Professor."

"Clearly they had planned a barbeque. Needed the gas as a fire-starter. Otherwise they might not have been able to crisp their weenies. And you know, no God-abiding Christian can tolerate a cold, limp weenie."

Rick laughed. "I have to admit you put up some good arguments, Professor. But my research indicates that these Christians deny even having weenies. It was bogus. I rest my case."

"You ought to shut your face, Wallace before somebody shuts it for you."

Rick spun around. PH was standing behind him, glaring at him. Rick felt the adrenaline rush through his body.

"You already tried that once, Pecker Head, and ended up hog-tied, as I remember." Rick's voice was low and cold. "But I still owe you one for that whack with the stick. So, if you think you want it, come ahead." He picked up a grade-stake and whacked it into his hand. "I don't think any-body here is going to do it for you."

PH stared at him, his mouth working, but no sound coming out. Finally he blurted, "You're fucking fired, Wallace. Get your shit, and get out of here."

"You ain't firing my chucktender, Pecker Head. Anybody gets fired around here, it'll be you." Henry stood up and whacked his grade-stake against the ground. "Good and solid. No knots in this fucker."

PH looked around for support. Seeing none, he beat a hasty retreat, hollering over his shoulder, "I'm reporting you to the Duke, Wallace. You too, Baldridge. All you fuckers get back to work."

"That boy has some problems," Côte said. "When he gives an order, nobody seems to give a shit. Kinda hard to run a railroad that way."

"He'll have some problems if he fucks with me, or Wallace," Henry growled. He laughed, bit off a chunk of his cigar, and spat it on the ground. "Stood up pretty good for yourself, Squirt. I didn't think you had it in you. Pretty fucking feisty."

"I owe that sonofabitch big time," Rick muttered, feeling shaky. "He'd have killed me with that grade-stake if he hit me right. And he's such a lying weasel. Fucker had the cops eating out of his hand."

"Do you think he's tied in with those Christians?" Teach asked. "I mean, why? What would he get out of the sabotage and all that?"

"I think he was after Cashman's job," Everett said. "I think he was try-ing to make Cashman look bad, so he got promoted. Fucker is sure not going to earn a promotion. Fuck, half the crew would quit."

"That Magus was his cousin," Rick offered. "Could've been doing the sabotage as a favor. That whole clan is pretty squirrelly." He told them about Gorse, and how he ended up in the trash can."

"All them Texas boys is weird," Côte offered. "I think it comes from pulling their puds out on the prairie."

"I thought they fucked the heifers," Henry said.

"Well, PH would've. But he couldn't get one to date him," Côte laughed. "Mooo. You ain't puttin' that little thing in me."

They were nearing the end of the drilling for the last shot by the time the job shut down, Friday night. "We'll be done here on Monday," Côte said. "Me and Henry will get to *fuck the dog* for a while. What you gonna do, Squirt?"

Rick shrugged, and tossed his lunch-bucket in the car. "They usually got some busy work somewhere. If they lay me off, I can always work for my father-in-law. He's always got plenty to do on the farm. I only got another couple weeks, and I'm done anyway. Hell, maybe PH'll get my ass fired. I don't know."

"That sonofabitch will get his," Henry growled as he dusted himself off. "He ain't much longer for this company, I'll tell ya. Monday might just be his last fucking day, too." He climbed in his car, backed carefully around, and then drove slowly out of the quarry.

Friday night, Rick and Ellen took in a movie. They swung by Rick's house on the way home, to see if his folks had come home early. Snuffy must have had the same idea, because he was lying on the front porch. Rick gave him a pat. They were about set to leave when the station wagon rounded the corner. "Damn near psychic, Snuff," he said. He got his keys and opened the house.

TK was driving. The whole family was tired and subdued. Even the Stooges just said "Hi" and headed up to bed. Rick helped TK and his father carry in the baggage. Rick's mother invited them to dinner on Sunday.

"Want a ride home, TK?" Rick asked.

"I'd appreciate it," TK answered. He threw his duffle bag into Rick's backseat, and climbed in. "You guys all married and everything?" he asked.

"Yep, signed, sealed and squealed," Rick said. "We're living in the little house for the next couple weeks." He told TK about their apartment, and solicited his help with the move.

"Sure thing," TK said.

"Well, how was the island?" Rick asked.

"Different," TK answered. "Real different."

That was all they got out of him. As they drove him home, Rick brought him up to date on all the events of the past two weeks. TK agreed that Magus's death-scene was bogus. "Heck of a clever exit, though. Probably high-tailed it to Canada. Cops will just close the case."

They left TK at the end of his road. He always preferred to walk in.

Saturday was a workday on the farm. Rick helped Edgar cut his corn, using a hand-sickle to make the starter rows. He and Ellen took a swim, and hit the sack early. Sunday, they headed downtown about ten in the morning. Ellen rode with Mora, and went to church. Rick just headed to his house to read the Sunday paper.

He got a cup of coffee and bummed a cigarette from his mother. He brought her up to date on the doings in town. She was particularly interested that Mora had come around. When Rick asked her about the island, she just said, "It was fine. We had a good time."

Rick's father always slept in on Sundays. He claimed that it was a command from Harry Lauder that a good Scotsman had to "Lie between the sheets his bed *adornin*." He got up about noon, and had a cup of coffee and small glass of scotch. Then he settled down with the New York Times.

Everything seemed the same, but different. Rick couldn't explain it. It was like the energy had gone from the house. Willa simply ignored her mother. There were no screaming fights. The Stooges all headed out to see how the world had changed while they were gone. Snuffy tagged along with Larry and Curly. Moe headed up to the playground to see if he could scare up a pickup game of baseball.

Rick stuffed his pipe, and sat out on the front porch. He realized quite suddenly that this was no longer home. It wasn't just the family that had changed. It was him. His center had moved from Maple Street to someplace else. It wasn't the farm, either. When Mora's little Chevy turned the corner, he realized wherever Ellen was, that was home.

Dinner was a quiet affair. Rick's mother was very solicitous of Ellen's wants and needs, but the conversation lacked the usual wit and snap that Rick associated with a family dinner. After dinner, Rick's father took a notebook and retired to the backroom saying, "Think I'll work on my poem."

Rick raised his eyebrows. His mother shrugged. "Started on the island. I don't know what he's writing, but I'm glad he is."

"It seemed kind of different at your house," Ellen commented on the ride home. "Is it because of me?"

"I don't think so," Rick answered. "I think something happened during their vacation. But I haven't got a clue. They're all weird, anyway."

"You don't know what weird is," Ellen said, suddenly serious.

Rick looked over at her. He wanted to ask what she meant, but he let the moment pass. Maybe it was better not to know. "Well, we don't need to carry anybody's problems. We'll be busy enough making sure our little family does okay."

Ellen snuggled against him. Rick speeded up a little, suddenly anxious to get home.

Monday was hot. It was hot when Rick got up and smoked a pipe and drank a cup of coffee on the stoop. It was hotter when he got to work. By the time they finished drilling the shot, it was over 100 degrees.

The dynamite crew had already spread piles of dynamite sticks next to the holes, on the front side of the shot. They had headed back to the magazine for another truckload. Rick could see the sticks soften and flatten. He was sure he could see fumes rising from the exposed stacks.

"That stuff will make you plenty sick, " Côte said, "unless you got a weak ticker. It's nitro glycerin. I seen a kid keel right over and die, working with that stuff on a hot day like this. But if you got a bad heart, you won't die on the job when them fumes is rising."

"Glad it ain't my job," Rick said.

PH drove up in his pickup. He sauntered over and looked at the field. "You drillers help the dynamite crew," he ordered.

"Not me," Henry said. "Ain't in my job description."

Côte shook his head. "Can't do it."

PH muttered something about mutiny. "You laborers, then. These old farts can worry about the equipment. You two help the dynamite crew."

"Shit, me and my big mouth," Rick muttered as PH walked over to talk to Blaster Bill. "I suppose I don't get a choice."

"I suppose you don't," Henry agreed. "Fuck it. You've done plenty of dynamite stuff. Can't let you *fuck the dog* with Côte and me. That wouldn't look good."

Rick and Big Fart walked down and met the dynamite truck. He hollered to Teach and Everett, "You're lucky day. You get two laborers, free of charge."

"Welcome to the club, boy," Teach laughed. "We got plenty for you to carry. Don't go breathing, though. That stuff'll kill you."

PH came down the hill to the truck. He was hollering orders as he came, but Rick couldn't figure out what he was saying. PH grabbed Everett by the arm, and spun him around, causing Everett to drop fifty pounds of Special Gel to the ground. He hollered something in Everett's ear. Everett looked furious, but then he smiled. He touched the bill of his baseball cap, picked up his box of dynamite, and started up the hill.

They carried and parceled out dynamite the rest of the morning. By lunch, the whole crew was nauseous from the fumes, and no one ate much. They sat, drank water or coffee, and smoked.

After lunch, Blaster Bill told them how he wanted the shot done. Then he went around and poked a blasting cap into a stick of Toval at every hole. Everett worked with Blaster Bill, and Rick worked with Teach to load and tamp the holes.

It was well after 3:00, when Bill began to wire up the shot. Teach asked Bill where he wanted to shoot from. Bill stopped and looked around. He absentmindedly rubbed his stomach where he'd taken a hit from the fly-rock. Finally, he pointed over the crest of the hill down in a hollow.

"You won't be able to see the shot," Teach said.

"That's all right. Everett can stand at the top of the hill and give me the all-clear, then head back into the woods."

Teach shrugged, and he and Rick unrolled the spool of blasting wire, walking over the crest of the hill, and down into the hollow. Then they went back and began the tedious job of cleaning the boxes and waste from the site. Usually, they saved the plastic bags to stuff in the holes on the next shot. But this was the last shot of this job, so they piled everything back into the dynamite truck.

The crew made their way to the quarry to take cover. Bill finished wiring the shot, connecting it to the blasting wire. Everett helped him carry the blasting machine to his protected hollow. Then they gave the signal that the shot was imminent. It was answered almost immediately by the blasting air-horns as the equipment shut down, and operators took shelter.

Henry was sitting on the lip of the quarry, watching the process, and chewing his cigar. PH came across the lower edge of the shot, and headed for the quarry, hands jingling in his pockets. Suddenly he stopped. He hollered at Henry, "You see my keys?"

Henry didn't say anything. He just pointed out on the shot. There about in the middle of the shot, the sun was glinting off a piece of metal.

"Shit fuck!" PH waved his hands at Everett at the crest of the hill, and took off towards the shot at a trot. He was about two strides from the piece of metal, when the shot went off.

As explosions go, it had a little more bang than they wanted, but there wasn't a lot of fly-rock. The bang was followed by a resounding thud, and a cloud of dust engulfed the area and rose slowly into the sky. There wasn't much doubt in anyone's mind that PH was history. As the dust settled, you could see the rock was broken and humped up in the center. There was a shoe laying on the surface a few feet down from the top.

"This is getting to be a habit," Côte said. "You'd think a grown man would have more sense than that."

Henry bit off the end of his cigar and spat it on the ground. "Sense wasn't PH's strong suit," he said. "Somebody better head down to the office and tell the Duke."

"I'll go," Teach said, throwing a rock or something against the wall of the quarry. He walked over and got into the dynamite truck. He started it up, backed around, and headed down the access road.

"What happened?" Blaster Bill had climbed out of his hollow and was standing on the edge of the quarry.

"That fucking idiot ran out on the shot. Not your fault, Bill," Henry growled.

Bill looked at Everett. Everett shrugged. "It was clear when I signaled," he said. "I give the high sign, and ran for the trees."

They all just stood and stared at the smoking shot. They were still standing there when the Duke drove up. Rick thought the Duke might go on a tirade, but he was very calm. "What happened?" He asked the question of Henry, ignoring Blaster Bill.

"Idiot dropped his keys out on the shot. Went running back. Everett had already given Bill the high sign. Stupid fuck should've known better than that."

The Duke looked at each of the others. Each man nodded. That's the way it was.

"Cops will be here in a few minutes. Don't leave. They'll want to hear your story."

They waited. They smoked, but they didn't talk. Teach had come back with the Duke. It was twenty-five minutes before the cops came. It was Avery and Redman. Redman looked at Rick, "Damn you are bad luck, boy. I'm surprised anybody will work with you."

The two detectives took a quick look at the shot. Then they told the Duke he could get a backhoe up and see if they could find the body. While the backhoe worked, the two detectives talked to each of the men. After they had been questioned, each of the men headed over to where the backhoe was working to help sift through the debris.

Rick was the last to be interviewed. He gave the same story. Avery grunted. "Well kid, that ends this case. We had pretty much concluded PH was working with Magus. Together they were responsible for all the sabotage and probably the bombing."

"Why? What was in it for them?"

"Best we can tell, they wanted to get PH into the super's job. Then they were going to swing some contracts to their own set of suppliers and make a killing on kickbacks. Shoddy concrete, stuff like that."

"Shit, Bob Strong would never let them get away with that shit."

"Yeah, well they had something on Strong. That's what got the whole scheme going. Seems he ain't filed his income taxes since 1955. They found out somehow, and were going to blackmail him. If that didn't work, they were going to arrange an accident. I guess his second in command ain't exactly one of the *Untouchables*."

Rick could believe Strong hadn't filed his taxes. Probably had money coming back from the government, he had so many kids, but hated to spend the time it took to fill out the forms. "Hope you guys aren't going to do anything to Strong."

"Nah. Just give him the word. The IRS will work that stuff out. But a guy like that has to be careful."

"Why did they kill Jensen?"

"We don't know, precisely. But we can't see how it could be anybody else. They certainly had the means and the opportunity. Who knows, maybe the union wanted a cut."

"I still think…"

"Forget it. We don't give a shit if Magus faked his death, or not. He's gone. All we could prove is misdemeanor level stuff. You ain't going to tell me PH faked it too, are you?

Rick shook his head. "No, that was real."

"We think maybe Duque had a hand in it. He owned some of the companies they had lined up. Maybe all of them. Of course, nothing happened, so all we have is suspicion."

"Huh? Jack North told me the Tycoon is selling out, and going back to Pennsylvania. Maybe this has something to do with that."

"Got him!" somebody shouted over at the blast site. "Least, I think it's him."

"Call in the coroner, Redman," Avery said. "You men. Leave him be, now. We'll take it from here. You can all go home." He walked slowly over to where the men were standing. Rick followed him, and then wished he hadn't. PH's body was not a pretty sight. Rick turned and headed back to his car, feeling a little guilty that he wasn't the least bit sorry. He saw something flash amid the debris. He picked it up. It was a piece of a Miller beer can, bent into a flat golden panel. He tossed it back on the ground.

Côte came up beside him. He scratched his head. "Now I gotta rethink this whole thing."

"What thing?" Rick asked.

"Life. Ya see I had it figured. Life was just the opposite of the movies. In the movies, the good guys win and the bad guys lose. But in life, the good guys get fucked, and bad guys get rich. But now, here we got Whitey, a good guy, and he gets rich. And we got PH, a definite badass bad guy, and he gets blown to smithereens. It don't make no sense."

Rick nodded. It didn't make any sense to him either.

Chapter 31

Teach

June 2002

"Grampa! Grampa! I broke it!" Ben's voice pierced Rick's reverie. He opened his eyes, and was somewhat shocked to be in the same quarry. "Grampa, come, please!"

"Coming Ben. What did you break?" Rick got to his feet and made his way across the quarry to where Ben was working the rock.

"The rock, Grampa. My fish. See."

Rick looked at the slab that contained the fossilized fish head. Sure enough, it had cracked right along the plane of where the fish head protruded.

"Don't worry Ben. Lots of fossils get broken. We can put it back together if we have to. Let's see if we can lift out the rock." Rick grabbed the edge of the slab and lifted. It came away easily.

"Hey, look Ben. Now you got two fossils." The slab had cracked precisely along the plane of the fish, and each side had a perfect fish replica.

"Wow. Two fossils." Ben reached in, and tried to wiggle the remaining block free. As it did, something else fell free. "Grampa, know what?"

"What, Ben?"

"Some guy isn't going to be able to drive his car. Look, he lost his keys."

Rick took the keys into his hand. The brass key tag said "Ferguson Ford" on one side. He turned the tag over. Etched into the reverse side were the letters, PH.

Rick held the keys in his hand, and stared into space. He was back in the quarry. PH had just yelled to Henry about the keys. Rick stretched his mind. Where was everyone else? He remembered Everett at the top of the hill. Côte was down in the quarry. Then there was the blast. And then…what? He remembered Teach throwing something against this wall before he went down to get the Duke. Throwing something. Something, maybe like maybe a set of keys.

"Come on, Ben, let's see if we can get this slab out. Then I want to go visit somebody before we head back to Aunt Willa's house."

He and Ben carefully removed the slabs. Together, they weighed a good thirty pounds. Rick fit them into the knapsack.

"I'll carry them, Grampa." Ben was eager.

Rick shrugged. "Okay. They're heavy, though. So soon as you get tired, let me have a turn, okay?"

Ben agreed. About fifty yards down the trail, Ben got tired, and Rick hefted the knapsack. Ben didn't ask for another turn.

It was slow going on the walk out. They startled a deer and a partridge. Finally, they reached the farm lane that took them back to the car. Ben ran ahead, and was waiting when Rick staggered to the car. He opened the door, and slid the knapsack behind the seat. He and Ben climbed in.

"Who are we going to visit, Grampa?"

"Mr. Merryweather. He used to be a teacher. An art teacher. I used to work with him on construction."

"Oh. Do you think he'll want to see my fossil?"

"You bet, Ben. I think he'll like your fossil a lot."

Rick thought about Mike Merryweather, as he drove the four miles to his house. Rick had seen him only once since that summer. Back when Ben's dad, Tim, was eight or so, Rick brought him around to visit Teach, expecting to find the same jolly, irreverent guy he knew in the old days.

But Teach was different; real different. His first wife had died of breast-cancer. He had a remarried a very straight-laced woman. He was a teeto-taling, born-again Christian. The visit had been uncomfortable, and Rick had never gone back.

Rick turned into the winding driveway with some trepidation. He parked the car and helped Ben out. Ben grabbed the backpack and lugged it to the door of the little white house, tucked neatly into an ancient apple orchard.

Teach was at the door when they got there. Rick was startled at how old he looked, and then realized that Teach *ought* to look old. He must be at least seventy-five. "Hi Teach," he said.

"Squirt? Is that you, Squirt? My God, you've gotten old. And who's this?" Teach bent down to Ben.

"I'm Ben. You know what?"

"No, what?"

"I found a fossil fish. You want to see it?"

"Why, you bet I do. Come in, come in." Teach ushered them into the little house. It was neat, but different than the last time Rick had been there. Something was missing."

"I try to keep it up," Teach said, sensing Rick's puzzled look. "But since Sarah died, it's a struggle."

"You're second wife died? Oh Teach I'm so sorry."

"I'm not very good at keeping wives," Teach said. "Would you like some lemonade or iced tea?"

"I'd like some lemonade," Ben said. "I'm thirsty. We've been digging fossils, Grampa and me."

"Iced tea for me, Teach. I'm a bit of teetotaler myself, these days."

"Ain't bad when you get used to it, is it?" Teach filled two glasses with lemonade, and one with iced tea. "You know I went to pieces when Junebug died. I was drinking myself right into the grave. Darn near got fired. Ed Silicheck, the principal, took me aside and said, 'You got one chance. Join AA tonight, or you're fired.' I couldn't afford to get fired. I had Sammy at home. God knows how he was getting along. So, I went. I haven't had a drink since. AA suggested we look to a higher power, so I wandered into the New Church of Christ on Front Street. I met Sarah that first night. She took charge after that."

"Lucky for you, I bet. It would be a hard thing to do alone. I never could stand being alone." Rick said, thinking of his own bad time when Ellen left.

"Mostly lucky. Sammy and Sarah never did hit it off. He quit school at sixteen, and bummed around the country. Somewhere along the way, he discovered he was gay. Sarah wouldn't have anything to do with him after that. She figured that was about as big a sin as there is. He also found out he had my genes, only better. Sammy is a fine artist. He and his partner live in Italy. We correspond by E-mail. Goes by the name, Sammy Jay. That was his mother's maiden name, June Jay. I told him with that name, he ought to be illustrating kid's books. So, just to spite me, I guess, he did one. Won a National Book Award. Ain't that something? You might have read his book, Ben. *Meadow Secrets?*"

"Maybe. Yup, I think I did. It had all the animals and where they hide, didn't it?"

"That's the one. Say, let's see that fossil of yours."

Ben got the knapsack and carefully picked out one slab. He laid it down on the floor with the fish up. Then he got the other slab out and laid it next to it.

"Two fish? Wow. I thought you said you found one fossil."

"It really is just one fossil," Ben said. "It broke right in the middle."

"That's a mighty fine fossil. That's about the best fossil fish I've seen. Hey, I've got some fossils," Teach took Ben downstairs to his game room. He opened a cabinet. Inside were dozens of fossils and geodes. "You can look at all these while your grandfather and I talk. If you get bored, there's a television over there with some dinosaur movies for the VCR. He left Ben carefully picking out each rock and fossil and examining it.

"How about you, Squirt. What have you been up to?" Teach asked.

Rick had been looking at one of Teach's paintings. "Painting again, I see."

"Yeah. It didn't feel right when Sarah was here. Now, it feels right. It fills my day. How do you fill yours?"

"I'm doing some consulting. Not so much as I did for a while, but some. My obsession is filling in the holes."

"Holes? What holes?" Teach sat in the high-backed rocker.

Rick sat on the sofa. He brought the key out of his pocket. "Things in my life that just didn't seem to quite add up." He jiggled the key in his hand. "Things where the answers we were given were bogus. Where pieces were missing." He tossed the key to Teach.

Teach caught it and looked at it. It was obvious he recognized it. Some memories can't be erased by time. He turned it over. "My God. PH. You don't suppose these were the keys…" his voice trailed off.

"We found it in the quarry. The one where we were parked. It was behind the fish, believe it or not."

"So he didn't lose his keys on the shot," Teach said.

"I went there to remember, Teach. I played the whole summer back like a mini-series. And I remember, just before you went to get the Duke. You threw something."

"They're all dead, you know." Teach kept turning the key over in his hand. "They were all in on it. I wasn't. Everett just gave me the key and said to hang on to it. But all the others were in on it. Henry, Everett, even Côte, I think. I don't think Blaster Bill had a clue."

"Yeah, I figured that. I wasn't sure about Côte. But I figured Henry and Everett were in on it for sure. But you know, it wasn't PH's death that bothered me. I mean, I don't really care who blew up PH, or whether he blew himself up. If ever a man deserved a quick trip to the last judgment, it was PH. But I don't think they killed him because he was a prick."

"No? Why else would they kill him?"

"I think they killed him because he knew who killed Jensen."

"The union guy? Who do you think did that?"

"You know, don't you?" Rick looked hard at Teach.

Teach smiled. "Yeah. I know."

"It was Everett, right?"

"It was Everett," Teach agreed. "How did you figure it out?"

"The barrel of beer. I remembered that Everett was already on the ground and behind the tree when the car exploded. It never registered at the time. But if he hadn't moved before the explosion, he would have been killed. He knew it was rigged. Which means he probably did it."

"You're right. But PH wasn't blameless. He pretty much goaded Everett into it, telling him the union was going to fire his ass. 'Unions got no place for old farts,' he'd say. 'Put you right out to pasture. Let you pound your pud.'"

"I believe that. Then I'll bet PH got Everett to help him sabotage the job. At least look the other way when those wild-assed phony Christians came in."

Teach nodded. "Yeah, but when old BVD gave his speech, Everett said 'no more.'"

"Then, it was probably a race to see who could kill who, first. I think Everett took a shot at PH, one Saturday when he was guarding the job."

"They never talked about it much," Teach said. "But I heard most of the story that summer after you left for college. Everett would talk to me, some. Henry let a few things drop. It wasn't too hard to put together. It was damn near just luck that everything worked so that PH got blown up. They just counted on him being stupid. And he was."

"Just an old man worried about keeping his job. Pretty easy to understand." Rick finished his iced tea.

Ben came up the stairs. "Grampa, can we go back to Aunt Willa's? I'm tired."

"You bet, champ. Say goodbye to Mr. Merryweather, and thank him for the lemonade and for letting you play with his fossils."

"I wasn't playing, Grampa. I was studying. You have some very good fossils, Mr. Merryweather. Thanks for letting me see them. I put them all back. And thanks for the lemonade."

"Well, you're welcome, Ben. It's been a pleasure having you come for a visit. I wish I had a grandson like you. Your grandfather is a lucky man."

Ben nodded. He put his fossils back in the knapsack.

Rick fished a business card out of his wallet. "It's got my E-mail on it. Drop me a line, Teach. Us dumb college uh-fellows got to stick together. We're probably the last of the old BVD crew left."

Teach nodded. "Yeah. That was the last summer I worked for BVD, but they got a few more jobs: Springfield, Windsor, White River Junction. But the old man died, and Charlie just never did recover from Stevie's death. I guess John Cashman and the Duke ran it. I heard the family sold out to Hanes right after they won a big job up around Derby Line."

Teach clapped Rick on the shoulder. He hefted Ben's knapsack. "I'll carry this out to your sports car," he said. "Consulting must pay pretty good."

"Good enough to pay for a rental car," Rick laughed.

Rick backed the car around, and headed out the driveway. In the rear-view mirror, he could see Teach bouncing the key chain in his hand.

They drove back through Springfield, and along old Route 5, the *Missing Link Road*, to locals. Rick noticed that the Jehovah's Witnesses had built a new Kingdom Hall on Route 5. There was a little old man sitting on a chair at the end of the church driveway. He had a box of pamphlets. For a second, Rick thought he recognized the man, but he wasn't sure, and didn't stop.

Chapter 32

I-91 South, Exit 40—Bradley Field

The Wallace family reunion was a great success. All the members of the family were talking to one another. They made a huge fuss over Ben. Uncles and cousins introduced him to cutthroat croquet. Everyone whooped it up when Ben sent his Great Uncle Steve's ball flying into the bushes.

Rick told them the true story of the Route 91 murders, but only TK took a real interest. For everyone else, it was just so much ancient history.

The party broke up about 8:30. Rick, Ben, and TK helped Willa pick up, and then all headed up to bed. Rick and Ben shared a room with double beds and a skylight. As they were getting undressed, Rick emptied his pockets onto the dresser. Among his coins and keys was a small white limestone pebble with a trilobite fossil. He had found it on the banks of the Mississippi a couple of years before.

Ben spied it on the bureau. "What's that Grampa?" He picked it up. "Oh, that's your trilobite fossil. How come you brought it?" He frowned. "I know. If I didn't find a fossil, you were going to drop it so I could find it, right?"

"Uh…well, I…" Rick stuttered.

"You thought I was a baby, and if I didn't find a fossil, I'd cry. That deserves a *nougy* for thinking I'm a baby." Ben leaped off the bed onto Rick's back, and rubbed his knuckles on the top of Rick's head.

"Hey," Rick bellowed. He dumped Ben on the bed and began tickling him.

Suddenly, there was a pounding on the wall. "Cut it out you two, or I'll come in there with the belt," Willa hollered.

"The belt?" Ben looked wide-eyed.

"The belt." Rick whispered, dragging up a memory of an old Bill Cosby routine. "Nine-feet long, six-feet wide, with little hooks that tear the flesh off your bones."

"Oh, no." Ben hid under the covers. He poked his head out and giggled.

Rick put his finger to his lips. "Shhhh," he whispered. "Even the walls have ears. See, there's one right over there."

Ben giggled some more.

"I'm sorry about the trilobite," Rick said. "I should have known that you are the world champion fossil hunter."

"I am," Ben said with certainty. He smiled and drifted off to sleep.

Rick lay on his twin bed, looking at the stars through the skylight. He played over the family reunion in his mind. His brothers, how could he have ever called them, "The Stooges?" Today, Chuck was the leading architect in Vermont. Larry was a "take-no-prisoners," environmental lawyer. And Moe, was the idol of thousands of teenagers, worldwide, for the powerful graphics in his best-selling video games.

And Steve. Steve hadn't even been there that summer. That was during what Steve called his "research chemist" career in Haight-Ashbury. Today Steve wrote poetry, and made a living at it. Not something many people accomplish.

The thought of poetry diverted his musings. His father had started writing again that summer. He didn't write very much before he died, just two years later—a victim of too much of what he loved most, tobacco, and scotch. Rick had once had the slim volume of poems. He had read them once or twice, but they were lost in a house-fire. He remembered the opening lines of the first poem, entitled "Pitcairn Island."

> "Land ho,' we cried, lips parched, belts knotted
> Minds twisted and shrunk.
> "Too many days at sea", says me.
> "Too many days at sea."
> But had we known Pitcairn's curse
> We'd have thrown our lot with Bligh.
> For a sure death is sweet music
> In Bedlam's pits.

Rick had always thought his father, a huge fan of the Bounty trilogy, was writing of the Bounty's crew. But now, remembering that summer, he wondered.

So much had changed with his father's death. His mother had lived off the Stooge's Social Security payments, spending a good part of it on cheap wine. One-by-one they dropped out of high school, and hit the road, each eventually finding his own path. Finding herself alone, his mother had made an effort to pull her life together, and find someone new to fill the void. Her unfortunate choice was George Gorse. The thought made Rick grimace.

"Do I have my answer?" He stared at the moon through the skylight. "I know who killed Jensen. I know who killed PH. Was that the question?" In his mind he stood back from the mosaic he had created, trying to get a perspective on the whole.

There were loose ends. Jack? Where was he now? The Tycoon? What happened to him? Rick didn't know the answers. Whitey and Annabelle, he knew, had done well. He had visited them several times. They had taken in Whitey's nephew and niece when his sister, Mayfair, had committed suicide. The two kids, now in their early forties, were running the restaurant and diesel repair shop, and had been, since Annabelle and Whitey died, just two days apart, back in 1995. Manny was a fantastic chef, and Diana was an even better mechanic than her teacher, and he was the best there had ever been.

"It wasn't just the hate," Rick whispered. "It was people just throwing the switch, and the guy who had been their friend, was suddenly a *murdering nigger*." He let that idea settle. It could have been the part of the story that bothered him most. Yet, the town hadn't gelled around the hate. They tested it. They tasted it. But it didn't seep into their souls. And, in the end, the people of Bellows Falls, the farmers, and even the hoodlums, had rejected it. And then Rick knew the question. "Why?"

He wanted the answer to be Whitey's answer, that "killing never stopped killing. Only love stopped killing." But somehow he couldn't feel that the town had taken a step quite that big. "Maybe it was only indifference," he muttered as he drifted off to sleep.

The day dawned clear, and cooler. Willa was already in the kitchen making coffee, when Rick got up at 5:15. Ben was sleeping peacefully.

He tiptoed downstairs, and accepted a cup of steaming brew from Willa. They sat and read the paper, and sipped their coffee. After a bit, Rick got up and refilled his cup. "Thanks for having us, Willa."

"You're always welcome. It was fun." Willa looked up. "What's bothering you?"

"I was just thinking about that summer. It changed my life. But you guys were being changed too. Whatever happened on the island, changed the whole way the house felt."

"That's true," Willa said. "TK and I waited out the next school year, graduated, and got married. We made our mind up that summer. You were our inspiration, you know. You and Ellen just getting married and charging off and doing it."

"I guess we did. But I guess I feel guilty that we never looked back. You guys could probably have used some big brothering about that time."

"You *stupe*, Rick."

Rick did a double take.

"Sorry. It's like looking in the mirror and seeing Mom looking back," Willa laughed. "I just meant, you were always there. We knew if we needed help, you'd be there. That's all that mattered."

Rick thought about sharing his thoughts on the love, hate, and indifference with Willa, and then decided it could only cause her to spend sleepless nights thinking about it.

Ben and TK came roaring down the stairs. "What's for breakfast, woman?" TK hollered. "We can't send these boys off with an empty stomach."

Willa rustled up eggs, ham, and muffins, washed down with juice, milk, and coffee. No one left the table hungry. After breakfast, Rick and Ben packed up, gave hugs around, and headed out.

Rick drove north to Springfield. He got on I-91 at the Springfield interchange, and headed back southbound. After a couple of miles, there was a sign indicating a rest area ahead. When they got to the rest area, he pulled in and parked. "Come on, Ben," he said. "I'll show you something."

The rest area had no toilet facilities, just a parking lot, and stairs that went up the hill. They climbed the stairs and went through an opening in the fence that had once sported a gate. The outline of the old access road Chip had bulldozed to the gravesite was still visible, and Rick and Ben followed it up into the woods. There at the edge of the clearing, was a large cut stone.

"Is that a gravestone? Who's buried here?" Ben asked.

Rick told him a little bit about Stevie DeBoni. He knelt down to see the inscription. Below Stevie's name, there was a second name. Rick brushed it off. Benito Vincenti DeBoni, 1888 –1966. And beneath the name there was an inscription, "He *bilt* good roads." Below the misspelled "built," was a small circumflex, Côte's mark.

They had plenty of time, so Rick exited at Route103, and headed into Bellows Falls. He toured the town slowly, telling Ben what used to be where. He turned up Maple, and stopped the car. Coming towards him was a wire-haired Airedale mongrel, walking gingerly like he'd just had a very good night.

"Hey, Snuff," Rick yelled. The dog stopped and looked at him, then swaggered on past.

"Do you know that dog, Grampa?" Ben asked.

"Nope, guess not, Ben. But I'm pretty sure I knew his great-grandfather."

As they drove through the square, Ben asked "Where are all the stores Grampa?"

"Gone, Ben. Where that hole is, there used to be a hardware store, and some other stores. There used to be four big grocery stores in town, and seven or eight corner markets. Now there's just a couple of gas stations selling junk food."

"It must be too easy to get on the Interstate and go somewhere else."

"You got it, Ben. You are pretty smart. But if you keep saying smart things like that, I may have to give you a *nougy*."

They headed out through Westminster, past the old Freighthaulers terminal, now Santee Trucking, turned by the Farmer's Market vegetable stand, and got back on Interstate 91. They joked, and talked, and sang, and the miles melted away. "There's our exit, Ben. Exit 40, Bradley Field." Rick turned off the Interstate.

"Grampa, sometimes I just have to say stuff, or I'll burst. What should I do when I just have to say stuff?"

"Write a book, Ben," Rick said, turning into the Alamo lot.

"Will that work?"

"Works for me."

0-595-65236-0

Printed in the United States
829000003B

9 780595 652365